# The Schiele Slaughters

# The
# Schiele Slaughters

## A Megan Crespi Mystery Series Novel

# Alessandra Comini

SUNSTONE
PRESS

SANTA FE

This is a work of fiction. Names, characters, businesses, places, events, and incidents are either the products of the author's imagination or used in a fictitious manner. Any resemblance to actual persons, living or dead, or actual events is purely coincidental.

Sunstone books may be purchased for educational, business, or sales promotional use. For information please write: Special Markets Department, Sunstone Press, P.O. Box 2321, Santa Fe, New Mexico 87504-2321.

Book and cover design › Vicki Ahl
Body typeface › Bernhard Modern Std
Printed on acid-free paper
∞
eBook 978-1-61139-320-0

———————————————————————————

Library of Congress Cataloging-in-Publication Data
Comini, Alessandra.
The Schiele slaughters : a Megan Crespi mystery series novel / by Alessandra Comini.
    pages ; cm. -- (Megan Crespi mystery series novel ; 2)
    ISBN 978-1-63293-025-5 (softcover : acid-free paper)
    1. Murder--Investigation--Fiction. 2. Art thefts--Investigation--Fiction. I. Title.
PS3603.O477S35 2015
813'.6--dc23

                        2014034385

———————————————————————————

**WWW.SUNSTONEPRESS.COM**
SUNSTONE PRESS / POST OFFICE BOX 2321 / SANTA FE, NM 87504-2321 /USA
(505) 988-4418 / ORDERS ONLY (800) 243-5644 / FAX (505) 988-1025

To Jane Kallir,
whose friendship and oeuvre catalogues on
Egon Schiele
have been invaluable.

# 1

The night watchman's body had no hands or feet.

The naked cadaver had been propped up on one of the museum chairs in bizarre imitation of the writhing man in the self-portrait above. In the actual painting, the life-size nude figure was minus the prop of a chair, twisting pathetically without hands or feet in an existential void. Black duct tape had been applied to the private parts of his body. The stark image was a self-portrait by one Egon Schiele. Next to it on the floor by the guard's mutilated body lay a black metal rose tipped in silver.

* * *

For those who knew the work of the Viennese artist Egon Schiele, this particular artwork was the culmination, in 1910, of the twenty-year-old artist's public self-punishment for the crime of masturbation.

His womanizing father, Adolf Schiele, had contracted syphilis around the time of his marriage and had infected Egon's mother Marie. She gave birth to three dead infants before Egon and his two sisters, Melanie and Gerti, were born.

All three children watched with horror as their father gradually slipped into a state of mindless, gentle insanity. A mere ghost of his former self, Adolf died when Egon was fourteen—a spectral vision that never left the artist.

Awareness of the venereal origin of his father's deterioration was partly responsible for the obsessive preoccupation with sex characterizing much of the artist's figural work throughout his short life. He died of influenza at twenty-eight, just days before the end of World War I.

In the Vienna of 1910, masturbation—a topic even Freud was uncomfortable discussing with his own sons—was an activity still believed to cause insanity. The "solitary vice" should be resisted, or at the very least punished.

* * *

In the contorted painting above the corpse, Schiele had publicly punished himself in a guilt-ridden, hand-amputating portrait that charged and changed his very physiognomy.

Not so with the night watchman. Anton Berg was instantly recognized by the three women guards who came on duty at Vienna's new Leopold Museum early the next morning. As one of the guards called the police they also noticed that the security cameras were not working. The next call was to the museum director, Johannes Ohm. He arrived before the police and was greeted by the horrified guards.

After taking in the gruesome scene, Dr. Ohm discovered that the screens in the command panel of the control area behind the cloak room had been disconnected. And no alarm had been tripped. Whoever had committed this murder and desecration knew what he was doing. It was a very bold operation. And the only possible point of entry and exit would have had to be the museum roof, where some leaking skylights were currently under repair.

The police wondered whether there might be more than one individual implicated. Was it possible that some of the protestors who had been loudly demonstrating in front of the museum last week were involved?

The demonstrators were members of the *Israelitische Kultusgemeinde Wien*—the Israelite Community of Vienna known as the IKG. They accused the Leopold Museum of owning confiscated works of art that had originally been seized from Jewish owners and Jewish galleries during World War II and not restored to the legitimate heirs. The IKG posters carried by the demonstrators demanded restitution and the police had had to rope off the belligerent protestors to allow bewildered museum visitors entry and exit.

Although no evidence of any wrongdoing by the Leopold Museum had been established, several claims concerning a few of the museum's iconic works had been filed by the IKG in the Austrian courts. These included works not only by the Expressionist Egon Schiele but also by his mentor, the Art Nouveau master Gustav Klimt.

One of the specific artworks in question had been Schiele's *Self-Portrait Nude Seated* under which the murder victim had been posed. But this lawsuit had been resolved last year in favor of the museum. And no claims had been lodged against Klimt's life-size *Kissing Couple*, in which two naked women knelt against a decorative background, locked in a sensuous kiss.

All attention had been focused on the corpse at the feet of Schiele's *Self-Portrait*. No one had thought to search the upper floor of the building until one of the policemen asked the trio of lamenting guards if they had done so. They looked at each other in alarm. No! Immediately, with the policemen and the museum director in the lead, they swarmed up the stairs and fanned out onto the second floor.

"It's the Klimt, it's the *Klimt!*" screamed one of the women, alerting her colleagues, the director, and the policemen, all of whom rushed into the room from where the shouting had come.

This time there was no human victim. But a crime had been committed. Someone had used a knife, sliced out the central part of the *Kissing Couple* and taken it. Next to the frame on the floor was a black metal rose tipped in silver.

# 2

"They'll just have to call back!" exclaimed retired history-of-art-professor Megan Crespi out loud to herself as she continued to lather conditioner through her hair in her London hotel-room shower. Staying, as she always did, in her favorite basement room of the Aster House at No. 3 Sumner Place, Megan was in no position to answer the room phone that was ringing loudly and incessantly. She had just finished exercising for some thirty minutes, waiting for the medium brown hair dye to do its job. It would take a good rinse now before she could gingerly step out of the shower, dry herself and blow-dry her hair. Reminding herself not to rush things at the age of seventy-seven even if she was physically very fit, she allowed the irritating phone to continue ringing. Finally it stopped.

Carefully rinsing out the conditioner, Megan wondered who could be calling her. Earlier, she had reported in to her best friend Claire Chandler, who once again had patiently agreed to babysit her beloved little Maltese dog, Button, back home in Dallas.

She did not expect any phone calls now since the secretary at the London Existential Psychotherapists office had checked with her just last night after she arrived at the hotel. The chairperson himself, Anthony Starling, had confirmed that her evening lecture, "Unwilling Prisoners: Tchaikovsky and his Wife Antonina Miliukova", was all set for seven o'clock tomorrow evening. He would be picking her up for dinner beforehand at five.

And now it was tomorrow. After dressing for the day in her *de rigueur* outfit of black Merrell shoes, black slacks, black vest with a plethora of pockets, and bright red blouse, Megan decided to go through her Power-Point presentation one more time before going up for breakfast in the cozy, multiwindowed sunroom of the hotel.

Lecturing with images is so darn *easy* nowadays, she thought to herself, marveling at the new technology—well at least new to *her*—and remembering with a grimace how for most of her teaching life she had carted around two bulky slide carousels for speeches she had given around America and Europe. Only rarely had her carryon not been opened and the mystifying carousels taken out for inspection.

Once, a security guard actually pulled several slides out of one of the carousels and held them up to the light. Unfortunately, they happened to be erotic works by Schiele and Klimt. The guard eyed Megan with ill-concealed surprise and disapproval before dramatically replacing the slides in the carousels and commanding her to pass on. He immediately whispered to the nearby security guards and in a few moments they were all laughing and pointing at her retreating figure.

Well perhaps it was odd that a *woman*, an older one at that, was lecturing on such artists. But Megan had discovered Egon Schiele back in her mid-twenties when she was in graduate school at Berkeley earning a Master's degree in art history. Her eyes had opened wide with admiration for the artist's frankness as she toured a small exhibition of his works assembled by her teacher, Professor Herschel Chipp.

Her new passion had taken her to Vienna, where both Schiele and Klimt had lived and worked. That was in 1963 and it was not her first trip to the splendid city. She had first seen and lived there at the end of 1956, the year of her graduation from Barnard College. Hugely enamored of her art history teacher there, a German professor named Julius Held, she persuaded her parents to let her continue studies at the institution Dr. Held had recommended, the University of Vienna.

But first, her father had insisted, she must visit her Italian grandparents in Milan. Proudly they took her to the *Cimitero Monumentale* where Toscanini was buried just a few steps from their own family mausoleum. Once inside, they dramatically pointed out to Megan a plaque already inscribed with her name and birth date, followed by a hyphen and a space. The names of her parents, her brother, Giangiorgio, and sister Tina were there as well, all with the frightening hyphen and space after their birth dates.

After two weeks of well-meaning but suffocating care, Megan had firmly bade the Nonno and Nonna farewell and elatedly boarded a train for Austria. She was headed for an adventure she could never have imagined.

The adventure was the Hungarian Revolution against Communist rule in the fall of 1956 when thousands of fleeing refugees filled the city of Vienna. Like other students she stopped going to class and pitched in to help at the different clothing distribution centers. Still today, she always thought of those difficult but bracing days whenever her business took her back to Vienna—her *Wien*.

Megan was yanked back to the present when the room phone began ringing again. This time she was in a position to pick it up and did so. An anxious voice questioned: "Dr. Crespi? Megan?" Instantly she recognized the voice of her cherished friend and colleague Johannes Ohm, director of Vienna's Leopold Museum.

"Hannes!" she exclaimed excitedly. "How have you found me all the way over here in London?"

"I didn't have your cell phone number, Megan, so I called your university and they told me you were in London, staying at the Aster House. I tried your room just ten minutes ago but there was no answer."

Megan refrained from explaining that she had been in the midst of dyeing her hair and asked instead, "What's up? You don't sound like yourself. Are you all right, Hannes?"

"*Ach, ja,* I am all right but something *terrible* has happened at the museum!"

"What? Has there been a fire?"

"Thank goodness not that. But something even worse than that. *The night watchman was murdered. But there is more! The hands and feet of his body had been severed...*"

"No! How horrible!" Megan interrupted.

"But still more, Megan. The mutilated corpse was carefully propped up on a chair right in front of our Schiele's nude *Self-Portrait*. The portrait itself had been mutilated with black duct tape over the genitals. And on the floor beneath it a black metal rose with silver tips had been left."

"But why? What was that supposed to mean?" asked Megan, feeling her skin tingle. "Did they leave a note?"

"No, nothing. No explanation. But there is still more to tell you. Upstairs we found that Klimt's *Kissing Couple* had been sliced out of its frame! The painting is gone and on the floor in its place was another black metal rose."

"But this is terrible, just terrible! And no note upstairs either?"

"*Nein.* Nothing to indicate *why* these awful things were done. Or who did them. But we think we may have an idea as to the reason for the outrage."

"What is that?"

"All last week the IKG was staging a protest against the Leopold. Things got pretty hot and there was a lot of shouting and pestering of the museum visitors. Finally the police had to rope off the protestors. That really made them mad."

"So you think one or more of the IKG members may have broken into the museum and actually murdered the watchman and carved out the Klimt?"

"It's a possibility. The IKG does have a lunatic fringe they cannot control, you know."

"But *murder*? Destruction of *masterpieces*?"

"I know. But there it is. This is what we have on our hands.

"And that is why I have called *you*. If you can possibly come, Megan, we want you here. With your expertise on Schiele and Klimt, we think that you might be able to shed some light on this double tragedy."

"But there are fine Klimt and Schiele experts right there in Austria, Hannes. Why add me to the mix?"

"Let's say it's your unique outlook and your special contacts that we value. After all, you were the stubborn American who just had to seek out the actual jail cell in which Schiele had been imprisoned. No Austrian had thought of doing so. Not even Schiele's relatives. Fifty years had to pass before you appeared on the scene. And your success in finding, photographing, and writing about the cell was instrumental in its now being a museum. The tiny prison town of Neulengbach is now a tourist attraction, thanks to Schiele *and* to your persevering search.

"So you see, Megan, we need your plucky American approach to things," urged Johannes Ohm. "You won't be caught up in the usual tangle of pride and prejudice that hampers the complex art history scene here. You'd be the unprejudiced outsider looking in, don't you see?"

"You credit me with too much, Hannes," responded Megan, touched by her friend's characterization of her and the lucky find she had made some fifty years ago.

"Please do come, Megan. You're already halfway here, after all."

"Well, if I do, I couldn't come until tomorrow, as I'm giving a lecture here this evening. But I will check the Internet and see if I can get a flight to Vienna that brings me in at a reasonable time."

"*Wunderbar!* I'll reserve a room for you at your usual hotel, The Römischer Kaiser, isn't it?"

"Yes, that's right, and would you please ask for a room in the back?"

"Consider it done," concluded a relieved Hannes.

After securing flight reservations on Austrian Airlines for early the next morning, Megan picked up her iPhone and called Claire with the news that she had agreed to continue on to Vienna after her London lecture and might she please keep little Button for a few more days? She explained what had happened.

"Of course," responded Claire indulgently, not surprised that once again a Crespi trip abroad had been lengthened.

The breakfast buffet was such that Megan was able to assemble her own favorite ensemble of cereal, blueberries, strawberries, banana slices, yogurt, and milk. After leisurely going over the text for her presentation that evening, she made her plans for the day. She would go to Sotheby's first and surprise her colleague there, Jillian Lloyd, head of sales. She wondered if Jillian had heard about the tragedy at the Leopold Museum.

Megan had to get her mind off the grisly events in Vienna. So perhaps after Sotheby's she would visit Hampstead Heath which was always a delight. And the John Keats House, with its portrait bust of Keats by the American sculptor Anne Whitney was nearby. Whitney was one of several nineteenth-century American women sculptors who went to Rome, and Megan had written and lectured extensively about them. In fact she had been able to acquire two sculptures by them herself.

The first was a life-size medallion portrait by Margaret Foley that showed a striking older woman's face in profile. "M. Foley, Fecit Roma, 1884" was carved into the rim of the marble medallion. Megan liked to think that the subject could possibly be Clara Wieck Schumann, the wife of Robert, and one of the first pianists to memorize pieces and give concert performances without the notes in front of her.

The second work, formerly in Megan's Dallas home, was also life size and a true treasure. It was Anne Whitney's statue of Lady Godiva, her "rippling ringlets" falling down her back and her modest garment still pulled in at waist level as she unclasped the "wedded eagles" of her belt. The Lady who rode naked on her horse through the streets of Coventry, clothed only in "chastity," was the heroine of Alfred Lord Tennyson's poem on the historical figure, "I waited for the train at Coventry...."

For years the lovely Lady had graced Megan's living room, but recently she had made a gift of the statue to the Dallas Museum of Art, pleased by the thought that so many more people could see and admire her there. In fact, the statue had become a focal point in the museum's audio tour and a stopping station for the many classes of schoolchildren who visited the museum.

Well, she would see how the day worked out. Maybe she could work in visits to two museums: the John Keats House *and* Freud's House. She could never get enough of the strange feeling of the great Viennese doctor's presence there. Perhaps it was the smoke from his cigars, she joked to herself.

She remembered an incident that happened a few days after her mother—a heavy smoker—died. Megan was walking through her parents' living room and had given her mother's favorite upholstered chair an affectionate pat. Immediately a cloud of smoke had billowed up from the chair—a preternatural last greeting.

After downing her daily "senior" pills, Megan walked three blocks from the Aster House down Old Brompton Road to the South Kensington Station and took the underground to Sotheby's on the always busy New Bond Street.

An unwelcome surprise greeted her there. In front of the establishment was a large group of protestors wearing what looked like police uniforms. They wore brimmed hats with the words, in German and in English, "*Kunstraub*/Art Theft." Occasionally lunging toward persons who had gathered to watch what looked like a movie promotion, the demonstrators handed out flyers. Megan made her way to the front of the crowd and before she could enter Sotheby's one of the flyers was immediately thrust into her hand. Its message urged that art looted by the Nazis should not continue to be auctioned off. "Don't sell! *Restitute!*" the message read.

Jillian Lloyd, a slender woman in her forties with a droll sense of humor, was taken completely by surprise when a beaming Megan appeared at the door of her office. They hugged each other and Megan asked right away if she had heard about the murder and happenings at the Leopold Museum. Jillian had not heard about it, so Megan filled her in with what details she knew. Both women expressed their horror at what had happened. Who could have done such a thing? And why?

Having no answers, Megan asked why the demonstration outside? What had sold on auction to have triggered such a fervent response?

"Oh, it's a townscape by Schiele," was Jillian's rueful answer. "A restitution lawsuit was slapped against it, hours after it was sold and shipped to the rep of an anonymous buyer. Don't think it will fly, however."

"I've heard that is becoming the fashion nowadays, filing restitution claims that may or may not hold water, but that cause delays and problems, or *issues* as everyone says nowadays. There simply are no longer *problems* in the world, only *issues*, have you noticed, Jillian?"

Jillian laughed in agreement. She hadn't really thought about it before, but Megan was right. Everything was an "issue" nowadays.

"By the way, Megan, we expected the Schiele to go for, highest, seventy million pounds, as it's not one of his better ones really—he left it unfinished and unsigned. But two buyer reps had a bidding war and the painting went for over one hundred and ten million pounds. Unheard of!"

"Amazing. Do you have any idea as to who the two anonymous competitors were?"

"We can't identify them for sure; their reps were new to us. And none of the veteran Schiele collectors bid on the work. But our guess is that the bidding war was between two Russians. You know that with the new billionaire class in Russia there is tremendous interest now in acquiring works by Schiele and Klimt. The most enterprising, ravenous you could say, of these collectors are based in St. Petersburg and Moscow.

"But these new buyers are inexperienced and have only superficial acquaintance with the artists' works. That Schiele townscape, for example, which was as I've said certainly not one of his best, went for the price I told you. And that doesn't include the percentage that Sotheby's garners, so the price was actually more than one-hundred-and-ten thousand pounds."

"Golly, that's almost a hundred and eighty-five million dollars!" exclaimed Megan, her mind adjusting to the new phenomenon of an elite class of avid Russian collectors of Western art. "Are you sure you don't have any specific leads, Jillian?" pushed Megan.

"Well, just between the two of us, I suspect that the painting was bought by Boris Ussachevsky, the billionaire grandson of the Russian Futurist artist and collector, Vladimir Ussachevsky. Boris inherited his grandfather's collection—all Western European paintings, incidentally—and is known to have been working to enlarge his Schiele holdings, none of which, by the way, are to be seen in his very successful St. Petersburg gallery, Solovey."

"Solovey? That's a lovely name. Do you know what it means?"

"Yes, I was told it means nightingale. So perhaps it only has visitors at night? Just kidding, Megan. Seriously, the only other Russian buyer I can think of who might have sprung for the Schiele townscape would be Ussachevsky's Moscow competitor, Alexandra Azarova, also a billionaire."

"Yes, I know Alexandra as a matter of fact. Met her when she was in Texas for a convention. She's very nice. And you might be amused by her gallery's name. It's the Gallery Rasputin; brings up cheery thoughts of assassination, doesn't it?"

Jillian snorted, then asked with interest: "Where is it?"

"At the Smolenskaya Embankment on the ground floor of one of the street's tallest buildings and near the metro."

"Oh, not a bad section of town at all."

"Well," said Megan, "both Ussachevsky and Azarova certainly sound like possible buyers. I am intrigued by the idea of a Schiele townscape of the Moldau River being somewhere on the Volga River."

"Well, Megan, enough of Russian intrigue. Let me show you something truly spectacular. We have a previously lost Schiele for our next auction! It's undergoing restoration right now but we are doing it in-house, so I can take you down to see it. Sorry I couldn't let you know about it before, but it's all been very hush hush."

The two friends threaded their way through the basement corridors of Sotheby's until they came to a large room at the back of the building. A restorer Megan knew from previous visits beamed at them. It was genial Rupert Wechseln from Mannheim.

"I thought this Schiele painting might tweak your curiosity, Megan," he said in greeting. After pleasantries had been exchanged and wry remarks quipped about the protestors outside, Megan, Jillian, and Rupert bent over the Schiele under restoration, examining it with reverence.

It was one of three known large 1910 self-portraits by the artist showing himself nude and in different tortured positions. One of them—the "seated" one—had been known for decades and had gone through various private collections until it was recently acquired by the Leopold Museum. This was the painting in front of which the night watchman had been found murdered and mutilated.

The other two self-portraits, reproduced in black-and-white in both of Janette Killar's oeuvre catalogues of Schiele's works, had been thought to be lost. But now one of the two missing self-portraits had been offered to Sotheby's by an anonymous owner through an intermediary.

"It's extraordinary!" Megan cried, amazed at the sense of agony emanating from the lean body, standing off-center, and this time with at least one hand and one foot intact. Schiele faced the viewer, with upper rippling torso bending far to his right, hands defiantly on hips—the right hand not perceptible— legs set slightly apart in what looked like an imminent fall to the ground. And yet there was no ground to fall upon. Like the Leopold Museum self-portrait, Schiele's naked body was posited in an empty continuum of unarticulated space. The figure seemed to be hurtling at the same time it was defying gravity. The expression on Schiele's face was fraught with anguish. His challenging eyes were enormous under a furrowed brow.

Rupert was at work restoring the garish yellow with which Schiele had painted his body and face. At the moment the yellow, laden with the dust of decades, was more buttery in color. The artist's bristling spikes of dark brown hair stood straight up from his head, as though electrified. Bright reds articulated the lips, nipples, and erect penis.

"This ithyphallic self-portrait might be a difficult work to sell to any museum," Jillian said musingly.

"Oh, I agree," responded Rupert immediately. "It's probably destined for a private collection rather than for a public, or should I say 'pubic' collection?" Two groans greeted his very bad pun.

After another twenty minutes Megan took her leave, thanking both her friends for the special treat of looking at the incredible new Schiele find.

Passing with some difficulty through the throng of demonstrators, Megan stopped at one of the many Tutti-Frutti yogurt shops that dotted London and treated herself to a multi-fruit shake. She had a lot to think about. If one of the two lost Schiele self-portraits of 1910—the standing one—had been found, perhaps the other one was extant after all. She reminded herself of how Schiele had shown himself in this second work, which up to now was only known in black-and-white reproduction, but which by common assent also had the body articulated in shrieking yellow. Schiele had shown himself, as with the other two self-images, frontally and naked. But this time he was kneeling. His arms were bent at the elbows and his hands, fingers tensed and splayed outwards, were held up away from his body toward the beholder. Another variation on punishment of or temptation to masturbate.

What a trio of self-purging, Megan thought. And yes, the Leopold Museum had been most courageous in exhibiting the unblinkingly frank work. Of course there had been a few individual visitor complaints, but fortunately, in worldly Vienna, no real problem. At least not until the murder yesterday, and the linking of the hacked corpse with the amputated image above.

And now she had about three hours before she should return to her hotel for a half-hour's lie-down—something that had recently become a ritual in her busy life. Luckily, after only thirty minutes or so, Megan always felt her energy revive and she was ready for whatever might come up. She did want to be especially rested for her lecture tonight.

A bit reluctantly Megan decided she had better visit only one of her two "cheer up" destinations: either the Freud House or the John Keats House. Choosing the latter, Megan took the underground out to Hampstead Heath. It was one o'clock in the afternoon and the sun was blessedly out, warming the March air.

It was an uphill walk from the underground station to the Keats House, and one she had always enjoyed. The streets, the little shops, and restaurants she passed were always interesting and filled with colorful characters. And there was one stationery store she always entered because of the unusual must-have gift items on display.

This time it was a sheet of thick gelatin stickers in the shape of penguins. Fondly remembering her spectacular Antarctic cruise with Claire Chandler two years ago, Megan bought two sheets of the adorable creatures, one for herself and one for her friend.

She decided to fortify herself for the Keats experience by stopping at a small café and having some tea and a sandwich. She took a table near a party of excited children celebrating the birthday of one of them. The father who was supervising his end of the long table had just finished reading *The Times* and, spotting Megan looking at him, asked her if she'd like to look at it.

"Oh, yes indeed. Thank you so much," Megan replied, surprised and pleased at this chance thoughtfulness. Over her tea she perused the front page. Under the fold was a long article headed by a startling headline: MAN DIES AFTER LITERALLY EATING HIMSELF TO DEATH. Megan could not stop herself from reading the article, but soon wished she had not. The details were appalling. A deranged man, living alone in the basement of a London apartment complex, had decided to sever and cook parts of his body which he would then slowly chew and swallow. Over a period of several weeks he had cut off all his toes, both his ankles, the fatty areas above his knees, parts of his thighs and strips of his inner upper arms. In each instance he had been able to staunch the flow of blood by cauterizing the exposed body part. Last to go were his testicles, and he was unable to stop the bleeding. Quietly, slowly, and apparently blissfully, he bled to death, writing out a note stating that he was the first man in history to eat himself and that he had done so "in penitence." The stamped but unsealed envelope in which the note had been found was addressed to "The Grand Master, Dr. Kurt Wagner, Castle Gemmingen-Eggaberg, Gmunden, Austria."

The man's distorted, blood-soaked body was not found until someone in the building complained to the landlord about the stench coming up from the basement. All of these facts had been given in detail in the salacious *Times* article. The international police had visited this Kurt Wagner, "the Grand Master," with the note addressed to him, but Wagner had denied any knowledge of the man.

Oh, yes, Megan *earnestly* wished she had not read the whole article. Now she could not put the image out of her mind. Perhaps a walk in Hampstead Heath would clear her mind before going on up to the Keats House. Turning toward the beckoning green meadow she dodged a runner and entered the park, walking briskly toward a hilly embankment. Mothers pushing baby carriages ambled alongside her and a large dog with a shiny black coat was happily fetching and refetching a ball for its equally happy owner.

Ah, yes, this was soothing, just the right thing to be doing. At the top of the hill three young people—a vocalist, a violinist, and a cellist—were performing old folk ballads. Just now, when Megan reached them, it was "Lord Randall."

Megan was enchanted and dropped a five pound note into the hat that was passed around. These youngsters, not one over twenty-five probably, were pretty professional and a CD stack of their recordings was prominently displayed. Megan could not help buying one of the CDs. It was appropriately titled *The Balladeers*.

She remembered her own total engagement with folk music when she was in *her* twenties. She had taught herself, with the aid of LPs played over and over again, not only the words to countless songs but also the traditional folk instruments: five-string and tenor banjos, twelve-string, and regular classical guitars. And she had learned not only English ballads, but American songs, inspired by Odetta and Cynthia Gooding.

The close-up barking right at her elbow of the ball-retrieving black dog brought Megan back to the present. All dark thoughts of the man who ate himself had vanished and memories of her days as a folk singer had left her in a buoyant mood.

Now she left the Heath and walked over to the two-story Keats House, set back from the street and inviting with its sparkling white façade and large friendly windows. After buying her entry ticket Megan headed straight for Anne Whitney's 1873 bust of Keats which had been lent to the museum by nearby St. John's Parish Church. Then she turned to a sentimentalizing oil portrait of Keats abandoning his open book to listen to a nightingale on Hampstead Heath. It was painted some twenty years after Keats' death by his great friend Joseph Severn.

Severn had traveled with Keats to Rome in 1820 in search of a warmer climate that might cure the tuberculosis that was devouring the young poet. The artist lived fifty-nine years longer after Keats's passing and Megan had discovered his tombstone alongside that of the poet in Rome's Protestant Cemetery.

She was much taken by the fact that Keats had not wanted his name on his own headstone. Instead he requested the poignant phrase: "Here Lies One Whose Name Was Writ in Water." But Severn, who had cared for and sketched the dying Keats, decided to add: "This Grave contains all that was mortal, of a YOUNG ENGLISH POET, who on his Death Bed, in the Bitterness of his heart, at the Malicious Power of his enemies, desired these words to be Engraven on his Tomb Stone." Severn was buried right next to Keats.

Megan remembered all this because she used to take her nineteenth-century art history class of some three hundred students on a slide tour through the Protestant Cemetery every year. Staring appreciatively at the Keats portrait now, she even remembered a few lines from the poet's "Ode to a Nightingale": "light-winged Dryad of the trees" singing "of summer in full-throated ease" in "some melodious plot of beechen green."

"Dr. Crespi? Can it really be *you*?"

Megan, who was five-foot four, turned to face what could have been her double as far as height and girth were concerned. Only this woman was younger and had jet black hair pulled back tightly in a bun at the top of her head. She wore an attention-getting purple pant suit and three-inch heels that clicked loudly when she walked.

Megan recognized, not without a sense of irritation and even dread, the Vienna gallery owner Éva Vidovszky from Budapest. This was the woman despised, if grudgingly admired, by most of the international art world for her ruthless acquisitions of restituted works originally in the possession of Jewish owners. Vidovszky had a nose for naïve new owners who did not fully realize the potential monetary value of the artworks that had come into their lives. Her ability to sweet talk, indeed if need be, intimidate potential sellers was legendary. Too often owners who had literally been talked out of possession of their works had appeared in established galleries to lament their loss and ask for advice on how to get their works back.

Unfortunately the answer was always the same: they had signed a legal contract to sell, hence they had no case to take to court, no matter how unfair, how odious the rushed transaction had been.

Megan remembered the astonishing story Schiele's older sister Melanie had told her about being drugged one evening by a visitor who, over a period of years, had rained constant attention and gifts upon her. That night, after dropping some sort of sedative in Melanie's tea, the visitor had produced a typewritten one-page document concerning "the safekeeping of Schiele artworks" which he asked her to sign.

Feeling quite groggy, the vulnerable old widow had unwisely granted his request. She did not realize the document stated that after her death, all her Schiele works would go to him.

What had actually happened after Melanie's death in the mid-nineteen-seventies was that Schiele's devoted nephew, Anton Peschka, Jr.—son of the artist's sister Gerti—filed a successful claim in court that declared the visitor's document had been signed under duress.

*The name of Melanie's visitor was Alexander Vidovszky, grandfather of Éva Vidovszky.*

"Well, and imagine meeting *you* here," Megan had replied, forcing a smile to her lips. "What brings you to London and the Keats House?"

"What brings *you* here, Dr. Crespi?"

"A love of Keats and a lecture this evening," Megan replied evenly.

"I too am a loooooover of Keats," Éva lied rapturously. "And I have been conferring with the director here, Mr. Natter. He is extremely interested in some Keats memorabilia I have fortuitously come by."

Yeah, "fortuitously" indeed, thought Megan to herself, imagining the shenanigans Vidovszky very likely went through to acquire them. "What do you have in particular?" she asked, hoping the dirty laundry list wouldn't be too long.

"I have several Keats letters to his betrothed, Fanny Brawne, and a lock of his hair in a gold square brooooooooch," Éva said smugly, her Hungarian accent growing stronger by the minute. "The museum will probably give its eye teeth—is that how you put it?—to acquire them."

"And you have proven their authenticity, of course?" asked Megan, suspecting that Vidovszky had no doubt paid good money to some unknown, self-qualified "expert" for authentication.

"But of course," replied Éva, irritated at Megan's tone.

"Well, good to see you, Dr. Crespi. Pity that I fly to Vienna this evening and will miss your lecture—that is, I presume that it is a lecture *you* are giving, yes?"

"Yes," Megan allowed, turning away with an abrupt farewell nod of her head. The happy visit to Keats had suddenly turned sour and she was eager to leave the irritating woman's presence. Briskly Megan walked back down to the Hampstead underground station and boarded the train back to South Kensington and her hotel, thoughts of Keats and Schiele in her head.

# 3

In the back office of the *Israelitische Kultusgemeinde Wien*—the IKG—agitation reigned. "Milton, you just went too far, far too far today!" accused his uncle Herman Levine. The two men sat facing each other at desks overlooking a noisy inner courtyard. Herman was literally shaking with anger; Milton looked defensive, his thumbs digging into the flesh of his clasped hands.

"But all I did was try to hurry things up, Uncle. And after all, I did succeed."

"You succeeded in giving the IKG a bad name, that's what you did, you idiot!"

"But look, Uncle, your people demonstrated for a whole week outside the Leopold and got nowhere except for some negative newspaper and TV publicity. What I did got us immediate attention and some sympathy from museum visitors," he whined.

Milton was referring to the "live performance" he and three young cohorts had just pulled off that afternoon at the Leopold Museum's café before being intercepted by the museum guards and placed under police arrest. Herman Levine had to go to the station off the Schottenring to bail them out.

The four teenagers had entered the Leopold Museum with retractable tape measures tucked in their pockets. They hurried past the artworks and made a beeline for the museum café. There, instead of taking a seat at one of the tables, they produced an instant "living" pantomime by commandeering a table in the middle of the long room. Tearing off his clothes in one quick motion, Milton Levine had jumped up onto the table and assumed an angular, kneeling Schielesque pose while the other three boys quickly "framed" him with their extended tape measures. All four began shouting "Restitute Egon Now! Restitute Egon Now!"

Visitors and tourists in the café were first amused then outraged by the incident and had applauded en masse when the guards escorted them out of the building.

The newspapers and television went wild over the day's story and the evening news featured the wild antic as one more example of the extremes to which the IKG would go to publicize its causes.

# 4

A strange ritual was taking place in the deserted ballroom of the ancient Schloss Gemmingen-Eggaberg. The castle with its vast grounds was situated on the northwest side of Austria's beautiful lake, the Traunsee, and connected to the picturesque town of Gmunden by a wooden pedestrian bridge of considerable length. Egon Schiele had once been photographed on this bridge in the company of his patron and adviser, the art critic Arthur

Roessler. The contrast between the two men could not have been greater: Roessler with hands on hips; the artist in an unwilling half turn toward the camera with the fingers of his right hand balled up tensely into a tight fist.

Nowadays the castle was closed to visitors but the ancestral owner, Baron Friedrich von Gemmingen-Eggaberg, an affable but rather gullible man in his mid-fifties, was definitely in residence. He was aware that Dr. Kurt Wagner, Grand Master of the Doppel-O Society, had convened his Inner Circle on this full-moon night in mid-March. The baron had gladly rented the Grand Master the entire east wing of his castle for the clan's occasional gatherings. He and his wife Marion were hugely indebted to the Grand Master for having saved the life of their teenage son Franzi in a boating accident on the Traunsee some two years earlier.

And now, in the castle ballroom, and bathed in bright moonlight, some twenty-four persons, all clothed in blood red caftans, moved together in an ever-closing ring. Slowly, they surrounded the large black case lying on a pedestal in the center of the room. Next to the case stood a tall, imposing man with red ringlets of hair that extended to his shoulders. He was dressed in a fur-trimmed black caftan and held aloft an unsheathed sword. He was leading the hypnotic chant: "Clothed in chastity, clothed in chastity."

As the group closed in on the Grand Master the chanting ceased. A new member was being initiated. In contrast to the other figures, his long tunic was white. He knelt before the pedestal, his head bowed and both hands on the black case.

"What bringest thou us, Wolf Schnitt, lowly novice?" queried the Grand Master, head of the small extremist cult he had founded in Vienna two years earlier. Since that time the sexual abstinence group—the S A—had doubled in number as Wagner's website, www.obliterateobsenity.org, known as the Double-O, or Doppel-O in German, attracted like-minded adherents across Austria and beyond. Membership was granted only to the proven fervent, however, and the Inner Circle of twenty-four practicing S As had met this evening for the first time in three months to admit the dedicated supplicant who had passed all but the final requirement for admission into their exclusive cult.

"I come bearing proof of my willingness to obey and carry out the commandments of the S A and the Doppel-O," answered the kneeling applicant, a large, muscular man with prematurely white hair and trim beard.

"And cometh thou clothed in chastity?"

"Aye, so cometh I," declared the kneeling man, standing up abruptly and letting his caftan fall to the ground. He was completely naked except for the leather chastity belt that encased his private parts.

The group murmured its approval.

"And hast thou fulfilled thy mission to obliterate obscenity?" asked the Grand Master solemnly.

"Aye, that I have," answered the applicant. "The Leopold Museum's naked Schiele has been censored with black duct tape as thou hast commanded. To remove the tape will also strip off all the paint. Restoration, if even possible, would take months and the museum will not dare show it to the general public again."

"And what of the perverted Klimt image on the museum's second floor?"

"That offence against nature has been severed from the canvas and left to rot." The applicant did not say where it had been left to rot, and the Grand Master did not ask.

"Thou hast done well. We have seen the newspaper and television accounts and know that thou art truthful."

Wolf Schnitt bowed his head in acknowledgement of the Grand Master's words. A plump, balding man standing directly behind him, second in command to the Grand Master, deftly slipped the applicant's caftan back on.

"But thou knowest we require the ultimate act. What proof hast thou that a habitual observer of obscenity—a Peeping Tom—has been eliminated?"

Slowly Schnitt raised the lid of the black case on the pedestal and folded it back. The circle of onlookers strained to see the contents. What they beheld was proof positive: two hands and two feet bathed in dried blood.

"Behold the extremities of the night watchman who was standing in front of the Schiele self-portrait admiring it. It is he whom I have eradicated."

The ring of believers resounded with murmurs of approval. The Grand Master took a step toward Wolf Schnitt and rested his sword lightly on the man's shoulder.

"Thou art hereby enfolded and received into the Sexual Abstinence Inner Circle of the Doppel-O Clan with its noble cause of obliterating obscenity wherever it may be found.

*"Today Vienna, tomorrow the world!"*

# 5

Megan's lecture for the Existential Psychotherapist Association had gone well despite the rude interruption caused by one member who insisted that Tchaikovsky's wife had *not* lived her last twenty years in an insane asylum. Other members of the association had shouted him down and the lecture had continued. Had Tchaikovsky's sudden flight from his marriage of convenience to quash rumors of his homosexuality triggered Miliukova's going insane? Megan ended with the composer's *Chanson Triste*, and two photographs, one of Antonina Miliukova, the other of the institution in which she had spent her final years. The Q and A session afterward had been lively and she and her host had not been able to leave until well after nine in the evening.

Back at the Aster House, Megan checked her e-mail, dumped the unwanted political solicitations, and set about answering the urgent and interesting ones till after midnight. Suddenly she was very tired. After all, the day had been quite full she told herself, thinking of her morning visit to Sotheby's and the fabulous Schiele artwork being restored there, then of Hampstead Heath and the unwelcome encounter with that bane of the art world, Éva Vidovszky. What was that woman really up to in London, she wondered.

Megan's flight to Vienna left promptly at eight o'clock the next morning and she passed the time working on the mystery novel she was writing, *The Mahler Murders*. Actually, she was glad to be continuing on to Wien, as there were a few Gustav Mahler details she wanted to verify. And a visit to the new Mahler section in the *Haus der Musik* on the Seilerstätte was always rewarding. The library alone matched that of her Mahler expert friend in Paris, Henri-Claude de La Granger.

It had been there, in Henri-Claude's guest room, that she had been bitten by his over-protective German Shepherd and taken to the local hospital. But the experience had not soured her on visiting Henri-Claude whenever she could. Right now, however, Paris was the last thing on her mind. She was in the middle of writing about Alma Mahler's active post-Gustav life when a voice over the loudspeaker announced their imminent arrival in Vienna.

Having only her carryon luggage to contend with, Megan hailed a taxi and fifteen minutes later was checking into her favorite hotel in the heart of the inner city, the Römischer Kaiser on the Annagasse. Unfortunately, the desk clerk apologized to her, they did not have a back room free. Would she mind a larger room for the same price—"Because you are such a loyal client"—in the front? And no, Megan did not mind too much, knowing that the pedestrian Annagasse was relatively quiet after nine pm or so.

Upstairs on the second floor she unpacked her beloved Prima Classe roller bag and her large black shoulder bag, and set her MacBook Air to charge. Then, by way of a fruit juicer café, she walked over to the Leopold Museum sipping her liquid breakfast.

"Please send her up immediately," commanded Johannes Ohm when the entry guard telephoned the Herr Direktor to say he had a visitor.

"Megan! Thank you so very much for coming to Wien," Hannes greeted her with genuine affection and a long hug.

"Oh, you know, Hannes, I am always ready to travel here, to my favorite city, but I am only sorry that this time it is under such horrible circumstances. Do you or the police have any idea now *who* might have done such a reprehensible act of vandalism? To say nothing of murder?"

"The police think it was the IKG. I am not so sure, however."

"Why is that? The IKG has done some pretty dramatic things in the past. I had to push my way through one of their noisy demonstrations in London just yesterday."

"And we also had a specific IKG event here yesterday, when four young protesters were physically removed from our café. But the IKG has never expressed disapproval of the *sexual* contents of the works whose ownership they contest."

"The two targeted paintings—was there any difference in provenance?" Megan asked.

"Well, the damaged Schiele self-portrait was in ownership contention until the lawsuit was concluded in favor of our museum last year."

"And the Klimt *Kissing Couple*?"

"It has a squeaky clean provenance and in fact was bought for the museum partly with government funds. So all is in order there.

"What I *am* very much struck by, Megan, is the fact that our two paintings were damaged in such a, shall we say, 'chaste' manner, covering up or literally cutting out any and all references to sex."

"Ah, I see exactly what you mean, Hannes. Sounds like an anti-pornography raid. But one that went wrong so the night watchman had to be done away with. But why such a brutal murder? Why cut off the hands and feet of the poor man? Could this be intended as a cult ceremonial of some sort?"

"That's exactly why I called you to come to Wien, dear Megan. We want *your* insights. And I wanted you to see *these* in person," Hannes said, picking up from his desk two black metal roses with edges tipped in silver. "One of these was left on the floor by each vandalized painting. What do you make of them?"

"I think of the black rose as a symbol of death," Megan said, reaching for the objects. "What about you?"

"Yes. However, I think..."

"But, Hannes, aren't you going to let me see what's happened to the Schiele and the Klimt?"

"Of course, Megan. Let's go upstairs to our restoration room."

What Megan saw was horrendous. Although most of Schiele's compelling nude image was intact, the genitals had been covered by thick black duct tape. It was applied across the body in an inverted T shape. Schiele's yellow legs, torso, and raised arms glistened above and below the tape.

"What a travesty!" Megan exclaimed with indignation.

"Yes, the work of a hypocritical prude who is obsessed by sex, I would imagine," said Hannes.

"Now let me show you our poor Klimt remains."

They walked to the other side of the restoration room. There, still clinging to its frame, was what was left of the painting, the central part of which had been sliced with a sharp instrument and ripped out. Only Klimt's decorative surround was left—an evocation of the cosmos with silver and gold spots of light above and a spangled green terrain below, rich with small colorful flower buds.

"This is just terrible," Megan murmured. "And there was nothing of the canvas center left behind?"

"Nothing. This vandal made off with the heart and soul of Klimt's painting."

"Well, if it were put up for sale, the whole art world would know from where it came."

"*Ja*. But if it goes into a fanatic's private collection..."

His cell phone rang. The expression on his face darkened as he listened to his caller and his mouth opened in disbelief.

"You'll never guess what's happened *now*," he turned to Megan after hanging up.

"What?"

"*Schiele's grave and tombstone have been desecrated!*"

# 6

Jillian Lloyd and Rupert Wechseln were conferring over lunch at Paolo's Italian restaurant near Sotheby's. Their heads were bent over a color photograph of Schiele's *Self-Portrait Nude Standing with Hands on Hips*. The right hand side of the work had already been treated with emulsion and the once bright yellow tone of Schiele's flesh had been restored to its original saffron tint.

"I just don't think the remainder of the Schiele restoration can be finished by the time of our next auction," Rupert lamented.

"I didn't think the damage looked too bad," said Jillian, thinking of the painting's glimmering hue that had already been restored to some of Schiele's flesh.

"Oh, most of the paint is in good enough condition despite the dark yellowing of the varnish. It is more the fact that the canvas had been rolled up for so many years. That's what is giving me severe problems. There is a roll mark in the middle of the body. I've slowly attached and marginally extended the canvas on wooden stretchers, yes, just as you and Megan saw. But it will take a judicious use of moisture and further stretching to work away the very visible warping of the surface along the whole width of the work."

"How long might that take," Jillian asked concernedly.

"That's the problem. I can't predict. Right now I'm running a wire from side to side and then I'll tighten it by twisting it ever so slowly around a dowel rod every few days."

"That sounds precarious! What else might you try?"

"If the wire doesn't work I'm going to attach a one-by-two piece of wood in the back along the middle of the painting, but I don't have much hope for that procedure; at the most it would improve things only slightly. Right now Schiele looks as though he has a layer of fat over his bare belly and that's just what we don't want," Rupert sighed.

The two walked back to Sotheby's and were surprised to find there were no demonstrators out protesting. They had been there when they had left for lunch but now they were nowhere to be seen. Instead several London policemen were fanned out around the building entrance.

"What's going on?" Jillian questioned the nearest policeman. "Where are the demonstrators?"

"We've rounded them up and dispersed them. We had to, considering what just happened inside the building."

"*What* just happened inside the building?" Rupert asked, feeling the hairs on the nape of his neck stand up.

"Someone has stolen a painting," curtly answered the policeman, trying to wave them on.

Quickly, the duo flashed their Sotheby's IDs and were allowed to enter the building. The agitated director of auctions caught up with them in the great hall.

"It's a disaster!" he shouted. "Your Schiele has vanished from the restoration room. *Please* tell me, Rupert, that you moved it to another location."

Rupert's face turned pale. The apprehension he had instinctively felt outside could not have prepared him for this.

"No, I have certainly not moved the Schiele. Jillian and I were just looking at it before lunch."

"Well, between then and now *someone* has been in the restoration room and taken the painting. The canvas was simply sliced from its stretchers. Our only hope is that the person hasn't had a chance to get out of the building with it. The front entry is covered and there are more police at the back entrance, so we're covered there."

"So the only place the robber could go is up," Jillian said, recovering slowly from the shock.

"The police are searching the upper floors and roof right now," the director assured them.

"They should, if we're lucky, have our man very soon. Sotheby's couldn't stand the scandal of a multi-million pound painting being stolen right from under its nose," he almost whined.

\* \* \*

Lorenzo Ladro laughed. It had been so easy. When the Grand Master

summoned him from Milan to Gmunden and Schloss Gemmingen-Eggaberg two days ago he knew that an important task must be in the offing.
And sure enough his Master had given him a *meraviglioso* assignment. He
was to fly to London immediately, find a way to access Sotheby's Auction
House, enter the restoration room in the basement without being observed,
and liberate the Schiele naked self-portrait under restoration there.

The red-haired Grand Master, Kurt Wagner, spoke in terse terms.
"Under no circumstances are you to allow the painting to be damaged any
more than it is now. You will have to roll it up, but you must bring it back
to me with no further damage."

"I am not to destroy it? But, Master, is that not against our obliterate
obscenity oath?" Ladro asked, confused by his orders.

"This is a unique and very special circumstance," Wagner answered
in a manner that brooked no further questions. Nor was he about to reveal
how it was that he knew there was a Schiele at Sotheby's. Not for nothing
did he keep a Sotheby's employee on his payroll. The man, Walter Holloway,
was a new member of the Doppel-O. The usual stiff membership dues had
been waived in his case as his position as night watchman at Sotheby's was
worth more than gold. Holloway had now grandly proved his loyalty to the
cause.

Ladro took his leave, headed for Vienna and caught a flight for
London that very afternoon. The next day, dressed in a hoodie and armed
with his cell phone camera, he joined the crowd of IKG protesters and
scrutinized the two-story white building with large twelve-paned windows
that constituted Sotheby's at 34-35 New Bond Street. At the roof level a
third, attic story had been created by building a setback, multi-windowed
enclosure. Hmm, promising.

To the left of Sotheby's and flush with it was an almost identical
building, also white with great windows. It rose two stories and, like Sotheby's, supported a rooftop enclosure framing two garret windows. A tall
chimney abutted the Sotheby's attic floor, however, and things did not look
promising as a route for entering the auction house.

Ladro sized up the building to the right of Sotheby's. Larger than its
neighbor, also with white facing, it rose three full stories with an attic garret

window and high-peaked roof abutting a large brick chimney. Along the balcony rim of this attic story, Ladro estimated, he could cross over to the Sotheby's roof unseen, drop down and gain entry through one of the three garret windows.

*Facile*, he decided. He would break in around noon the next day, a time when most of Sotheby's employees would be eating in their offices or out for lunch. Unlike at night, the motion detectors would be off. For now, with a free evening ahead of him, he welcomed the opportunity to observe night life on the Strand. He took a few photos of the rooftops involved, then headed for the tube station that would take him to the Strand and Twinings' Tea Shop for a bit of quaint English nourishment. Later he would cruise Trafalgar Square, and, just for fun ponder how one might break into Buckingham Palace. After all, an intruder had once come upon Queen Elizabeth to the astonishment of both, and the British papers had a hay day reporting the event.

The next day at noon, armed with a round leather blueprint carrier, Ladro approached his quarry. Everything went as planned. In fact it was easier than he had anticipated, since, once he crossed over to the Sotheby's building, he found that the back stairs went all the way up to the roof. Silently and cautiously he descended. He met no one on any of the landings, and no one was in the basement corridor when he entered it. After checking out several rooms, the doors of which conveniently had glass panels, Ladro found what he was sure had to be his goal. Looking through the glass panel he saw an oversized table that took up most of the room. On it, turned face up, was a canvas upon which the naked figure of a man was painted. A side table held a variety of brushes and bottles, and a pair of white surgical gloves had been carefully placed beside them.

Ladro was in and out of the room in seconds. His great Cressi Borg knife cut neatly and swiftly along the four wooden stretchers that held the large painting and it sank neatly onto the table below. Rolling the canvas up quickly in his blueprint carrier, Ladro pressed it against his jacket and ran back up the staircase to the roof. No one had seen him, although he had certainly heard plenty of jovial conversation coming from the different floor levels. But thankfully no one was on the stairs. It was a bit more difficult to climb back out of the garret window he had broken into and hoist himself and the leather carrier up to the adjoining building's balcony rim, but he made it on the second attempt. No one below had spotted him: all attention was on the shouting demonstrators. Two hours later found Ladro at Heathrow waiting to board his flight back to Vienna.

The Grand Master would be pleased.

\* \* \*

The Grand Master was indeed pleased. Paying Lorenzo Ladro off handsomely upon his arrival at the Schloss in Gmunden, Kurt Wagner, his hair flying about his face, went in search of the castle owner, Friedrich von Gemmingen-Eggaberg. The baron's wife informed him that her husband had gone into town on business, something to do with the Brahms Museum. Wgner thanked her, then walked briskly over the wooden bridge toward town.

He reached the *Kammerhofmuseum* a few minutes later and entered the Brahms memorabilia room. Sure enough, there was the baron with the museum director, both facing a short woman whose black hair was swept up in a bun at the back of her head. She was wearing a purple pant suit and heels that clicked when she walked.

Éva Vidovszky was haggling with the baron, who was silently studying something in his hand.

*A fenébe!* she exclaimed in Hungarian to herself. Out loud she assured the unresponsive man: "Believe me, it is the genuine article. The two-page letter is in Brahms' own handwriting and the envelope, as you can see, is addressed to his surgeon and amateur musician friend Dr. Theodor Billroth. The contents of the letter concern an essay Billroth had begun titled '*Wer ist musikalisch?*' and they give us Brahms' reaction to the scientific answers essayed by his brilliant colleague. This letter concerning 'who is musical?' is priceless!"

"So what is *your* price?" asked the baron evenly, handing the envelope back to Vidovszky. An approaching Kurt Wagner stopped in mid-step to hear the woman's answer.

"Sixty thousand Euros for the letter, twenty-five thousand for the envelope."

"Make it seventy thousand in all and I will present your case to the mayor of Gmunden."

"No, I cannot do that, Herr Baron. The historic stamps on the front of the envelope and Brahms' return address on the back, of Bad Ischl, where he was visiting his good friend Johann Strauss, make this a unique Brahms item. I cannot go below twenty-five thousand for the envelope. Why, sold separately it would fetch possibly thirty thousand or more, who knows?"

The Éva Vidovszky reputation for hard bargaining was living up to its name.

The baron hesitated, reaching for the envelope and turning it over and over again.

"I'll tell you what, Herr Baron," cooed Vidovszky. "If you invite me up to your Schloss to see your Albrecht Dürer collection, you can have both letter and envelope for seventy thousand."

"Who has told you about my Dürer collection?" asked the baron sharply, furious that a commercial dealer would have the nerve to ask to see the unique Gemmingen-Eggaberg collection of the German Renaissance artist's work. It had been passed down from one generation to the next for over four centuries. Art historians and museum directors had importuned the family for decades, pleading to see the collection which was known to have, in addition to graphic works, a second self-portrait of 1500 by the great Nuremberg artist. But even though the present generation of Gemmingen-Eggabergs had fallen upon hard times financially, the baron had protected the family heirlooms and refused to allow public access to the Dürers. The idea of selling the collection was anathema.

Catching sight of Kurt Wagner in the room, the baron acknowledged his presence with a quick nod.

"Why, Herr Baron, it is common knowledge that you have a superb collection of Dürer—even a self-portrait!"

"You will have to excuse me now, Frau Vidovszky. I will put in a good word for your Brahms items with the mayor, but that is all I can do."

With that the baron nodded his head in dismissal of the pushy woman, shook hands with the harassed director, and exited the Brahms room with Wagner. The two men, who were on a first-name basis, walked energetically back toward the castle, exchanging indignant comments on the impossible personality of the ubiquitous Vidovszky woman. Why didn't she just stay put in her Vienna Antiquariat gallery instead of running all over Europe peddling letters and memorabilia of the famous? The fact that she had sold Schiele's *Nude Self-Portrait Seated* to the Leopold Museum in Vienna had brought her instant fame, then notoriety when the provenance of the painting had been vigorously, if unsuccessfully, contested by the Austrian IKG.

When the baron and Kurt reached the Schloss, Kurt touched his arm and said in a hushed tone, "Fritz, the Schiele *Self-Portrait* has arrived."

"Arrived?" An expression of relief and joy crossed Fritz's features. *Schloss Gemmingen-Eggaberg would be saved!*

Once again Fritz marveled at the timely arrival in his and his wife's life of the mysterious Dr. Kurt Wagner from Vienna. First, he happened to be nearby, two years ago, when their teenage Franzi would have had a fatal boating accident were it not for Wagner, who risked his own life to save their son. They felt endlessly indebted to him. Then, a few months later, the mesmerizing giant of a man, who was clean-shaven with a long thin nose and red hair that fell to his shoulders, had approached them with an unusual but highly attractive proposal.

He, Wagner, founder of an international anti-pornography group—the Doppel-O Society—desired an absolutely private site at which to convene the Inner Circle of the Society on a regular basis. In exchange for permission to use the uninhabited east wing of the Schloss he would pay not just handsomely, he would pay extravagantly. He named a monthly sum that was impossible to turn down.

And now Wagner had come into possession of a valuable nude self-portrait by Egon Schiele that had long been thought to be lost.

"And as promised, I will give you one half of the sum I obtain when it is sold," Kurt was saying to Fritz. "In exchange, you will accept that money as payment for six acres of land in the forest behind your castle."

Of course it was understandable that the leader of a society against pornography, intent on "obliterating obscenity," would wish to unload what many would describe as obscene. Fritz had a general idea as to what the asking price could be for such a "lost" work, and now Wagner not only had it in hand—by what means Fritz really did not wish to know—but apparently he also had a buyer for it. Kurt told him he was leaving for Russia that very evening.

Mystified but elated, Fritz could only repeat to himself that the Schloss and all its adjoining lands would be saved!

\* \* \*

A full day had passed. The London press knew that a painting had been stolen from Sotheby's but exactly what had been taken had not been disclosed. Now Jillian Lloyd and Rupert Wechseln were consulting with the director about when to release a detailed description of the stolen Schiele self-portrait to the newspapers. Public awareness of the subject matter might tip off museums and potential buyers should they be approached, at least those who were above adding stolen works to their private collections.

"But it's such an *embarrassment* for us," Sotheby's director almost whined. "It is the first time in our history that a purloining of such magnitude has taken place. And god knows what further damage to the canvas has occurred."

"Perhaps just because of the damage the work will be difficult to sell?" Jillian asked hopefully.

"I do know eventually we shall have to inform the police as to what exactly was stolen. But that means instant media coverage," the director fretted.

"I recommend you do it sooner rather than later," Rupert urged. "And at the same time we should contact members of Restorers International to be on the watch for such a canvas. Even if they are unacquainted with Schiele's work, a half-restored canvas should be a pretty easy item to spot. We should circulate a photograph to them immediately, to the police, and definitely to the media. That way the image will go viral," insisted Rupert.

Jillian sighed. "What an ironic way for Schiele to have the publicity he always craved."

¬

Hannes and Megan were in his 2011 Volvo station wagon headed for Schiele's cemetery, the Friedhof Ober-Sankt-Veit, in Vienna's Hietzing district. Neither one of them spoke but they were thinking along similar lines. They dreaded what grisly scene might be awaiting them at the cemetery. After conferring for a moment with the gate keeper, Hannes drove straight down a side lane toward Schiele's grave. Megan spotted the grave of the opera singer Christel Goltz, who died in 2008. A few turns further down a policeman and two cemetery workers were standing by Schiele's tall tombstone. Mounds of dirt were on either side in front of it. A woman was urgently talking to the policeman. Several journalists and photographers were also on the scene.

"*Ach! You* here, Felicitas!" Hannes cried as they got out of the car. Turning to Megan he made the introductions. "Megan, this is Frau Professor Felicitas Geduld, the founder of Vienna's Egon Schiele Society. Felicitas, this is..."

"But we *know* each other!" both women cried out at the same time, embracing.

"Oh, what terrible circumstances to be meeting under," Felicitas moaned, pointing to the desecrated tombstone behind her. Megan took a few steps closer. What she beheld was worse than she had imagined. The two larger than life bas-relief figures on the stone pillar at the head of the grave had been attacked with a hammer and chisel. The faces of Egon and Edith Schiele were almost unrecognizable, so many gashes had been cut into their features. The two nude figures had been further damaged. Schiele's groin had been ground down while his wife's bare breasts were completely chiseled out. Across the mutilated figures large red spray-painted letters spelled out the words: "Obliterate Obscenity!"

"And that's not all," groaned Felicitas, pointing to the grave itself.

Megan had been concentrating totally on the sculpture. Now she lowered her eyes and saw what Felicitas meant. An attempt had been made to shovel dirt out of the grave. Mounds of earth lay on either side, and the top of the uppermost coffin—that of Schiele's—had been partially uncovered. On it had been placed a single black rose tipped in silver.

Hannes made a sudden start. "This desecration is the work of a cult! Megan! Felicitas! The black rose of death has to be the symbol of the Doppel-O. Surely you've heard of it? The Double-O cult?"

"Is that the lunatic fringe of the IKG?" asked Megan quietly, still stunned by their discovery.

"Oh, no, the Doppel-O is some sort of secret society here in Austria," explained Hannes. "They have a website. People who have tried to find out more information have given up because the society charges a huge sum of money—some two thousand Euros—merely for the privilege of answering personal questions. It seems the society has a series of tests, as well as more Euro demands, before one can finally meet the clan members face to face."

Hannes went over to talk to the policeman and two cemetery workers.

"I guess nothing can protect an artist from posthumous hatred," brooded Megan, thinking of the animosity that must have triggered the vandalism at the Leopold Museum just the day before this staggering discovery at the cemetery.

"Are you sure your Schiele Museum is not a target now?" asked Hannes, returning to the women.

"We will take every precaution. I only learned about what happened here at the cemetery a few hours ago."

The trio discussed the depressing situation a few minutes more, then broke up.

"Where would you like to go now, Megan?" Hannes inquired.

"Back to the Römischer Kaiser, if you please," she answered, suddenly feeling quite tired. "We'll get together again tomorrow morning, all right?"

"Prima!"

When Megan climbed out of Hannes' Volvo after the drive back to downtown she heard her phone ring in the outside pocket of her shoulder bag. The ID said "Claire Chandler." Quickly sitting down in a quiet nook off the lobby Megan answered.

"You don't know how good it is to hear your voice, Claire. It's been a terrible day. Gruesome things are going on here."

"Well, then steel yourself, honey. And be sure you are sitting down. I have some frightening news to tell you."

# 8

Tall, slender, and with a head of spiked dark brown hair very much like Schiele's, billionaire Boris Ussachevsky sat alone in the spacious back office of his elegant Gallery Solovey near the Hermitage in St. Petersburg. With a feeling of immense pride he slowly scrutinized his newest Schiele acquisition. It had cost him a bit, but it was worth it. At the last Sotheby's auction in London he had successfully bid against his closest rival in Russia, Alexandra Azarova, whose huge Gallery Rasputin in Moscow was one of the best known in Russia.

Yes, that was a triumph!

Never mind that the Schiele townscape—obviously from the year 1911—had been left unfinished and unsigned. He, Boris, expert on and lover of Egon, knew exactly what the artist had intended. And he had already attended to the addendum of Schiele's characteristic box-encased printed signature. He had placed it on the lower left of the canvas and dated the painting 1911. Now he was waiting for the smell of fresh oil paint to fade.

The townscape was gorgeous. It showed ancient Krumau's main bridge and the horseshoe bend of the Moldau river with ancient two-and three-story houses fronting the dark blue water. The scene was without figures—quite typical of Schiele when he was painting town-and-landscapes. Views of Krumau—Schiele's mother's hometown—were especially prized by Boris. This was the town where, seven years after his father's death,

Schiele had experienced a visitation from him. The impressionable artist had written about it at length.

It was strange, Boris thought, that Schiele had never portrayed the father whom he later worshipped. At least in memory. In actuality Adolf Schiele had been distressed by his young son's concentration on drawing to the exclusion of all else. In fact one evening, when he came home from his work as Tulln's stationmaster, he found the whole living quarters of his apartment above the station lined with drawings of trains winding in and out of the rooms. In one angry sweep Adolf had swept up the drawings and thrust them into the fire, shouting at Egon to get to his neglected homework.

Despite this one known instance of Schiele senior's intemperate attitude toward his son's work, in later life the artist yearned for the father he had lost when he was fourteen. He had worked out his longing in several allegories over the years—a famous one showed two monks, the younger one in front, confronting the viewer, the other one behind him, seemingly blind and stumbling into the younger man.

While experts like that Megan Crespi of Dallas, of all places, believed the back figure to be that of Gustav Klimt, he, Boris, knew for certain that the figure was Adolf Schiele. He could *feel* it. Why he could almost be the reincarnation of Schiele himself! And the last time he had communicated with Crespi about his interpretation she had allowed that the allegory could have two meanings.

This was all Boris needed. Hadn't the young Schiele always found father figures? Arthur Roessler the art critic, for one, and the kindly Heinrich Benesch, for another. And, more importantly, Gustav Klimt himself had taken on the young Schiele. While he was still studying at the Vienna Academy of Art, Egon had suddenly appeared in the older master's atelier garden with a portfolio of his drawings. "*Hab ich Talent?*" he asked. Klimt had looked through the drawings silently, then answered: "*Viel zu viel!*" Yes, Klimt had been right to tell the young boy that he had "much too much" talent.

Yes, as a boy Schiele was the Mozart of art—precocious, original, and hugely productive. That productivity continued as he grew into manhood, painting in three categories: radical portraits and self-portraits, lyric town-scapes and landscapes, and mysterious allegories.

How right, Boris thought, his painter grandfather Vladimir had been to acquire some of young Schiele's drawings directly from him, back in the early 1910s. Most of them were agitated self-portraits naked or half clothed; others were nude portraits of his younger sister Gerti. These searing images of angst Boris did not have on display in his gallery. He kept them shielded from public knowledge in his faraway dacha Solovey on the lake at Votkinsk, the childhood home of Tchaikovsky. Being there, looking out at the lake, was, Boris had always thought, like being at Swan Lake. Yes, whenever he was at his dacha Solovey—a small replica in wood of King Ludwig's Neuschwanstein palace—he could relax completely and give himself over to being with Egon and Pyotr Illyich.

A closet gay like Tchaikovsky, enormously wealthy, and with no rel-atives to care for, Boris could totally unwind in their felt presence. He was eternally thankful to his grandfather, whose Futurist canvases, like those of Kazimir Malevich, were in high demand. Only two weeks ago he had sold Vladimir's *Brown on Brown* of 1918 to a South American buyer for an extremely lucrative sum.

Sales of his grandfather's works had picked up recently, as historians were reevaluating the role of Russian Futurism versus that of the slightly earlier Italian Futurism. And his grandfather had exchanged works with Umberto Boccioni during the Italian's three months in Russia. The Boc-cioni pieces were selling almost as well as Vladimir Ussachevsky's paint-ings.

This was good, since the Schiele Krumau townscape he was now admiring had been expensive. Alexandra Azarova's middleman had let slip her name as that of his competitive bidder at the London Sotheby's auction. Azarova's "anonymous" representative at the auction had then been bribed by Boris' middleman, and so they learned that Azarova had given her representative a cutoff figure. With this information Boris knew exactly how much he would need to bid to secure the Schiele painting. Of course he had to pay a handsome bribe to Azarova's representative, but it was worth it. At last he, Boris, owned a Schiele townscape!

And now an Austrian by the name of Max Valentin had contacted him from Vienna offering him a Schiele direct, no auction house involved. It was a colossal find, Valentin had assured him. A life-size Schiele self-portrait nude. It was one of three known large images from the year 1910 in which the artist showed himself completely naked. The last of the series, stylistically, was in the Leopold Museum. The one Valentin was offering showed the naked artist standing front and center, leaning to the viewer's left, hands on hips, and boney legs slightly apart.

Boris had immediately consulted the updated Janette Killar oeuvre catalogue he owned and found a black-and-white photograph of the life-size work. Along with two life-size nude portraits of the artist's sister Gerti, it was described as one of two lost nude self-portraits of 1910. All of them—the two self-portraits and the two Gerti portraits—were designated as "present whereabouts unknown."

The question of previous ownership, of provenance, would have to remain unanswered for now. Boris was awaiting delivery of the Schiele and the delivery would be made in person by the mysterious Herr Max Valentin.

* * *

"What could possibly be 'frightening' news, Claire," queried Megan, slightly irritated that her friend would begin their long distance call in such an unsettling fashion.

"Well it *was* frightening, at least for me. But don't worry, all is well now. This is what happened. I'm out at your lake house with Button, taking care of the pool repair as you asked. Now, you know that Button has been doing very well since becoming blind; that he has managed to find the doggie door, our bedrooms, and his water dish."

"Yes?" said Megan, hating the suspense.

" Well, last night Button came upstairs as usual when I was preparing for bed. He was out of my sight for only a few moments while I brushed my teeth. But in that short a time he somehow wandered further afield than usual and he fell through the railings of the upstairs balcony onto the floor below!"

"What? *Fell?* But that's a distance of eight feet!"

"No, no, Megan, he is okay, absolutely okay now. When I rushed down to see him he was lying on the floor below the balcony. He was on his side, not moving, and there was a bit of blood coming from his mouth."

"How terrible!" Megan breathed.

"Because it was late at night I couldn't get in touch with the local vet, so I just gently picked up what I thought was the body of a dead little Button and put him on top of a towel on the couch, stroking him all the while. A few minutes went by—I was crying—when all of a sudden I saw him move slightly, then stretch his front feet, then his back feet! I was so relieved. He seemed to be trying to ascertain whether anything was broken. He got to his feet and essayed a few steps. Minutes later he was slowly wagging his tail and asking me to hold him. I was never so relieved in my life!" Claire concluded her amazing account.

"A blind dog recovered from an eight-foot fall? This is really incredible!" exclaimed Megan, her voice rising in excitement.

"When I got him to the vet the next day, she examined him all over and found absolutely no broken bones. She said that it was probably because he *was* blind that there was no damage. He was unaware that he was falling and so didn't tense up. It's a miracle, honey, it's a miracle."

"You are so right! Poor little darling doggie. No wonder you said you had 'frightening news' to tell me. Whew! Please take an iPhone photo of him and send it to me right away. Okay?"

"I've already done so. You'll see it when you have a chance to check your e-mail."

Megan brought Claire up to date on the day's events and then went upstairs for a quick lie-down before dinner. Thoughts of little Button chased through her mind.

Fritz von Gemmingen-Eggaberg could hardly wait to find his wife Marion after he parted company with Kurt Wagner, who was off to Russia that very afternoon. Fritz was actually whistling a tune when he found Marion on the couch in the family den playing with their blue-eyed cat Maya.

"Darling, I have wonderful news!" he greeted her, bending over to give her a kiss.

"What is it, sweetheart? I haven't seen you in such a good mood for ever so long."

"The thing is, well, we are going to be able to keep our Dürer."

"Can this be true?" Marion jumped up to look him square in the eyes.

"*Ja, ja,* it is going to be true. And it's thanks to Kurt Wagner. Thank god I agreed to let him convene his Inner Circle Doppel-O meetings here. He has paid me back a hundredfold in rent always, but now he is about to reward me a hundred thousandfold."

"Do explain!" urged Marion, sitting back down and drawing Fritz to the couch beside her.

"You know that Kurt and his dedicated cult are violently opposed to pornography."

"Yes, I've looked several times at his fervent website about 'obliterating obscenity.'"

"Well, one of his agents has procured a major Schiele work to offer to a billionaire Russian client. The man is a Schiele fanatic and evidently will pay any price for the artist's work. This painting is a naked self-portrait done when Schiele was nineteen or twenty years old. It had always been considered lost. But somehow Kurt found where it was—he didn't tell me the details—and he is leaving with the painting today to meet with the client he has in Russia. Kurt will then have enough funds to buy the acreage he wants in the forest back of the Schloss as a permanent home for his Doppel-O clan."

"So the Gemmingen-Eggaberg Dürer has indeed been saved. Oh,

Fritz, I'm so happy! What marvelous news. We must tell Franzi right away. He already adores Kurt. Now he will love him even more for having saved Dürer for our family."

\* \* \*

Kurt had not told Fritz everything. Always a man to hedge his bets, he would be visiting a second potential buyer in Russia: Alexandra Azarova of Moscow. In fact, he would offer the Schiele to her first. That is why he had booked a Lufthansa flight first to Moscow, then, after a day there, he would fly on to St. Petersburg. Let the two of them fight it out. He was his own Sotheby's incarnate and he relished the role.

As he sat lounging comfortably in his business class seat, he thought back to the irritating incident he and Fritz had experienced that noon at the Brahms Museum. With all her faults Éva Vidovszky did have a point when she asked to see Fritz's very private Albrecht Dürer collection. It was something he too had desired very much to see, but so far his friendship with Fritz and Marion had not developed to the point where he could ask such a favor—a request that had, without exception, been turned down by the family when approached by scholars, museum directors, and, heaven forbid, commercial galleries.

Once he had tentatively tried questioning their son Franzi, who in a sense was indebted to him. But the boy was mute on the subject, obviously well-schooled in the family tradition of never discussing the collection. But, oh, how he would like to see the self-portrait that the collection was reputed to have. Rumor had it that the painting was a second Christ-like self-portrayal by the twenty-eight-year-old German master. It was painted in the same century-turning year, 1500, as was the well-known *Self-Portrait Frontal* in Munich's Alte Pinakothek.

Although not conveniently near Alexandra Azarova's gallery, Kurt had nevertheless booked an overnight room at the modern Park Kultury Posutochno Apartments, where he could cook a meal in his own kitchen. Which is just what he did when he arrived, ravenous, at two in the morning. He had brought his crab cakes and kit salad with him. And the Schiele canvas, still in the leather roll. He had opened the roll only once just to see how much restoration would have to be done by one of his two potential buyers. He was rather shocked at the warping of the partially restored canvas, but he would downplay the amount of time that would be required to bring the picture to its former golden glory. Here was an obscenity that the museum public would be spared. Whichever of his two clients bought the Schiele, it would most probably go into their private collections, never to be seen again.

How gratifying it was to fulfill the Doppel-O mission while at the same time bringing in a fortune to benefit his growing society. The permanent home he would provide Doppel-O members in the pine forest behind the castle would attract new members. His cause would be carried out not just on the European continent but also in North America, where some of the most perverted works of art were housed in immoral museums, contaminating the public every day of the week with their displays of sex and nakedness. Yes! His sect would grow and they would have a common home. May the obscene Schiele go to the highest Russian bidder!

# 10

Since she was in Vienna and would not be having dinner with Hannes until seven o'clock that evening, Megan, after a short nap, decided to go out to see what sort of job Felicitas Geduld's Schiele Society had done in reproducing the artist's last home and studio. Actually the building at Wattmanngasse No. 6, where Schiele had lived, was now empty of residents and boarded up. The Schiele Society had been unsuccessful in trying to buy the building from a foreign owner. All the Society could do was to have the building next to it, Wattmanngasse No. 8, affixed with a plaque indicating that Egon Schiele had lived in the adjacent building at No. 6. They had, however, been able to take over the ground floor of No. 8 and it was there that the artist's studio had been reproduced. Megan was eager to see how that had turned out.

She exited her hotel and walked the three blocks over to the opera house and a bank of taxis. Some seven minutes later she was at Wattmann-gasse No. 8.

Nodding to the pleasant woman at the desk opposite the entry door, Megan looked around the room. Photographs of Schiele taken in 1914 before the outbreak of World War I by fellow artist Anton Josef Trčka adorned the walls. Originally in brom silver, they had been enlarged and took up all sides of the room. The riveting photographs captured Schiele's contorted pantomimes still-stopped by the camera in poses reminiscent of the German dancer Mary Wigman's angular body language. Ah, but to see the images blown up to life size! What a treat. Some of the images caught the artist displaying his arcane language of the hands, with fingers stiffly apart or welded together in tense and terse positions. One photograph showed the artist's face twice, with the back one in apparent conversation with the front one. This double image paralleled Schiele's dark double self-portrait allegories in which the back figure seemed to threaten or control the front figure.

Other photographs dated from earlier or later periods in the artist's short life span. They documented the dark passage from youthful bravado to angst-filled, staring poses, to a more relaxed but always succinct body language. One photograph showed the artist posed in front of the large glass cabinet he had built and painted black. There he kept his favorite objects and books. Another photograph showed him seated in one of the two black chairs he had also carpentered, his body tense, with fingers balled up into fists.

It was almost like being with Schiele in person, Megan thought, as she walked around the well-lit room. One photograph caught her attention: it showed Schiele seated and holding a little three-legged wooden horse, the same one depicted at the top of a rare still life by the artist. Megan had seen one of the wooden horses in Schiele's collection in person when she became friends with the artist's two sisters in the 1960s: Melanie, the older, serious, honest and genuine; Gerti, still the coquette with a mind that jumped compulsively from subject to subject. Her long-suffering son, Anton—Toni—Peschka, Jr. would always have to direct his chattering mother back to the conversation at hand when Megan interviewed her about her brother. Melanie, on the other hand, was eager to relate stories about her talented brother, and it was from her that Megan had learned the famous story of Egon's visit to Gustav Klimt that resulted in the older artist's pronouncing he had "much too much talent."

Now, as Megan studied the photograph of the artist and his beloved little carved horse, she remembered that Melanie, who had inherited one of her brother's wooden horses, had shown her how, with a bit of effort, the horse's head could be flipped back. Its hollow body contained a key to the cellar and its storage rooms at his home and former atelier at Hietzinger Hauptstrasse 101.

Megan had actually talked Melanie into visiting the building once where, after taking photographs of the edifice from the outside, they went inside and down the basement steps to the cellar, hoping against hope that there might be some forgotten Schieles down there. Nothing had come of their little foray, but it gave them plenty to laugh and brag about.

The disappointing object of their research was the cellar where, during World War I, Schiele had apparently stored some of the larger paintings he was working on. Correspondence from the artist to his friend Arthur Roessler indicated that he was at work on "an extraordinary series which will benefit all of Wien." The art world had not found out, however, to what the cryptic sentence was referring, as nothing in either the Wattmanngasse or the Hietzinger Hauptstasse studios or cellars after Schiele's death matched up with the letter to Roessler. Arthur Roessler himself, who would become Schiele's main biographer, putting together several books on the artist based on his writings, was at a loss as to what the "extraordinary series" might be. It was apparently a secret that Schiele had taken to his grave.

Or was it? Megan wondered if one of the little wooden horses Schiele collected had been preserved in the special hiding place in the artist's black display cabinet. She knew that this vitrine, along with the artist's two chairs and the great standing mirror that had reflected so many agonized self-portraits, was now at the Wien Museum. It might be worth a visit to that museum just to check. It was too late to go today, especially since she was meeting Hannes for dinner and she wanted to be fresh for that.

The ticket taker at the little Wattmanngasse Schiele Museum waved Megan on into the inner room, pronouncing her a senior citizen and declaring that entry was free for her. Jolted, Megan was suddenly reminded that she was seventy-seven. Okay, but truly this museum should be charging something more than what she had just started to pay. She had been told that several dozen tourists showed up each day to visit.

The inner room, which was down a long, narrow hall, contained a few academy drawings by Schiele—expert studies from antique plaster casts—and some early portraits of his family—his mother, his two sisters, and above all his Uncle Czihaczek, who controlled the family purse strings.

As Megan studied the early works, marveling at their already apparent virtuosity, she heard a loud shout from the ticket taker, who had left the front room for a few minutes to go to the bathroom.

"*Nein, nein!* she was shouting. Megan ran back along the corridor to the front room where the woman was now on the phone, calling Felicitas. What had so alarmed her?

"Oh, no!" Megan exclaimed, looking at the walls of the room. Black spray paint had been applied to all the Trčka photographs, obliterating in each case the head and hands of the artist. What a travesty!

Who could have committed such a mean, deranged act? And *why*? Megan walked from photograph to photograph, surveying the damage and also trying to calm down the agitated ticket taker.

Felicitas Geduld got there within a few minutes and, in shock, silently surveyed the damage.

"Remember what Johannes Ohm said about the cult group Doppel-O," Felicitas finally enjoined Megan. "It has to be them. The IKG doesn't carry a grudge against Schiele. They're all about restitution. About checking out provenances. Vandalism just isn't their thing."

"Do we know who the head of the Doppel-O is?" Megan asked.

"Yes. It is a very strange Viennese man, Dr. Kurt Wagner—a medical doctor. He is the founder of the cult. And he is extremely elusive. Journalists and photographers would give their eye teeth to interview him, but he keeps a low profile. Which is pretty difficult if what I hear about him is true."

"What's that?" Megan asked.

"Except for the fact that he has red hair and not dark brown, he looks exactly like Albrecht Dürer's portrait of himself. You know, the one from fifteen hundred when Dürer was twenty-eight, the frontal portrait in which he shows himself with long curly locks of dark brown hair down to his shoulders. Well the one known photo of Kurt Wagner shows him wearing his hair in ringlets down to *his* shoulders. Pretty weird, eh?"

"Yes, that would be striking," Megan allowed.

Felicitas laughed mournfully. "Maybe Wagner thinks he is a reincarnation of Dürer?"

"Or equally likely, of Christ," proposed Megan, "which I think is what the Dürer portrait meant to imply. Hmm. So this modern, Dürer-like Christ leads an antipornography sect that has chosen Schiele as its antiChrist."

"I hadn't thought of it that way, but what you say makes a lot of sense—scary!"

"This means every single Schiele painting that has any nudity in it, his drawings also, are all, all in jeopardy," Megan pronounced.

"Listen," she continued, "Hannes and I are having dinner this evening. Let me discuss it with him. Perhaps he has some ideas as to who could have done this."

"Yes, that's good," said Felicitas. "He may have some leads. But let's try to keep this vandalism attack to ourselves for now. You can tell Hannes, of course, but I don't want to call the police into it just yet. That would bring bad publicity to the museum."

\* \* \*

"On the contrary, even bad publicity is good for the Schiele Museum," Hannes maintained over dinner at the Italian restaurant *Sole*, one of Megan's favorite restaurants on the Annagasse and only halfway down the block from her hotel. "The Klimt atelier already has some seventy-five to ninety visitors a day. News of the vandalism would without a doubt double attendance at the Schiele Museum."

"Well, I hadn't really thought of it from that angle," Megan said.

"What you don't know yet, Megan, is that I did go ahead and contact the police after you phoned me with the news of the paint spraying."

"Oh, no! Felicitas expressly said not to!"

"No, it was the right thing to do. Do you want to know why? The police think they have a suspect. In fact they're pretty sure they know who it is."

# 11

"What do you *mean* Megan Crespi is in Wien?" angrily asked a surprised Kurt Wagner. He had placed a call to his second-in-command, one Arnold Moll, after a few hours of sleep in his Moscow hotel.

"Well she is, Grand Master. She was spotted yesterday going in and out of the Leopold Museum in the company of its director. Then later she turned up at the Schiele gravesite with him. Only hours after I had carried out your command to render damage to the tombstone and leave our black rose on top of Schiele's coffin. That took some digging, I can tell you."

Moll hoped his successful assignment concerning desecration of the artist's gravesite would cheer up the Grand Master. But Wagner was fixated on the topic of Megan Crespi.

"That settles it. This Crespi woman is responsible for awakening America to Schiele. She's been publishing on the artist since the nineteen sixties! Now there are dozens of competitive American collectors thirsting for his filthy work. And yet if Crespi doubted the provenance of a Schiele work, most of those same collectors would be turned off and not buy. Crespi is a malignancy in the art world that must be excised. We have an excellent opportunity to do just that, now that she is in Wien again."

"What do you want us to do, Master?"

"What I want you to do is contact our new initiate Wolf Schnitt immediately and set him on the woman. I can't think of a better person for the assignment."

"Oh, I agree, Master, I agree," Arnold said hollowly, hugely disappointed that *he* had not been given the assignment.

"And impress upon Schnitt that we do not know how long Crespi will be in Wien. You must find out where she is staying—probably at the Römischer Kaiser, where she has been known to hold court in the past. And Schnitt must move with all haste. He must make it look like an accident if at all possible."

Invigorated by the thought of putting America's proselytizing Schiele scholar out of commission, Kurt went out to the apartment's well-stocked kitchen and prepared a hearty breakfast for himself. As was his habit, he downed a full carton of milk with it. Over a second cup of coffee his thoughts turned to America's other Schiele proselytizer, Janette Killar, owner of the Galerie St. Sebastian in New York. Not only did her gallery continuously find and sell Schiele items, her detailed oeuvre catalogues of the artist's work were used around the world for ascertaining the provenance of each of the artist's many paintings and works on paper. *Verdammt!* Damn! Killar was a nonstop promoter of Schiele pornography. Perhaps he should give Schnitt two assassination assignments and send him to America after the Vienna job was completed. Or if Megan should slip out of Austria before Schnitt could get to her he would have a second opportunity if he went to America for the Killar cut.

Yes, he liked the idea. It was actually brilliant. Two for the price of one.

Kurt telephoned Arnold back and communicated to him Schnitt's further possible assignment. Then he turned his thoughts to today's meeting with Alexandra Azarova. He would be bringing Schiele's long lost *Nude Self-Portrait Standing with Hands on Hips* with him.

# 12

"So who do the Vienna police think spray painted the images in the Schiele Museum?" Megan asked Hannes over her *Sacher Torte*—a calorie boost she could never turn down when in Wien. They were sipping their coffee after a delicious dinner. Hannes looked at her meaningfully. "They are absolutely certain it is that lunatic IKG demonstrator who was arrested yesterday for pulling off a ridiculous stunt at our museum while you and I were at Schiele's gravesite."

"An IKG member?"

"Yes. A young ruffian named Milton Levine."

"I don't understand, Hannes. Isn't his and the IKG's interest in *restitution* of Schiele works to their rightful owners? Why would he want to damage *images* of Schiele. That just doesn't connect."

"I suppose I would rather believe it was a kid than entertain the possibility that Doppel-O is involved. Then we would really be dealing with loonies."

Megan thought quietly for a minute. "Look, Hannes, we've had three separate Schiele incidents in two days: the duct taping of his self-portrait, to say nothing of the murder of the night watchman, in your museum; the desecration of Schiele's grave and tombstone, and now the spray-paint job on the Trčka photos of the artist at the Schiele Museum. To me they all seem undeniably related."

"I'm afraid you're right about this. I suppose I've been in a state of denial. It would all be so simple if all three incidents had been the work of the IKG. If it makes you feel any better, Megan, the police are also investigating the recent activities of Doppel-O, but so far nothing they can pin down. They are a mysterious society, connected primarily in terse code on the Internet. We know nothing about their meetings, if indeed they are held. The big chief, Kurt Wagner, lives here in Wien, but is rarely seen. His employee, if you can call him that, Arnold Moll, also lives here, but seems harmless enough. All we know about him is that he is a geek paid by the Doppel-O. He is their webmaster, and as far as the police know, that is his only employment."

"Oh, Hannes, you've certainly given me something to think about. I'm going to stay on for a few days, I think. There's something I want to check out at the Wien Museum tomorrow."

"Can you tell me what it is?"

"I'd rather not for now. It's just a hunch, really."

\* \* \*

Next morning's breakfast at the Römischer Kaiser, although without blueberries, was a very satisfying one and Megan felt reinvigorated. She was sitting in her favorite place, the table next to the street window that commanded the whole room. She watched the tourists from various countries settle in and listened with amusement to their plans for the day, refraining from joining in with her own enthusiastic suggestions.

She had a day's plan of her own and she better get a move on. Hurriedly passing the lounge by the reception desk on her way to the elevator, she did not notice the lounge's only occupant, a lean, silver-haired man with trim beard absorbed in his newspaper. As it was still quite cold outside and indeed looked as though it might rain, Megan put on the bright red parka that Polar Cruises had provided for her visit to Antarctica two years ago. She had kept her parka, although there were few occasions when the weather called for something like that in Dallas. But now it was just the right thing. Underneath she was in her usual black slacks, black vest with numerous pockets, and a red blouse.

Exiting the hotel, her favorite shoulder bag hanging heavily in place, she walked toward the Ringstrasse, crossed it, and within minutes had entered the Wien Museum, flashing her press pass—a treasured item she had been issued when writing art criticism for some of the American art journals. Of course she could have called up to the museum's director, Dietrich Mann, with whom she had a good relationship, but for the time being she preferred that he not know she was in his museum.

Slowly, and panting a bit, she climbed the stairs to the second floor rather than taking the elevator farther down the hall. Anything to get a little weight-bearing exercise in, she thought courageously. Walking past the paintings by Schiele, Oskar Kokoschka, and Arnold Schönberg in front of which she usually lingered, she headed straight to the black wooden cabinet with glass doors that had once held the contents of Schiele's prize collection of books and small art objects.

It was empty now but Megan knew, from Melanie's vivid description, that there was a small side drawer at the bottom of the cabinet that worked on a spring release if one knew where to find it. She did. Hoping against hope that the object she was seeking would be in the little drawer, she looked quickly around the room. That early in the morning there was only one other person—a tall man with prematurely white hair and a bit of beard. Soon he moved on to another room.

There was no guard around. Megan gauged the viewing field of the overhead surveillance camera above her head. It did not encompass the cabinet. Within seconds she had stooped down by it and found the spring release. The side drawer slid open without making a sound. Quickly Megan felt inside the drawer. There was something in it. She pulled it out. It was one of Schiele's little wooden horses. Success!

Okay, I need this just for today. I am truly only borrowing it, she told herself as she slipped the horse into her parka pocket. She headed to the ladies room and went inside. No one else was there. Taking the horse out of her pocket she examined it. This one had four legs, so it was not the one in Trčka's photograph. Carefully Megan pulled its head back and found what she was hoping to find. A key. Was it the key to Schiele's basement storage room in the Hietzinger Hauptstrasse building? She tucked it into one of her vest pockets and then walked quickly back to the Schiele cabinet, returning the horse to its home.

Tomorrow she would inform Dietrich about the secret drawer and the little horse. He would be thrilled to display it of course. But, just for today, she needed its contents—the long forgotten key.

# 13

Kurt Wagner, alias Max Valentin, looked at his watch. He was due at Azarova's Gallery and Museum Rasputin in an hour. Familiar with Moscow's vast metro system he sipped his milk carton for a while longer, then dressed, picked up the leather roll with its precious Schiele contents and strolled over to the metro station at Park Kultury, a mere five-minute walk from his Posutochno hotel. He took the red circular line metro, unbearably crowded as usual, two stops to the Smolenskaya Embankment and headed for the tall building in which the gallery was housed. He was right on time.

Alexandra Azarova—tall, slim, brunette, and beautiful—stood up from her desk in the front room of her gallery and blinked her eyes in disbelief. Except for the red color of his hair, her visitor could have passed as a modern-day reincarnation of Albrecht Dürer.

"Why, Herr Valentin, I thought you were Albrecht Dürer making a visit to me," she said in flawless German.

"Yes, people often see a physical similarity between the great Renaissance master and myself. I consider it a compliment. And even more, I consider it a compliment that you would receive me on such short notice."

"Oh, but who could not agree to meet with you when you are bringing along such a rarity?" With a bit of disbelief Azarova eyed the leather roll the man was carrying. A Schiele, *rolled up*?

Anticipating her question, Wagner said quickly, "Yes, unfortunately the Schiele came to me in this roll. But the damage, except for a crease in the center, is not great and a good one half of the painting has already been restored."

"Shall we go into my inner office?" Azarova asked, waving her hand toward an ornate door behind her. On either side of the door was the gallery's present exhibition on "Degenerate Art"—twentieth-century artists like Max Beckmann, Oskar Kokoschka and Marc Chagall whom Hitler and the Nazis had deemed degenerate—*entartete*. An enlightening exhibition, it dramatically matched up canvases approved by the Third Reich with those denounced by the regime. The works spoke for themselves—saccharin or pseudo heroic versus the malaise of angst that had descended upon modern artists in the first decades of the twentieth century. A traveling exhibition, it was originated by Harriet Goodhue, noted director of Montreal's Art Austria Museum.

The inner office was luxurious with a black leather couch and matching armchairs grouped around an imposing mahogany desk. Alexandra elected not to sit behind the desk, however. Instead, smiling, she motioned Valentin toward a long table alongside a pair of French doors, inviting him to lay the Schiele roll on the well-lighted table.

If this should turn out to be the genuine article with proper provenance, she thought to herself, it would be a fabulous acquisition. And it would make up for her loss of the Schiele townscape at the recent Sotheby's auction. Her St. Petersburg rival had outbid her on that one. She wondered whether or not this Max Valentin had approached Ussachevsky, but she decided not to ask until she saw the painting, heard its provenance, and learned the price Valentin was asking.

Slowly and with extreme care, Kurt Wagner removed the rolled up canvas from its carrier and began to unroll it on the table. The painting was just as he had described: a "blister" bulge across the center and one half of the artwork already restored.

Azarova's first reaction was that it was a genuine Schiele. She was acquainted with all of the Killar catalogue images of lost works by the artist, and this was definitely one of them. Schiele's portrayal showed himself standing naked and facing the viewer, his hands defiantly on his hips, his hair standing on end as if an electric current had pulsed through him.

She pondered the possibility, however, of whether or not the painting might be a forgery, remembering that after Schiele's death his brother-in-law Anton Peschka had "finished" some of his drawings and added signatures to others. Still, she had always thought that was as far as he ever went. Could someone else, in more modern times, have created an exact replica in oil of what was reproduced in the Killar catalogue? Azarova was well acquainted with the Leopold Museum's nude Schiele self-portrait, its color hues and its tight brushwork. No, this unstretched canvas was definitely not a forgery. But finishing the restoration would be tricky. What would Herr Valentin's asking price be. Considering these complications?

She asked.

"In dollars I am asking two hundred million," Valentin answered without hesitation.

"Good heavens! That is a pricey sum, considering the restoration work that has to be done, work that could last months and months."

"I have taken that into consideration. But the work is unique. And it is Schiele at his most provocative, his most confrontational. Certainly nineteen-ten was his best and most popular year."

"I shall have to think about this, Herr Valentin. For starters, what is the provenance?"

"Bother provenance! Here before our eyes is a long-lost Schiele from his most original year, and you ask about previous owners. Who cares?"

"I care! It could have been stolen, for example, from its present-day owner. Or, such a theft could go back to Nazi times and become the subject of a restitution lawsuit."

"Well, I can assure you that the owner, who asks to be anonymous, has the work legitimately—it's been in the family since shortly before the end of World War I."

"I am going to have to think about this very hard, Herr Valentin. You have an undisclosed provenance. You have a painting in poor condition with a terrible blister bump and half of it still needing restoration."

As if he had read her mind, Valentin said: "Do you have a reliable restorer here in Moscow? Could you find out how much it would cost to have the painting restored?"

"I could probably get someone I trust from the Pushkin State Museum to come see the Schiele here this afternoon."

"If you and he, or she, can come right away, I will wait here with you, if that is all right. But I must tell you that I am leaving this evening for St. Petersburg and..."

"Say no more! Of course I am aware that you will be showing this Schiele to Boris Ussachevsky. He recently outbid me for a Schiele townscape at Sotheby's, as you probably know."

"You can't blame me for approaching your competitor. I don't intend to start a bidding war but..."

"Of course you do, Herr Valentin. Please don't take me for being naïve. Let us wait for the restorer to come here this afternoon and then we may be able to talk business."

"That seems reasonable."

"And now would you like some real Russian tea perhaps?"

"Thank you. And after that I should love to inspect the interesting degenerate art exhibition you have on right now in your gallery."

"Very good. I think you will be surprised by some of the works on the walls. And remember, they are all for sale," Azarova said in half jest.

Valentin made a wry smile and raised his hands as if to dismiss such an idea.

Azarova jangled a bell on her desk and within minutes a smiling white-haired woman brought in two large tea cups and a plate with crackers and cheese. She was immediately joined by another employee carrying a large engraved metal samovar with decorative handles. Azarova pored tea for them both and they settled down to making small talk, each eying the other trying to fathom what the ultimate Schiele transaction might be.

# 14

As she exited the Wien Museum, Megan noticed that the lone man who had been on the second floor with her, was ambling along behind her. Could he by any chance be following her or was their exiting the museum at the same time just chance? She laughed at her suspicion, but after seeing the desecration of Schiele's gravesite the day before, anything connected with Schiele was possible.

She decided to test things by walking straight over to one of her favorite monuments in Vienna, the Brahms memorial near the Karlsplatz opposite the Musikverein. It always gladdened her heart to see the eloquent 1908 life-size marble memorial to one of her favorite composers. In the distant past when she was a student in Vienna, she had asked a friend to photograph her seated in Brahms' lap. The lamenting lady with the lyre sculpted to one side of the composer's feet did not seem to take offence at Megan's brief intimacy with Johannes.

This time Megan paused for a long time in front of the impressive monument by Rudolf Weyr. It was right on the short route Brahms used to take from his three-room apartment at Karlsgasse No. 4, past the mighty baroque Karlskirche where Alma and Gustav Mahler had married, and on to the Musikverein building on the other side of the Ringstrasse.

Megan imagined she could hear Brahms' footsteps. But then she realized she actually *was* hearing footsteps. They advanced at a steady slow pace toward her back. Abruptly Megan turned on her heel and stared directly at the man with white hair and trim beard who was passing by behind her. He did not look at her or break his stride but walked slowly on past her.

It had to be her imagination, Megan reassured herself. Returning to the task at hand she walked briskly toward Otto Wagner's beautiful subway station at the Karlsplatz. Her self-assigned mission now was to take the G4 U-Bahn seven stops out to Hietzing and then walk to Hietzinger Hauptstrasse 101. She would access the basement, if possible, and see whether the key she had found at the Wien Museum was the key to Schiele's former storage site, That is, if the storage area still existed now, some hundred years later.

Glancing around the U-Bahn station as the train pulled in, she was relieved to see that the platform was empty, and in her car there were only a few people, including a large family group. Yes, the idea that anyone was following her was silly. She remembered wryly that this was also what she had thought, wrongly, when last in Vienna in hot pursuit of a missing Klimt painting known only as the Secretum. There had been several killings for Klimt before the situation was dramatically resolved.

No drama this time, thank goodness, Megan told herself as the train pulled into the Hietzing station and she hoisted up her shoulder bag.

Without looking back she walked slowly toward Hietzinger Hauptstrasse, enjoying the fresh air and the different building facades.

Wolf Schnitt had also exited the train at Hietzing. Keeping back on the platform stairs, he had jumped on board at the very last minute. Now he took the other side of the street, lagging a block behind Megan. He was surprised to see her suddenly disappear. She had entered a building up ahead on the Hietzinger Hauptstrasse but he was too far away to see the number. *Verdammt!* He would have to case several apartment houses on the left side of the street now.

It was thrilling for Megan to be back inside the doorway of Hietzinger Hauptstrasse 101. It was such a pity that the building had recently been turned into condominiums, making it impossible for the Egon Schiele Society to petition the government to declare his lodgings there a national treasure. Megan thought that if she could get inside the building, before trying to get inside the cellar, she might even climb the stairs to the top floor where Schiele's atelier had been and see if she could possibly talk her way inside, just for the fun of it. Perhaps the new dwellers in that attic apartment would be more willing than the previous ones to let her in. She had gotten nowhere the times she had tried before, back in the 1960s and then again ten years ago.

But now, how to gain entry into the building? She studied the roster of names on the inner wall. Which bell belonged to the attic apartment? As she was pondering this, a pleasant looking woman in her mid-forties with a very full shopping bag on her arm entered the covered entryway where Megan was standing. She gave a slight start to see someone that close to the door.

"What are you doing here?" she asked suspiciously. Megan explained that she was hoping to contact the residents in the attic apartment.

"Well, that would be me and my husband, but why do you want to contact us?"

Megan could not believe her good luck and quickly explained why she was there and what a privilege it would be to see the interior of the historic apartment and look out of the very windows the artist Egon Schiele once had. She related how he would wave startling self-portraits out the window to catch the attention of a young attractive Edith Harms, who lived in the apartment house opposite him. His ploy had worked and the couple married in 1915, just days before the artist had to report for military duty in Prague.

Listening with growing interest to Megan's story, the woman introduced herself as Marie Garrard and motioned Megan to come inside. Yes, if she didn't mind the stairs, she could look around.

How fantastic! Megan was excited beyond measure to have at last this unique chance to examine the quarters that once belonged to Schiele. The two women slowly climbed the five flights of stairs to Marie Garrard's flat. The front door opened on to a large room with French windows facing the street. From photographs Megan knew that this was the room that had been Schiele's atelier. She walked to the windows and looked out onto the street and the building opposite. Yes, waving a self-portrait out the window could indeed attract the attention of anyone sitting on one of the balconies opposite. Quickly Megan took a photograph of the view with her iPhone. Always adding to Schiele documentation, she thought to herself, even after a lifetime of work in pursuit of the artist.

As the two women descended to the ground floor, Megan told her new friend that she would like to go down to the basement, just in case, somehow, there was a memento of some sort pertaining to Schiele.

"Oh, but you won't be able to get into it," Marie said. "The cellar is locked. But I'd be happy to let you in," she continued, jangling her house keys.

A few minutes later Marie had unlocked the cellar door and together they entered the huge underground room which was damp and smelled of mold despite the wooden floor that had been built over the earthen flooring.

"Hardly anyone keeps things down here nowadays," Marie told Megan. "As you can tell it's not only dark—just this one light by the door—but moldy."

"Well, I see, or rather smell what you mean, but even so I'd like to walk around. There used to be subdivided storage spaces here. They're all gone now, I see.

Megan decided to check the walls, lined as they were with sagging, empty shelves. She felt the walls and the shelves—no, nothing unusual here, just dirt. As she reached up to scan the top shelf of the back wall with her right hand, her shoulder bag slipped from off her left shoulder and clunked down to the basement floor. Stooping to pick it up, Megan saw an indentation in the wood planking. A flat brass ring was folded into a matching groove in one of the boards.

"Ha! Marie, there's something here!"

Megan dug into her shoulder bag for her laser flashlight and beamed it on the floor. Faintly visible was the outline of what looked like a trap door. She wondered if the key she had taken from Schiele's horse might come into play, and sure enough, after sweeping the dust away with her shoe, she could see a keyhole on the surface of the wooden door. Holding her breath, she inserted the precious key. It worked! Slowly the creaking sound of a lock turning could be heard.

"Stand back," Megan warned, "I'm going to try and lift this thing. I think it's a…" She could not think of the word in German for trap door, "…a hatch of some sort."

"How exciting!" Marie exclaimed, coming right up to where Megan was bending over. Seeing that Megan was getting nowhere she offered: "Here, let me help."

With their combined strength the door in the floor began slowly to move upward. But they could lift the trap door only so far, not quite two feet high.

"We're getting nowhere," Marie panted. "Something is blocking it. Let me get my husband to come help." With that she climbed back up the cellar stairs, leaving Megan alone. She kept trying to lift the heavy trap door higher but to no avail.

Within minutes Marie was back, her husband Oskar in tow, and after introductions, the women made way for the small but powerful man who, after a first tentative effort, kicked a stub of wood caught in the hinge out of the way and then pulled back the trap door all the way.

"*Einfach!*" he declared. Oh, sure, Megan thought, simple for *him*. Accepting profuse thanks, Oskar, who had little interest in what his wife or Megan were up to in the foul-smelling cellar, went back upstairs.

With the trap door now folded completely back, the two women peered down at what looked to be a primitive staircase. Megan's flashlight picked out the wooden steps, all of slightly different heights, and the two women climbed carefully down to the subbasement floor. The dark chamber they were now in was surprisingly wide and high. Megan's light illuminated nothing but some slender bars of wood, all of them painted black, all of them around five feet high and all propped against the wall in regular groupings of four. There was nothing else.

Nothing else except, *wait a minute*, these bars, these rims aren't just happenstance. They are assemblages for *frames*! *Empty frames*!

*  *  *

Wolf Schnitt was getting tired of waiting for his quarry to reappear. He had taken up his stance in a doorway and was keeping watch on the entryways of two adjacent residential apartment houses across the street, Number 101 and Number 103. Surely the Crespi woman must have entered one of the two buildings. He dodged a woman with two children entering his doorway and maintained his watch. So far *nichts*. Perhaps Crespi was visiting friends. There was no telling how long she might stay if that were the case. And how, on such a residential street, was he going to make her elimination look like an accident. No, the best thing was to wait it out and follow her back to the U-Bahn. He might find an ideal opportunity on the train platform—just one push was all it would take.

*  *  *

Nauseated by the dank odor, Marie Garrard had left Megan to muse over the basement chamber alone. "Just push the basement door tightly to when you come up," she had said. "It will lock by itself." Megan had thanked her absentmindedly as she continued to stare at the potential wooden frames.

Yes! If you space two of the five-foot long wooden bars at top and bottom to encompass a five-foot height, and then place two more of the five-foot bars vertically, you have a 60-by-60-inch frame. She counted off how many "frames" could be put together by the narrow beams of wood propped up in groups of four against the cellar wall. Seven.

*Seven!* That was exactly the number of panels that Schiele was working on the last year of his life. The artist had told no one, not even

Arthur Roessler, what he was painting, but merely that the works would be of utmost significance to all of Vienna.

But these unassembled frames were empty. What had they been intended to hold that could be so important for Vienna? Megan wondered if they could be Schiele's allegorical answer to Klimt's famous Vienna University panels representing *Philosophy, Medicine,* and *Jurisprudence.* It was certainly true that during all of his short painting career, say from 1909 to 1918, Schiele had demonstrated a penchant for dark, mysterious allegories. Allegories he explained to potential but mystified patrons that encompassed existence and death.

But would Schiele have had *seven* allegories? Usually painters delivered themselves of four allegories, such as the four seasons or the four elements. But seven? Well, yes, it was entirely possible that Schiele was creating a row of seven allegories responding to some seven realms he had in his head. After all, there was in existence a sketch he had made on graph-ruled paper showing an octagonal building identified as "Mausoleum," along with a floor plan dividing the building into eight walls. Some of the walls bore identifying words such as "earthly existence," "ideology," "passions," and "stages of life."

Or perhaps Schiele had begun creating a row of seven portraits that could somehow embody the labels he had written out? Megan thought of the electrified, startling portrait Schiele had painted of his fellow artist Paris von Gutersslöh. She had recently revisited the 1918 portrait in its handsome setting at the Minneapolis Art Institute. It was life-size and would certainly measure at least five-by-five feet with the portrayed seated in one of Schiele's black wooden chairs, his arms and hands up in creative energy, the slightly indicated background charged with vibrant brush strokes. Could he personify "ideology" perhaps? And certainly a Schiele self-portrait could symbolize "passions."

Megan automatically thought about the extraordinary Schiele self-portrait she had been given decades ago by the Fogarassy family of Graz. They had presented her with the double-sided drawing—a rowboat seen from above was on the verso—in celebration of Megan's earning her PhD at Columbia in 1969. What a gift! Printed by the artist on the sheet of paper was the signature and date, 1913, and the word *Erinnerung—Re-membrance*. The drawing, with yellow and green highlights, showed Schiele with raised right hand, standing in a loose sort of double tunic that reached to his knees, his back to the viewer. He was in the act of drawing, to his left, a male figure with a beard and, as if interrupted in his task, the artist had turned his head back toward the viewer, a quizzical expression on his face. The man he was drawing was Klimt. And both were presented as monklike figures, removed from the world.

Also years ago, Schiele's sister Melanie had bestowed upon Megan an early 1909 black crayon drawing by her brother: a drawing in which a tall, gaunt figure facing front and on the left was overlapped by the decorative robe of a second standing figure on the right and in profile. The front figure was Klimt, the back figure a young, aspiring novitiate who, Melanie had told Megan, was Schiele. Over the years Megan had marveled that two pictures showing Schiele with Klimt had been entrusted to her. Quite recently she had donated *Remembrance* to the Dallas Museum of Art, but every nuance of Schiele's keen line was locked in her memory.

One of the Trčka photographs, she recalled, had also shown Schiele standing in front of a large figurated canvas he had named *Procession*. Could this photograph be a clue as to whom Schiele had intended to include in the procession? Was it perhaps an entire row of seven hermits or monks? Was it possibly a protest against a hypocritical Viennese culture that publically expressed moral outrage at the frankness of modern art, but privately collected what could be termed pornography, beginning with Klimt's and Schiele's explicit renderings of naked models?

Megan pondered the number seven. Why that number instead of an even number? Did seven have a special significance for Schiele? Not that she knew of. She would ask Hannes when she returned to the Leopold Museum for lunch with him that afternoon. She glanced at her watch. Good heavens, she was going to be late! Pulling the trap door back into place, and leaving it, on instinct, unlocked, she ran up the basement stairs and closed the cellar door firmly behind her as Marie had requested. She hastened out to the street. An empty taxi was driving by and she hailed it.

From his sentinel spot on the Hietzinger Hauptstrasse a frustrated Wolf Schnitt was left speechless as Megan quickly entered the taxi and zoomed away toward town.

# 15

"Restoration could take several months but I could make it look as good as...*old*!" playfully emphasized the Russian restorer from the Pushkin Museum.

"And what might a full restoration cost?" Alexandra Azarova asked. She and Kurt Wagner, alias Max Valentin, were standing on either side of the Schiele canvas which had been carefully laid out by Igor Borodin and temporarily pinned down by four heavy wooden slats which Igor had brought with him to Azarova's Gallery Rasputin.

Igor rolled his great brown eyes up in slow calculation of the labor and time needed to restore the compelling image before him to its former self. Particularly troublesome would be matching the recent yellow hue given the body, the leftward leaning upper part of which had been restored. The arm and leg to the viewer's right was still in its original faded state and the staring face with its wide eyes needed touching up as well. The swollen bulge across the center of the canvas was the most troublesome. With a deft use of varying temperatures the welt could slowly be brought down but extreme caution would have to be exercised.

Finally Igor spoke. "I calculate it would cost you, or anyone else for that matter, somewhere in the neighborhood of two million rubles or close to fifty-eight thousand US dollars."

Kurt held his palms up as though in self-defense. No amount of questioning by him changed Igor's figures, and with a rueful but firm explanation for the expense that would be involved, the restorer took his leave.

"Igor Borodin is the most respected restoration man in Moscow," Azarova said, "so I think we have to take his word concerning how much work would be involved."

Seeing the look of disappointment on her visitor's face, she continued: "In short, you have a unique Schiele self-portrait from the bonanza year of nineteen-ten in your possession, but it is in partially ruined condition, and cannot be sold as is. And then there is the overriding question of previous ownership of the painting. Whether there are any pending restitution claims. I would need to have specific provenance documentation as there is none in the Killar catalogue. There it is designated simply as 'present whereabouts unknown.'"

Kurt thought for a minute. He wanted to sell the painting now, not cart it around Russia and Europe. Finally he said: "Give me an offer including the restoration costs to yourself that you would be willing to make."

"No, no, you do not understand, Herr Valentin. I am not in the business of restoring paintings, no matter how potentially magnificent they may be. I buy and sell works, the previous ownership of which is scrupulously documented, and I keep a few for my small museum, but I do not handle damaged or undocumented pictures under any circumstances."

"But the client I represent does not wish to have his identity revealed," Kurt lied desperately. "Nor has he told me who the previous owner or owners were. Can you not tell me what you would be willing to pay *today* if restoration, say, were not necessary?"

"I can give you a general notion as to what I think the painting would be worth, presuming it is restored to its former magnificence. With proper provenance, mind you, it could well be worth the equivalent of one hundred and fifty million American dollars."

"This is what I have been waiting to hear. Perhaps I shall be in touch with you tomorrow afternoon," concluded Kurt as he began carefully rolling up the canvas.

He realized that he was getting nowhere with this wretched woman who insisted on an "impeccable" provenance. That was something he could neither improvise nor provide. He had not anticipated such complications.

After he left her gallery, Azarova watched his figure disappear down the street and heaved a sigh of relief. "What a dreadful man!"

The very next morning the international media and the Moscow papers were full of the news that a valuable Schiele painting had been stolen from Sotheby's of London. The subject matter was a life-size nude self-portrait by the artist.

# 16

In the taxi taking her back to her hotel Megan could not get the discovery of seven "frames" in Schiele's Hietzinger Hauptstrasse basement out of her mind. She was terribly excited about having come upon a possible explanation of the artist's future plans. In his letters of 1918 to various patrons Schiele had frequently referred to a project involving "monumental art."

Her thoughts went back to the Mausoleum sketch she had thought about earlier. She had examined it carefully in years past, even drawing her own copy of it in the *Studiensaal*—the study room—of Vienna's great Albertina Museum, where so many of the artist's graphic works were housed.

Thinking back to 1963 and her early days at the Albertina, Megan remembered with a smile how, when she first began studying the Schiele drawings there, the guards referred to her as "Fräulein Crespi." But after her discovery of the Neulengbach prison cell where the artist had been incarcerated, she was addressed respectfully as "Frau Crespi." The careful sketches she had made of each Schiele drawing had served her enormously well, making her familiar with each year of his ever-changing drawing style and positioning her as an expert on the many Schiele forgeries that came her way.

Now she was calling on that knowledge as she imagined what Schiele might have had in mind for his mausoleum. Perhaps he intended it as a memorial to Vienna's fallen sons in the Great War. But how would this be an "immense benefit" to the city, as he had written? Perhaps he did indeed have allegories in mind. And if so what would they have addressed? Birth, life, and death were constant motifs in his work. Perhaps a grandiose progression through the stages of life? Something his mentor Klimt had done before him in his allegories for Vienna University.

Megan's ponderings were interrupted by the arrival of her taxi at the back entrance to the Römischer Kaiser. Once in her room she flopped down on the bed, relieved to have a chance for a catnap before lunch with Hannes. But no sooner had she started to doze off than the phone rang.

"Hallo, Megan. It's Antal Maack. I just learned you're in Wien! Why didn't you let me know?"

"Oh, Antal, dear. I didn't tell you, because I didn't know I was coming."

Antal Maack was an old and treasured friend from Megan's days at the University of Vienna in 1956. But a few weeks after the fall semester had begun the Hungarian Revolution took place. Because she had a station wagon, Megan made several trips a day to the Austro-Hungarian border to pick up Hungarians who had made it across into Austria and bring them to Vienna.

One of the Hungarians she met during those unsettling days was a handsome, dark-haired young man with light blue eyes named Antal Maack, who, in addition to his native Hungarian, spoke Italian. He also played the piano. Megan was a flutist. With Italian and music in common their friendship had blossomed, linguistically, musically, and, briefly, romantically. After Megan returned to the US, they had continued their friendship through the years, including Antal's several marriages and divorces.

Megan herself had remained single, devoting all her time to her profession as a professor of art history, first at Columbia University for ten years, and then at Southern Methodist University in Dallas, where her mother had founded the Italian Department and her father had opened a portrait photography studio. It was from him that Megan inherited her passion for photographic documentation—something that had served her well in her lifelong pursuit of the works and related sites of various artists and composers.

Now she was jerked back to the present as Antal asked: "Of course you've heard about the Schiele desecrations and the murder at the Leopold?"

"Yes, that's actually why I'm here," Megan said, filling him in on everything except the Hietzinger Hauptstrasse find, which, somehow, instinct told her to keep to herself. She still needed to digest what she had found there.

"When I heard about the damage done to the Schiele self-portrait nude, I began worrying about my own Schiele nude. Do you think the nut who did this could be targeting private collections as well?" Antal asked Megan.

He was referring to another 1910 canvas by Schiele, a life-size nude portrait of his younger sister Gerti. Placed front center against a background void, and seemingly seated, with one arm bent inward at the elbow, she stared out challengingly at the beholder. Back in the early 1960s it had come up for auction at Vienna's Dorotheum. Antal, just starting his law firm and his own collection of Schieles, had bought it for a song. With the same yellow tonalities as Schiele's own nude self-portraits of 1910, the picture glimmered in Antal's apartment on the first floor overlooking the busy Herrengasse and was his pride and joy. His succession of wives had not felt the same way about the painted occupant who held sway on the wall next to the French doors in Antal's small, cozy den. After his third divorce Antal had remained single, filling his apartment rooms with Schiele drawings and with his other passion, toy trains and their winding tracks. His maid could only shake her head at the dusting involved by this grownup man's toys.

"Surely no one could breech my security with its motion detector," declared Antal. There had been a few occasions when the maid or he himself had forgotten to turn it on, but he did not mention these.

"I certainly hope not. But there is more to the story. Schiele's gravesite has also been the target of vandalism, did you know that?"

"Yes, I saw it in the paper and it was covered on TV last night."

"And did you hear about what happened at the new little Schiele museum on the Wattmanngasse?"

"No. What?"

"All the Trčka photo blowups of Schiele in the front room were viciously spray painted yesterday."

"How outrageous! But that sounds more like a kid's mischief than the work of the intruder who killed the Leopold night watchman."

"Right. But what mystifies me, and Johannes Ohm, is the sudden outbreak of such *hatred* toward Egon Schiele. Why? And who hates with such vehemence?"

"I see what you mean," replied Antal.

"The most useful suspects are the lunatic fringe of the IKG," Megan mused, "but their cause is restitution, not wrecking. Antal, have you heard of the Doppel-O organization?"

"No. Sounds scary."

"Apparently it is an obscure sect devoted to stamping out pornography in public places. Hannes and I think they are the more likely suspects. But very little is known about their leader, their membership, or even their actual location. In fact I'm meeting Ohm for lunch to talk about all this shortly. Why don't you join us?"

"Delighted to. What time are you meeting?"

"At one-thirty, over at the Leopold. Why don't you meet me at the Römischer Kaiser and we'll walk over together."

"Done. I'll be there in about ten minutes," Antal said. His apartment on the Herrengasse was not far from Megan's hotel or Beethoven's Pasqualatihaus on the Mölker Bastei. Megan wondered if she had been too impetuous, inviting Antal to join Hannes and her for lunch, but after all the two men did know each other and were, as was the case so often in prickly Vienna, friendly rivals in things concerning Schiele. Anyway, Antal's take on the matter at hand just might be useful.

# 11

The rain began in earnest just moments after Kurt Wagner had checked into his St. Petersburg hotel as Max Valentin that evening. His boutique hotel with just twenty-five cozy rooms, the Art-Hotel Rachmaninoff, was just to his liking—quiet, but in the historic district and just behind the Kazan Cathedral. Munching on an apple he had taken from the reception desk, Kurt turned to the TV's local pornography channel. One of his favorite programs, *Slave for a Day*, had just started. Tonight it featured a sailor's visit to a Hamburg whorehouse that specialized in S/M. Some nonsense about the man's request to be stripped naked and tied with his back to a four-foot revolving wooden wheel that dominated the bordello's "playroom." Two naked women turned the wheel slowly, bending over the sailor and administering occasional, licks, bites or whip lashes. Although properly incensed, Kurt soon turned the channel off. He needed his wits about him for the next day.

* * *

The sun was trying to come through the mist that had descended upon the city during the night. At precisely ten in the morning Boris Ussachevsky opened the door of his Gallery Solovey and surveyed the artworks on display with pride. He had acquired enough Russian and Italian Futurist works to hold a thematic exhibition, "The Artist Sees the City." Most of the paintings were devoted to colorful, geometrized views of buildings and crowded squares, but a few of them presented pedestrians in multiple time sequences, giving the works a feeling of slow motion. There was the usual array of Vladimir Tatlin, Natalia Goncharova, and Kazimir Malevich along with several spectacular canvases by Umberto Boccioni. Boris was justifiably proud of the collection he had put together. The show had gotten rave reviews in the paper and people were already beginning to stream into the gallery.

Pressing the morning paper under his arm, Boris walked quickly toward his office, nodding at the receptionist and greeting a client he knew on the way. He closed the door behind him, sat down at his desk, and then opened up the newspaper to the sensational article he had come upon over breakfast. So! An Egon Schiele self-portrait nude oil had been stolen from Sotheby's of London two days ago and today a certain Max Valentin from Austria was bringing him a "rare" Schiele nude self-portrait from 1910.

Once again he paged through his Killar catalogue of Schiele's works with its small black-and-white reproductions of the one known and the two "lost" self-portraits of 1910: the standing self-portrait nude with hands on hips, and the kneeling self-portrait nude with huge hands and fingers flailing upward. Ah! To own one of those!

Yes, he had succeeded in obtaining the poignant Krumau townscape by Schiele, but he had never dreamt he might be able to acquire a Schiele self-portrait in oil. And how many times had he compared the Trčka photographs of Schiele with his own face—the resemblance was uncanny. It was destiny that was bringing this rare Schiele to him.

For Boris things were beginning to add up in a new way concerning the missing pair of nude self-portraits painted during the young artist's first full year out of the Vienna Academy. Where one 1910 lost painting was, could very well mean that the other one was very possibly hidden away in the same private collection, wherever that might be.

If Boris could, by some miracle, pull the location of that private collection out of Max Valentin when they met, then perhaps he might have a chance to dispense with a middle man and approach the owner directly. Boris wondered if Valentin would also be contacting that Azarova woman in Moscow. Well, he had outbid her once recently; he could do it again if necessary. If the Schiele were the genuine thing, that is. And if it were, he would stop at nothing to acquire the painting for his private delectation. Never mind that it had been stolen from Sotheby's. That was Sotheby's problem.

*　*　*

Kurt had decided to stretch his legs and walk to the Gallery Solovey from his hotel. Even so, he was a bit early for his eleven o'clock appointment with the owner, so he slowed his pace and took in the architecture around the Hermitage—such a blend of old and new, the ancient imperial style versus the garish *nouveau riche* statements of self-worth. It was in one of the latter commercial buildings that he found the eye-catching facade of Gallery Solovey, an oasis of pseudo Art Nouveau décor in the desert of square building blocks wherein it was housed. Paired nightingales spelled out the name of the gallery above the door.

Walking up to the receptionist Kurt discreetly announced himself and was instantly greeted in person by a tall, slender, brown-eyed, man of about forty-five. His dark brown hair was spiked and stood on end. Motioning Valentin into his office with a welcoming smile, Boris invited him to roll out on his well-lit work table the contents of the leather roll hanging from his shoulder. Inconspicuously he pressed a button under the table that activated the video camera hidden overhead. A few minutes later the two men were gazing at Schiele's standing self-portrait nude, one-half of which had already been nicely restored.

"But this answers the description given in the news this morning of the Schiele painting that was stolen from Sotheby's!" exclaimed Boris, feigning shock. He was actually hugely pleased that this was the very work before him.

"Yes, it is one and the same. The anonymous source I represent approached me two days ago, asking if I knew of any private collectors who might wish to buy the Schiele, no questions asked. This is why I have come to you. I know your reputation as a discreet dealer."

"What does your anonymous seller hope to get for the sale of this badly damaged Schiele?"

"The damage can be taken care of by any competent restorer, and you know that. The painting itself is enormously valuable because of the fact that it is one of three known large 1910 self-portraits by the artist in the nude."

"Any restorer worth his salt would refuse to work on the painting without reporting it to the international police," responded Boris, happy to begin downgrading the desirability of the artwork for legitimate museums and buyers. He planned a campaign of devaluation that would leave this Max Valentin man happy to sell and at a much lower price than the painting, even without restoration, was worth. The chess game had commenced.

\* \* \*

When Megan and Antal walked into the Leopold Museum they were greeted at the entrance by Hannes himself. Eagerly he led them to his office, expressing pleasure at seeing his friendly rival in the acquisition of Schiele works.

Hannes had news for them. The police had raided the office of the IKG this morning and found black spray paint that matched the paint sprayed on the Trčka photographs of Schiele. An arrest had been made. It was young Milton Levine, nephew of the IKG director Herman Levine. And, he had pleaded guilty. Guilty of a noble cause, he maintained. He was merely trying to draw public attention to the plight of unrestituted Schiele works. His attention-getting device was the symbolic blotting out of the artist's face and hands in each Trčka photograph. After all, they were only enlargements; the original photographs had not been involved.

Megan shook her head in disgust and said: "But once again, what the IKG does is amateur stuff. A protest, a demonstration, a paint spray job. Nothing like the murder of a guard or defacing or cutting out actual works of art, as with the Leopold's Schiele and Klimt."

"And how is the desecration of Schiele's grave explained?" added Antal. "Surely the Levine boy did not admit to that sort of destruction?"

"No, no. He was pressed on that subject and said he had no part in what happened at the cemetery. And I believe him," answered Hannes.

"But after lunch," he continued, "I want to show you, Antal, the Schiele and Klimt damage. Megan and I didn't have much time yesterday with them as we headed straight out to Ober-Sankt-Veit when we heard of the vandalism out there."

The threesome sat at one of the corner tables in the Leopold café overlooking the Museum District square. The IKG protestors were back, this time holding signs that said "Show Us Our Schiele!"

"How ridiculous," scoffed Hannes. "The painting is in restoration, not restitution. And the masking tape is providing a real problem for our restorers. We can't afford to damage the paint by removing it whole piece. It has to be done millimeter by millimeter. And it could take months."

"Will you be putting it back on view?" Antal asked.

"You bet we will. The museum refuses to be intimidated by some crazy madman."

"But of course you will be increasing the security," theorized Megan.

"Oh yes, we've already done so. But more remains to be done and we need to get funds from the state to do that."

"That's the problem with government-owned institutions," Antal said. "They are in competition with each other. Everybody wants a piece of the financial pie."

"I need to update my own home security system," Antal continued thoughtfully. "Right now I have motion sensors. That is when I remember to turn them on at night. During the day, if I'm out and she leaves, my maid usually takes care of such things. Do you think I should have anything else, Hannes?"

"Well, motion sensors and securely locked doors and windows are all excellent defenses, but video cameras with a continuous feed are also desirable, that is if you have someone to man the post at all hours."

"At my home in Dallas," Megan volunteered, "I have a motion sensor box by the front door that, when triggered barks loudly, like a very large dog. Only recently did my letter carrier catch on that it was an electronic bark."

"That's a good idea," responded Antal. "I think I'll adopt that one. Nifty concept." Then, turning to Hannes, he asked: "Is there any progress on finding out who is responsible for your museum's disasters?"

"Megan agrees with me that it could be the strange new cult that advocates banning of so-called pornographic works in public museums. Perhaps you have heard of it. They call themselves the Doppel-O Society. The two "O"s stand for the English "Oliberate Obsenity," which has no direct onomatopoeia translation into German, no *Klangmalerei*. Perhaps a good German parallel could be *"Protestiert gegen Pornographie,"* but then it should be "Doppel-P," which sounds scatological in either English or German, so I can see why they avoided it. 'Double pee' hardly conveys what this strange and dangerous cult group wants its message to be."

"Where is this Doppel-O sect located?" Antal asked.

"No one knows exactly. We do know that the head of the sect, the Grand Master, as he is called, has a home in Wien, but talk is that he is rarely there; travels a lot proselytizing, converting converts to his cause."

"And they are on line," Megan volunteered. "Their website is www. obliterateobscenity."

"And it's followed by a dot org, though how they manage to be a legitimate, tax-exempt organization is beyond me," Hannes added.

"Surely the police will come up with something solid soon," Antal said.

"Oh, that's what we're counting on," Hannes answered. "We've urged them to interrogate the website originator, and they have done so, but no results."

Antal's phone rang suddenly and he discreetly turned away from the table as he took the call. His face turned ashen. "What?" he barked, causing other people in the café to turn and look at him. Antal listened a few seconds more, then hung up and turned to Megan and Hannes with a look of horrified incredulity.

"It's the maid. My home has been broken into and the Gerti portrait has been spray painted!"

\* \* \*

A good half-hour had elapsed since Kurt Wagner offered the stolen Schiele to Boris Ussachevsky. Both men were sticking to their respective positions, but Boris seemed to have the upper hand. Emphasizing the need for a complete disclosure of provenance—about which he cared not a whit unless it led to yet another Schiele self-portrait in private hands—and on condition that the transaction would be conducted secretly, Boris allowed that he might be interested in acquiring the work. Privately, he knew that this extraordinary portrait of in-your-face sexuality would go directly into the secret collection out at his Votkinsk lake villa.

Kurt was in a quandary. As with his dealing the day before with Azarova, he was in no position to disclose a provenance for the painting which had been out of circulation for so many decades. It had been by extreme good luck that the Doppel-O's London member Walter Holloway had noticed that a large painting designated as by Egon Schiele was under restoration at Sotheby's. Wagner thought about how he had immediately put Lorenzo Ladro on to the job and that mission had been accomplished without a hitch. The subject of the painting was fair game for the Doppel-O, and this time it had been dealt with before it could contaminate an innocent public.

Now he had a truly priceless, if slightly damaged, painting on hand which he was extremely eager to sell in order to buy acreage for the establishment of a permanent base for his Doppel-O cult. From Austria dedicated converts could be sent out to various museums around Europe and eventually to the Americas and Israel to eradicate pornographic holdings forced upon a naïve public. Corruption of museum visitors must be halted, even if it took theft and violence. Any means could justify such a noble end. Now, as he faced the Russian, he decided to play a trump card.

"If I pay for the restoration and it is done to your satisfaction, what would you be prepared to offer me for this riveting work?"

"That is assuming I would be interested in buying it," answered Boris immediately, sensing he had the advantage now. "I have no doubt that restoration of the original colors could be successful and ultimately unnoticeable, but there is that welt across the middle of the canvas. To reverse that damage would take time, a lot of it. I would not be prepared to make you an offer until I see the restoration results."

"But that could take months!" Kurt let escape before he could conceal his agitation.

Boris allowed the smallest of smiles to cross his lips. Obviously the man in front of him was looking for a quick sale. Time was on the buyer's side, not the seller's.

* * *

"Oh, no!" Megan and Hannes had voiced their disbelief at the same time after Antal's announcement of the Schiele vandalism at his home.

Abandoning their lunch table they quickly accompanied Antal to the front of the museum where he hailed a taxi. "Don't tell *anyone* about this yet," he admonished them as the car drove off.

"How can it be?" asked Hannes as they watched Antal's taxi leave. "So far the attacker has focused on public objects relating to Schiele—his painting in our museum and his grave site. We do not count the juvenile attack on the Trčka photographs."

"It is extraordinary," said Megan. "Antal's collection of Schiele is very private; few people even know that he is a collector. And, as he said, his home is armed with a motion detector. Perhaps the maid had left on errands and forgotten to turn it on?"

"We will know more when we learn from Antal the extent of the spray paint damage and whether a note of some sort has been left," replied Hannes. "Let us hope the damage can be repaired. This is as bad as what duct tape does."

*  *  *

Back at his flat on the Singerstrasse in the center of town, Arnold Moll carefully replaced his can of black spray paint in the cabinet under his kitchen sink. It had taken only a few seconds, once he climbed to the first floor balcony of Antal Maack's apartment. Unbelievably the French doors were unlocked! Silently he pushed them inward and spotted the Gerti portrait on the wall next to him. He aimed his spray can directly at the painting, covering the exposed parts of the body.

"The Grand Master will be thrilled to hear my news," he said out loud to himself. He was quite sure that Herr Maack would not remember they had met at the Miniature Train Convention in Salzburg last year. Both were collectors of nineteenth-century toy trains and all that went with them, from lengths of tracks to tiny stations and signal towers. And both had started to pick up the same coal-burning little engine at the same time.

Laughing at the coincidence, the two had fallen into a far-ranging conversation that encompassed music and art, specifically the collaboration of the two Gustavs—Mahler and Klimt—at the great 1902 Beethoven exhibition held at the Vienna Secession. Moll bragged that he owned a few pencil studies by Klimt for the Beethoven frieze, specifically his drawings of the lone knight who would pass through an underworld of ugly monsters before reaching the celestial heights of pure love and *Freude*—joy. Impressed by Moll's holdings, Maack found himself bragging about his large early 1910 Schiele life-size portrait of his sister, mentioning that the artist had presented her naked and that she presided on the wall by his desk.

As soon as he had gotten home from the unusual encounter Arnold had looked up the year 1910 in his copy of Killar's Schiele catalogue. There were two life-size portraits of Gerti that qualified. Both were nude, or rather naked, as the subject exuded a simultaneous sense of intrusion and angst.

He could not tell which one his new acquaintance owned—the one seated with outstretched right arm bent at the elbow, or the one standing with face averted and arms protectively crossed against the body—but it was handy to know that a Schiele of such importance was in private hands in Wien.

In fact, awareness of this arcane bit of information had been one of the factors that had interested the Grand Master in him when they first met in cyberspace two years ago. They had exchanged views on ways to obliterate the obscenity that was prevalent everywhere, contaminating the minds of the young and outraging their elders. Pornographic pollution was the first step toward criminal behavior and something must be done, Wagner had declared passionately. Extreme measures were necessary, since the police rarely bothered with such things. Witness, for example, their lax attitude toward prostitution. At night any number of women for sale paraded in the underground U-Bahn station right in the center of town at the Opera Passage. And the walls of the men's room there were caked with corrupt images drawn one on top of the other. God knows what the women's restroom looked like!

When Wagner learned that the short, mousey little balding man Arnold Moll was a professional webmaster, he invited him to produce a website for the new cyber community he wished to found. It would be committed to eradicating public obscenity, not in toilet stations but where publicity would immediately follow, in museums. And later the question of pornography in private collections would be addressed.

Well, he, Moll, had advanced the second mandate that very day. His chance acquaintance with the Gerti portrait owner braggart had allowed him a first strike, one of which not even the Grand Master had conceived.

\* \* \*

Boris waited silently a few minutes, watching his Austrian visitor squirm. But his heart was pounding with excitement. The Schiele was magnificent, even in its present state. He had to have it. And he, Boris, could do the restoration. The fact that Valentin was eager to get rid of the stolen canvas was only too obvious. He continued to stare silently at the painting on the table. Soon it would be his.

Unable to bear the silence any longer, Kurt Wagner/Max Valentin made a proposal. "What if we forget about my providing a provenance and you absorb the restoration costs at your leisure here in St. Petersburg? What would you be prepared to offer me in such a situation?"

Ah, now we've gotten to the crux of the matter, thought Boris. This man has no idea of the provenance of the painting stolen from Sotheby's and restoration clearly doesn't appeal to this man in a hurry.

"Given those two factors, I could offer you seventy-five million US dollars."

"What!" exclaimed Kurt. "Why this masterpiece is worth at least twice that!"

"Possibly it might be worth more if, one, the provenance were made public; two, it were guaranteed not to be the subject of an international restitution lawsuit; and, three, the restoration was successful. But as things stand now, seventy-five million is all I would care to invest in a painting that is damaged and has a flawed history."

Kurt made a dramatic move to roll the canvas back into its leather holder. Boris evinced no reaction.

"I must tell you," Kurt announced, "that I have a figure from the Gallery Rasputin that is far and away higher than the sum you have offered me."

"Then you must have a provenance, since I know quite well that Alexandra Azarova buys nothing that does not have a squeaky clean history of ownership."

"We had not yet discussed that aspect of the sale," Kurt lied lamely. He was playing out of his league and he knew it. He forgot to continue rolling up the Schiele and stared helplessly at the St. Petersburg billionaire gallery owner.

"All right, Herr Valentin," Boris said after a further minute of silence had gone by. "For an immediate and totally confidential sale I will offer you, without provenance documentation and without restoration, the sum of one hundred million US dollars, not a cent more.

"Done," said a greatly relieved Kurt Wagner. "When would I be receiving payment?"

"Now. I'll write you a check on my Swiss bank account payable in US dollars," answered Boris, walking over to his desk and sitting down.

"How shall I make it out?" he asked.

"I too have a Swiss bank account, but it is under the pseudonym Kurt Wagner, so please use that name."

A few minutes later the Grand Master of Doppel-O exited the Solovey Gallery, his dreams of a permanent home for his cult within palpable reach of being realized. An Austrian Airlines flight back to Vienna left late that afternoon and he would be on it.

# 18

Back in her room at the Römischer Kaiser, Megan thought she would stay one or two more days in Vienna. She needed to restore Schiele's cellar key to its home in the toy wooden horse and then tell the museum director, her friend Dietrich Mann, about the precious hidden treasure in the secret drawer of the black cabinet on display in his museum.

And she wanted to go along with Hannes tomorrow morning when he met with the police detective who had been assigned to "the Leopold case." Also now there was the damage to Antal's Schiele portrait of Gerti to follow up on. She had just talked to him on the phone and he was about to take the vandalized canvas over to the Belvedere Museum for restoration. Might she have dinner with him this evening to talk everything over, he asked her nervously. But of course, Megan had assured him. We shall rack our brains together as to who could have done this terrible thing.

That evening after a prolonged dinner with an agitated Antal at the nearby *Wienerwald* restaurant on the other side of the Annagasse, Megan decided it was high time to call Claire and find out how little Button was doing, and if he were fully recovered from his frightening fall of the day before.

When she got through to Claire and they had discussed at length Button's amazing full recovery, her friend reported that she had picked up the mail at Megan's house and that there was a hand-addressed letter for her with a variety of beautiful Russian stamps.

"Who from and what city in Russia?"

"Well, the return address says Sonja Oppenheimer, thirty-three Pervomaiskaya, Kaliningrad, Russia."

Oh yes, that's the new Russian name for Königsberg. You know, Käthe Kollwitz's hometown up in far north eastern Prussia. I was there about ten years ago to photograph what was left of the old town after World War II. The British bombings destroyed most of the buildings, including, unfortunately, the two houses in which the artist grew up."

"So do you know this Sonja Oppenheimer person?" Claire asked.

"It doesn't ring a bell with me except that one of Schiele's closest friends was an artist named Max Oppenheimer. He died in the mid-nineteen fifties in America."

"Well, perhaps this is a relative," Claire said enthusiastically.

"How about opening the letter and let's find out?"

"Oh, good! I was hoping you'd say that." Claire slit the envelope open and began reading the letter. It was written in charmingly quaint English:

Honored Professor Doctor Crespi,

    Because you are famous authority of Egon Schiele I you write for consultation, hoping you can me help. Shortly I am approached by Éva Vidovszky who me say she from Austrian tax office, she know I have Schiele paintings, and she need see. I say her no but she is persisting, persisting, and so I her show one not in good condition as it in hot Austria attic many years. She say she can fix and present me with London firma document I to sign for fixing for free. I not like surrender my solitude so she say she do it all anonymous and I pay no tax.

    Now I hear from her no more and I have read in newspaper and see on television that a Schiele painting is from the London firma stolen! Can you help me, esteemable Professor Doctor Crespi to find out what is happen to my Schiele painting?

    Yours in greatest honor,

    Sonja Oppenheimer

    Telefon 7 4012 376 7754

"Wow! That is quite a letter!" cried Megan, a sense of excitement coursing through her veins. "And it may very well shed light on some of the things that are going on here in Vienna."

She brought Claire up to date on the latest Schiele events and wrote down Oppenheimer's telephone number. Claire promised to scan the letter with her iPad and e-mail it on to her right away.

"Now, be careful, Megan," warned Claire, aware that her impetuous friend might make a hasty decision like flying off to another country on short notice. Not that she minded keeping sweet little Button. It was just that she was always a bit anxious on Megan's behalf when she was abroad on art business. She remembered the several missed, thank goodness, attempts on her friend's life when she was helping to solve the mystery of a missing panel by Klimt.

"I will be, don't worry," concluded an animated Megan, suddenly alert to a possibility of linked happenings in the Schiele world.

"From now on I will wear my new Google Glass," she promised herself out loud, pulling out her Internet-connected eye ware. "You never know when you might want to snap a photo without people knowing."

# 19

It was a fatigued but relieved Kurt Wagner who arrived back in Vienna late that evening. He went straight to his apartment in the heart of the city on the Spiegelgasse and checked his answering machine. There was a message from Arnold Moll saying he had wonderful news. Kurt looked at his watch and decided it was too late to call Moll, but he would do it first thing in the morning.

However, it was not too late to respond to a second communication. It was a mysterious, excited message left by Lorenzo Ladro. Wondering with irritation why he was being contacted—hadn't he paid the man a regal enough sum?—he got through to him in Milan just as he was going out the door.

"Good that you have called me back, Grand Master. I have news of something I think will be of interest to you. I have learned from one of my associates who works there, that a private collector has contacted Milan's Galleria La Scala and has sent them the photograph of a Schiele that he wishes to sell. The photograph shows a completely naked portrait of the artist's sister from early years. It too is a large oil. Same size as the one I brought to you from London. Are you interested? Shall I see about 'organizing' it for you?"

Wagner realized immediately Ladro must be talking about the other nude portrait from 1910 that the artist had made of his sister and, though pictured in Killar's catalogue, it was listed as "whereabouts unknown." It never rains Schieles but it pours, he thought to himself.

"Yes," he answered evenly. "I would be interested. And at the same price and same delivery location."

"Agreed. This will not happen soon, I am afraid, as the goods are not yet in the oven, if you understand what I mean."

"All right," Wagner said, suddenly feeling immensely tired, tired even of Schiele. "Contact me when you have news, then," he said, hanging up and shaking his head to clear it from Italian machinations.

Then, with privacy for the first time since leaving St. Petersburg,

Wagner gazed long and joyously at the check Boris Ussachevsky had written out to Kurt Wagner. Tomorrow he would route it to his own Swiss bank account, one he had created years ago in his own name. True to his word, he would give half of the Schiele proceeds to the baron, thereby securing ownership of the acreage within the forest that stretched behind the Schloss.

He had already envisioned how he would want the communal meeting house to be built. It would be a replica of the long houses he had seen on the Haida Gwaii islands off British Columbia. There, underneath a six-beam pitched roof with a smoke hole in the center, he had witnessed the stunning ceremonial dances of the Haida Gwaii Indians around a giant log fire in the center of the room, the initial flames reaching up to the round ceiling opening, and the intoxicating smell of burning cedar filling the great room. It was then and there that he had determined he would found a commune for his Doppel-O and that they would convene in a ceremonial safe house removed from the outer world. The thickly forested land behind the Schloss was ideal for the sort of isolation he had in mind.

The private method Kurt had discovered for strengthening his "clothed-in-chastity" way of life was to view and critique pornographic films. It was exhilarating to the point of orgasm to deny to the last moment the sexual urgency that welled up in him as he watched the films. Unlike Schiele, who cut off his hands compositionally in guilt for the solitary vice, masturbation for Wagner was nothing to feel guilty about. It was an expediency that left him free to think about the things that really mattered, most particularly expanding the Doppel-O membership in other countries. So far he only had agents in London and Milan.

The next morning after a hot shower and with a carton of fresh milk next to him, Wagner telephoned Moll. The excitement in Moll's voice crackled with electricity.

"Grand Master! In your absence I have successfully engineered the Doppel-O's first censorship of a pornographic Schiele in a *private* collection!"

"Excellent, excellent," Wagner said approvingly, mildly surprised that his personal geek had left the secure capsule of cyberspace to do battle in the real terrain of the outside world. "Which work, which collection, and how?"

"The life-size obscenity depicts Schiele's sister Gerti *naked*!"

Wagner sat up with a start. Just last night he had been informed by Ladro that there was a Schiele nude portrait of Gerti for the taking. Was this it?

"Go on. I'm listening."

"It was acquired decades ago by the Hungarian lawyer Antal Maack who lives here in Wien and who recently let slip to me the fact that he owned it. You remember, I told you about him."

"Ah ha! That would be one of two nineteen-ten portraits in oil Schiele did of his sister. Tell me, is she standing or sitting in the painting?"

"She seems to be sitting, although there is no chair or background whatsoever indicated."

"Yes, that would be right, I know now exactly which one it is. And the only information Killar gives is that it was in a Dorotheum auction. I forget the year but I am certain no buyer is mentioned.

"But now tell me, Arnold, how did you manage to gain access to the obscenity?"

"I was able to find out where Maack lives on the Herrengasse and the good thing was that I did not even have to enter his flat. It was a matter, rather, of accessing his inner courtyard balcony on the first floor and then pressing open his unlocked French doors. I pushed the curtains aside, leaned inside, spotted the canvas to my right on the wall, and aimed my can of black spray paint directly onto it. I didn't even set off an alarm and I was out of there in the equivalent of one minute. I just had time to toss a black rose on the floor."

"You have done exceedingly well, Arnold, exceedingly well indeed."

"Oh, thank you, Grand Master. Praise from you means everything to me."

"And of course there must be absolutely no Internet mention of your success. The Doppel-O organization can never be associated with the courageous activities of its members. This is the vow we have all sworn to uphold. Our website continues to wage general war on pornography but never discusses the specific victories of war. This you understand?"

"Fully understood, Grand Master, fully understood."

"Well, I have encouraging news for you as well, Arnold. My trip to Russia was a success. We now have the finances necessary to acquire the land for our commune at Gmunden. Once the deed of sale has been signed we begin building immediately."

# 20

As Megan, dressed in her red parka and black wool beanie, walked through the Karlsplatz to the Wien Museum after breakfast to return the borrowed Hietzinger Hauptstrasse key to its nesting place inside Schiele's toy horse, she again had the feeling of being followed. Several times she stopped abruptly and turned around, but she saw no one who aroused her suspicions.

After entering the museum, she nodded to the guard and again walked up the stairs to the second floor instead of taking the elevator at the far end of the entry hall. Good exercise, she reminded herself. Eagerly she walked into the room that contained Schiele's furniture. Three early museum visitors, Australian from their accents, were moving around the room slowly, commenting on the paintings. Megan had to linger quite a while before the enthusiastic group took the stairs down to the gift shop. As soon as they did, she moved with alacrity to the cabinet, bent down to release the side-drawer spring and slipped the Hietzinger Hauptstrasse key back into the hollowed out body of Schiele's wooden horse.

So intent was Megan on her restitution mission that she did not notice the tall white-haired man with trim beard who stood in the adjacent room keeping her in his line of sight. He quickly stepped away when Megan stood up. This time instead of taking the stairs down right away, Megan walked to the next room and leaned over the polished wooden balcony that circled around the permanent scale model of Vienna's inner ring buildings as they looked in the year 1900. The display had always fascinated her and she could never take enough photographs of the historic buildings lining the Ringstrasse. Pulling her iPhone out she began taking panorama shots, something she'd never done with this particular exhibition before.

The activity was so totally engrossing that she was unaware of the man who crossed over to the top of the stairs she would be taking down to the main floor. Megan's back was to him as he stooped suddenly to loop a trip wire around the banister at foot level. Crossing quickly to the other side of the staircase he drew the wire taut and with one quick tie expertly fixed it in place. A moment later he was back in the room from which he had come. From where he now stood he had an unobstructed view of the staircase.

Reluctantly, Megan stopped taking her panorama shots. She really must go down to the desk now and ask to be announced to her friend, the director. Hurrying to the staircase while trying at the same time to tuck her phone back into her shoulder bag's outside pocket, she was distracted as she took the first step. She was not to take another. The trip wire flipped Megan head first down six steps to the landing below. Instinctively she extended her hands and elbows to take the full impact of the fall and landed in a heap, her parka bunched up under her, her woolen cap askew.

"*Was ist geschehen? What has happened?*" yelled the museum guard on the first floor as she ran toward the landing. The three visitors in the museum shop rushed back into the museum to see what had happened. As they ran up to the landing where a prone figure was lying motionless, the tall man at the top of the staircase quickly unlooped the trip wire from the balustrade and made his way to the elevator down the hall. In the pandemonium taking place he was able to exit the museum without being noticed.

She could not have survived such a fall, thought a triumphant Wolf Schnitt as he strode to the Karlsplatz. His first mission as a full-fledged member of the Inner Circle of Doppel-O had been accomplished.

*Megan Crespi had been dispatched and, just as the Grand Master had commanded, it looked like an accident.*

# 21

The baron sat at his desk in the castle and stared with disbelief and delight at the check Kurt Winter had handed him. It was a check made out to Friedrich von Gemmingen-Eggaberg for fifty million US dollars.

"This is marvelous," said Fritz at last. "Now, Kurt, let us examine the bill of sale and if you are in agreement, my notary will come right over to the Schloss and we shall both sign it." He felt a slight twinge of regret at the idea of selling even the six acres under question, but these were hard times for the castle and, of equal importance, the Dürer legacy could now remain in the family. All this for the sale of six acres of land that could not even be seen from the Schloss.

As he mulled this over the thought came to him that, as a signal of his gratitude, he might show the serious redheaded man before him who looked so much like Dürer, the master's self-portrait. Of course that would be breaking with family tradition, but the baron was exceedingly grateful to Kurt Wagner and he thought highly of his cause to stamp out pornography.

*Ja!* He would do it. A few minutes later the two men were standing in the family library, a huge two-story room with leather bound volumes shelved from floor to ceiling and spanning three sides of the room. On the far wall opposite the entry, surrounded by book shelves, hung a second version of the famous Dürer self-portrait of 1500. It was set off by a lavish gold frame. Wagner stared at it silently, strangely unmoved by the sight of his Doppelganger.

The silence was finally broken by the baron, who had been gazing at Wagner intently.

"I see you are of two minds about this painting," he said.

Kurt Wagner hastened to remonstrate but the baron continued. "You may well have observed that the image before you is not genuine. This is simply an excellent copy. We keep the actual self-portrait in a secret room. Here let me show you."

The baron removed a large leather volume at shoulder height next to the Dürer image, pulled down a lever that had been hidden by the book, and the whole picture panel slowly began to revolve inward. When it had finished its half turn a small inner room was revealed. The walls were hung with precious Dürer etchings and woodcuts. On the center wall, framed simply in black, hung a luminous oil painting that returned Wagner's gaze. It looked just like the image outside but this was the real thing. Like the Munich self-portrait, this one was a bust rendition of Dürer staring out frontally from within a dark surround. Frontality, at that time, was usually reserved for depictions of Christ. On the upper left, Dürer had dated the picture 1500 and had signed with his monogram A and nestled D. On the upper right he had printed in Latin an inscription in silver lettering against the dark background.

It read: "I, Albrecht Dürer of Nuremberg portrayed myself in everlasting colors aged twenty-eight years." While Wagner reverently read the inscription out loud, the baron marveled at how the man before him, his hair the same shoulder length as Dürer's, looked like the Renaissance master. It was as though Dürer had come to life and was standing next to his portrait. The similarity was striking: the same full lips, long, thin nose, high cheekbones, and light eyebrows.

The baron broke the silence. "Now you understand, Herr Wagner, why I am willing to sell you six acres of the Gemmingen-Eggaberg estate. It is as though, either through chance or some will of fate, you are the reincarnation of the great German master himself."

Humbled, Kurt Wagner, bowed his head and murmured: "May I be worthy." Inside him a, jubilant voice declared: "You have been chosen by God himself to follow in the footsteps of this great artist. You are the modern-day Christ, striving to bring purity to an impure world."

# 22

A dazed Megan slowly regained consciousness. She was surrounded by the three Australian tourists and a solicitous guard. They had been joined by the museum's worried director, Dietrich Mann. She could hear their voices but when she opened her eyes she saw nothing. It was dark.

Very slowly, just as she was told her little dog Button had done after his fall, Megan tentatively stretched out each arm and leg. Nothing seemed to be broken. But...

"Lie still," one of the Australians advised. "You may have a concussion."

"What happened? Where am I?" asked Megan groggily.

"You've had a fall down our staircase, dear Megan," Dietrich answered, aghast to see his American friend collapsed on the staircase landing of his museum. He had no idea she was even in Wien.

"Oh, Dietrich. What a strange way to see you. I was on my way to your office." Megan had used the word "see" but in fact she wasn't seeing anything. Everything was black, no matter how wide she opened her eyes.

"An ambulance is on its way," soothed Dietrich. "Can you remember anything about what happened?"

"Yes. I remember," Megan murmured. "Something was in my way on the first step as I started to go downstairs and I tripped over it. I went shooting down on my wrists and elbows. Thank goodness I had my parka on because I think it helped break my fall."

"All right. Be still. Don't move anymore. I've called an ambulance and we'll get you to a hospital. They'll check you out there."

"Whatever you say, Dietrich," Megan said, sinking back gratefully into her parka. "And thank you for your concern," she nodded sightlessly to the guard and the Australian visitors.

The ambulance arrived within minutes and Megan was expertly transferred to the AKH—Vienna's General Hospital, the *Allgemeines Krankenhaus*. The physician who took her case, Dr. Benjamin Gerhardt, examined her carefully and instructed that x-rays be taken. He looked at

Megan's badly bruised wrists and elbows which were black and blue and quite swollen.

"You must have used your wrists and elbows to break your fall. They will become more swollen. Your blindness is very likely the result of a concussion and is most probably transient. I wouldn't be surprised if it cleared up in an hour or two." He left the room and a nurse entered, ready to wheel her off for x-rays.

"May I give you a number to call on my behalf?" asked Megan, worried about the appointment with Hannes and the police she would be missing.

"Of course. Here, I'll dial it for you on my phone."

A minute later Megan was telling a concerned Hannes what happened and where she was.

"My wrists and elbows are banged up, but the scary thing is that I can't see. The doctor says this will probably pass, but right now I'm as blind as a bat, and it's frightening!"

"Megan, I'm coming right over to the hospital. Inspector Ludwig can meet with us later."

"Thank you, Hannes, thank you," said Megan, hugely relieved to hear the voice of a caring friend.

About twenty minutes later Dr. Gehardt reentered the cubicle where Megan had been placed after x-rays had been taken and took her hand. "You are a very lucky woman, Frau Crespi. Your x-rays show no broken bones, so all we have to do is wait for your sight to be restored. I'm going to give you a supply of pain killers and I'd like you to take the first one now."

The nurse guided Megan's hand to a glass of water and handed her a pill. Megan gulped it down, then immediately asked for a second glass of water. She felt dehydrated. She was also feeling terribly helpless and depressed. Not to be able to see? Her whole profession had depended on her sense of sight, to say nothing of her life itself. She kept opening her eyes wide, hoping each time that light would dispel the darkness, but nothing. There was no change.

The minutes passed like hours. The sounds of other patients being admitted to the hospital emergency clinic reached her ears and Megan was left alone, lying on the narrow bed in her cubicle. She felt around her cautiously and realized she was hooked up to a heart rate monitor. What *was* her heart rate she wondered, looking toward where the readout would most likely be. Blindness greeted her effort. How could she get used to this?

Suddenly a warm hand clasped her arm. "Megan," said Hannes gently. He had found her room location on the blackboard chart at the emergency room entrance and was appalled to see how black and blue her arms and forehead were. Megan opened her eyes and stared at him blindly.

"Oh, Hannes, thank god you are here!" A tremendous sense of relief flooded over her and with it her sight returned, albeit somewhat blurred.

"Oh, oh, oh! I can *see* you, I can *see* you, Hannes!"

"*Ach, ja,*" said Dr. Gerhardt, entering the cubicle. This is exactly what I thought it would be, a simple case of transient blindness due to the slight concussion you have had. The blurry vision will clear up and I don't think you will have any other symptoms. You are free to go now. But you must get a lot of rest and continue to take the pain pills for the bursitis your elbows and wrists will present."

Megan was ecstatic to be able to see again and realized her empathy for unsighted persons had just increased a hundredfold. She used to wonder whether it would be worse to be deaf or to be blind, and now she had her answer. After all, she could always *hear* music in her head, seemingly fully orchestrated. She just couldn't hum it the way she heard it. Never mind. If I have to choose I now know which it would be, she consoled herself. She felt better already despite the stinging soreness of her wrists and elbows.

"You know what, Hannes," she said bravely as he helped her to his car, "let's go on back to your office. I feel well enough now."

"Not on your life," responded Hannes vehemently. "You are going to have a lie-down, an all-day one if necessary. And stay home this evening." A few minutes later he pulled up to the back entrance of the Römischer Kaiser and came around the car to open the door for her.

"All right, Hannes, I think you are probably right about my needing rest right now," Megan said gratefully.

A few minutes later, without even taking her parka off, Megan was stretched out on her bed, her arms and legs wrapped around a pillow. She fell asleep immediately.

When she did awake several hours later she saw that it was already four o'clock. She felt much better, thanks to the pain killer pills Dr. Gehardt had given her. In fact, she felt hunger pangs. Perhaps she was even up to having dinner with Dietrich Mann if he could make it on such short notice. He was still at the Wien Museum when she called and he was thrilled to learn of Megan's improved condition and that, most importantly, no bones had been broken. But he nixed the idea of their going out to dinner.

"Are you crazy? You just had a fall and a concussion this morning! You stay put, Megan, and if you're really hungry I will bring a picnic dinner over for both of us. How about around six o'clock? And should you feel well enough after that, *only* if you're up to it, Megan, we could walk across the street to the *Wienerwald* for dessert."

"I suppose you're right, Dietrich. Even though I feel much better now. And my vision is almost back to normal."

"You bet I'm right. Expect me at six."

Megan felt uplifted. If she was hungry, she was well. Food, rather than Schiele or bodily aches, was front and center in her mind.

# 23

At her modest old home in Königsberg—now called Kaliningrad ever since its annexation by Russia following World War II—Sonja Oppenheimer was busy foraging in the attic among her father's works for the single large Schiele oil remaining to her. Now in her late eighties, Sonja had always kept both Schiele self-portraits rolled up in the attic, just as her father Max had done when he moved from Vienna to Königsberg in East Prussia.

None of her Königsberg friends or acquaintances even knew of the existence of the two paintings, or that she had a large store of her father's works as well. And Sonja had kept it that way until last week when that frightening tax office lady Éva Vidovszky appeared at her door, insisting she inspect her Schiele holdings. Finally Sonja had relented, but only partially, laboriously bringing down from the attic to appease her the first Schiele piece she chanced upon, the rolled-up canvas of what turned out to be the artist's *Nude Self-Portrait Standing with Hands on Hips*.

That seemed to satisfy the woman, who then expended her energy in scolding her concerning the terrible condition the painting was in. A few flakes of yellow pigment had sprinkled onto the table top when they unrolled the canvas. How could Frau Oppenheimer ever have thought of rolling up the canvas? Sonja had explained truthfully that this was the way she had inherited it and that she had never taken a look at the painting until now. She could clearly see the welt running across the middle of the canvas and the faded coloration, so she was actually glad when Vidovszky offered to have the painting restored on her behalf.

"If you allow me to take this damaged work to Sotheby's of London for restoration," Éva had told her, "I will report it in its damaged state to the Austrian tax office and you will not have to pay taxes on it." Relieved by this offer, and accepting the signed "receipt" Éva Vidovszky officiously wrote out, Sonja had, foolishly—she now realized—allowed the tax lady to leave with the canvas roll for London.

Just why her father had so treasured the two Schiele canvasses, Sonja had never really comprehended. A fellow painter and close friend of Schiele's, Max Oppenheimer acquired the two works from the artist himself in 1912, just weeks after his release from a Neuelengbach country jail. Schiele had been charged with keeping pornographic works in his garden-house studio where child models were exposed to them.

With no place to keep the two controversial large paintings back in Vienna, Schiele had asked Max to store them for him. Then, taking a different motivic tack after his prison experience, and casting himself as a hermit, monk, or saint, Schiele, soon riding the crest of increasing success, apparently forgot that the two juvenile 1910 works were still with Max. When Egon died in 1918 of the Spanish flu, just as World War I was ending, Max held on to the paintings, keeping their existence a secret.

This action was partly out of professional jealousy. Schiele's jerky psychological portraits were still sought after while Max's work was just beginning to be recognized, and even then only as a painterly version of Schiele's existential portrayals. Max's portraits of Arnold Schönberg and Heinrich Mann were eventually acquired by major museums in Switzerland, but more for their sitters' fame than for their artistic quality.

Three months before the Anschluss of March 12, 1938, Max rolled up the Schiele works in his possession along with a number of his own drawings and paintings and took them for safe-keeping to his grandparents' home in the Prussian port city of Königsberg, near the Polish border. Staying one jump ahead of the Nazis and their mission of destroying degenerate works of art, Max left Europe for America, but not with his paintings. His brother Jakob, a close friend of Arnold Schönberg and a Judaic scholar, also left most of his belongings behind and migrated to America with his wife and daughter.

There was great irony in Max Oppenheimer's choice to hide his works from Hitler in Königsberg. Earlier in the decade, in 1933, at that very city, Hitler had given a rousing speech, broadcast by radio for the first time, to the entire German nation on the eve of the Reichstag elections. He also visited nearby historic Tilsit and had himself photographed on the Neman River bridge, thus righting the wrong done the defeated Germans there by Napoleon and Czar Alexander I of Russia at the beginning of the nineteenth century. Hitler returned to Königsberg on the twenty-fifth of March in 1938, just two weeks after Austria was annexed into the German Third Reich.

Max's daughter Sonja, though born in New York, had moved to the ancestral home in Königsberg as a teenager after her father died in the mid-1950s. There in the attic she found her father's many rolled up paintings as well as a couple identified on the outer paper sheath as "E. S." Two of her father's works had been placed on easels. Not being particularly enamored of the "overwrought" Expressionist art of her father or Egon Schiele, Sonja had left the paintings in peace, expending her professional energies on a long career in nursing. She had never married. Now retired, she lived a comfortable life on a generous pension, tending to her much-loved garden, leaving the world alone and hoping it would leave her alone.

Now, after the fuss on television and in the newspapers about the theft of *her* stolen Schiele from Sotheby's, she was indeed curious as to the subject of the other Schiele painting still in her possession. She had already written the American Schiele expert, Megan Crespi, whose home address in Texas a local museum researcher had provided her, and she was hoping for a speedy answer.

Despite the labor involved of climbing so many steps, she decided to carry the Schiele work downstairs to examine it. Perhaps it too should be restored. Obviously, it was worth something after all these years. The media coverage of the Schiele painting she had let go to the tax lady had made that pretty obvious. Clearing her small dining room table of its setting for one, Sonja cautiously began to unroll the canvas. Then she stopped. Miniature flakes of faded yellow paint sprinkled out onto the table. Horrified, she immediately rolled the canvas back in to itself and slowly carried it back to the attic. Only an expert should deal with this. Éva Vidovszky's scolding was well merited, she told herself. She hoped Professor Crespi would contact her soon.

# 24

While Megan waited for six o'clock when Dietrich was going to be bringing over a picnic dinner for them both, the idea of another phone call came to mind. One that would not be about her state of health which was rapidly boring her, but about her main passion, Schiele. Picking up her phone she reached for the piece of paper on which she had jotted down the telephone number of that worried woman who had written her in such quaint English from Königsberg, Sonja Oppenheimer. Talking to her about Schiele matters would certainly make her forget about Crespi aches and pains, and they truly *were* aches and pains.

She took another pain killer, then placed the call. An answering machine stated the same brief message in German, English, and Russian: "You have reached Haus Oppenheimer. Please leave a message and speak slowly."

Megan started to leave her name and had barely pronounced the final syllable when a woman's strong voice said joyously: "Frau Doktor Crespi? Here is Sonja Oppenheimer. I so hope you can help me. Thank you so very much for calling me."

"Of course! I am happy to do so. Please do tell me from the beginning about the visit from Éva Vidovszky and how it came to pass that you assigned your Schiele painting to her for restoration at Sotheby's in London."

Sighing with relief, Sonja told Megan at length about Vidovszky's visit and her frightening announcement that back taxes were due to the Austrian government on any Schiele work she might possess. Vidovszky had told her that since the end of World War II Austria had an agreement with both Germany and Russia concerning the taxing of national treasures still in private hands. Tracing the Oppenheimer family had led Vidovszky from Vienna to New York to Königsberg. She was acquainted with the fact that Sonja's father had been a friend of Schiele's and she was investigating lost works by Schiele.

A few weeks ago, Vidovszky told Sonja, she had been contacted about Schiele's lost works by one Adolf Peschka-Schiele, great grandnephew of Schiele. This Adolf was a self-described "last living" relative of Schiele's and to emphasize his legitimate if remote relationship, he had added his great grandmother Gerti's maiden name Schiele to his own surname Peschka.

The thing was, Vidovszky had explained to Sonja, Peschka-Schiele was a fanatic. He was hell bent on filing restitution claims on all known Schieles that did not have water-tight provenances. As the artist's only living relative, Adolf lay claim to such works. He had several law suits in progress at the moment in Austria and abroad. And now he was on the track of any Schiele works the artist might have traded with Max Oppenheimer. He was looking for Oppenheimer descendants, and he had asked if Vidovszky knew of any.

"Does he think *I* have a Schiele work?" Sonja had interrupted Éva Vidovszky's long narrative. Vidovszky had reassured Sonja that she was sure Peschka-Schiele did not even know about her; he was only searching for possible connections in New York.

However, Vidovszky had continued, it would be wise to move the painting out of her house, out of Europe even, and get it into restoration in England, before existence of it in Königsberg became common knowledge. And, she emphasized, she would report it as damaged to the Austrian government so that no back taxes would be levied. Did she have any other Schieles, Vidovszky had quizzed repeatedly. Sonja had been too frightened to tell her the truth.

"But I can tell you, Frau Doktor," Sonja concluded her long story, "I feel that I can trust you. You live in Texas, far away from the imbroglios of Vienna. The truth is I do indeed have one other Schiele canvas in my home. In fact I attempted to look at it just this afternoon but realized it was too fragile to unroll completely."

"Considering that one of your two Schieles has disappeared and may never be recovered, what would you now wish to do with your other Schiele?" Megan asked concernedly.

"I think I do not want to have it in my house any longer. I do not want people importuning me as the Vidovszky woman did and as this Peschka-Schiele might do. *Ich will meine Ruhe!* I want my peace! The best thing to do, I suppose, would be to restore it and sell it through a reliable agent or established gallery. Or simply *give* it to the Belvedere Museum in Wien. Yes, I think that would be better. I do not need the money. Let Schiele return to his homeland."

Megan thought for a moment. There was one restorer in Russia in whom she had faith and one established gallery owner in Russia she trusted. They were Igor Borodin of the Pushkin Museum and Alexandra Azarova of the Gallery Rasputin in Moscow.

"If I can arrange it, would you permit me to send to your home a Russian restorer and a Russian gallery owner, both of whom I trust implicitly?"

There was a silence.

"Only if *you* come with them, Frau Doktor Crespi. I need to have someone with me whom I can trust. To be my advocate. Oh, please say yes, that you will come to Königsberg and see the Schiele with me."

The last thing Megan wanted was to tell Sonja Oppenheimer that she was not in the greatest shape to travel. But the prospect of being on the spot when a Schiele canvas thought to be lost for decades was unrolled was too enticing. And if, as seemed highly likely, the painting proved to be the other nude self-portrait from 1910—the kneeling one—then she absolutely had to be there.

Megan heard two voices in her head. One was Claire's saying "Steady, now, steady," and the other was her own voice saying "Yes!" A second later she heard herself saying the latter out loud to Sonja Oppenheimer.

# 25

Adolf Peschka-Schiele had concluded his business in London. It was unsuccessful. He had conferred at length with Sotheby's head of sales, Jillian Lloyd, and with the auction house's restorer, Rupert Wechseln. What they had told him about the Schiele painting undergoing restoration there made sense. The Killar catalogue's black-and-white reproduction matched in every detail the life-size portrait stolen from Sotheby's. Yes, it was one of the two 1910 lost self-portraits in the nude—the one in which Schiele was standing. And apparently the colors, when totally restored, would match those of the Leopold Museum's great 1910 nude self-portrait seated with arms raised and lower legs cut off.

But no matter how he tried, Peschka-Schiele was unable to wheedle out of Sotheby's discreet employees just who had offered the painting for auction. Company policy forbade disclosure of private clients was his only answer. They would not even reveal from what country the individual came. If only he could have gleaned which *continent*!. If it had been Europe, the source might have been in Austria, but then why not go to Vienna's Dorotheum Auction House? If the owner was from North or South America or Israel, then he might have been the descendant of resettled Austrian or German Jews. Adolf had made as complete a list as possible of contemporary Jewish owners of Schiele works, both oils and graphics, and he had methodically researched the families and their far-flung descendants.

One name stood out from the others. Jerome Schwartz, Director of the São Paulo Museum of Twentieth Century Art in Brazil. He was the grandson of Schiele's early patron and dentist, Peter Schwartz. Schiele traded portrait sketches of his family for dental work, and in early 1913 he had painted a life-size double portrait of Peter and his teenage son Paul. It was a psychological masterpiece with the sensitive younger Schwartz visibly challenging the confining orbit of his old-fashioned father.

Schiele had done a father-son portrayal once before in 1913, and with a similar tension between parent and offspring, Heinrich and Otto Benesch. This double portrait was now in the Linz Museum in Austria. But the Schwartz double portrait had been left behind in Vienna in private hands when the Schwartz family hastily emigrated to Brazil a few weeks before the Anschluss. Killar's catalogue did not give the name of the family; merely "Private Collection." Adolf Peschka-Schiele knew that Jerome Schwartz had tried repeatedly, but always unsuccessfully, to determine the whereabouts of the portrait of his grandfather and father. Wherever it was, it was worth a fortune. But did the present-day owner know that?

This was Adolf's way of dealing. Approaching naïve, unsophisticated inheritors of Schiele works and talking them out of owning them. His only rival in this tactic was the Hungarian antiquities dealer Éva Vidovszky, whose Antiquariat in Vienna offered everything from a lock of Keats' hair or an envelope addressed by Johannes Brahms, to the occasional Klimt or Schiele or Kokoschka drawing—all for astronomical prices.

It was mortifying that it was she, and not he, who had, by a twist of fortune, come across Schiele's masterpiece of 1910, now in the Leopold Museum. It had been a janitor who discovered the painting languishing in the attic of the apartment complex he was asked to clean out when it changed over to condominium ownership. Not knowing what to do with such an old and odd painting of a writhing naked man, he had taken it to the Antiquariat down the street for advice and evaluation. The Antiquariat was owned by Vidovszky and she gave the janitor all of five hundred Euros for his find. Both parties were enormously pleased by the transaction. As for the painting's later acquisition by a city museum, the janitor remained blissfully unaware, since he never read newspapers and did not own a television set.

* * *

Megan's phone conversation with Sonja Oppenheimer had been exhilarating. Following through on her promise to the worried lady, she immediately dialed another Russian telephone number. Alexandra Azarova was delighted to hear from her Texas friend. Megan had been her hostess when she flew to Dallas for an international art dealers association convention several years ago. She had arrived two days early and after Megan had picked her up from D/FW Airport, their talk had turned to Alexandra's busy work schedule. She told Megan about the cherished retreat she owned an hour outside Moscow, a small dacha she had inherited from an uncle. It was located by a little lake and had a lovely view of the water.

"What you say amazes me," said Megan almost in disbelief. "Not far from Dallas I too have a lakeside retreat with a fine view of the water! And it has a tree house guesthouse I built for visitors, complete with bathroom, microwave, and cable TV."

"Oh, this I have to experience," Alexandra cried. "A tree house guesthouse? Only in America! Or should I say only in Texas? Please, can we forget the museums in Dallas and go there instead for two days?"

Megan was only too pleased to skip the cultural tour of the city she had given so many times to visitors. They made a quick stop at her home to pick up a surprised Button and a few overnight things, then headed northeast out of Dallas on Highway 75 for the seventy-minute drive to Lake Bonham, near the Oklahoma border.

On the way they discussed the shady dealings of her St. Petersburg competitor, Boris Ussachevsky. It was indeed fascinating that his grandfather Vladimir had known and bought drawings from Schiele during his study year in Vienna in nineteen-thirteen. But surely Vladimir could not have bought *seventy* of them, which was the number of Schiele "drawings" the Solovey Gallery had offered for sale over the past two decades.

A few of the works were indeed by Schiele and pictured in Killar, but most of them were well-done forgeries, combining recognizable motifs from genuine works and hence producing convincing "previously unknown" works. It took a true Schiele expert like Janette Killar or Johannes Ohm or Megan herself to detect the difference. And Alexandra had developed quite an eye for Schiele forgeries herself.

Her opinion of Boris Ussachevsky was at an all time low, needless to say. She wondered that none of his clients had ever questioned the credentials of the works they bought. But then most of Ussachevsky's clients were not Russian, they were Japanese or South Korean, eager to add Schiele to their collections.

Now, after promising Sonja Oppenheimer that she would come to Königsberg, Megan was talking to Alexandra on the phone, urging her to join her in Königsberg. The Schiele painting, although in poor condition, should be exciting, a real find. It was very probably the kneeling nude self-portrait of 1910. And would Alexandra kindly see if she could persuade their mutual friend Igor Borodin to come as well? They could take a flight together and Megan would meet them at the Königsberg Devau airport.

As it worked out, Boris was only too willing to accompany Alexandra on the "first responders" flight, as he phrased it. He had missed out on restoring the Schiele nude self-portrait Alexandra and Max Valentin had shown him, so he would be more than pleased to restore this latest discovered work by the extraordinary Austrian painter.

By e-mail they coordinated their flights to arrive in Königsberg on the afternoon of the day after tomorrow, as all three of them needed at least twenty-four hours to finish up commitments and work at hand. Also, having another full day to rest up from her fall sounded good to Megan. But a chance to return to the north Prussian birthplace of the great artist Käthe Kollwitz also meant another opportunity to photograph the scant trace of the ancient city that World War II bombing had left intact.

Megan looked at her watch. There was still time to call Claire and her sister in Dallas before Dietrich arrived with his picnic dinner at six o'clock. She would break the news of her fall at the Wien Museum and emphasize her quick recovery. Then she would inform them of her expanded itinerary. Just as she had expected, they both made a big fuss over her health and the time needed for recovery, but Megan was telling the truth when she assured them that she was greatly improved. There was only the inconvenience and pain of the swollen elbows; her wrists already felt and looked a bit better. And just think! The black and blue spots made her face look "interesting."

# 26

"*But that is simply not possible!*

She *has* to be dead," protested Wolf Schnitt, his eyes wide with surprise. He had traveled out to Gmunden the next morning to tell Kurt Wagner in person of his success in disposing of Megan Crespi. He was standing in the Grand Master's office in the Doppel-O wing of Schloss Gemmingen-Eggaberg.

"She was seen walking with a man outside her hotel last night. She looked in terrible shape, but she is *alive*, so my man tells me."

His man was Arnold Moll, who happened to be walking on the Annagasse the previous evening when he saw Crespi. He recognized her from photographs on the back of her Schiele books. She was leaning heavily on the arm of a male companion and they were slowly entering the *Wienerwald* restaurant. Moll followed them inside and took a seat at the periphery of the room where he could watch them as they were led to a table in the back of the restaurant.

"But I clearly saw her tumble hard all the way down the stairs to the landing below. She wasn't moving when I left the building. Naturally I thought she was dead."

"She *should* be dead! After all she's in her late seventies, I think," said Wagner. "It's a miracle that she survived such a fall.

"The question now is," he continued, "what is she up to, how much if anything does she suspect about the Doppel-O, and how long will she be in Wien? My man followed the couple back to her hotel. So that confirms what you found out, that she is staying at the Römischer Kaiser."

"What can I do to make things right?" asked a desperate Schnitt.

"Nothing except try again. Go back to Wien immediately. Haunt her hotel. Check into it if you have to. You've got to get her alone if possible. Collateral damage would raise too many questions."

"I'll leave immediately. And this time I won't fail, Grand Master." Wolf Schnitt bowed to the red-haired man, then turned on his heel and left the Schloss.

\* \* \*

During dessert the evening before at the *Wienerwald*, Megan had told Dietrich about the secret drawer in Schiele's black wooden cabinet and its contents: the little wooden horse and the key inside.

"The key to his Wattmanngasse studio?" Dietrich asked, raising his eyebrows.

"No, oddly enough, it is the key to the Hietzinger Hauptstrasse cellar storage room. A trap door there leads to a small basement room that was empty except for a few narrow boards of wood. I was able to get down inside and count them. They were stacked up in an unusual way: sets of four, and all the same length—five feet. What I realized, after counting them all, was that—if nailed together—they could be seven frames for seven large, five-by-five-foot paintings!"

"That's intriguing, to say the least," mused Dietrich. "Is it known whether Schiele was working on that many paintings at any time in his career?"

"Yes, he had written Arthur Roessler that he was involved in painting an entire series of works. The only trouble is we don't know whether they were allegories or townscapes or portraits. The artist never specified the subject matter. All he wrote was that the series would benefit Vienna."

"Is there nothing in the Killar catalogue that points to what Schiele was doing, say during the war years?"

"I can imagine his doing a series during this time, especially toward the end of the war when his military duties were not so demanding, but there are no likely artworks with a continuous theme in the oeuvre catalogue. Well, let me correct that. Schiele was painting a number of mysterious allegories."

"But you have no real leads?"

"Well, there is one thing you might call a lead. In nineteen-eighteen, the year of his death, Schiele made two sketches on a single piece of paper of what looks like a temple seen from the side and then also from above. The double drawing is labeled in his handwriting 'Mausoleum.' The building is octagonal in shape so if you don't count the entrance wall that leaves seven wall surfaces onto which a large image could be hung. So it looks as though Schiele might have been planning to place his paintings in this templelike mausoleum. To repeat his words, he was working on an extraordinary series that would benefit Wien."

"Well, that is a puzzle," Dietrich said. "Perhaps your Königsberg trip will shed some light on this conundrum."

"I wouldn't count on it. I believe the painting there is from that early nineteen-ten trio of full-size nude self-portraits, one of which is in the Leopold, the second of which is the one stolen from Sotheby's. That leaves us the third one which, as pictured in Killar, shows Schiele kneeling with hands and arms raised. Up to now it has been designated as 'present whereabouts unknown.'"

"Well, what a find that would be. I wish you luck and safe travels," Dietrich said, just a tad jealous that this American art historian might once again be in on a great Schiele find. He pictured how, because of her discovery of the provincial jail where Schiele had been incarcerated, Neulengbach now had a thriving little museum, bringing any number of tourists to the town, and drawing them away from *his* Wien Museum. Recently Neulengbach had created a "*Schiele Weg*"—a Schiele Way—with twelve markers designating locations having to do with the artist's stay in the village. Another tourist draw. And now this elderly scholar from Texas had come up with an important, previously unknown, new Schiele fact: the hidden drawer in Schiele's art cabinet in his very own museum!

"Please be careful, Megan," Dietrich had said as he helped her limp back across the street to the Römischer Kaiser. A very tired Megan smiled. It seemed as if everyone were telling her to be careful. Well, she would certainly watch more carefully where she was walking now and hope never to lose her balance again.

*  *  *

Boris Ussachevsky cursed himself.

He had just ruined a Schiele. And not just any Schiele. It was *the* 1910 nude self-portrait standing which he had intimidated the naïve Austrian Max Valentin into letting go for a mere one hundred million US dollars.

Oh, he had been so clever. He was so sure he could restore the faded painting himself. Hadn't he done a superb job on the Schiele townscape he had bought at Sotheby's recently? The fact that it was unfinished and not signed had not deterred him. With great care, and applying the exact same colors and brushwork that Schiele used, he had finished the Krumau view and fashioned an absolutely credible signature and date, 1911, on the lower left of the canvas.

Naturally Boris thought he could renew the faded yellow color of Schiele's body on the left side of the painting now before him. The other side had already been handsomely restored. The black contours, so angular and aggressive, were intact, but could use a little touching up while he was at it. The background was an off-white, more dirty cream than ivory, and, at least it seemed to him, needed no refurbishing. However, when Boris began fortifying the thick contour lines with black paint, actual dirt fell off the lines and polluted the adjacent cream background. Not only that, he had not waited long enough to renew the yellow hue of Schiele's body after blackening its contour, so when he did apply yellow paint it began to congeal with the black lines of the body.

Patience! He simply had not practiced patience. He could have done it if he had not been in such a hurry. Or could he? Now he was beginning to have self-doubts. Yes, he could have taken the Schiele to a restorer, but who in Russia could he trust not to reveal that he, Boris, was in possession of a major artwork just recently stolen from Sotheby's? There had been only one other dealer in Russia with the means to buy the Schiele even in its half-restored state and that was his Moscow rival Alexandra Azarova. Valentin had obviously lied to him that he had an offer from her to buy the canvas. Azarova was a stickler for provenance, and now she knew it was a stolen work of art as well. Why, she might even have informed the police by now about Valentin's offering it to her. And of course she would know that the Austrian most probably offered it to him as well. Had she perhaps told the police of this possibility?

All the more reason to take the fabulous work—as it would be again, once he had more time to work on it—to his dacha in Votkinsk. There it could be hidden away with his other Schiele oil. Not a soul in St. Petersburg knew about his second home in remote Votkinsk, some 870 miles to the southeast.

If he alerted his pilot now, he could leave on his private jet—a two-engine Gulfstream G650—this very evening.

Yes. That was it. It was his duty to shield Schiele from prying eyes. And at the same time he would continue trying to ascertain the identity of the anonymous client who had offered it to Sotheby's in the first place. That client might also own the other 1910 nude self-portrait, the one in which Schiele showed himself kneeling. Perhaps he should contact that crazy Peschka-Schiele man and tap his brain. After all, he could offer an enticing sum to buy any Schiele in private hands he might know about. That might bring results.

"Egon, forgive me," Boris said out loud. "I shall restore you to your former magnificence at our beloved Votkinsk."

# 21

Feeling almost herself the next morning, despite her aching elbows and wrists, Megan called Hannes and they set up a time for Inspector Ludwig to meet them at the Leopold Museum in the early afternoon. They wanted to go over things related to the killing of the night watchman and to the Schiele and Klimt damage at the museum. And of course the Schiele spray painting at the house of Antal Maack.

After a leisurely breakfast in her favorite breakfast nook with its view of the Annagasse, which at that moment was being pelted with rain, Megan put on her black beanie and red parka—the two pieces of clothing that had, mercifully, helped to break her fall—and walked slowly over to the Ringstrasse. Once there, she headed in the direction of the Kunsthistorisches Museum, the Parliament, and the University, all of which gave onto the magnificent Ring. Although those buildings were to her left, Megan took the far right side of the Ringstrasse so she could walk past the handsome Mozart memorial, an image of which always crowned the lecture she used to give on the changing image of Mozart.

Watching her slow progress from the other side of the Ring, as she stopped to gaze at the joyfully rippling baroque monument, was Wolf Schnitt, who had also exited the Römischer Kaiser Hotel. He was now entertaining the mad notion that if he could somehow get near Crespi when she had to cross the streetcar track that ran around the Ringstrasse, perhaps he would have a chance to stage an "accident." She was probably on her way to the Leopold Museum and would have to cross over the track.

Schnitt was unaware of the fact that he himself was being keenly scrutinized by a short woman with black hair pulled back in a bun and wearing a smart red raincoat and black slacks. Knowing Megan Crespi's favorite hotel from the American's previous Vienna stays, Éva Vidovszky had come to the Römischer Kaiser that morning on the off chance that she might find Megan Crespi at breakfast and get her take on the Schiele happenings afflicting the city of Vienna. Also, of course, to see what if anything she knew about the possible location of Sotheby's stolen Schiele.

Just as Vidovszky entered the Annagasse from the Kärntner Strasse crossing, she saw Megan actually exiting the hotel and coming up the street toward her. But before she could quicken her pace to intercept her, she also saw a man come out of the hotel, his eyes boring into Crespi's back as he moved to the far side of the pedestrian street, slowing his pace to match that of Crespi. Thinking his movements rather odd, Vidovszky entered the store on the corner, where, unobserved, she could watch both persons through the windows of hats on display. Was the man following Crespi?

She watched them both walk past the opera house and take the Ringstrasse toward the Mozart memorial to the southwest of the Burggarten. Megan stopped in front of the statue and the man behind her halted as well, a good twenty paces away. Vidovszky also stopped and waited. As though on a three-dimensional chess board all three figures were paused.

A streetcar passed noisily by on the other side of the Ring in the direction of the opera house. The noise seemed to awaken Crespi from her Mozartian reverie and she continued walking slowly down the Ringstrasse toward the university. She had decided to enter it briefly just to revive memories of her classroom days there so long ago. A good shortcut would be to cut across the streetcar tracks now so she could walk down the University side of the Ring.

Megan saw another tram coming toward her in the direction of the opera house, but it was still down at the university, so plenty of time to cross the Ring. Then she remembered what Claire had said to her about being careful, and decided to wait. The two different persons walking slowly behind her also came to a stop.

Suddenly it occurred to Megan that there was a special exhibition on right now at the Belvedere Museum. It had the engaging title, "The Women of Klimt, Kokoschka, and Schiele" and was co-curated by her friend Janette Killar. Wouldn't that be a more positive way to spend her time?

To the puzzlement of her two observers, Crespi abruptly turned in her tracks and crossed the Ringstrasse in front of an oncoming streetcar. She began walking purposefully back in the direction from which she had come.

What was the woman up to, wondered both her trackers. Would she be turning right and perhaps enter the Kunsthistorisches Museum, or walk past it and the Natural History Museum opposite, and on to the Leopold? Either choice would make tailing her a bit more difficult, as they too would have to cross the Ringstrasse streetcar tracks in between station stops.

But no, Crespi continued on in the direction of the opera house at a relaxed pace. She seemed to be conserving her energy. Well, this was enough zigzagging for Éva Vidovszky. Knowing clients would be waiting for her, she turned off the Ring to enter the Volksgarten and return to her Antiquariat on the Herrengasse. She would drop in on the Römischer Kaiser later that afternoon and if Crespi wasn't there she would leave a note for her. She looked up at the sky. Dark clouds were beginning to form again and she could smell more rain coming.

Crespi had just reached the opera house crossing on the Ringstrasse as a streetcar pulled into the station stop. Not needing to increase her pace, Megan easily caught up with the tram and boarded it. Seconds later the streetcar pulled off in the direction of where Megan would switch at the Schwarzenbergplatz to the D tram toward the Upper Belvedere.

Schnitt's view of his unpredictable quarry was blocked by the same streetcar that Crespi had boarded. When it continued its course there was no one in a red parka on the platform. Schnitt decided she must have entered the *Opernpassage*—the major underground pedestrian crossing at the opera house with entrances on all four sides of the Ringstrasse. He ran to the entry on his side and, ignoring the escalator, raced down the steps. There was no sign of the Crespi woman. Had he failed his mission *again*?

\* \* \*

Peschka-Schiele had returned to Vienna empty handed so far as information was concerned having to do with Sotheby's stolen Schiele. Late in the evening as he was relaxing to television he was surprised to receive a phone call from the famous billionaire owner of the Solovey Gallery in Russia.

"This is Boris Ussachevsky calling from St. Petersburg. Am I speaking with Herr Peschka-Schiele?"

"Indeed you are, Herr Ussachevsky, and of course I know who you are. Your sales of Schiele drawings are known around the world."

"I am calling to see if I can learn anything from you concerning the recent dreadful events in Vienna in regard to Schiele."

"I see." Adolf wondered why the man was really calling. "Well, so far the police have not identified the killer of the guard who was murdered at the Leopold. Nor has there been any break in the case concerning the defacement of the Schiele self-portrait there or the theft of the hacked-out Klimt *Kiss* painting."

"What a pity. And how about the desecration of Schiele's grave? Do they have any idea who did that?"

"Probably the same person who spray-painted the photographic blowups at the Schiele Museum the same day."

Boris got to his real point for calling. "And any progress on the other Schiele that was brazenly kidnapped from Sotheby's in London?"

"If you mean do they know who did it, no. There has been talk of an anonymous client who had handed it over to Sotheby's for restoration before putting it up for auction, but so far it is not public knowledge as to who that person is."

"And any private insights, you might have?"

"I wish I did have a private insight. But the so-called anonymous client could have been from Austria or outside Austria so far as I can guess. Sotheby's is keeping the person's identity to itself. Possibly not even informing the police."

"Yes, I would think that they dare not break their confidentiality agreement with a client. But can you imagine the insurance claim they may have to pay?"

"It would be enormous," said Adolf. "Then perhaps the world will know who the anonymous owner was. But if the painting has gone into private hands it may never be unearthed.

"Just one thing, Herr Ussachevsky," continued Adolf. "Do you think that the other lost Schiele nude self-portrait of nineteen-ten might possibly belong to the same anonymous client?"

"An interesting idea," allowed Boris, drawing the unproductive conversation to a close.

"Well, sorry I could not be more enlightening, Herr Ussachevsky."

"Ah, but it is my honor to have talked with a Schiele descendant."

After they said goodbye both men came to the same conclusion. The other lost Schiele was also, almost certainly, in the possession of Sotheby's anonymous client. There was, floating out there, an enormously valuable Schiele to be had.

* * *

Megan switched tram lines at the Schwarzenbergplatz and a few minutes later she got off the streetcar near the entrance to the grounds of the Upper Belvedere where the "Women" exhibition was being held. As she walked to the entrance she remembered reverently that the elderly composer Anton Brückner had died in the little *Kustodenstöckl* on the left. Climbing to the second floor of the Belvedere where the exhibit was being held, she was surprised to encounter quite a crowd, even though the show had opened several months ago. It took a few minutes for her to thread through the museum visitors before she spotted what she guessed had to be a highlight of the exhibition—two portraits by Klimt and by Schiele of the same person, Fräulein Friederike Maria Beer.

Megan had met and interviewed "Fritzi," as she asked to be called, a number of times in the 1960s when they both lived in New York. They had struck up a long friendship that even took Megan to Honolulu when Fritzi moved there. And yes, there they were, the two fascinating life-size portraits side by side, the earlier one by Schiele on the left, and the one by Klimt, done two years later, in 1916, on the right.

What a contrast! In Schiele's portrait of her, Fritzi was shown upright, knees and arms bent, with plunging bare feet, flailing arms, grasping fingers, and oval head turned toward the spectator in a fixed, blank stare. The zigzag body was plummeting into unarticulated space. Schiele had stripped Fritzi of any explanatory environment—mattress (upon which she was actually lying), pillow (which she had her arms around), or room (the artist's studio)—and instead jettisoned her into an existential, angst-filled *void*.

Megan remembered what Fritzi had told her about the portrait's reception at home. The family maid had exclaimed: "Oh! My mistress has been painted and she looks as though she lies in the tomb!" Perhaps because of this tomblike aspect, Fritzi had then commissioned Klimt to portray her. "Why do you come to me?" Klimt had asked her. "You have already been painted by a very good artist."

"Ah, yes," Fritzi had replied. "But *you* will immortalize me." Flattered, Klimt accepted the commission and produced one of his most spectacular icons of femininity, posing Fritzi standing, frozen, and facing the viewer against an animated oriental background of warriors on horseback. She was shown fingering the fur lining of a coat that had been turned inside out—Fritzi's idea.

She further recounted to Megan what she told the artist as he painted her: "I said to Klimt that I wished I had the courage to wear my coat the way I would like to, with its fur on the inside and its beautiful *Wienerwerkstätte* lining on the outside." Klimt had caught her moment of courage and had indeed immortalized his sitter.

Except for one blow of fate decades later. Fritzi had allowed the Klimt portrait of her to be shown at a London exhibition, and when it was returned to New York during a month of sleet and snow, it encountered a strike by airport workers and the crate containing it was left outdoors on the tarmac for two weeks.

"The painting was a ruin!" Fritzi had exclaimed to Megan. "I simply slid off the canvas. I was no more." A superb restoration had done as much as it could, but ever after, for Fritzi at least, it was no longer by Klimt's own hand.

As Megan gazed at the pair of portraits and listened to the comments of passersby, she realized that most viewers took it for granted that Klimt's was the earlier, more mellifluous Art Nouveau rendition and Schiele's the later, with its Expressionist emphasis on pathos and angst. The professor in Megan refrained, with great will power, from correcting the visitors. After all, there were the informative didactics right next to the two paintings.

To Megan's question regarding what Schiele was like to sit for, Fritzi had informed her with relish: "He was shy and quiet. He did not look at me at all with the same penetrating eyes that Klimt did." When Megan asked what he looked like, Fritzi had responded: "He was tall and thin and spoke with the Viennese intonation, but not in heavy dialect. He dressed normally, but even so he stood out in a crowd. One could tell there was something unusual about him. That fantastic head of hair! Those outspread ears! He really appeared rather spectacular."

All these personal details had been confirmed for Megan by Schiele's sisters Melanie and Gerti who were also still alive when she first began researching the compelling artist.

Another life-size canvas in the exhibition caught Megan's attention. On loan from the Basel art museum, it was the famous double portrait by Oskar Kokoschka, showing himself with a very recognizable Alma Mahler floating in a stormy realm—*Die Windsbraut*—*The Bride of the Wind* or *The Tempest*. Alma was sleeping peacefully alongside Oskar, who was wide awake, steadfastly staring through the storm. And speaking of storms, the rain clouds outside were beginning to gather ominously.

Looking down at her watch Megan realized two hours had elapsed and if she wanted a bite to eat before meeting with Hannes and Inspector Ludwig, she had better get cracking. She walked back to a streetcar stop by way of the Lower Belvedere and its wondrous array of Franz Xaver Messerschmitt's self-portrait busts in alabaster or lead, grimacing in varying throes of emotion. Again she thought to herself what an impact these faces from the eighteenth century must have had on the young Schiele, newly arrived from the provinces in imperial Vienna.

This time upon arrival at the Leopold Museum, Megan went directly to the café for a sandwich and a welcome solo sit-down before joining Hannes in his office.

Inspector Ludwig had not yet arrived.

"Take a seat, please, please! How are you feeling, dear Megan?"

"I am actually much better. Still have some swelling in my wrists and elbows and my face is a fright, as you can see, but otherwise my old energy seems to have returned and I'm not in too much pain, just a little creaky."

"I'm so very glad to hear that," answered Hannes sincerely.

Just then his secretary announced the arrival of Inspector Ludwig and they rose to greet him.

"We have a possible break in the case," said Ludwig, coming to the business at hand immediately. "The London police, with Sotheby's permission, have now released to us the name of the owner of the stolen Schiele. It seems she had asked Sotheby's to restore the canvas before putting it up for auction. Her name is Sonja Oppenheimer and apparently she lives right here in Wien."

That was odd, Megan thought to herself. Yes, she knew about the existence of Sonja Oppenheimer and that the Schiele nude self-portrait standing had been in her possession. But she lived in Königsberg, not Vienna. And she, Alexandra Azarova, and Igor Borodin were about to visit her the very next day *in* Königsburg. What could all this mean?

"We have her address. It's on Herrengasse, number eighty-seven."

"But isn't that where the Hungarian Éva Vidovszky's Antiquariat store is?" asked Hannes, looking bewildered.

"Ah! I think I can explain," Megan announced, suddenly piecing it all together. "I've been in contact both by letter and more recently by telephone with a Sonja Oppenheimer who lives in Königsberg, not Wien. I know, from our lengthy conversation, that it was Éva Vidovszky who visited the lady in her own home and talked her into letting her take the Schiele to Sotheby's for restoration and eventual sale. So Sonja Oppenheimer is the name Vidovszky must have given to the auction house then, and not her own."

"But why would she do that?" Ludwig asked, his forehead lined with inquiring wrinkles. "Perhaps because Vidovszky knew ahead of time that the painting was going to be stolen?" continued Ludwig, answering his own question.

"Are you saying that Vidovszky *arranged* for the Schiele to be stolen?" Hannes asked incredulously.

"No, no, it's just a thought. I'm trying to think of any and all possibilities."

"But Vidovszky would not have wanted the Schiele stolen *before* it was restored. No, it has to be someone else," Megan said.

"I think it must have been stolen for the person who has it now, whoever that might be," Hannes commented.

"Yes, that sounds possible," said Megan. "If we find out who has it now, we will also learn, most probably, who stole it in the first place."

"Or it could be a question of seller and buyer: the person who absconded with it intended to sell it and found a willing private collector who had no scruples about acquiring a stolen artwork," speculated Ludwig.

Hannes turned to him. "I think your best bet is to interrogate Éva Vidovszky. Check out her passport: it should show that she has recently traveled to Russia."

"But what if she declines to show you her passport? Would you have any legal recourse? Are there any charges that could be preferred against her?" asked Megan.

"That is just the problem. We have no cause to interrogate her as things stand now. Merely knowing that hers is the name given to Sotheby's is not enough."

"Still, you could interview her to ask if she has any ideas as to who could have stolen the work and who might have it now."

"Yes, that much we can and will do. You both might like to come along when we visit her in her shop."

"Could we do it right now, today?" asked Megan, turning to the inspector. I have a flight out to Königsberg tomorrow. And actually I'll be visiting Sonja Oppenheimer herself, along with two art experts from Russia. It's all been prearranged and perhaps we can find out more about Vidovszky's role in all this."

"We can go to her Antiquariat right now if you like," answered Ludwig. "All three of us."

No sooner said than done. Megan donned her parka and adjusted her hat for the outdoors, which for a woman from Texas still seemed quite chilly for March. The trio made their way down through the museum exit and toward Ludwig's police van. It had begun to rain again. Well, this should be quite an interview, reflected Megan, warming to the task of quizzing the notorious art dealer who thought nothing of pretending to be from the Austrian tax office and thus intimidating a solitary old woman into entrusting a major Schiele artwork to her.

This could be most interesting. Megan rubbed her hands together and smiled at her two companions as they entered Ludwig's police van.

# 28

What had begun as a March shower had turned into a full-fledged rainstorm. People were huddling in store entrances. After having checked out the Leopold Museum and other nearby museums where the Crespi woman might have gone to, Schnitt was heading back to the Römischer Kaiser Hotel. But now it was starting to hail. He took improvised shelter in the entryway to St. Anna's Church on the Annagasse. The hail was turning vicious, so Schnitt stayed put. But one figure was fighting the storm—a woman in red holding a large shoulder bag over her head. Hurriedly making her way down the narrow Annagasse, she passed within inches of Schnitt before starting to cross over to the Römischer Kaiser on the other side of the street.

By god, that's Megan Crespi, Schnitt suddenly realized. Without another thought he whipped out his Whetstone folding knife and lunged toward her, the blade extended. No one else was on the street and Crespi was still a few feet from the hotel. Schnitt lunged, plunging his knife into the nape of her neck. Without a sound his victim fell to the ground on her stomach, a jumbled red bundle on the hail-pelted street. Schnitt struck again, this time the knife blade entering between two ribs in her back on the left side. He repeated thrusts between the woman's ribs until it was clear that the heart had been thoroughly punctured. He wanted to turn the woman over and smash her face in but the need to leave the scene before other people arrived was growing by the second. With a last plunge of his bloody knife blade into Crespi's neck, Schnitt ran up the length of the Annagasse, turned right on the Kärntner Strasse, and blended in with people taking shelter in the open doorway of the Malteser Church of the Knights Hospitaller. *Megan Crespi was no more.*

Or at least so Schnitt thought.

# 29

"Madam Vidovszky should be back any time now," the alarmed receptionist at Vidovszky Antiquariat, Ildiko Hartleben, assured Inspector Ludwig and the man and woman with him.

"What is her schedule for today?" asked Ludwig.

"She was here late this morning for a business appointment, but then she left again about thirty minutes ago. For where, she did not say."

"What about this afternoon? Any appointments or clients coming here?"

"No appointments as far as I know."

Ludwig's phone rang. His eyes opened wide as he listened to the message. "We'll come immediately," he said as he hung up.

"You'd better come too," Ludwig said to Ildiko Hartleben. "Your employer has been killed. Stabbed to death."

* * *

The hail had stopped when Ludwig's police van came to a halt at the Seilerstätte entrance to the blocked-off Annagasse. Its four passengers hurried past the police ropes to the crumpled body of Éva Vidovszky. She had not been moved, a sheet covered her. The concierge at the Römischer Kaiser had identified the woman from the documents in her shoulder bag, which lay a few feet away.

Inspector Ludwig pulled away the sheet.

Megan was aghast. She had no love for the victim, but to see her murdered and in a pool of her own blood was another thing altogether. And there was something else. Vidovszky was wearing a red raincoat with hood up.

"Why, Megan," Hannes gasped. "*You* could have been mistaken for her, especially in your red parka!"

"I think, Hannes," said Megan in a hushed undertone, "it is the other way around. *She* was mistaken for me. We are the same height and build, and today because of the rainy weather, she wore her raincoat, one which just happened to be red and have a hood like my parka."

"Do you really think..."

"I do," Megan interrupted Hannes. "The coincidence is just too great to overlook. And now I have to wonder if my fall at the Wien Museum was an accident. I don't remember being pushed, but I do remember tripping over something, that I know for sure."

"But why would anyone want to kill you, Megan?" Hannes asked in alarm.

"Well, in the eyes of an organization like the Doppel-O, I could very well be considered a purveyor of pornography because of my books on Schiele and his sexually explicit images."

"Did this Vidovszky woman have any enemies you can think of?" Ludwig was asking Ildiko Hartleben, who hesitated, looking numbly at the group, an answer totally beyond her.

"So many you could fill a book with them, but they could all be classed as 'irritated' rather than hostile," Hannes answered for Ildiko, turning to Megan for corroboration.

"Right," Megan seconded. "Many who did business with her were irked by her methods, but certainly not enough to kill her! The fact that she was found right here in the Annagasse just steps from my hotel must mean she was intending to catch me here and probably quiz me about all the recent Schiele happenings. That's the way she operated. Maybe even try to ascertain if I knew about the existence of Sonja Oppenheimer."

Ludwig looked at Megan and Hannes solemnly. "Of course we must wait for the coroner's report, but it would seem, based on the sadistic slaughter of the Leopold Museum night watchman and now the multiple stabbing of Frau Vidovszky, we have a maniac on our hands."

"The question now is not why, but who," Megan said.

"What do you mean, Frau Professor?" asked Ildiko.

Hannes answered on behalf of Megan and Inspector Ludwig. "The reason why seems to be the charge so often lodged against Schiele when he was alive, pornography.

"As to the 'who,' we have every reason to believe that a cult group, the Doppel-O, self-described on the Internet as being devoted to the cause of obliterating obscenity, is behind the killings. The problem is, we have no proof. And no real suspects."

"Only happenings and related incidents," Megan added. "Such as the desecration of Schiele's grave, the spray-painting of photos of him at the Egon Schiele Museum—although the culprit in that case has been caught—and the spray-painting of Antal Maack's Schiele portrait of his sister."

Ludwig added: "And let's not forget the strange item left behind in three of the incidents. The two metal roses we found in the Leopold, the one we found on Schiele's grave, and the one on the floor of Antal Maack's apartment."

"I am instructing our computer techies down at the department to hack into the website of the Double-O clan and come up with some names for us," Ludwig declared. "We know the identity of the webmaster—Arnold Moll—and we'll find some reason to haul him down to the station, you can bet on that."

"For now, Megan, it is good that this is your last night in Wien," said Hannes concernedly. "It seems that where you are staying is a matter of public knowledge. I think you can't leave Austria soon enough if indeed the murder of Vadovszky is a case of mistaken identity."

"But why would Professor Crespi be in danger?" asked Ildiko Hartleben, incredulously. It seemed she knew enough of her employer's shady dealings not to have been too surprised at the brutal physical attack on Vadovszky which had turned deadly. But this professor from America?

Hannes answered for all of them. "Because Professor Crespi has been for many years a leading scholar on the artist Egon Schiele. And even today she is involved with the artist because she is curating a major exhibition of his portraits for the Art Austria Museum in Montreal.

"*So she could be considered the world's number one promulgator of pornography, by Doppel-O standards.*"

# 30

The moon seemed to have come up early this mild March evening at Villa Solovey by Votkinsk. Closer to the lake, Boris Ussachevsky had laid a straw basket of field flowers at the base of the modern life-size bronze monument raised in front of the lake in honor of Tchaikovsky. Boris did not like the bronze effigy of the great man very much, but he still felt the need to honor it. Pyotr Ilyich was shown seated on a park bench, one limber leg crossed over the other in an attitude Boris found definitely fey. Or was Boris being unnecessarily protective of his idol?

Certainly this evening was one in which he could rejoice as far as his other idol, Egon Schiele, was concerned. During the long weekend Boris had taken off from his gallery affairs, he had been able to right the restoration wrongs he had committed in St. Petersburg. In fact, Boris had actually improved upon the genitals, highlighting the penis so there could be no doubt that it was erect. Schiele would have approved, he was certain. Did he not know Schiele better than anyone?

Now, with the smell of fresh paint in the air, his refurbishment of the Schiele painting was drying nicely. The original amber tone of the skin had been perfectly matched with Sotheby's original restoration and the enhanced black contour lines practically glistened. And the once-blemished spatial void was again just that—a void, unsullied by any trace of paint grains.

Boris was in such a good mood that he decided to do something he had never done before: climb up the pedestal of Tchaikovsky's monument and sit on the bench with the composer. No one was around, why not do it and take a selfie while he was at it? In two boyish leaps he was astride the statue's legs, facing his idol. Giving him a quick kiss on the mouth, he turned and slid onto the bench to the right of the statue where there was just enough room for him to be wedged in the embrace of the composer's left arm. In another second the photograph had been taken—a perfect double portrait with grey Swan Lake behind.

Yes. He had rectified the wrong he had done Egon, and as a reward here he was communing with Pyotr Ilyich and nature. Life could not be better.

Or could it? The conversation Boris had with Peschka-Schiele recently had whetted his acquisitional appetite. *Was* there yet another Schiele 1910 nude self-portrait to be had? If so, where could it be? In Austria, somewhere in Europe, the United States, Japan?

These questions continued to race through Boris' mind after he walked back to Villa Solovey. The idea of owning the other 1910 Schiele nude self-portrait—outstripping even the Leopold Museum—began to obsess him. Perhaps he might even be able to acquire it by legal means so that the world could know of his acquisition. All things were possible in the Schiele world.

* * *

At Vienna's Schwechat airport early the next morning Megan boarded a Finnair flight for Kaliningrad, which she stubbornly insisted on calling by its previous German name, Königsberg. There would be a brief stop in Warsaw. Only reluctantly had she revealed her latest peregrination plan to Claire and her sister. She thought she had them pretty much calmed down by the end of their conversations. It had been a bit of a fight, however, and she had a lot of future explaining to do. Wisely, she did not mention yesterday's mayhem that took place practically on the doorstep of her hotel. Or that the murder could have been intended for her. No, that would keep, and she too must stop thinking about it herself.

She was looking forward to meeting up with Alexandra Azarova and Igor Borodin at Kaliningrad's small Devau Airport, about five miles from the city. She knew that it had been enlarged since she was there in 2004, but she was sure that the dismal contemporary city that had become Kaliningrad in modern-day Russia would be just as thin-skinned as it had been back then. Rumor was that because Vladimir Putin's former wife Lyudmila was from Königsberg, he had force-financed a Potemkinesque transformation of the buildings lining the route into town from Devau Airport to give the impression of a grand boulevard. She would try to take her two friends to the old districts of Maraunenhof and Amalienau where some of the old buildings from Kollwitz's time had escaped British bombing.

The brief stopover at Warsaw provided Megan with Internet access and she soon made contact with Alexandra and Igor. They had just landed at Devau and would be waiting for her there. Megan was almost the last to reboard her plane, so taken was she by some very small Bose earphones on sale in the airport shop. Back in her seat she readjusted her Google Glass. So far there had been no need to use the spectacles, but considering that she and her Russian team would be looking at Sonja Oppenheimer's Schiele today and that the lady might be skittish about Megan's photographing her holdings, she had decided to wear the wonderful, if expensive, contraption.

A somewhat refurbished Devau Airport greeted Megan's eyes when her Finnair flight pulled up bumpily on the short runway at noon. Alexandra and Igor were standing outdoors by the customs area and waved vigorously when they spotted Megan carefully climbing down the passenger stairs from the plane. A few minutes later, after hugs had been exchanged and clearing a very perfunctory customs achieved, the three friends were in a taxi heading for the Radisson Hotel where Megan had stayed before and enjoyed. At the front desk she asked that they be assigned rooms on the sixth floor, where a fine view of the city's partially restored old cathedral could be had. It had been left a pathetic husk in World War II. This request was accommodated and twenty minutes later they reassembled in the hotel lobby.

Megan had telephoned Sonja Oppenheimer from her hotel room and was joyously received. Sonja asked if they could come over that very afternoon.

"That's why we are here," Megan assured her.

They had fixed the hour for two o'clock, she told Alexandra and Igor, adding "So that gives us just time for a leisurely walk around the old cathedral. It's only a long block away on the Kneiphof island and there's something I want to show you." Her friends were intrigued.

Megan led them past the front of the gothic cathedral to the northeast corner and stopped before a simple, tall attached mausoleum with free-standing pilasters. "Have a look at who's buried here," she said eagerly. "It is with a categorical imperative that I command you to find out." Her friends were mystified.

"Immanuel Kant!" suddenly exclaimed Igor, reading the simple identifying legend in Cyrillic on the interior wall. On another wall only Kant's name was given, and that in Roman lettering. "I knew Kant was from Königsberg, so I should have guessed whose mausoleum this was before you went on expostulating about categorical imperatives."

"How appropriate that he would be so honored," murmured Alexandra, "since he spent his whole career at Königsberg University. So that is what you so wanted us to see, Megan?"

"Nope," replied Megan mischievously. "This is just a bonus. Keep following me." She led them behind the cathedral to the southeast corner.

"Here! See?" Megan pointed to a tall tombstone. The bas-relief bronze face of a man was affixed to it and below the image was the name Julius Rupp and the dates 1809-1884.

"Do you know who this is?" Megan asked excitedly. Blank faces gazed at her. "It's Käthe Kollwitz's *grandfather*! The pastor! And the portrait head is by the sculptor herself." Megan could hardly contain her pleasure at knowing about this grave and its meaning. She had taken a number of photographs of it on her previous trip to Königsberg. And in particular she had photographed the barely readable grim injunction on the tombstone: "*Wer nach der Wahrheit, die er bekennt, nicht lebt, ist der gefährlichste Feind der Wahrheit selbst.*" "He who does not live according to the truth he confesses is the greatest enemy of truth itself."

Megan was a fervent admirer of the great pacifist Kollwitz and her powerful work, both graphic and sculptural. And she had made it a point when teaching about World War II always to include Kollwitz's passionate admonition: "*Nie wieder Krieg!*" "*Never again war!*" Once a former student had e-mailed her: "I know what your lecture was on today. Saw your students coming out of the auditorium and some were crying, so it had to be the Kollwitz lecture." He was right. It had been. Now she beamed at her colleagues as they walked up close to the effigy and read the inscription.

"But now we have to hurry if we are going to get to Frau Oppenheimer's in time," Alexandra said, glancing at her watch. They walked back across the square to their hotel and hailed a taxi. Some ten minutes later they had located 33 Pervomaiskaya in one of the old neighborhoods that had mostly survived British bombing and Russian invasion.

Sonja Oppenheimer had been watching out a front window of the small, wooden, three-story house and came out on the front porch to greet them. She led them to the sparse parlor and offered them tea. Politely they accepted, wondering how soon they might reasonably bring up the reason for their visit.

They did not have to wonder. Right after tea was served, Sonja burst out: "As soon as you your tea have drunk we together will go to the attic and down bring the Schiele roll." Rarely had Megan sipped hot tea so quickly or refused biscuits that were offered.

A polite five minutes later the trio followed Sonja slowly up the stairs to the attic floor. Its single dark room ran the length of the house. Canvases, both rolled and a few on stretchers, were everywhere. It was obvious that many of Max Oppenheimer's works had been stored there for decades. Two of the artworks were on easels—one a portrait of a gesticulating man, and the other of a women. He was, unfortunately, always and only a secondary Schiele, Megan thought to herself.

"I brought down only one of the two Schieles for that dreadful woman, Vidovszky," said Sonja quietly. There was a brief silence. The trio had unanimously decided not to tell her what had happened to Éva Vidovszky. Sonja spoke up: "Let's take the other one downstairs and look at it in the good light there is over my dining room table."

Exerting extreme care, Igor picked up the heavy canvas roll marked "E S AUCH" and led the way down the stairs to the dining room. Noting Sonja's fragility as she descended the stairs, Megan wondered how she had ever managed to carry such a heavy canvas roll down two flights of stairs for Vidovszky.

Although Igor was unhappy about unrolling the old canvas, he knew it would be necessary to open it partially at least just to be sure it was the one by Schiele and not one of Oppenheimer's many stored artworks.

From his bulging briefcase Igor pulled out a sizeable white linen cloth and placed it on the dining room table. He put the large roll on top of it. The overhead lamp provided good light and the group stood at the far ends of the table to give Igor room to work. At his very first cautious movement a minuscule pigment of yellow paint fell out on the linen cloth.

This is the other lost 1910 nude self-portrait, Megan thought reverently, eager to see the life-size figure that she knew would be kneeling with elbows and hands up.

Slowly Igor extended the roll a bit more. Yellow ochre brush strokes filled the canvas edge. That was odd, thought Megan. The background should be a creamy white, only his nude body should be yellow, and Schiele's brushwork in 1910 was not so clipped. The brushwork she was now looking at had been pulled away, not laid down.

No more pigment fell to the table so Igor unrolled the canvas some twelve inches more. The left edge of a male body was revealed, but it was dressed, not nude. Igor pulled another twelve inches, exposing the full figure. Megan gasped. The figure was not Schiele!

"See if you can unroll the whole length of the canvas without damaging it," she commanded tersely, now intent upon seeing the complete painting. She realized that this canvas was much broader than would be necessary for a single self-portrait or portrait. There was no doubt that the work was by Schiele: the abrupt application of paint matched his style of 1913 and the thin angular contour lines were characteristic of that year as well. As the full canvas came to view the people around the table gasped as one.

*It was the lost double portrait of Dr. Peter Schwartz and his son Paul.*
\* \* \*

Even if short, it was a most interesting phone conversation Arnold Moll had with the desk clerk of the Römischer Kaiser Hotel the morning after the Vidovszky murder. He had pretended to be Megan Crespi's nephew in an effort to ascertain whether or not she was still in Wien. The Grand Master wanted to know, *urgently* wanted to know where she was. Wolf Schnitt had failed again. Just as with the previous attempt to do away with Crespi, Schnitt had reported success to the Grand Master only to be proved categorically wrong by that evening's stunning television news. The noted antiquariat dealer Éva Vidovszky, who had sold the Leopold Museum its prize Schiele painting, had been stabbed to death in the center of Wien on the Annagasse. There was no known motive and clues as to the identity of the murderer were at present not forthcoming. A leak to the press also indicated that a certain Sonja Oppenheimer of Kaliningrad might have some connection to the case.

Arnold Moll had been informed by the helpful desk clerk that Frau Professor Crespi had checked out of the hotel early that morning and had taken a taxi to Schwechat for her flight to Kaliningrad. Moll immediately Googled the name Sonja Oppenheimer and learned that she was the daughter of the Expressionist painter Max Oppenheimer who had died in New York in 1954. Her present whereabouts were unknown.

Moll did not need Internet affirmation to conclude that this must be one and the same Sonja Oppenheimer connected somehow with Vidovszky's antiquariat. If Vidovszky had contacted her, that could mean only one thing: Oppenheimer had a Schiele artwork. He could be in Kaliningrad by late this evening. Perhaps he could intercept or obstruct whatever Crespi was up to.

All this he told the Grand Master who alternated between fulmination over Schnitt's second failure to eliminate Crespi and an almost desperate receptivity to Moll's plan. It was a plan that could result in the taking out of yet one more obscene Schiele. Yes, Arnold Moll had his blessing. By all means go to Kaliningrad. Immediately.

\* \* \*

The four people standing around Schiele's *Double Portrait of Peter and Paul Schwartz* in Sonja's Königsberg house were still in a state of shock.

"But this portrait has been lost ever since the Anschluss," remonstrated Alexandra, almost whining. "How could it have ended up in Max Oppenheimer's collection? It was owned by Schiele's dentist, after all. Why would he have given it to another painter? And one who was a fellow Jew just as the Anschluss was about to take place?"

Megan answered for all of them. "Perhaps just because the Anschluss was imminent. Perhaps Dr. Schwartz had no place to store it before leaving

Austria in such a hurry and so he left it with Oppenheimer, who must have been making preparations to ship his own collected oeuvre out of the country. At least Max had a remote destination away from Austria and Vienna to send the artworks to, up in northeastern Prussia."

"Yes, yes, that must be exactly what happened," breathed Sonja, grasping the table edge with both hands. "This is too much excitement for me. I must sit down."

Megan helped her to an easy chair and brought her a welcome glass of water from the kitchen while Igor and Alexandra continued to admire the surprise Schiele. The life-size work was extraordinary in its tightly knit sense of presence despite its faded condition. Schiele had contrasted the standing figures of father and son not only in terms of size, age, and physiognomy, but also in terms of personality. Peter appeared as an active, self-confident man who responded readily to the world about him. But his son Paul was shown as a young man absorbed in his own thoughts, deferential to the authority of his father and passive in response, but alert to his own world—an intense dreamer very much in tune with Schiele's own nature.

The left arm of the older Schwartz, who was on the left, was raised to shoulder height and extended toward Paul on the right, thus bridging the canvas and the gap, both spatial and emotional, between the two standing figures—the father pointing, the son clasping his fingers tightly together. Schiele's geometric brushwork fracturing of the background into kinetic emblems denoting directions, energies, and intensities, strengthened the painting's central statement about the inbuilt tensions and ties of a father-son relationship. It was indeed one of Schiele's major works.

Turning from Sonja to gaze at the double portrait once more, Megan noticed the strong resemblance between the son Paul and his own son Jerome, whom she had met recently in Dallas when he was on his way back to Brazil from a business trip to New York. She had remarked on the uncanny likeness of the painted Paul in Killar's catalogue to him and he had sighed, wondering if that double portrait of his father and grandfather would ever be unearthed?

Now they could give him a phone call and let him know that the lost work had indeed come to light. Remembering that she had her Google Glass on, Megan maneuvered around the table and with the controlled blinking of her eyelids took several shots. Alexandra and Igor, although close by, were unaware of what she was doing. Just as well, Megan thought. These photos are merely to send on to Jerome, not for any real documentation.

Igor now turned to Sonja, who was still recuperating in her chair, and assured her that restoration of the painting was indeed possible. The flaking had been minimal, the condition of the whole only faded, not damaged.

Somewhat abruptly, Alexandra asked Frau Oppenheimer what she would like to do with the painting now that it had been found.

"Oh, please! Please! One thing at a time!" Sonja said, fanning herself with one hand and leaning back fatigued in her chair.

"Things are going too fast for her, and I don't blame her," Megan whispered to Alexandra, ever the art dealer, and Igor, ever the art restorer. She spotted the upright piano in Sonja's living room and asked Sonja if she would like to hear a few old-time songs.

"Ah, yes, that would be most lovely," Sonja replied immediately, smiling gratefully to her would-be benefactor. Even though Megan only played the piano by ear, she had a repertoire of songs ranging from the nineteen-tens through the nineteen-fifties that she used to perform with her father, who played the violin and mandolin.

Although the piano was badly in need of tuning, it was passable and soon Megan was softly playing songs that ranged from *La Vie En Rose* and *Perfidia* to *Arriverderci Roma* and *Muss I* Denn. Soon everyone was more relaxed and smiling and the Schiele stress was temporarily alleviated. For her two Russian friends Megan played *Katinka*, embellishing it with octave runs. They even joined in the chorus. The magic of music, Megan thought to herself.

"You know what I should love to hear now, dear Frau Professor?" asked Sonja, feeling less overwhelmed.

"Anything, as long as it is in the key of C or C minor," Megan answered happily.

"I should love to hear something from *Show Boat*."

Vastly surprised, Megan obliged with *Can't Help Lovin' Dat Man* and

*Ol' Man River*—both songs she had carefully worked out over the years.

As the last chord died away Sonja spoke up, her voice firm and controlled. "Thank you. And I know now what I should like to do with this Schiele of which I have been the unknowing caretaker all these decades. I should like to give it to its rightful owners, the heirs of Peter and Paul Schwartz, if there are indeed any heirs."

"Indeed the grandson of Dr. Peter Schwartz—Jerome Schwartz—is alive and has been looking for the double portrait all his life," Megan was quick to assure her. "He lives in Brazil where his family fled after the Anschluss. And he is in fact the director of a highly regarded museum there."

"Could we contact him immediately?" Sonja asked.

"Yes, yes, such a wonderful restitution can definitely be arranged, Frau Oppenheimer," Alexandra said, interrupting what was going to be Megan's enthusiastic answer. "But you should receive some financial remuneration—let us call it 'rent'—for having safely stored the artwork for so long. After all, you are in possession of a master..."

"No, I am not interested in that. I have my pension and that is quite sufficient for me," Sonja forcefully interrupted Alexandra. "I want that my life is *simplified* not complicated."

"Frau Oppenheimer," said Megan, "I have Jerome Schwartz's telephone number right here in my phone. Would you like me to call him? It's about nine o'clock at night there in São Paulo right now."

Sonja Oppenheimer clapped her hands together with delight. "Let us do it, let us do it immediately!"

Igor and Alexandra exchanged silent glances. There was too much at stake here, things were going too quickly. Crespi was too impetuous. Still they held back. Certainly they would not want to go against Frau Oppenheimer's wishes.

Megan dialed Jerome Schwartz's number and handed the phone to Sonja when she heard his voice answer. "Speak to him in English," she prompted Sonja.

"Olá?" Jerome repeated.

"Mr. Schwartz, here is speaking Sonja Oppenheimer, the daughter of Egon Schiele's good friend and fellow painter Max Oppenheimer."

"How grand! Yes, I know Schiele was very good friends with your father."

"I am calling you to tell momentous news that the double portrait of your father and grandfather is found in my attic!"

"Can this be? Is this a joke?"

"No, is true. Here I hand you over to a friend you know." Sonja passed the phone back to Megan.

"Jerome, hello, it's me, Megan Crespi, and every word you just heard is true. Schiele's double portrait has been quietly sitting in Frau Oppenheimer's attic ever since the Anschluss. Her father sent it up, along with his own canvases, from Vienna, out of Hitler's way. It is slightly faded, but safe."

All four persons in the room could hear Jerome's excited response: "*Fabulous*! This is absolutely *fabulous*!"

"Here is Frau Oppenheimer again for you," said Megan, passing the phone back to Sonja, who was frantically gesticulating to her.

"Here is what I shall like to do, Mr. Schwartz. Next to me is excellent restorer from the Hermitage, Gaspadin Igor Borodin, and also worthy Moscow gallery owner, Gaspazha Alexandra Azarova, both friends of Doctor Professor Megan Crespi. I propose we trust the Schiele to them for taking to Moscow and restoration if you are agreeable to expenses."

"Oh, both names are *famous* here in Brazil and I should like nothing better than to place the Schiele in their hands temporarily for restoration and afterwards perhaps victorious exhibition in Azarova's Gallery Rasputin. Perhaps we could all meet there at the opening?" Sonja conveyed what Schwartz had said, then handed the phone back to Megan.

Megan looked around the room. Everyone was smiling openly. "We all love your idea, Jerome, and we shall do just as you suggest. But to be on the safe side," she said, looking at her companions meaningfully, "would you kindly fax us permission to do so. Here, I'll hand you over to Alexandra and she can give you her office fax number."

"Fabulous!" repeated an overjoyed Jerome.

Igor was the next person to talk directly to the proud new owner and he gave Jerome an estimate of what the restoration costs would be.

The delighted Brazilian responded in a more businesslike mode: "I know of your high reputation and I authorize you to begin restoration at once under the financial terms you have just outlined."

Megan could see that Sonja's strength was beginning to wane. She suggested they put off till tomorrow returning to the attic to find the second Schiele 1910 self-portrait. Since the wrapper on the double portrait had said "E S AUCH,"—"E S ALSO"—that must mean the second original roll labeled merely "E S" was still upstairs.

"But take the double portrait with you *now*," urged Sonja Oppenheimer. "It will be safer with you, even in a hotel now." She would not take no for an answer. "I need time to recover," she said as the taxi they had called pulled up. "Let us meet tomorrow again at two o'clock. You have brought me and Mr. Schwartz and Schiele great joy."

# 31

Behind Schloss Gemmingen-Eggaberg at Gmunden, the Grand Master of the Doppel-O, stood studying the progress of the day's construction on the first building to be raised in the clear-cut forested acreage that now belonged to him and his clan. Clad in a long, loosely belted, fur-trimmed black robe, he scanned the cedar-lined interior with its six mighty wooden piers. They spelled out the dimensions of the rectangular meeting house he had dreamed about building ever since his introduction to the long houses of the Haida Gwaii. In another two days the simple wooden edifice, with its secret cellar for himself only, would be completed. Impatient to have the long house finished quickly, he had doubled up on work crews. It had been well worth the extra expense.

At last he could convene his members in a safe house where no cyber eyes or ears from the outside world could monitor events.

Then shall I, the Albrecht Dürer of the new millennium, lead the pure of heart to their rightful dominion. There shall I declare our war on obscenity to have begun. The first of the pornographers to fall shall be Austria's own Egon Schiele—that serpent in our own mother nest.

Kurt Wagner, alias Max Valentin, alias the Grand Master, walked to the center of the flooring and ceremoniously laid down an object. It was a black metal rose with silver tips.

\* \* \*

Arnold Moll's Finnair flight set down at Kaliningrad's bustling Khrabrovo Airport a few minutes before eleven o'clock that evening. He rented a Volvo station wagon and drove straight to the Skipper Hotel overlooking the Pregel River. Thanks to the Internet, he had already located the address of the city's only resident by the surname of Oppenheimer. He would be paying that citizen of modern Russia a call early the next morning.

\* \* \*

Megan was already downstairs having breakfast at seven in the morning when Alexandra and Igor appeared. She was in a jolly mood she told them because she had just realized that, with their whole morning and early afternoon free, they could hire a chauffeur and be driven in style out to see the town of Tilset where Napoleon signed the peace treaty with Alexander I of Russia on a raft moored in the Neman River—a treaty which deprived the defeated Kingdom of Prussia of almost half of its territory. The two Russians looked unconvinced.

"But this was the time and place when Prussia's beautiful Queen Louisa threw herself on the ground in front of Napoleon and begged his mercy for her country, don't you remember? There is a wonderful painting showing them—after she stood up again—before Tilsit Cathedral. Do you know it?"

"Yes, but that is a myth about her kneeling on the ground," laughed Igor affectionately, amused by the American's passion for history, especially when women were involved. "We were taken there as schoolboys to see this great event in Russian history."

"Well, *I* was never taken there as a *schoolgirl*," Alexandra said, "and it sounds like a very good idea. A morning outing in nature would be lovely."

"There is a famous racehorse breeding stable near Tilsit that I wouldn't mind seeing," allowed Igor.

"And we could pick up some good Tilsit cheese," added Alexandra, imagining some appetizing slices on thin crackers.

That was enough for Megan. While the Russians ate breakfast she conferred at the front desk and arranged for a chauffeured car to pick them up promptly at nine o'clock for the hour-and-a-half trip.

* * *

Sonja Oppenheimer could hardly fall asleep. She was filled with joy. Good had come of bad. What the Vidovszky woman had begun in deceit, Megan Crespi had righted with sincerity, integrity, and helpfulness. How generous it was of her and the two Russians to travel to Königsberg. And how gratifying it had been to notify Jerome Schwartz that the missing Schiele had been found! Yes, it had been a wonderful day in her otherwise humdrum life.

Early the next morning Sonja woke up in the same joyous mood as the night before. After breakfast she decided to play her piano, something she had not done for years. It would help pass the time until two o'clock, when her new friends would return. Oh, why did I put them off until then, she thought. I had imagined I'd be far too tired to deal with another day of Schiele discoveries, but I'm not at all tired now.

The brash ring of the front doorbell resounded over the sounds of Sonja's piano playing. Ah! Perhaps Professor Crespi and her friends have decided to come early. That would be wonderful. Sonja went to the door and opened it. Facing her with an ingratiating smile on his face was a short, plump, mousey little man who addressed her in German. Was she Frau Sonja Oppenheimer, formerly of New York? When Sonja answered yes, the man immediately gripped her by the shoulders and pushed her inside, kicking the door closed behind him with his foot.

"*Where is your Schiele painting?*" Arnold Moll hissed into Sonja's ear.

"Who are you? What do you want?"

"I want your obscene Schiele painting. Where do you keep it?" Moll said, looking around at the sparsely furnished interior. He put his thumbs to Sonja's throat and pushed hard. She gagged and tried in vain to pull away.

"Tell me. Now!"

He released the pressure momentarily.

"It's, it's in the attic," Sonja gasped.

Moll took a choke hold on the trembling woman and held it until she passed out. He continued to exert maximum pressure until breathing stopped. Then, checking to see no one else was in the house on the first or second floors, he bolted up the attic stairs. Opening the door, he was greeted by a hoard of rolled and unrolled canvases, a couple of them displayed on easels. No Schiele was in sight. He began examining the rolls, the ones closest to the door first, and within seconds he found a roll marked "E S." Not waiting to check any further, he descended the stairs with the roll tucked under his left arm. Stepping over the prone body of Sonja Oppenheimer he opened the front door and looked around to see if there were any pedestrians on the street. No one was in sight and the street was empty of passing cars.

Closing the door behind him, Moll walked calmly to the Volvo station wagon parked in front of the house, loaded the canvas roll in the back, and headed for the Russian border. He had determined to drive back to Austria with his precious cargo rather than risk taking a plane flight with possible baggage examinations. And he would wait to contact the Grand Master until he arrived in Gmunden. He had something colossal to show him. Wolf Schnitt was out; he, Arnold Moll was in. From now on he would be, exclusively, the Grand Master's right-hand man in their holy war against obscenity and all those sheltering it.

\* \* \*

The racehorse-breeding farm on the way back from historical Tilsit had multiple equestrian stables and a ring where the handlers exercised the horses. Megan and her friends had arrived at a fortuitous moment when the horses were being fed. They were allowed inside the stables to watch and were able to get very close to the horses, who were extremely curious and friendly. The time passed swiftly and when Igor looked at his watch it was already noon. They had better get going if they wanted to be at Sonja

Oppenheimer's on time. Knowing that in all likelihood they would be transporting another canvas roll to their hotel, they asked the chauffeur to wait as they pulled up to Sonja's house at five minutes past two o'clock.

Megan led the way up the front walk and rang the doorbell. There was no answer. She rang it again. Still no answer and there was no sound of anyone bustling in the house. They waited a few seconds, then Megan rang again.

"Try the door," Alexandra suggested.

Igor pushed the door gently and it swung wide open. A terrible sight greeted their eyes. Sonja Oppenheimer, her skin still a bluish color, lay crumpled on the threshold, her wide brown eyes staring blankly. She was quite dead.

"Oh my god! How can this have happened?" Alexandra screamed.

Igor knelt down beside the woman, automatically feeling for a pulse. It was in vain. "What's that?" he asked, pointing to a small object next to Sonja on the floor. Megan looked where he was pointing and knew instantly what it was: a black metal rose tipped in silver. She began to tear up. "It's *my* fault," she cried, "we should have warned her to be on her guard. We shouldn't have left her alone. We should have realized she could be in danger!"

"Of course it's not your fault, Megan," Alexandra said reassuringly. "It's not our fault. Someone obviously found out she has Schiele artworks. Or it's possible they followed us knowing that we were in search of Schiele. But to *murder* the dear lady because of that?"

"Perhaps she tried to resist him, keep him from coming inside," Igor said.

Suddenly it dawned on all of them that Sonja might have been robbed. Robbed for the Schiele canvas. Igor led the race up to the attic. Ominously the door was wide open. Megan and Igor began checking the identification on the canvas rolls in the front of the room. All of them were labeled "Mopp."

"Keep looking," instructed Alexandra, "while I go down and call the police. We can't wait any longer to report this."

It took some time to convince the Russian desk sergeant at the police station that a murder had been committed. Finally she agreed to dispatch a squad car to the house at 33 Pervomaiskaya. Another ten minutes passed. Igor and Megan came down the stairs empty-handed. All the rolls and stretched canvases were labeled or signed "Mopp."

"The Schiele has been taken and apparently nothing else," Igor said gloomily.

"I suppose the only positive thing about this is that we have confirmation now that Sonja did indeed have the other Schiele self-portrait still in her attic," Alexandra said slowly.

Megan made no comment. She was still horrified at the spectacle of death by the front door. And she was trying to come to terms with the possibility that because *her* life was in danger, visiting Sonja had imperiled her as well. The presence of a black rose was more than a signature of death. It was an irrefutable connection to the recent Schiele events in Vienna.

Just then an approaching siren was heard and the worried trio hurried to the doorstep to meet the police.

An efficient official took down their statements, checked their passports, taking smart phone shots of the identifying photographs inside, and, after a lot of questioning, finally cleared them to return to their hotel.

It was a very gloomy trio that reunited in the lobby of Kaliningrad's Radisson Hotel that evening. All their flights left shortly after eight o'clock and their taxi was already waiting outside to take them to the Devau Airport. Igor and Alexandra would be flying directly back to Moscow with the precious Schiele double portrait roll as carryon luggage. Megan was due to repeat the Warsaw-Vienna trek, an itinerary that would get her back around two in the morning. But it was worth it. She wanted to get out of what had been a murderous Kaliningrad. Was her own life in danger in this Russian city as well? The spectacle of poor Sonja Oppenheimer was not to fade anytime soon.

And what did returning to Vienna have in store for her? She had accepted thoughtful Antal Maack's offer to put her up in the guest room of his own flat. She had confided her horror to him at the thought of returning to the, in her eyes, blood-spattered Römischer Kaiser Hotel. Despite the very late hour, she knew Antal would be up and awaiting her with words of comfort. He would understand when she told him she wanted to go back to America as soon as possible. But within hours she would receive terrible news from Dallas.

# 32

Peschka-Schiele was not sure what the unusual Schiele drawing he had found at the Antiquariat Vidovszky meant.

When he heard of the rebarbative owner's death his first reaction was *good riddance!* His second reaction was to get himself over to her Antiquariat and offer his aid to what he knew would be an overwhelmed receptionist, as Vidovszky had no immediate family. Ildiko Hartleben had accepted his offer to help with gratitude. Naively, she opened up Vidovszky's file cabinet in the inner office and asked him to begin checking through the files for any works out on loan for approval while she began taking down the artworks hanging in the front room.

Having access to his dead rival's files was more delicious luck than Adolf could ever have imagined. Eagerly he drew out the files on Klimt and Schiele. The Klimt file was thin but it contained a very interesting color photograph. It showed a ragged-edged image of two naked women kissing. Ah ha! This is the Klimt *Kissing Couple* that was sliced out of its frame at the Leopold Museum the night someone killed the night watchman there and vandalized the Schiele *Self-Portrait Nude Sitting*. On it was marked "offer rejected."

How was it that Vidovszky had access to this photograph? Did that mean she also had had access to the painting remnant? Had she sold it to someone? Had someone come to her with it? Well, he would check that out later. The main thing was to examine the thick file pertaining to Schiele he had placed upon Vidovszky's desk.

Eagerly, he opened it. Enlarged black-and-white photographs of every lost Schiele reproduced in Killar greeted his eyes. All of them were heavily annotated with suggestions of provenance as well as notations concerning dead-end leads as to possible present-day owners.

And then, in a folder all its own, he came upon a peculiar original drawing by Schiele. Peculiar because it was neither a portrait nor a townscape nor landscape. It was a black crayon drawing on graph-ruled paper of a large octagonal building seen from above. On top was written, in Schiele's distinctive script, the word "Pantheon." Then above seven sides of the octagon were the words "Art," "Music," "Literature," "Science," "Medicine," "Philosophy," and "Love." Nothing more. What could this mean? And was the drawing referring to an actual building or the plan of an imagined building?

Schiele had written one additional word on the bottom of the sheet of paper: "Krumau." Ah! Not so enigmatic, thought Adolf to himself. The old castle town of Krumau, in present-day Czechoslovakia, was the birthplace of Schiele's mother and a place much loved by the artist. He made several visits to the Bohemian town and in 1911 moved there with his seventeen-year-old lover and model Wally Neuzil, seeking solitude for his work, away from the "gossip, intrigue, and jealousy of Vienna," as he put it.

During the Great War, in 1917, Schiele had been assigned to guard duty at Krumau and in the evenings he was able to work on his paintings. He had written to a patron that he was working on an extraordinary series and that it would benefit all of Wien. What the series might have been about had remained a mystery. Now Adolf wondered, could the series have been completed and if so, could it have been stored in Krumau when the artist was suddenly transferred back to Vienna in 1918?

The appellations referring to art, music, literature, science, medicine, philosophy, and love might mean that, like his older colleague Klimt, Schiele was engaging in allegory. All during his painting career Schiele had painted obscure allegories, some featuring himself, sometimes even the self doubled. Other allegories depicted dead or melancholy mothers holding small babies. Peschka-Schiele sat bolt upright in Vidovszky's chair.

Yes! That was it! It was entirely possible that Schiele had *completed* the images intended for this pantheon and, because of the war, had left them in storage somewhere in Krumau. Why had no one thought of this before? Oh, but I am a clever man, Adolf congratulated himself. Somewhere in old Krumau, with its narrow cobbled streets and great river bend, there must be an octagonal building, probably small, perhaps built over another building in this town of gothic, renaissance, and baroque overlappings. All he needed was to go to Krumau—Český Krumlov, as it was called nowadays—and begin looking.

With his smart phone Adolf carefully photographed the precious Schiele drawing before transferring it to his briefcase. He then commenced the tedious work he had volunteered to do. Well worth the tedium, he smiled to himself.

*Tomorrow I leave for Krumau!*

\* \* \*

Although it was after two in the morning, Antal Maack was waiting for Megan at the terminal in Vienna. "Oh, how wonderfully *dear* of you," Megan cried joyfully. Minutes later they were in his car heading for Antal's apartment on the Herrengasse. Megan filled him in on the happenings at Königsberg. One joyful, the discovery of the Schwartz double portrait, and the other tragic, the murder of Sonja Oppenheimer and theft of the other Schiele in her attic.

"But how is *your* Schiele?" she asked, pulling herself away from the jumbled narrative that she realized was pouring forth nonstop from her.

"Ah, Gerti has already been restored to her former self. The spray paint was easy to remove, so the restorer told me, and the damage to the surface was negligible. So she will greet you when we get home. Your bed is all made up and you can go straight to bed, as will I."

Megan did pause at Antal's den to say hello to the restored Gerti, then gratefully went off to the guest room for a much-needed sleep. They would meet up in the morning, but she was to sleep as long as she wanted, Antal had instructed her.

Surprisingly, Megan was wide awake at the break of dawn the next morning and she felt rested and restored. Antal heard her moving around and went to the kitchen to fix one of his guest's favorite Austrian breakfasts:

*Palatschinken*—thin crêpes, seasoned by Antal with a lemon flavor. Megan could hardly believe her nose as she became aware of their heavenly scent. They sat down, ate, talked, drank coffee, and laughed. Soon Königsberg seemed far away.

When Megan's phone rang she was tempted not to answer, but seeing her sister's photo on the caller ID, she changed her mind. Tina's voice sounded strained and serious.

"Megan, the police just called me. Last night there was a break-in at your house!"

# 33

It had been a long and arduous trip for Wolf Schnitt, beginning at seven-forty-five in the morning out of Vienna, then switching flights at London's Heathrow airport, and finally arriving at the Dallas/Ft. Worth Airport a little after seven that evening. Having nothing to declare, he passed through customs without a hitch. The glass cutter and suction cups in his checked bag had not been detected.

Schnitt had done his Internet research well. The Hotel Lumen to which he directed his taxi driver was just across the street from Southern Methodist University and its Meadows School of the Arts. Megan Crespi's home was on the other side, only two blocks east of the campus. He had memorized her address: 4222 Willow Way. He merely needed to walk across the school's campus and east to Willow Way. This he would do in the wee hours of the morning when the neighborhood was asleep. Right now he would fit in some sleep of his own.

Six hours later Schnitt's alarm sounded and he woke, still feeling tired but up to performing his self-assigned task. Dressed in black shirt and pants, he walked quickly through the SMU campus and exited on Willow

Way. The Crespi home was a two-story corner house surrounded by a low, red brick wall. From across the street Schnitt surveyed the house. A light was on in the middle room of the second floor. Looks like your traditional burglar light, Schnitt concluded. He knew the house was empty because Crespi, who lived alone, was still in Europe.

Schnitt decided to avoid the front door, which was brightly lit by two floods, and walked around to the back. The iron gate in the wall opened inwards onto a narrow cement walk that led up to the rear entrance of the house. Getting close to the house he looked into the kitchen box window that was filled with a collection of various objects in blue glass. He could clearly see beyond them to a light bulb hanging from the oven vent. It was attached to a timer. Another burglar light. The back door was a metal-framed, full-length glass panel. The inside privacy blind was closed.

Schnitt tried to pick the two locks. The lower one gave almost immediately, but the upper one was obviously a bolt, he realized after numerous attempts with different keys failed. The alternative was to cut out the glass panel. Taking his glass slicer out of his pocket he deftly began working, starting at the upper right corner of the door. Then he noticed a sign by the doorbell to his right. "This property protected by the University Park Police." Schnitt stopped. The sign looked old and weather beaten. It was probably out of date he told himself. Why should the Crespi house be protected by the police rather than by a standard burglar system? He noticed another sign by the doorbell. It read "ADT security." Uh huh, Schnitt thought. A little too much signage. I bet she doesn't have a burglar system at all. Just signs. And lights on timers.

He continued his work and while he was cutting the glass he rehearsed what he would do once he entered the house. What he was after was Crespi's Schiele. Well known in Schiele circles, and once thought lost, it was a vile little self-portrait, no larger than twelve-by-twelve inches, showing the artist naked and standing over a mirror looking down at his dangling private parts. Disgusting! He would take the painting and bring it to Vienna unharmed. The Grand Master could destroy it himself and he would be redeemed in his eyes. If he hadn't killed Crespi at least he could relieve her of the obscenity she had the gall to keep in her home.

The glass panel came free from its moorings and lifted away neatly when he applied his two suction cups. He set it down on the ground against the house and stepped cautiously through the empty frame, pushing aside the blind. The moment his foot touched the kitchen floor Crespi's motion detector kicked in and a siren began to wail. It was so loud the whole neighborhood could hear it.

*Verdammt!* He had to act quickly. He gauged he had at least five minutes to search the house. The kitchen opened on to a long hall hung with prints on both sides. Traversing it Schnitt burst into a dining room lined with crammed book shelves, then onto what was obviously the living room with couch and chairs facing each other. A harp was by the fireplace. On the walls hung three small paintings—none was the Schiele obscenity.

Schnitt ran into what had to be a music room—a large area with a piano, drum set, and string bass. A few more paintings on the walls, but not the Schiele. So Crespi must keep the thing upstairs.

The siren seemed to wail even louder. Schnitt raced up the stairs and entered the front part of the house lit by the burglar light in the middle room—nothing. Just bedrooms. He ran to the back of the house, through a large study with more books, and found a final bedroom—the master bedroom. More pictures on the wall but again no Schiele.

Out of the corner of his eye Schnitt glimpsed a night light illuminating the adjacent bathroom. There on the wall by the mirror over the sink was the unframed Schiele. What a place to keep a painting! My god, did the woman *shower* with it? He grabbed it off the wall and sprinted to the staircase.

"*This is the University Park Police. Come down the stairs quick time and identify yourself.*" Another male voice from the dark stairs below commanded: "*Get the hell down here!*" The two policemen had no way of knowing if the intruder were armed.

Schnitt had no place to go so, on a desperate impulse, he yelled and hurtled down the steps hoping to topple the men below. Instead he was stopped in his charge by two bullets. One hit his throat, the other hit his heart. The blood-spattered Schiele fell to the ground.

Had he been alive to know, Schnitt would have been gratified to see that the groin was blotted out by blood, his blood. But he was dead, quite dead. The quick-thinking University Park Police had done their job.

# 34

"Wait! Megan! Are you there? There's more to tell you," Tina said to her sister who had been stunned into silence on the other end of the line. "The intruder was caught, but the police who answered the call had to shoot him. He's dead."

"Oh my god," Megan murmured. "Do they know who he was?"

"They said he wasn't from around here. The ID on him—a passport— showed he was Austrian. The name on the passport was Wolf Schmidt, or maybe it was Schnitt. That's all the police know. It will be in the paper tomorrow, although your address of course will not be revealed.

"The police called me right after they shot the burglar. Said he had a painting in his hand and..."

"Was it the *Schiele*?" Megan interrupted.

"Yes," Tina answered. "But don't worry, it wasn't damaged except for some drops of blood on it. I've already taken it over to the Meadows Museum on campus and their restorer is cleaning it up. It should be okay," she said.

"Thank you, Tina, for thinking so quickly. Now tell me, was there any damage done to the house or my things?"

"I've gone through the house very carefully, every room, and every-thing looks okay, except for the back door where the glass was cut out. A repairman has already been to the house to fix it."

"Thank heavens for that, at least."

The two sisters talked a while longer and then hung up, each of them feeling a modicum better. Megan explained to a worried Antal what had happened and he immediately got on line, looking for a Vienna Wolf Schnitt. The best he could come up with was an W. E. Schnitt, hairdresser. Now that made sense, he joked with Megan, trying to cheer her up a bit. That did indeed make her smile as she knew "*schnitt*" meant "cut" in English.

Turning her thoughts to booking a flight back to Texas, she asked Antal if she could do so on his computer as her laptop was out of juice. Antal reluctantly turned over his computer to her, expressing his dismay that she would be leaving Wien so soon.

Before she had a chance to beam up American Airlines, another call came in on her iPhone. The photo identification this time was that of her friend Janette Killar. Janette was not only the author of the Schiele oeuvre catalogue, but co-director of New York's venerable Galerie St. Sebastian.

"Megan? So glad I caught you still in Vienna. Listen. I've been contacted from Vienna by an heir of the Eva Benesch estate. He says he is in possession of a handwritten diary he thinks I might be interested in."

"Wow! That could only be one thing: the lost diary Schiele kept while in prison. I *told* you it existed, and that Eva Benesch had *almost* showed it to me until I told her I was good friends with Christian Nebehay, owner of the famed Nebehay Antiquariat in Wien."

"Yes, yes, but no one has ever seen the original and some Schiele scholars think the whole diary was a fraud, as you are aware. Even though it was published by his friend Arthur Roessler after Schiele's death, and then by you in English translation," said Janette.

"Well, you know that my unshakable view is that even if Roessler did embellish things, the diary did exist, perhaps only on sheets of paper. Now, from what you tell me, it sounds as though it truly does exist."

"That is, if the diary this client is offering is Schiele's."

"But who else's could it be? This is so exciting!"

"Yes, exciting. But, actually, the provenance is all wrong. Roessler hints that the diary was given to *him*, so how did it get into the hands of Eva Benesch?

"Perhaps it was passed on to Heinrich Benesch senior and he passed it on to his son Otto who passed it on to his wife Eva?"

"That's a pretty big perhaps," scoffed Janette. "And if Otto did inherit the diary, he would have given it to the Egon Schiele Archive at the Albertina Museum, since he was the director of that formidable institution for so long."

"Can't beat that logic," Megan conceded.

"But, actually, the point of my call is that since you are still in Vienna, could you make a visit to this client and see what it is that he is offering?"

"Of course! I haven't set a return date for my flight back yet, so I'd be more than happy to visit your source and take a look at the 'diary.'"

"Oh, great. His name is Erich Danzig and he lives at number thirteen A, Johann-Strauss-Gasse, right off the Wiedner Hauptstrasse."

"Oh, sure, I know where that is. Does he give a phone number?"

"Yes. Are you ready to take it down or shall I e-mail it to you?"

"Good. How about your e-mailing it to me right now, as we speak."

"Okay. I can't wait to hear from you about what this Danzig guy is offering. And Megan, don't mention any possible price. Let me do the bargaining, yes?"

"You mean I can't buy it for myself for a pittance?" Megan joked.

After the two friends finished their jousting and hung up, Megan turned to a wondering Antal and explained what was going on.

"And you know what, Antal, I would like it very much if you went with me to visit the man."

"You couldn't stop me!" exclaimed her old friend, feeling loyally protective of this undaunted scholar who had spent half a century in the footsteps of a Viennese Wunderkind who lived so briefly yet left such riches.

Megan made no flight reservations that day. Instead she dialed the telephone number Janette had e-mailed her. A very amiable young-sounding man answered, affirming that he was indeed Herr Erich Danzig. Megan explained she was a colleague of Janette Killar, who had asked her to take a look for her at the item he had offered her.

"Why of course I would be pleased to show you the diary, Professor Crespi, but would you be greatly offended if I checked with Janette Killar first?"

"Certainly not," answered a not too surprised Megan, who was accustomed to Viennese suspicion. "Why don't you phone her and when you've confirmed things we can get together."

"I'll do it right now," Erich said.

Megan decided to unpack her laptop and charge it up if she was going to remain in Vienna another day or so. Anton had pleaded with her to continue staying with him, and as she really had no desire to move back to the Römischer Kaiser, she had readily agreed. The guest bedroom had a handsome small desk and comfortable swivel chair so she felt quite at home setting up her work items. They included her favorite pen and this year's edition of the small Italian diary she had kept ever since graduating from college. Her university had asked that she donate her fifty-plus years of diary-keeping to its archives and she had agreed. But she had to laugh at the picture of a future scholar trying to figure out not only her miniscule handwriting but also which language she was writing in, as she always chose the shortest word in the languages she knew for whatever she was writing.

Her iPhone began playing Massenet's *Méditation* from *Thaïs* and she picked it up quickly. It was Erich Danzig and there was a pleasant bounce to his voice.

"Janette Killar has just sung your praises to me so loudly I think I'm going deaf. I do apologize for checking on you, Frau Professor, but in Wien we do have to be careful when dealing with restitution issues. And that is what this diary perhaps was. Could you come and see it sometime over this weekend?"

"How about this afternoon?"

"Perfect! Would two o'clock be good for you? And shall I give you directions?"

"Oh, I know how to get there, thank you. Would you mind if I brought along a colleague who owns a Schiele painting?" Megan really would feel better if she had someone with her. Her latest experiences in Vienna and Königsberg had taught her caution.

"A Schiele owner? How very interesting. Yes, by all means, bring your friend along."

Antal was feeling a thrill of excitement. It was like old times, he thought, having adventures together with Megan. He thought about the time they had infiltrated the Moulin Rouge on the Walfischgasse together and how a tipsy Megan had emerged with the cabaret doorman's cap on her head, a treasured trophy she kept over her desk while she lived in Vienna during that student year of so long ago.

At a quarter to two that afternoon they walked over to Antal's Fiat and headed for Erich Danzig's apartment on the Johann-Strauss-Gasse. A few minutes later a pleasant young man with dark curly hair and penetrating brown eyes was showing them into a very modern apartment. The living room had a collection of some six guitars on the wall above the sofa. Megan and Antal immediately felt at home: this was a civilized dwelling. Erich insisted on serving some plum brandy before they got down to business. He was a locksmith by day and a dedicated folk singer by night, he told them readily. Then, clearing the coffee table, Erich disappeared into the next room for a minute. Megan and Antal looked at each other raising their eyebrows in silent, excited anticipation.

Erich emerged with a leather box in his hand and sat down in one of the arm chairs facing the sofa where Megan and Antal were seated. Proudly, he put the box on the coffee table

"This once belonged to my grandmother, Anna Benesch, the younger sister of Eva Benesch," he began. "She was a collector of Klimt and Schiele drawings. And she was a good friend of Adele Harms, Schiele's sister-in-law, who gave her this box shortly before her death. But like so many Jews in Vienna at the time of the Anschluss, my grandmother was relieved of her collection. She herself died at the Mauthausen concentration camp, but her daughter, my mother, survived because she had married a Swiss businessman, Werner Danzig, and lived in Switzerland during the war. After the war she spent years trying to find out where her mother's drawing collection had gone—whether or not it was dispersed to all four corners of the globe or had remained intact.

"The IKG helped her track the collection down and they determined that it was last in the possession of one Herbert Schindler, the CEO of Hapibier. That's a new beer best known for supplying the campers at rock festivals with on-site chilled beer.

"Now I wondered what the owner of a boutique brewery would be doing with a group of Klimt and Schiele drawings, so I contacted him. He was most forthcoming, said he had inherited them from his father. But he informed me that he had to sell the drawing collection to a wealthy American lawyer in order to raise the funds to begin producing his Hapibier."

"Complicated!" Megan commented, trying to keep track of all the names.

"It gets more complicated," continued Erich with a wry smile. The lawyer, Pierre Haroche, lives in New York and at first refused to see me. When he finally relented and allowed me to see his drawing collection—my *grandmother's* collection, mind you—he first had me sign a document attesting that under no condition would I institute a restitution lawsuit, since he had bought the drawings from Herbert Schindler in good faith."

"*Ach*! It would take a battery of lawyers to sort this all out," Antal exclaimed in knowing exasperation.

"Pierre Haroche made me acutely aware of that," conceded Erich. "He knew I didn't have the money to fund a major lawsuit, one that could most probably last years and years. But we got along very well—I actually sang several folk songs for him—and at the end of my visit to him, because I had to sign that indemnity statement, he gave me this box as a sort of consolation prize. He told me it contained papers in Schiele's hand. They had been put there by Adele Harms—Schiele's sister-in-law and my grandmother's friend, as I've told you. Adele gave the box to my grandmother, and the box remained with the drawings when they changed owners from an anonymous Nazi collector to Schindler father, to Schindler son, to Haroche.

"Since he didn't read German, Pierre Haroche was not interested in the papers inside, he told me. He had not alerted the world of Schiele scholarship to their existence because he had a thriving law practice and simply did not want to be bothered. But he did tell me that if I ever needed or wanted money the Schiele papers inside the box could be valuable.

"Well, now my fiancée and I are getting married," concluded Erich Danzig, "and I do need some money. That's why I contacted the dealer Janette Killar in New York. I saw that she had authored that huge book documenting Schiele's work, what do you call it? Oh, yes, an oeuvre catalogue. Or catalogue raisonée? We e-mailed back and forth and Killar told me she might be interested but would have to see the papers in person. So it's my good luck that you, Dr. Crespi, are here in Wien."

"Might we look at the papers?" Megan asked, trying to control her impatience.

"Of course. I went thought them once, several years ago, but they all seemed like outbursts of self-pity and for me, at least, made dull reading. So I tied them back up again."

Megan suppressed her annoyance, indignant that anyone could think even a single line by Schiele was "dull."

Erich handed the leather box to her. Anton leaned forward to see what Megan withdrew from the box. It was a packet of irregularly sized paper sheets bound with a string. Megan carefully untied the knot and removed the constraining string. She looked at the first ragged sheet, holding it up for Antal to see and discreetly photographing it with her Google Glass. Schiele's flamboyant cursive script was unmistakable. It began with the date 17 April 1912 and the outcry:

Thirteenth, thirteenth, thirteenth—thirteen
times the thirteenth of April! I have never
thought of the thirteenth superstitiously,
fearfully, and yet now a
thirteenth day of the
month has become
calamitous for me. For on 13 April 1912
I was arrested and put under lock and key
in the Neulengbach district courthouse.

A sheet later came the artist's description of his cellar prison cell:

A hell! A hell, not <u>the</u> hell, but a base,
vulgar, dirty, miserable, shaming hell is this
into which I have been thrown unexpectedly.
Dust, spider webs, cough spit, sediment of
sweat, also tears have sprinkled the scurfy,
crumbling plaster of this room. Where the
bunk touches the wall the stains are the

thickest and the limy whitewash has been
rubbed off. As though polished, the bricks
are like blood smears, all smooth and with a
dark, fatty shine.

Only the button for the electric bell above
the head of the bed does not belong, it is
present-day, is modern. And so I know that I
am not dreaming. I live, experience—unless
all life is just a dream in which there are
nightmares.

Megan stopped short and exclaimed. "Oh, yes! See here how Egon
refers to the electric bell on the wall over his head. He included that bell
when he sketched the interior of the cell."

Antal nodded empathetically while Erich looked vaguely interested.

"And when I discovered the cell, there it was, the bell and its long
black cord, still on the wall!

"Ah! Here's a poignant entry," Megan continued, holding up the page
for 18 April. She read aloud: "I must live in my own excrement, breathe
in my own poisonous, sticky fumes. I am unshaven—I cannot even wash
myself properly. Yet I am a human being!"

"Terrible!" exclaimed Antal.

"And here is one that relates to the corridor he drew outside his cell,"
Megan said excitedly, recalling how everything she saw in the long hall had
conformed to Schiele's drawing of so many years ago:

Drew the corridor before the cells, with the
rubbish that lies in the corners and the
equipment used by the prisoners to clean
their cells. Fine. Gave me equilibrium. I feel
not punished but purified!

"Oh, and here is what you could call his manifesto, right here on this
page, dated twenty-two April:

Primordially eternal is God. Man calls
him Buddah, Zoroaster, Osiris, Zeus, or
Christ, and timeless like God is that which is
most Godlike after him, art. Art cannot be
modern; art is primordially eternal.

"Yes," Megan declared, pretending a calmness she did not feel. "This
is certainly Schiele, as he cries out in agony at being imprisoned. He could
not understand that Klimt or Roessler did not come to his aid. But both of
them were away for the summer, so they didn't know about his being in jail.
Let's look at another page," she said, cautiously picking up the next sheet.
    "Yes, and here, this page for April twenty-fifth, here is what became
Schiele's credo in prison. Listen:

Yesterday: cries—soft, timid, wailing; screams—loud, urgent,
imploring; groaning sobs—desperate. Fearfully desperate. Finally
apathetic stretching out with cold limbs, deathly afraid, bathed in
shivering sweat. And yet, for art and for my loved ones I will gladly
endure to the end.

    "These are the words with which Schiele entitled his last of four
self-portraits done in prison. Done for the only time in his life without
the aid of his full-length standing mirror, the one he had begged from his
mother for his first studio and the one which he took with him as he moved
from place to place."
    As Megan continued looking at the pages, each of which she held up
for the benefit of her Google Glass and Antal, she realized that the "end"
of the diary was missing. Missing were pages 22 through 30 in the original
1922 edition of Schiele's prison diary as published by Arthur Roessler. She
could tell now what Roessler had amplified, to put it kindly. He had, in a
sense, "wrapped" the diary with a foreword and a long afterword, although
the pages had purported to be pages from the diary.
    And "pages" was perhaps the wrong appellation. The uneven sheets,
obviously torn along a ruler or some straight piece of wood, looked as

though they had been torn in half, then quartered from a larger sheet, most probably one of his sketchbook pages. Heinrich Benesch, whom he would portray in a double portrait with his son Otto in 1913, was the only one in Vienna who knew Schiele was in prison. He had brought out to the Neulengbach prison watercolors and drawing material for the artist.

She continued to look carefully through the material, saddened once again by the artist's obvious agony. He was, after all, only nineteen when he began his series of nude self-portraits in 1910, and only twenty-one when he was arrested.

*Then came the question Megan always hated.*

"How much do you think I could get for this?" Erich asked.

"You know, Herr Danzig, I could not possibly say. I am only an art historian. You would have to turn to someone familiar with the market. And probably not someone in Vienna. I will say that you were quite wise to turn to Janette Killar, as she is truly *the* world expert on Schiele."

"So, I must wait until she sees them in person then," said Erich sadly.

"But that shouldn't take too long," Megan encouraged him. "Send them on to her right away by FedEx or some other carrier, but insure them for, say, ten thousand Euros."

Erich's eyes brightened with joy. "You really think they might be worth *that* much?" he asked.

Megan could see he was a child in the world of adults, concerning things pertaining to Schiele. She knew the letters were worth far more and that there could easily be a bidding war between private collectors who would probably ferret them away.

So she advised Erich: "Why not make it your stipulation that the collection of letters be offered to museums only? That way these historical documents—and they are historical—would be preserved and open to Schiele lovers and scholars."

"Super!" Erich responded. "I think my grandmother would have liked that very much. I'll bundle them up today and go to my local FedEx. It's just over on Favoritenstrasse."

A few more pleasantries were exchanged and then Megan and Antal made their farewells and walked to the car.

"Whew!' they both exclaimed at the same time. "Out of the hands of babes, oft times come jewels," Megan paraphrased limply. She would have wonderful news to relate to Janette. *Schiele's prison diary existed!*

# 35

Krumau never looked better. The sun was bouncing off the green treetops and red-gabled roofs of the town, creating velvet pockets of shimmering shadows on the ground. Adolf Peschka-Schiele left his black Mercedes-Benz in one of the many parking lots outside the ring of buildings and outer fortification walls that demarked the inner city, which was limited almost exclusively to pedestrian traffic. By foot he crossed the first of two bridges he would have to go over before entering the old town. The second bridge, far more dramatic and longer in span that the first bridge, deposited him directly alongside the Hotel Dvořák's outdoor garden café and he stopped there for a cool drink before continuing. The temperature, for the end of March, was surprisingly warm. To think! Just a few days ago there had been a ferocious hail storm in Wien, and now here in Bohemian Krumau, just two-and-a-half hours away by car, he needed to take his jacket off!

Refreshed from the cold beer, Adolf began to study the two books he had brought with him. One of them was an old Baedeker guide book to the general Bohemian area from 1910, and the other a 2014 Baedeker featuring Česky Krumlov, now in the Czech Republic. What he was looking for was any sort of structure, imperial, religious, civic, or private that had an octagonal shape. One building, hexagonal in shape was given quite a bit of attention. Not far from the main square, it had served as the assemblage center for Krumau Jews being rounded up for shipment to Theresienstadt. Terrible. After some thirty minutes of fruitless study looking for an octagonal building, Adolf gave up. For a while, trying to formulate a plan, he sat watching the large groups of enthusiastic tourists crossing over the bridge. Below the bridge on the blue water a colorful array of dedicated kayakers fanned out in both directions.

. Who would have thought that old Krumau on the Moldau would ever be such a tourist destination, he wondered to himself. Well, he concluded, it makes sense, as the thirteenth-century town was one of the best preserved and least damaged by wars in Europe. He gave a last look at his 1910 Baedeker, studying the town plan. None of the buildings described in the very thorough guidebook had octagonal plans.

I will simply search on foot, Adolf resolved, draining the last of his beer, which had by now become as warm as the weather. Purposefully he began striding through the old town's main street toward the ancient castle compound. It sat astride a mighty rock promontory on the far side of the curving loop of the Moldau and culminated in the church of St. Vitus with its tall bell tower.

When he got to the town square he stopped, struck by the massive six-sided stone fountain surrounding the town's tall plague monument. Well, if the Krumauers could build hexagonal structures they could build octagonal ones as well. He studied the buildings fronting the square but they were all straightforward, mostly rectangular in plan, including the town hall. No polygons here.

His scrutiny of the town square, however, sparked an idea. Why not try to find the building that served as the military garrison during World War I? Where Schiele had been stationed on guard duty? Looking around him, Adolf approached the oldest-looking individual he saw, an elderly man sitting with his wife at one of the outdoor cafés.

"Do you by any chance know where the military garrisons here during the two world wars were located?" he asked the man. His interlocutor raised his shoulders and spread his hands out before him, indicating that he did not speak German. He looked pleadingly toward his wife.

She spoke out in German: "My grandfather knew about such things. He used to point them out to me when I was a child. One is out of town somewhere, but the other is where there is a museum now—an art museum, I think."

"An *art* museum? Do you mean the Egon Schiele Art Centrum?"

"Yes, that's the name. His mother was from here."

Adolf thanked the woman and began walking down to wide Široká street, where he had planned to go later in the day. Entrance to the museum, formerly the town brewery, was through a small inner courtyard, and there was certainly nothing octagonal in sight. He made his way through the several rooms that comprised the museum. An exhibit on the artist's life and work was flanked by a few original drawings and watercolors. There were replicas of furniture designed by Schiele.

And a continuously playing videotape presented the co-founder of the museum, Serge Sabarsky, who related the history of Schiele and the museum. Although Sabarsky died in 1996, Adolf still considered him a rival in Schiele research. A rival who had the money and resources, through his New York gallery and Austrian background, to ferret out Schiele works before Adolf could get to them. Yes, sneaky Sabarsky had always been one step ahead of him.

The building would indeed have made a good prison garrison, with its dark cellar arches, Adolf thought, but there was nothing octagonal about them, On his way out he stopped at the gift shop and bought himself a few black crayons, modern versions of Schiele's *schwarze Kreide.*

After some moments of checking out the street's architecture, Adolf decided to walk over to the garden house where Schiele had lived for a few months with Wally in 1911. Tucked into the town's stone fortifications, it too was now a museum, with a fine view of the river. Another dead end though as far as being an octagonal building. Adolf could envision the compelling town views Schiele had painted of what he occasionally entitled *The Dead City.* But there were no octagonal buildings in these canvases. In fact, Adolf was beginning to wonder whether such a building existed or if it were only a project Schiele had envisioned but never completed.

Had he wasted his time by going to Krumau? Hot, perspiring, and disillusioned, he walked briskly back to the two bridges over which he had entered the old town and to his car which was parked in the shade of the outer fortifications wall. He started the motor up briskly to get the air conditioning going and passed an irritatingly slow vehicle in front of him. He passed it too fast, evidently, because he immediately heard a siren behind him. A police car overtook him and pulled him to a stop.

Did he realize he was going twenty kilometers over the speed limit? Did he know his passport was out of date, the policeman asked after examining it. Adolf was thunderstruck. He had indeed allowed renewal to pass him by, and there had been no passport check when he entered Czechoslovakia that morning.

"You'll have to follow me to the station," the officer declared. Cursing his luck, Adolf obediently followed the police car back to the outer walls of town and pulled up behind it when the car came to a halt. He blinked and rubbed his eyes in disbelief.

*The police station was an octagon.*

# 36

The Grand Master had every reason to feel pleased as he approached the "prison" cell he had had installed underneath the long house. Access to this cell was through the trap door the workmen installed in the northeast corner of the long house floor. When the trap door was raised, access to the cell was by way of a narrow metal ladder that stretched steeply up from the cell's earthen floor. Ventilation was provided by narrow tubes that ran along the side of the cell and opened up into ordinary-looking vents to the outside. The cell had also been outfitted with electricity.

No one was around and it was getting dark. Wagner picked up some of the items he had brought with him and descended into the cell. He had to make several trips. First came the simple plank bed, then the two sawhorses that would support it, and then the thin mattress. All was as described by Schiele in his prison diary.

Working feverishly and breathing heavily, Wagner positioned the items, then closed the wooden trap door upon himself, and lay down on the narrow bed. Just as Schiele had done. Wagner lay there for some ten minutes, *feeling* Schiele, feeling his thoughts, his discomfort, and his resolution to "persevere to the end," as the artist had written on his final self-portrait in prison.

Then Wagner arose and with his heavy Swiss pocketknife carved the initials "M H" into the trap door above him. Initials Schiele had observed and recorded in the exact 1912 drawing of his prison cell and its door. This would be exclusively his, the Grand Master's cell for contemplation and, yes, for repentance. Repentance for each missed opportunity to apply the principles of the Doppel-O to pornography or to purveyors of pornography. Persons such as Megan Crespi, Janette Killar, and director of the Leopold Museum, Johannes Ohm.

And the cell would also be the place for punishment. Whenever Wagner felt the stirrings of sexual desire that welled in him as he censored the erotic television programs he monitored, he would descend into the cell for punishment—self-lashing—and penance. Not even his closest associates, like Arnold Moll, would know of the triple purpose of this unique cell created down to the smallest detail in the likeness of Schiele's cell at Neulengbach.

Yes, the Grand Master was pleased.

# 31

Crossing the border—Russia's, Poland's, and the Czech Rebublic's—had been without incident for Arnold Moll. Although the customs official at the Russian border had picked up the Schiele canvas roll, he only did so to remove it and see what else was in the back of the Volvo station wagon. Moll had spent the night in Warsaw doing nothing but sleeping; he had no taste for things Polish, except the occasional model train engine or carriage cars he had ordered from one of Poland's toy antiquarian dealers.

Now dropping down to Brno in the Czech Republic during his second day on the road, he decided to drive up the hillside overlooking the city to admire Mies van der Rohe's recently restored Villa Tugendhat. Walter Messerschmitt had lived there during the war directing the manufacture of jet engines. And when the Soviet army reached Brno they had destroyed the interior and turned the house into a stable.

Moll's aesthetic senses satisfied by the long white horizontal lines and great glass windows of the building, he returned to his car and headed straight for Vienna. He would stay at his own place that night, then the next day he would drive to Gmunden. He had something for the Grand Master, something beyond the Master's wildest imaginings.

*  *  *

Megan had good news for Janette. Back at Antal's apartment she gave her friend a quick call relating the interesting turn of events. The prison diary was genuine, she told her, only not written in book form, but rather on quartered sheets of drawing paper. She would soon be e-mailing her the photos she had taken with her Google Glass. Megan asked Janette what she knew about Pierre Haroche, the lawyer who had given Erich Danzig the boxed papers.

"Oh, that plague of New York galleries!" responded Janette. "He is a regular gallery ghost, always trying to make a trade in his favor. He has several times tried to trade up one of his Klimts or Schieles for a better work. We won't do business with him but he haunts us on a regular basis. Bad news all around."

Concerning Schiele's diary notes and that some pages in the Roessler edition of the diary were absent in the Schiele papers, Janette was especially interested. She was pleased to think that the thorough stylistic analysis of Roessler's presentation conducted by her father matched the missing pages. Yes, it was clear that Roessler had provided both the beginning and much of the end for the diary.

After talking to Janette and e-mailing the diary photographs she had Google Glassed, Megan decided it was high time she checked on little Button. Claire Chandler, the ever-patient dog sitter, answered the phone immediately upon seeing that the caller ID was Megan. Button was just fine. He had completely recovered from his terrible fall. How about Megan? Had she recovered from *her* fall? And how did the sudden trip to Königsberg turn out? Did she find the Schiele artwork she was looking for?

"No, but we found one we were *not* looking for," Megan told her. "And it is a biggie. The famous double portrait of Paul and Peter Schwartz, no less. Its location has been unknown for decades."

Claire was duly impressed, but the main thing on her mind was the attempted burglary and shooting at Megan's house. She hated to think what would have happened had Megan been *in* the house. Did she know who the man, identified as Wolf Schnitt from Austria, was?

"No," answered Megan truthfully, hoping that by now Inspector Ludwig had put together a dossier on the dead man. She tried to make light of the event but Claire would have none of it.

To put Claire and herself at rest, Megan finally said: "Look. Suppose the man, for some unknown reason, had wanted to do away with me. Now he's dead, so there's no reason to worry about me anymore. *I'm* not going to."

"Yes, but the fact that he's from Austria..."

"I understand what you're saying," Megan interrupted, "but the police here are doing a thorough investigation. We will find out about this man, and we will find out who his associates were. I'm still inclined to think that he wanted my Schiele painting, not my life."

"But how could he have known that you own several Schieles?"

"It's not a secret, Claire. Janette's catalogue lists me as the owner of certain works, that's one way he could know. When I lend Schieles out to museums or exhibitions, I usually have them say 'collection Megan Crespi, Dallas', just for the fun of letting people know that Dallas has more than just Cowboys."

"Well, still, I don't like it. Do you know if he was ransacking your house, looking for the other Schieles?"

"Well, with the exception of the self-portrait found with Schnitt, all my other Schiele works are at the Dallas Museum of Art at present. The police say nothing was disturbed in any of the rooms of the house, and Tina confirms that. She went over the rooms very carefully; said all the artworks were where they always hang, which I found comforting."

"So when are you coming home?" Claire asked, still worried about what might be in store for her dear friend.

"I don't know yet. I need to consult with the police here and with Johannes Ohm of the Leopold Museum. There are leads concerning this Schiele mess that are beginning to come together. It seems that there is a Vienna-based organization on the Internet called 'Doppel-O'—you can look it up if you want—and that their cause is to 'obliterate obscenity,' hence the double O. It's obvious that to them Schiele's naked figures, especially if they are shown engaged in erotica, are obscene."

"I will look the organization up on line," conceded Claire. "It certainly sounds like a real possibility as far as motive is concerned. I don't think that even the lunatic fringe of the IKG Vienna restitution group that's always demonstrating, would do damage like that."

"I agree." Megan decided that she would not tell Claire or her sister about the murder of poor Sonja Oppenheimer in Königsberg until she got back to Dallas. She had told Hannes and Inspector Ludwig about it that morning and they had set up an appointment at the police station for the following day at one o'clock, giving Ludwig time to consult with the Russian police.

She was eager for Ludwig's input. Surely by now the Vienna police had managed to find out more about the Doppel-O clan's actual activities. So she fudged about when she would be returning to the States. She needed to do some catch-up business at Art Austria in Montreal. An exhibition she was curating on Schiele's portraits was being assembled there. All the catalogue essays were in, the galleys proofed and ready for the printer.

Or was she unconsciously putting off returning to Dallas because of the intrusion into her own space, the rape of her own home?

# 38

Peschka-Schiele hardly minded paying his speeding ticket at Krumau's police station, he was so charged up by his discovery that the station was in an octagonal building. Settling the outdated passport charge was more serious, but after promising to renew it as soon as he returned to Wien, Adolf was allowed to leave.

The odd thing was that he did not seem to be at all in a hurry to quit the building, the sergeant on duty noticed. Instead he was asking questions about how old the building imbedded in the city wall was and did it have a cellar perchance? Told yes, he asked if he might please see it. The sergeant looked at his commander, who had come to his office door, and after considering the request for a few seconds, he nodded his head in silent assent.

An off-duty officer led the way down the basement stairs to a corridor that opened up onto a huge octagonal cavern. It was empty except for a few dilapidated file cabinets. Seven of the support arches had been bricked up and plastered over; the eighth arch constituted the entryway.

"Any idea what is behind all this plaster?" Adolf asked the officer.

"No idea," answered the man, bored.

He added an astounding piece of information, however. "We've been told that when the building is razed, the cellar will be excavated."

"When is that going to happen?" Adolf pushed, alarmed by what the man had said.

"Oh, whenever it gets sold. It's for sale now and we're about to move into our new station down the road."

"You mean this building is up for sale?"

"Sure. Didn't you see the sign outside?"

Adolf had to admit to himself that he had been so wildly excited by the octagonal shape of the building, wedged as it was between the outer city walls, that he had not registered anything else. Now the thought that Schiele's allegories could be behind those bricked walls was hammering at him with an insistency that was impossible to ignore.

On the drive back to Vienna, Adolf thought over his options. There was one man he knew of in Europe who not only had the means to buy the Krumau building but also a driving interest in Schiele and his work. That was the Russian who had telephoned him so recently: Boris Ussachevsky. As soon as he got back to the city and had calmed down, he would call St. Petersburg and inform Ussachevsky about this amazing turn of events.

How to fund this without surrendering the Schiele canvases to the Russian would be a tremendous problem. Perhaps he could get Ussachevsky to agree that whatever was found behind the arches would be divided between the two of them. He would e-mail Ussachevsky his photograph of the artist's drawing of the "Pantheon" octagonal building, with its specific locale identification as "Krumau." That should persuade the Russian to buy the building quickly. After all, nothing could beat the fact that Adolf was in possession of a mind-blowing piece of Schiele information with amazing potential.

# 39

Inspector Ludwig arrived early at the Leopold Museum the next day for his meeting with Johannes Ohm and Megan Crespi at one o'clock. He had made progress concerning the man shot in Crespi's home in Dallas, as well as coming up with some interesting information on the Doppel-O clan.

After looking around the ground floor, he climbed the stairs to the director's office and the two men greeted each other genially. They waited for Crespi, who called up precisely at one o'clock.

"Come right up, Megan. Inspector Ludwig is already here and he has news for us."

The three sat down around Ohm's conference table facing each other.

Ludwig opened his briefcase. He drew out an item that had been faxed to him from Dallas. It was a police photograph of Schnitt's corpse. Two bullet-entry holes were at the throat and the heart. The body's face was intact. Did Megan recognize the man?

"No, not at all," answered a mystified Megan. "I'm pretty sure I have never seen him."

"We have identified your burglar," Ludwig announced, "and why he traveled to Dallas to invade your home and attempt to steal a Schiele painting is perhaps solved now." Megan and Johannes looked mystified.

"His name was Wolf Schnitt. He was an investment broker with Herz & Herz in Döbling. Seems he had been missing from his job for several days now. His secretary directed us to his apartment here in the city."

"So how does an investment broker link up with our Schiele?" asked Johannes.

A second item was brought out from Ludwig's briefcase. It too was a photograph, but Inspector Ludwig kept it face down.

"Before I show you two this, I would like you, Dr. Ohm, to tell me exactly what you found in the museum after the murder of the night watchman."

"Um, there was the strangely placed body of the poor guard underneath the self-portrait by Schiele. The painting had been censored with duct tape. In addition, we discovered, upstairs, that our treasured Klimt painting, the *Kissing Couple*, had been sliced out of its frame with a knife or something sharp. Only the gold, decorative background was left: the two kissing figures were gone."

"Exactly what we found when we came in on the scene that morning," confirmed Ludwig approvingly. "Now have a look at this, both of you." He turned the photograph over.

Megan and Hannes leaned forward. The image showed the two nude women locked in a kiss from Klimt's *Kissing Couple*. The edges around the embracing figures were slightly uneven.

"Does this mean you have found the missing Klimt?" Hannes asked eagerly.

"Yes. We found the missing Klimt at Schnitt's flat. Yesterday."

"But what would an investment banker be doing with a fragment of Klimt in his home?" mused Hannes.

"And why would he have tried to get my Schiele painting and come all the way to Dallas for it?" asked Megan.

"Ah, and now for the missing link," Ludwig announced, quite pleased with himself. "We have hacked into what seems to be the membership of the Doppel-O cult, the one we have suspected all along. There are some forty members. Although they all have code names, the moniker 'Devoted Dispatcher' came up twice."

"So you see, Megan, I was right!" cried Hannes in consternation. "*It was no accident that you fell down the stairs in the Wien Museum.* Schnitt must have pushed or tripped you. And it must have been this same Schnitt character who killed the Vidovszky woman, thinking she was you!"

"At least the danger is over now," Megan said slowly, but not feeling any real relief. She could not help but think of what had happened to Sonja Oppenheimer, also the owner of a nude Schiele self-portrait. Wolf Schnitt couldn't have been in Russia one day and the States the next. Or could he? She gave an involuntary shudder. Was there another person capable of murder in the Doppel-O organization?

"So what do we do next?" she asked.

"That depends on what the Doppel-O plans to do next. The brief description of the group's aims and beliefs on the website cites purging pornography from public and private places. It doesn't say who the first offender to be targeted is, but I think it's pretty clear now that it's Schiele."

"So the Klimt in Schnitt's apartment was a personal souvenir, I suppose," Johannes ventured.

"That, or perhaps he hoped to sell it." Ludwig said. "After all, there are those shady dealers here and abroad who would handle such a thing. And there are collectors worldwide who would gladly buy a stolen Klimt, even a fragment of a Klimt."

"And what about the head of this self-righteous, dangerous cult?" Megan asked.

"Yes, we have known the identity of the so-called Grand Master for quite a while. His name is Kurt Wagner. But there is no blemish on his record. He is a medical doctor who hasn't practiced in two decades, yet he seems wealthy enough. For the past two years he has rented out one of the wings of the Gemmingen-Eggaberg castle in Gmunden. Now it seems that he has bought several acres behind the Schloss and is engaged in some construction there—probably an assembly room for the cult. Or a private dwelling for himself."

"How can you find out more about him?" Johannes asked.

"We have the address of his flat in Vienna, but we haven't been able to find him there. And we have no grounds for a search warrant. So we plan to visit Gmunden tomorrow morning, and if we don't find him there at least we can talk to the Schloss's owner, Baron Friedrich von Gemmingen-Eggaberg."

"Could we go along with you?" Johannes asked for himself and Megan.

"I was just going to ask if you two would be willing to come along. Fine. Excellent. Shall I pick you both up in front of the Leopold tomorrow morning at nine o'clock?"

Both Megan and Hannes eagerly nodded their assent. After Ludwig left, the two friends continued to talk about the week's whirlwind events, including the murder at Königsberg.

"I suppose we'll never know how it was that Sonja Oppenheimer had in her possession, without even realizing it, yet a third Schiele painting," Megan mused.

"Or that we will ever learn where the two nude self-portraits went to," Hannes added. "The first one, the standing one that was stolen from Sotheby's—the police still have no hint of where it is now. And now the second one, the kneeling one, is also in the hands of a thief. There is some hope that this one might appear on the market, but not much, since the whole art world knows it is a stolen work by now."

"If it was stolen by a member of the Doppel-O, then its fate is pretty well determined: destruction," Megan said glumly.

"Or maybe the thief wanted it for himself," suggested Hannes.

"At least Jerome Schwartz will have Schiele's double portrait of his father and grandfather restored to him."

"Yes, and that couldn't have happened if you and your two Russian associates hadn't visited Sonja Oppenheimer in Königsberg. So you can pat yourself on the shoulder for that."

"I'm not taking any kudos until we find where the two stolen self-portraits are now," said Megan obstinately. To tell the truth, she did not have much hope that they would be found.

"You realize, don't you, Hannes, that Antal Maack's Gerti portrait might have been stolen for eventual destruction if it hadn't been in a heavy double frame. All the vandal could do was quickly spray paint it from the balcony, then toss down his metal rose, and leave before anyone was the wiser."

"Has Antal beefed up his security since then?"

"You bet he has. Now there are security cameras in every room. Don't you think, Hannes, that other owners of Schiele artworks that could be considered lewd and erotic should be warned?"

"With all this publicity on TV and in the newspapers, they are probably all aware of the danger. It would be quite a job to ferret out each and every owner of Schiele *drawings*, as opposed to owners of paintings by him."

Hannes paused. "I can think of one person who probably has in her head the names of almost everyone who does own an erotic drawing."

"So can I," said Megan smiling for the first time. "Janette Killar."

Peschka-Schiele had e-mailed his photograph of Schiele's octagonal drawing to Ussachevsky. Now he placed a call to him and explained the great potential of his find.

"I understand the import of what you are saying," said Boris after he had listened intently to the Krumau story that the ingratiating descendent of Schiele had to tell him on the phone.

"Is there anything that can be done about it?" Adolf asked tremulously.

There was a long silence on the other end of the line. It continued. Adolf almost spoke again but thought better of it.

Finally the voice of Boris came over the line. "I shall fly to Vienna tomorrow. You shall pick me up the following morning at the Hotel Bristol on the Kärntner Ring at precisely nine o'clock. Understood?"

"Yes, Herr Ussachevsky, yes."

"What is the make and color of your vehicle?"

"It is a black Mercedes-Benz."

"Quite right. I shall see you day after tomorrow and you shall drive me to Krumau."

"Yes, th, th...*thank* you," Aldolf began stammering, thrilled by Ussachevsky's decision to come to Krumau immediately.

\* \* \*

The next morning Inspector Konrad Ludwig pulled up at the Leopold Museum precisely at nine o'clock and beamed a greeting to Megan and Hannes who were waiting on the curb. Ludwig was driving a roomy black Opel Corsa. Megan motioned Hannes to sit in front while she spread out comfortably with her capacious shoulder bag in the back seat. The talk was optimistic as they began the three-hour drive to the summer resort on the Traunsee, so beloved by Brahms.

When they passed the highway turn-off for Sankt Pölten, where Schiele's trial had taken place, they talked about the judge who had ceremoniously set fire to one of the artist's drawings. And once again Megan felt indignation that the judge, a Dr. Stovel, was himself a collector of erotic drawings in a more "acceptable" form. He was an avid collector of the nineteenth-century Austrian Jesuit artist Franz Stecher. This artist was mentally unbalanced, and his works reveal a morbid pornographic mingling of religious and sexual elements, done in a feeble neo-Blake style.

Stovel, in fact, displayed the neurotic obsession with the erotic in permissible disguises which was part of the overrefined sensualism of Vienna during Schiele's lifetime. It was that social hypocrisy against which the twenty-one-year-old artist had rebelled so flamboyantly. Just as his contemporary Sigmund Freud was exposing hidden secrets of the psyche, Arnold Schönberg was rejecting the musical cloak of chromaticism, and Adolf Loos was condemning decoration as criminal in architecture.

After the trauma of imprisonment, Megan told Ludwig, Schiele had latched onto the allegorical role of outsider from society, assuming in his self-portraits the guise of hermit or monk or martyred saint, as with Saint Sebastian. Imprisonment had shown the artist that being an artist did not make him sacrosanct, did not place him above the laws of society. Only gradually did he pull out of this antisocial stance as demand for his riveting portraiture and nostalgic townscapes began to grow. The two determining factors for this gradual change in his work—from angst to empathy—were the outbreak of World War I and his marriage to Edith Harms.

Hannes explained to Konrad—by now they had all moved to a first-name basis—that Schiele, along with his rival Oskar Kokoschka, had actually redefined portraiture in Vienna. It was not a person's status, but rather a person's state of soul that mattered. They had concentrated on the *existential* as opposed to the environmental aspect of their sitters. But after the start of World War I, Schiele, especially, had stopped imposing his own psychological interests on his sitters. Instead he showed identification with his subjects, even including items from their environment—a chair, books—instead of positing them in a void as he had done earlier.

"So," asked Konrad, "you think that, if Schiele had lived, he would have become mellower and less self-involved?"

Megan eagerly answered for Hannes: "Yes, we all think that his portraits would have been more gentle, less reactive, more reconciliatory, more painterly, and certainly more acceptable to the general public. No more arrests for pornography!"

"What were the charges against him anyway?" Konrad asked, his police interests peaked.

"Kidnapping, statutory rape, and public immorality," Hannes answered. "The first two charges were brought on by the fact that Schiele had housed for one night a teenage girl who had run away from home. These charges were brought against him by the girl's father, who later withdrew them."

"But the third charge," Megan took up the tale, "the one of 'public immorality,' stuck. It was alleged that Schiele, while entertaining and drawing child models in his studio, had, through careless or willful display of erotic drawings, contributed to their corruption. The stacks of drawings in his bedroom—some one-hundred and twenty-five of them—were confiscated, and it was one of those that the smut-loving judge ostentatiously burned in the Sankt Pölten courtroom."

The car occupants were silent for a while. Konrad took the highway turnoff for the Traunsee, then coming upon the Gmunden outskirts, the trio decided to stop at a fast food restaurant before dropping in on the owner of the Schloss. Konrad had telephoned the baron the day before and set up a one o'clock appointment for the three of them.

Driving up to the back of the castle after lunch, they passed by, unknowingly, the acreage Kurt Wagner had bought from the baron. It would be up to the baron to tell them where Wagner's land was. On the phone, Konrad told Megan and Hannes, the baron sounded quite forthcoming. He didn't anticipate any problems interviewing him.

The parking area behind the Schloss was relatively large and Konrad pulled up as close to the back entrance as possible. A servant opened the double doors and showed them into a long hall that gave onto a magnificent L-shaped den lined with book shelves featuring numerous leather-bound books. The view out the windows encompassed Gmunden town and the Traunsee.

While they were taking this in, a large cat strolled into the room and imperiously looked them over. A woman's voice was heard calling to her, "Maya? Maya! Where are you?"

Within seconds the tall, blonde baroness entered the den and smiled a welcome to the visitors.

"My husband will be down in a moment," she assured them. "Meanwhile I shall take this naughty cat away so she doesn't bother you." She scooped up a very vocal Maya in her arms and quit the room, tossing a smile back at the guests.

Another minute passed and then the baron entered the room, apologizing for the delay. He had been looking for the bill of sale made with Wagner to show the police inspector. Introductions were made and then the baron urged everyone to sit down, taking an armchair for himself.

"Now, how can I help you?"

"Herr Baron, we are here to inquire, if you will, about the connection of Dr. Kurt Wagner with you and Schloss Gemmingen-Eggaberg."

"Well, our whole family is indebted to Dr. Wagner because he rescued our son Franzi from drowning a couple of summers back. Since then our friendship has grown and I agreed to lease him an unused wing of the castle for business meetings with members of his organization. And more recently, I sold him six acres of unused forestland behind and out of sight of the castle. Here," the baron said, leaning forward and extending his hand toward Ludwig, "here are the terms of sale, including the specificity of site."

Ludwig studied the document at length, then remarked: "I see you have given him the right to build on the land providing the edifice or edifices cannot be seen from the road or the castle."

"Yes, that is correct."

"Do you know if he has initiated construction of anything on the grounds yet, Herr Baron?"

"Yes, I believe so, as there have been several tradesmen's trucks passing the castle on the lane that leads from our back parking area into the forest where Dr. Wagner has his acreage."

"But you have seen no structures yourself? I mean you or the Frau Baronin or your son, none of you have walked over there?"

"Well, I do not think that would be proper, now that the land is his, not ours, do you?"

"I am sorry to persist, Herr Baron. Have you been in communication with Dr. Wagner?"

"Oh, yes. He telephoned me just yesterday to ask if he could come for the remaining items in the castle wing he had leased from me."

"And did he mention anything about the acreage you sold him, anything about how it was being used?"

"No, nothing about that, and I didn't ask him, as I believe that is his private business. I know only that he was enormously pleased that his organization would have a permanent site to hold meetings."

"And may I ask what you know about his organization?"

"I know that it is called Doppel-O and has somewhat of an international membership. I do not know specifically what the number of members is, but from their gatherings here at the castle, I would say between twenty and twenty-five, no more."

"Could they be the so-called Inner Circle?"

"I wouldn't know about that."

"And are you aware of what sort of business the Doppel-O does?"

"Yes, Dr. Wagner has told me, and his website confirms it. His organization is devoted to removing public exposure to pornography, especially in public restrooms, schools, museums, films, and television. I think that is a noble endeavor. Surely you have watched the lowering of standards in dress, manners, and conduct of the younger generation, inspired by the trash they see all around them and on television."

"And you are aware of what the name of his organization stands for? The Doppel-O?"

"Yes, but of course I am. 'Obliterate Obscenity' in English. It is a dramatic appellation, but it certainly communicates its goal."

"Are you cognizant of the recent grotesque events concerning Egon Schiele in Wien, Sir?"

"Are you referring to the terrible butcher murder of the guard at your Leopold Museum, Herr Dr. Ohm, and the desecration of the Schiele painting?"

"Yes, we are," answered Ludwig for the group. "And also to the vandalizing of his grave and tombstone as well as the spray painting of another Schiele in a private collection."

"Well, I did not know about the Schiele in private hands, but I did read and hear about the damage to the Leopold Museum's Schiele and Klimt, and to the gravesite, yes."

"One more question, Herr Baron, if I may," Ludwig asked quietly. "Have you talked about these Schiele happenings with Dr. Wagner?"

"No, actually. We only spoke briefly on the phone when he called yesterday. But I do expect to see him when he comes over to pick up the remaining Doppel-O items in the east wing."

"Could we take a look at those items?" Megan broke in suddenly.

"That would be very helpful," Ludwig confirmed.

"I don't suppose there is any harm in that. I think it's mostly just furniture. But yes, we can go over and take a look. I don't imagine that would harm anything. May I offer you some libation first?"

Almost simultaneously Ludwig, Megan, and Hannes declined, Ludwig adding that it was a long drive back to Wien.

"Then kindly follow me," the baron said, leading the way out of the den and back into the long hall. They took a left turn at the other end and entered an equally long hall that ran to the east. This hall opened into a large room that must have been used in previous centuries for a ballroom, as there was a musicians' balcony at one end.

They looked around. Indeed, just as the baron had said, there was only furniture in the great room. Some forty chairs, a long table, and a large chest of drawers. Megan went over to it and carefully opened one of the drawers. It was filled with neatly folded robes. One of them was black, with a fur trim, and a second one was white. The rest of them were red. Megan pulled open the other three drawers of the chest: more robes, all red. Perhaps some forty of them.

She returned to the top drawer and started to lift the black robe up. She felt something metallic brush her hand.

*It was a black metal rose with silver tips.*

# 41

The conversation in Adolf Peschka-Sciele's black Mercedes on the long drive to Krumau was not nearly as animated as the one in Inspector

Ludwig's car had been. Boris Ussachevsky was not a loquacious man. But his striking resemblance to Egon Schiele could not be ignored. The same spiked hair, the same large, startled eyes, the same full lips, and even the same pale complexion.

Adolf tried to pull him out by speaking of Schiele's incessant drawings as a child of the trains that ran under the family's window. Their apartment was above the Tulln railroad station where Schiele's father was the station master. Thus the boy's fascination with trains was understandable, witness the only smile ever caught on camera of Schiele—the one of him at about ten years old, proudly clutching a locomotive.

Did Herr Ussachevsky know the story about the time Schiele's father had come upstairs from work to find drawings of railcars and locomotives stretched throughout the four rooms of the apartment? No? Well, his father was so angry—Egon had not done his homework—that he picked up the drawings and threw them into the ceramic potbelly stove. Egon was inconsolable for several days afterward.

This traumatic tale from Schiele's childhood brought Boris out a bit. He asked Adolf: "Do you have any idea why Schiele never portrayed his father? Seems he drew everyone else in the family—his mother, his two sisters, his uncle—but never his father."

"It does seem strange, doesn't it? I think probably because when he was nine, ten, and older he saw every day what his mother could no longer conceal from her children: their father's steady progression into syphilitic insanity. He began inviting invisible guests to the dining-room table and insisting that the children speak to them, for instance. Things like that. And then you've seen the harrowing photograph of him with Gerti in which he looks indeed like the emaciated ghost of the man he once was."

"Yes, that must have been terribly unnerving," admitted Boris thoughtfully, pleased to have this insight into Egon's childhood, so similar to his own. He too had lost his father when he was fourteen.

"And yet," Adolf continued, proud of the fact that his given name was the same as that of Egon's father, "the boy was sure of his artistic calling even as a ten-year-old. You recall the frontal portrait he drew of himself at that age, bust-length and solemn, with demanding eyes. Well I think I know what it was modeled on. Albrecht Dürer. You may know Dürer's frontal self portrait fingering his fur-lined cloak in Munich?"

"Yes, I do. It is indeed a riveting portrait, presenting himself as though he were Christ," Boris answered. He was intrigued by the possible iconographical connection of a young Egon identifying himself with the great German master.

The two men were silent for awhile. Then Boris decided to bring up the subject of the vision Schiele had of his father once in Krumau.

"What do you think triggered Schiele's hallucination that his father appeared to him during a visit to Krumau?"

"Perhaps because his father, already in a deranged state, had once tried to commit suicide there," Adolf theorized.

"Although he may not have portrayed him ever," said Boris, "his father was constantly in his thoughts from what I know. I have my own ideas about the subject matter of Schiele's large nineteen-twelve allegory, *The Hermits*."

"Oh? The one in which Schiele shows himself as a monk standing with arms akimbo in front of another monk who seems enfeebled, with eyes closed and who, Crespi and others think, must be Klimt?"

"Yes, that one. I, however, do not think the back figure is Klimt at all. I think it is Schiele's *father*."

Adolf was struck by the Russian's theory. It might explain why the second figure was shown as blind and helpless, almost bumping into the front figure. If this were the correct interpretation then Schiele would be showing himself as surviving where his parent did not. Certainly something to consider.

He thought about the symbolism of the two red winter cherries Schiele had depicted on the lower left side of the large canvas: one clinging tenaciously to its upright branch, the other fallen to the ground. This hardly subtle symbolism pointedly referred to the two men, one full of promise and defiance, the other tired and in a state of senility. And this was the canvas onto which Schiele had inscribed a triple assertion of himself as artist: his signature and the year were pointedly printed in white against the dark background.

Adolf began to wonder if the octagonal plan labeled "Pantheon" he had found in Vidovszky's office might have a significance beyond being allegories of the different arts. He knew that all his life Schiele had wanted to create new allegories that incorporated the gravitas of Klimt but spoke to modern concerns and times. The older artist had been fascinated by the beautiful façade, elegant and multifaceted. But Schiele wanted to penetrate beneath society's façade, to plumb his own and others' psyches. One of his outlets in the new age of cultural angst was to turn to landscapes and townscapes. The "dead" city of Krumau, as he often titled his views, played a prominent role in this. How fitting, then, that the pantheon he envisioned would be located in that particular city, his mother's hometown.

The time had passed more quickly than Adolf realized and soon Krumau's outer town walls came into sight. He pulled the car up to the parking area in front of the octagonal police station and was gratified to hear Ussachevsky give a quick gasp.

"This has to be what Schiele was referring to in his drawing," Boris said, gazing at the building set into the wall, three of its octagonal walls jutting out toward the street.

"Now you see why I shared my discovery with you. We must save the Schieles hidden within the bricked-over cellar arches."

Boris jotted down the telephone number of the real estate company emblazoned on a large sign in front of the building. The idea of getting close to Schiele through the medium of the building in front of them appealed greatly to Boris.

"We should get moving on this right away," he said to Adolf.

"Don't you want to look around inside the building, go down into the basement?"

"Yes, of course I do. Let's go inside."

The two men, so different in appearance—the Austrian short and balding, the Russian, tall, slender, and with a head of Schiele hair—got out of the car and walked to the police station's entrance. Inside a constable looked up from the front desk at them inquiringly. Adolf stated that he had been there a few days ago to pay for a speeding ticket, and he was afraid he had left his briefcase down in the basement. Might they go down and take a look?

*182*

"What were you doing in the basement?" the constable asked. "Tickets are paid for up here."

"Oh, I was so fascinated by the octagonal shape of this building that I asked if I could take a look at its foundations. A very kind Inspector took me down to the cellar and that's where I think I may have left my briefcase," Adolf lied with no compunction.

"All right, but you'll have to go down by yourselves. The station is undermanned today and I'm the only one here."

Trying to conceal his elation, Adolf led Boris down the basement steps. The two men walked down the long hall, then stepped into the great cavern that was the cellar. Adolf found the light switch, flipped it, and the seven arches were revealed.

Boris went straight over to one of the plastered arches and held his hands out, taking approximate measurements. Then he exclaimed: "These arches are easily high and wide enough to take the largest of Schiele's canvases. I wonder when the arches were filled in and by whom?"

"Perhaps, since Schiele was stationed in Krumau during the war and in this very building, he bricked them in himself, hoping to protect the paintings until the war was over," Adolf said.

The two men studied Adolf's iPhone photograph of the octagonal building Schiele had drawn. Not wanting to press his luck, he had not brought the precious original drawing with him. Schiele's view was from above and clearly showed the entrance arch they had just walked through. There they were, each of the other seven walls identified by those words "Art," "Music," "Literature," "Science," "Medicine," "Philosophy," and "Love."

"It's interesting that only two of the allegory titles match those of Klimt: 'Medicine' and 'Philosophy,'" Boris commented.

"Do you think Schiele encompassed the field of medicine as one of his seven cultural staples because of his fear—with so much sexual activity—of contracting syphilis?"

"Sounds possible," said Boris. "In fact I think that is a good idea. The range and frequency of Schiele's sexual encounters, especially in his adolescent years, might well have been a form of black magic, warding off the terrible fate of his father.

"Well, why don't you take shots of all seven of these walls and then let's get out of here and over to the real estate office," commanded Boris, pleased that Adolf had agreed with his theory of why "Medicine" had been one of Schiele's allegorical categories.

A pleasant, middle-aged woman with black hair and bangs greeted Boris and Adolf at the real estate office, which was further down the outside ring of Krumau's ancient fortification.

"Ah, yes, the police station property," she answered when they told her why they were there. "It was looked over last week by a Czech soap manufacturer from Prague, but he said that the building in its present state was useless. That he would have to raze the thing and fill up the ancient cellar underneath it."

Adolf looked pale.

"Has he made a bid?" Boris asked calmly.

"No, not yet, but he is checking with his main office and a bid should be coming in a few weeks."

"And the price your agency is asking?"

"We've listed it at four million Euros. Of course it's not going to go for near that, but that's what my boss has priced it at. It's been up for sale for almost a year now, while the new police station was being built, and the soap company is the first real interest we've had. Hard to sell a building that's attached to not one but two historic walls that can't be touched, if you know what I mean," the agent answered garrulously.

"Well, I am interested in acquiring the building as is," Boris announced, looking the woman right in the eyes. "Here is my offer and it would be in cash, payable today: three million, five hundred thousand Euros. And I do not wish to quibble."

The agent's eyes opened wide. "Let me telephone my boss," she said, waving them to two chairs. She disappeared into an inner room and was back within minutes, a wide smile lighting her face.

"My boss says yes, if we can get the paper work and payment today."

"I am amenable to that. I have one stipulation, however."

"What is that?"

"The building must be vacated immediately."

"That too can be accomplished. The new police station is ready. It's just been a question of logistics."

While the two conducted their business Adolf consulted his iPhone again, zooming in on a map of the old town. He could see how the outer city walls circled the small river city almost completely. The octagonal police station was not discernable, pity. But what a dream come true, he congratulated himself.

Then a sobering thought assailed him. Ussachevsky was paying for the building. What would he, Adolf, have to pay for the Schieles within? Would they split fifty-fifty? He had been so hell bent on saving the site that he had not thought out the consequences. Well, the Russian may have the money to buy the building, but *he* had the moral and legal right to the property inside. And it was he, after all, who had found the Schiele drawing, understood its portent, and initiated the project. No, the Russian would have to be content with a division of the contents on a fifty-fifty basis. That was all there was to it.

Adolf Peschka-Schiele was the great grandnephew of Schiele. What he could not know was that Boris Ussachevsky considered himself the reincarnation of Schiele and that *any* work by the artist belonged to him.

# 42

Arnold Moll had not yet returned the Volvo station wagon he had rented in Königsberg to the downtown Hertz rental near his flat in the Singerstrasse. He needed it to transport the Schiele roll to Gmunden. The Grand Master would be astounded. Of this he was certain.

But he wanted to be sure Herr Dr. Wagner wasn't at his Vienna flat on the Spiegelgasse before he made the long drive out to Gmunden. He called the Grand Master's cell phone. It rang six times before transferring the caller to the message box. Moll briefly stated that he was back in Wien from his Königsberg mission and was eager to see him, then hung up.

Almost immediately Moll's phone began ringing. It was the Grand Master. He gave Moll no chance to say anything. Instead he engaged in a tirade against the dead Wolf Schnitt. Did Moll know that he had, without orders, on his own initiative, and knowing Crespi was in Vienna, decided to fly to Dallas and steal her Schiele? The little one showing him naked and standing over a mirror? Did Moll know that? Well, after two failed attempts on Crespi's life, the idiot had botched even the simple burglary job. The police had been alerted by the house alarm system. They shot him dead. Did Moll know that?

Moll tried unsuccessfully to interrupt the tirade deafening his left ear.

Without pausing the Grand Master continued. How could this latest and promising initiate into the Doppel-O's Inner Circle have failed his mission and them so miserably? His disastrous actions could have imperiled the clan, did Moll realize that?

At last Kurt Wagner stopped for breath, giving Moll a chance to speak. "Yes, Schnitt had been a disaster, and yes, it is possible he may have endangered the Doppel-O. But he, Arnold Moll, his trusted second-in-command, had something colossal to hand over to the Grand Master. Was he in Wien or at Gmunden?"

"I am in Gmunden. What is it?"

"I believe it would be better not to discuss it on the phone. But I will leave for Gmunden immediately. And I do believe what I have to show you will make up in part for the terrible disappointment Schnitt has caused you."

"All right then, come, and when you arrive proceed directly to our long house. It is now ninety-nine percent finished." Kurt Wagner did not mention that the replica of Schiele's prison cell was completed. The cell was for himself alone.

Four hours later Moll drove beyond the Schloss back parking area and turned left on the new gravel lane that led through a half-mile of heavy pine forest to the clearing where the new long house stood in all its fresh glory.

Kurt Wagner's bleating motion sensor had signaled the approach of Moll's car and he stepped out of the doorway to meet him. Moll smiled a wan smile and motioned him around to the back of the station wagon. He touched the trunk open button on the dashboard and joined the Grand Master as the trunk lid slowly rose.

"What do you have here?" Wagner asked, looking at the large roll of canvas that had been set crossways in the back.

"Grand Master, I have brought you the other lost Schiele nude self-portrait."

Wagner stared first at Moll, then at the rolled up canvas.

"So you have done it!"

"Yes, Grand Master. It comes to you straight from Königsberg where I recovered it from the house of Sonja Oppenheimer. It was in her attic, untouched, for all these years."

"Let us bring it inside the long house immediately. I must see it."

As the long house still lacked furniture, the two men placed the 60-inch wide by 60-inch high canvas roll on the floor of the empty room. The only furnishing was a large oriental rug in the far northeast corner. Despite a small sprinkle of yellow paint flakes, Moll and Wagner cautiously continued to unroll the canvas. An extraordinary, if faded yellow sight greeted their eyes.

There he was, the young Schiele, quite naked, facing the viewer and resting on one knee, the other bent outward. The genitals were clearly visible. The artist's left hand rested on the thigh of his raised left leg, the tense fingers stretching upward. The right arm, bent at the elbow, supported Schiele's extended right hand with three fingers flailing upward, the thumb and forefinger joined to create an "o."

The artist's tortured features focused on his right hand, communicating an expression of extreme concentration. *His eyes squinted.* This may have been the first time Schiele had signed his work with this secret signature, as the German verb *schielen* means to squint. Later a hostile critic would write of his work: "this artist squints at what others already see."

"You have done well, Arnold Moll, exceedingly well," said Wagner finally.

"Thank you, Grand Master, thank you. What shall we do with the painting? Destroy it?"

"I think not," Wagner said thoughtfully. "There are two possibilities. The first is that we could cover the disgusting genitals as they deserve to be covered and then hang it here in the long house as an inspiration to us all."

"Yes?"

"And the second possibility is that I offer it, as is, to the Russian billionaire who bought the Sotheby's nude self-portrait standing. That would be a financial bonanza for the clan."

"Which are you inclined to do, Grand Master?" Arnold Moll dared to ask.

"You will leave this matter in my hands. I shall decide later what is to be done. For now we shall leave it unrolled, to prevent more damage. Help me carry it over to the far side of our lodge where the rug is," he said, pointing to the northeast corner of the building.

As Moll helped move the canvas, he noticed, extending out a few inches on either side of the oriental rug, what looked like a carefully carpentered, almost invisible trap door in the wooden floor.

But he said nothing. Who was he to question the Grand Master's doings? The trap door, if it were that, might well lead down to a special room for new initiates. Yes, that was it. The general Doppel-O members were unaware of the Inner Circle of S A elite, the Sexual Abstinence adherents of whom that cursed Wolf Schnitt had been such a disastrous member. Initiation of new S A members should be conducted in a secret chamber. How farsighted the Grand Master was!

* * *

In the grand ballroom of Schloss Gemmingen-Eggaberg with the baron, Johannes Ohm, and Konrad Ludwig, Megan's inspection of the black robe in a chest of drawers had displaced a black metal rose with silver tips.

She looked around quickly. The three men were in spirited conversation, with Inspector Ludwig still questioning the baron. Some instinct told Megan not to reveal her discovery while the baron was in the room. Discreetly, she opened her shoulder bag, took out a lens-cleaning cloth and carefully picked up the rose, wrapping the cloth around it, and placed it in an empty side pocket of her bag. It would be most interesting to divine whose fingerprints were on the rose back in Vienna. And it could possibly be a nail in the coffin of the so-called Grand Master of the Doppel-O sect.

She rejoined the men and heard the latest of Ludwig's questions for the baron. The question was a key one.

"Do you know whether or not Dr. Wagner might be at his acreage right now?"

"Of that I have no idea, sorry. I did notice that the construction vehicles regularly passing through my back parking lot all last week were no longer in evidence yesterday or today."

"And, just to confirm, he did not set a fixed time for coming round to pick up the final furniture items from this grand ballroom?"

"That is correct. But he did not need to set a time. Dr. Wagner is always welcome at the Schloss."

Yes, Megan thought, I did the right thing. Better not to let this somewhat naïve castle owner know about the black rose she had just come across.

A few minutes later they were saying their goodbyes to their amicable host. As they returned to the car, Konrad announced to their eager agreement that it was time for them to take the gravel lane that led into the Doppel-O's new acreage and ascertain whether or not Kurt Wagner was on the grounds.

After they were in their car seats Megan said: "Wait a minute, Konrad, don't start the engine yet. I have something to show you both." She drew her metal booty out of her bag pocket, tucked back the surrounding lens-cleaner cloth, and held it up for the two men to see.

"I found this in the top drawer of the chest of drawers in the ballroom."

"Oh, my god!" Hannes exclaimed. "It's the same black metal rose that was on Schiele's gravesite!"

"And on the floor of Antal's flat when his Gerti portrait was spray painted," Megan added.

"And on the floor of the Leopold," Hannes said grimly.

"You were right, Megan, not to touch the thing with your hands. We should be able to lift a whole set of fingerprints from it."

"That's what I was hoping," Megan replied. "It's also significant, I think, that I found the rose within the folds of the only black robe in that chest of drawers. The other robes, except for one white one, were all red."

"Keep it in your purse, Megan, until we get back to Wien," Konrad commanded as he started up the car. "Now let's see what's on the Doppel-O compound, what has been constructed."

They had only driven a few feet down the gravel lane when they met a Volvo station wagon coming toward them in the opposite direction. Making way for the car to pass, Konrad carefully scrutinized the driver, a male of about middle age and size with a bald pate.

After the man passed them, Konrad asked: "Did either of you two recognize him?"

Both Megan and Hannes had to answer in the negative.

"But I got his license number," Megan said with satisfaction.

"Good, but no need," said Konrad, "my car's overhead camera photographed it." Megan's eager amateur detective status was taken down a notch, but nevertheless she was in wonder at modern technology.

The police car proceeded slowly down the lane. About a mile further along they entered an area that had obviously been newly cleared. A large rectangular wooden structure stood before them. Beyond the building was parked a sizzling blue Porsche. It was a hybrid, Konrad commented, as they got out of the car.

They walked past a stack of cedar logs and up to the double door in the center of the building. Konrad knocked. Silence. Konrad knocked again, then tried the door. It was locked. The trio began walking the length of the building, peering into the windows. All they saw was a large empty room with a small recessed circle of dirt lined with rocks in the center. On the near side there was a narrow kitchen and what was obviously a small half-bath beyond. There was no furniture and no carpet, except for an oriental rug in one corner of the building. The roof had a raised, circular piece of metal in the center over the fire pit.

They walked around the back of the building. No sign of anyone. The forest took up its thick foliage again and there were no paths in sight. The parked Porsche could mean someone was around, but it could also just be stored there. Hard to tell, and they didn't have all day.

"Well, I guess we've come to a dead end," Konrad said reluctantly. Megan and Hannes couldn't help but agree, and so they all climbed back into the police car for the long drive back to Vienna.

* * *

The Grand Master had seen Arnold Moll off some five minutes before the police car pulled up. In those five minutes he had moved the Schiele canvas off the rug, rolled it up loosely, and pulled open the trap door, which was attached to the rug by almost invisible thin wires. Gingerly he picked up the Schiele and climbed down the ladder, pulling the trap door closed above him, which in turn pulled the rug back into place over the trap door. He stepped into the cell and tenderly unrolled the Schiele self-portrait. Wagner's toolbox was still in the cell and within seconds he carefully nailed the painting to the wall facing the head of the narrow cot. His work done, he lay down on the cot, his red hair wet with perspiration, and heaved a sigh of pure joy.

*Now before this unholy icon of obscenity he could exercise the three factors that had inspired his founding of the sexual abstinence Inner Circle of his Doppel-O: contemplation, repentance, and punishment.*

# 43

"How is it that you, Megan, came to discover Schiele's prison cell in the first place?" asked Konrad on the long drive back to Wien from Gmunden.

"Oh, let me tell the story!" cried Hannes eagerly, looking fondly at Megan.

"Go ahead," encouraged Megan, curious to hear another person's account of what jump started her scholarly career on Schiele.

"Well, at the advanced age of twenty-eight...isn't that right?"

Megan nodded assent.

"At her advanced age, back in nineteen sixty-three, she realized that not a single scholar had bothered to visit the village of Neulengbach since Schiele's arrest and imprisonment there. So she got herself to the town just a few weeks after arriving in Wien to study the artist's drawings in the Albertina Museum."

"Yes," Megan intervened. "It was there that I studied the drawings Schiele had made in prison with the watercolor and drawing materials Heinrich Benesch had brought him. In addition to four distraught, harrowing self-portraits, he also depicted his grim surroundings: the cell, with its narrow bunk bed and the initials 'M H' carved into the door, the corridor outside, with its wash bucket and mop, and the outside 'door into the open,' as he titled it."

Hannes picked up the tale. "She arrived in Neulengbach armed with a letter of introduction written by the director of the Albertina, Walter Koschatzky. But when she showed it to the desk clerk at the entrance to the district courthouse—the only building in town large enough to have a basement—the official took umbrage at being urged by a metropolitan official to be cooperative. Her being a foreigner didn't help," he laughed.

"Megan, why don't you take it up from here?"

"Oh, all right. The clerk told me that I could not enter the building, that there were *"wichtige Regierungspapiere"*—important government papers stored inside. Nothing I could say, not even that I had come all the way from Texas helped. So I walked away. But not too far away. I stood behind a large tree, collecting my thoughts. Then the noon bell rang and all the courthouse workers swarmed out of the building, including the clerk who wouldn't let me in."

"So what do you think this girl from Texas did then," laughed Hannes. "She walked in *backward* while the others were walking out. Then she spotted the stairs that led down to the basement and took them. Down there she saw the cellar corridor just as Schiele had depicted it, even with a wash bucket and mop standing on end, and the six cell doors. All she had to do was verify which of the six cells had been Schiele's."

"Let me guess," volunteered Konrad. "She looked for the door that had 'M H' carved on its inner side."

"Right you are, Konrad," approved Megan. "It was cell number two and I photographed it from exactly the same perspective that Schiele had drawn it, then took a close-up shot of the initials. Then I turned to photograph the cell's far wall and guess what was there?"

"Important government papers?" asked Konrad.

"No," said Hannes. "There was only firewood, neatly stacked for the winter. That was all."

"You can bet I photographed that too," laughed Megan. "Yes it is true that I discovered Schiele's prison cell, but if I hadn't made careful copies of the artist's prison drawings at the Albertina, I probably wouldn't have had the ability to identify exactly which of the six cells had been Schiele's."

"I am beginning to think we need you on the Vienna detective squad," Konrad said only half-jokingly, thinking about the dogged discovery of a cell that had been Schiele's fifty-one years earlier. And now it was over a hundred years since the artist had been incarcerated. Yet he, his words, and his work were as alive for them today as though it were yesterday.

The trip back did not seem nearly so long as more Schiele stories were exchanged and Megan told them about the informative and sometimes just plain bizarre interviews she had had with Schiele's relatives and sitters. For example, Adele Harms, the artist's sister-in-law, had begun her life story for Megan's Tandberg tape recorder with the sentence: "My father, like all Germans, was bisexual."

As they were approaching Sankt Pölten, they saw two cars—one of them with dented side doors—on the shoulder of the highway. Wondering whether the accident had been reported, Konrad pulled up. Megan and Hannes got out to stretch their legs. One of the two men involved glanced at them after he had finished giving his side of the story to Ludwig. He drew back a step, then said boldly to Megan, "Aren't you Megan Crespi?"

"I am," Megan replied, surprised.

"Yes, I know your face from your book jackets." This had happened to Megan before, but never in Austria.

"Isn't it *terrible* what has happened with Schiele just now in Vienna?" asked the man, expressing exaggerated dismay.

Megan and Hannes nodded solemnly in agreement. The man blabbered on. "Why, why, why would anyone want to destroy paintings by one of our country's greatest artists? And his gravesite? And, oh, when I think of the damage done to the Leopold's glorious Schiele self-portrait and to the artist's elegant, *elegant* portrait of his sister, it's just too awful."

When they were back in the car and on the road again, Megan asked Konrad the name of the man who had come over to talk to them.

"Um, Arnold Moll," he answered. Then he gave a start. "Wait a minute! Isn't that the name of the webmaster for the Doppel-O?"

"Yes, indeed," Megan affirmed, feeling a sudden, warning warmth rush through her veins. "But the real question is: *how did he know about the damage to Antal Maack's Gerti portrait, since news of it was never made public?*"

* * *

The bleat of the motion sensor above his Schiele prison cell replica had not alarmed Kurt Wagner. He was expecting no one. Arnold Moll had just left, and now he desired solitude. Whoever was there could look in vain for him. Wagner contemplated for another ten minutes. Then the motion sensor bleated again. Whoever had come had now gone.

Nevertheless, it was time to go up to the Schloss and retrieve the furniture still in the grand ballroom. The baron and his family were about to leave for their summer villa in Italy and were busy in their wing of the castle. Wagner had arranged to meet two brawny workmen from the town of Gmunden at three o'clock. They were there waiting for him when he pulled up in his Porsche. Wagner let them in the back portal of the Schloss, nodding to the footman who recognized him with a smile. A few minutes later the forty chairs, a table, and a heavy chest of drawers were placed on the flatbed rollers the men had brought with them. They pushed their loads to the back door and to the parking lot where their truck was pulled up. A few minutes later the furniture was safely unloaded and placed inside the long house.

Wagner paid off the workmen, then arranged the chairs in a circle, and dragged the chest of drawers over by the oriental rug. He opened the top drawer just to check on how crumpled the robes might be. They were very crumpled, so he removed them, spreading them out on the chairs for some air. Hadn't he put one of the Doppel-O black roses in that drawer? He looked for it. No sign of one. Oh well, he must have put it somewhere else. But nevertheless it was a bit strange, because he vividly remembered storing one rose with his black robe, just to be ready for the next initiation. He would check his carefully monitored supply when he was back in Wien.

* * *

Moll was in a state of shock. He had just met, face to face, the woman whom the Grand Master had decreed should be obliterated. Obliterated for promoting obscenity. He had actually seen her without her knowledge, the night he had chanced upon her leaning on a male companion's arm as they entered the *Wienerwald* restaurant on the Annagasse. The blasted woman had written *three* books on Austria's most perverse painter, Egon Schiele. His erotic drawings were equaled only by those of Gustav Klimt.

Well, Klimt was next on the Grand Master's list. That promised to be a much more complicated mission, however, since so many of the older artist's drawings of erotica were in the hands of private collectors.

Hadn't it been a triumph for him to access the Gerti portrait at Maack's flat in Wien? And hadn't the new initiate Wolf Schnitt been a disaster? *Two* opportunities to dispatch Crespi and both of them fiascos! It would have been better if the Grand Master had given him the assignment straight away. Hadn't he always proven his loyalty and competence? Who else could have devised such a striking website, could have coded the member names, have devised a whole alphabet of ciphers for the instant translation and retranslation of messages? Yes, it was he, and he alone who had made the Doppel-O web pages indecipherable to the public gaze and police scrutiny, yet easily understood by members who had the ingenious code.

He was indispensible to the Grand Master and it was high time he acknowledged it. Yes, he would ask Herr Dr. Wagner for the privilege, the right even, of being designated the clan's Dedicated Destroyer.

## 44

Konrad Ludwig dropped Hannes off by the Leopold Museum, then drove Megan to Antal's flat. She barely had time to kick off her shoes and collapse on the living room couch when her iPhone rang.

"Professoressa Crespi?"

"Yes?"

"This is Raiberto Bresaola in Milano. We have been in epistolary contact some years ago when I first opened my Galleria La Scala in two-thousand and seven."

"Oh, yes indeed, I remember well. How is your gallery doing?"

"We have been doing quite nicely, thank you, but now we have a mammoth problem and I am hoping you might be willing to help."

"Oh, dear! What is the matter?"

"Well, lately we agreed to buy an early Schiele oil painting that was offered to us by what we thought was an impeccable source. The owner, who lives in Rome, said he had had it in his family going back two generations. We saw that it was listed in the Killar oeuvre catalogue as 'present location unknown,' but the black-and-white photograph of it matches exactly the original oil we now have here in the gallery. We determined that it had to be the same: the artist's nude portrait of his sister Gerti. It measures sixty-by-sixty inches, quite large."

"But this is fantastic that the painting has turned up," Megan said enthusiastically. She thought she would not mention that she actually knew where the other sixty-by-sixty inch "lost" portrait of Gerti nude of 1910 was—at the home of her friend Antal Maack. She especially did not mention it because of the spray-paint attack it had suffered. Antal had not wanted the vandalism reported to the press. She wondered whether the Milan Gerti might be in similar danger.

"Yes, of course it is wonderful that an Egon Schiele has come to light,"

196

agreed Bresaola, "but now we suddenly have a restitution claim against it. And we've already paid the client for the painting."

"Has the claim been initiated by a man named Adolf Peschka-Schiele, by any chance?"

"But how did you *know*! Yes. That is the man, and the letter of intent on his behalf comes from an Austrian lawyer who is well known for restitution cases."

"Hmm. Can you tell me more about your seller? You say ownership goes back two generations."

"Yes, and the man—he's in his mid-fifties, I would say—showed me all the pertinent papers. We were very, very careful, I have to say. The documents showed that the painting came from his grandmother's family."

"And what was the grandmother's surname, do you know?"

"I do. You can't forget it if you recall the history of America's Manhattan Project at Los Alamos during World War Two."

"I don't understand," Megan said becoming irritated that Signor Bresaola was dragging out what should be a simple ticking off of information.

"Oppenheimer," enunciated her interlocutor dramatically.

Megan's ears picked up. How could that be possible? She knew that Schiele's fellow artist Max Oppenheimer had gone to New York after the Anschluss, not Italy. But wait a minute. Didn't Max have a younger brother who also migrated to America with his family—his wife and daughter? Yes, she remembered his name now, Jakob. A Judaic scholar who had to leave great portions of his library behind. His daughter never married, Megan knew that about her, but not her given name or if she stayed in New York.

She asked: "Oppenheimer, you say?"

"Yes, Oppenheimer."

"And your client's name?"

"Simon Oppenheimer."

"And ownership of the Schiele goes back to his grandmother, you tell me?"

"Yes. I have all the family details. His grandmother was Dinah Oppenheimer. She was the daughter of Jakob Oppenheimer, brother of the painter Max Oppenheimer. The family was originally from Vienna but they migrated first to Königsberg, then America to New York. There Dinah met and married an Italian and they moved to Rome in the nineteen-sixties, but after a few months they divorced. She gave the daughter from that marriage her own surname. Then that daughter, Rebecca, had a son, Simon, who was born out of wedlock. He is therefore, as he said, the grandson of Dinah Oppenheimer."

"Well, in this circumstance Signor Bresaola, you have a most unusual lawsuit against you. It's the reverse of many restitution cases in some respects. You have a non-Jewish collector suing for the return of property 'stolen' by a Jewish owner."

"I had not thought of it that way, but I see what you mean. Apparently this Peschka-Schiele is the real thing. I mean as far as his being the great grandnephew of Egon Schiele."

"Yes, that is real enough. Are you aware that he is what you could call a 'professional' complainant'? That he has a number of restitution lawsuits in progress both in Austria and abroad?"

"No, I was not aware. *Diavolo!*"

"Was there any publicity about your acquisition in the Italian papers or television?"

"No, not yet. We only received the artwork at the end of last week and, as it was quite faded, we sent it out to be restored. We weren't going to display it or put it up for sale until restoration had been completed. So, no, there has been no publicity."

"And yet Peschka-Schiele knew about the sale," Megan mused, once again disgusted by the greed and pushiness of the man who so obviously cared not about Schiele's work but only about its market value.

"Oh, I can tell you how that happened, Professoressa. It was another remote descendant of an artist. He lives in Rome and apparently made Simon Oppenheimer's acquaintance there."

"The man's name?"

"Peter Ucciky, the grandson of..."

"...Gustav Klimt. Yes, I know about *that* man," Megan interrupted harshly, recalling how he had dramatically laid claim to a number of Klimt paintings at the conclusion of what turned out to be a dangerous assignation of multiple interested parties in Girdwood Alaska. She had written about this harrowing experience in her first murder mystery, *Killing for Klimt*.

"Well, it seems that Ucciky recently sold a large allegory by Klimt for several hundred million Euros, as you no doubt know. He advised Simon Oppenheimer that he too could be a millionaire. Instead of keeping the family heirloom in a closet, since it was too graphic to display, he should approach a gallery like mine. Until today, when the restitution notice came, I was just happy that he came to me first."

"I agree that this is quite a predicament," sympathized Megan.

"Yes, but we too have lawyers. The reason I have called you is about something extraordinary related to this legal mess."

"Yes?"

"Simon Oppenheimer is also in possession of some twenty Schiele watercolor drawings. They are unsigned and undated, but they certainly look like Schiele's work. They are all portrait studies. A number of them look like the sketches of the composer Arnold Schönberg reproduced in *Killar*."

"Ah ha! This sounds extremely interesting."

"But, regardless of possible restitution problems, we need to have an expert confirm that the drawings are in fact by Schiele. And who better than the author of *Egon Schiele's Portraits*? So I am wondering if you might possibly consider flying over from Texas to take a look at them yourself."

"As a matter of fact, I am in Europe right now. I'm talking to you from Vienna," replied Megan, her passion for travel tweaked.

"Oh! Might we dare hope that you could make a side trip to Milano?"

Megan was intrigued by the idea. Also by the idea of getting away from Wien for a while. And she had not yet made reservations for her return flight home. She found herself saying yes to Bresaola and that she could fly to Milano the next day if flight reservations were to be had.

"I shall make reservations for a round trip for you immediately, Professoressa Crespi. I presume you would be returning to Vienna after visiting here? And do you have any hotel preferences as to where we can put you up?"

"One day in Milano should do it," Megan said, "don't you think? And as for hotels, something near your gallery, please."

"We can certainly do that. We are actually in the Galleria Vittorio Emanuele, at the La Scala end, so we could put you up in the Galleria at the Seven Stars Hotel at the duomo end. How would that be?"

"Perfect! I love walking around the Galleria."

"*Allora*, I shall call you back as soon as your flights and hotel reservation have been confirmed. And thank you, *mille grazie* Professoressa, for agreeing to come."

After they rang off, Megan turned to a silently inquiring Anton and described in detail and in chronological sequence what had taken place.

"Why don't you come with me, Antal?" she asked impulsively.

"Just what I was going to suggest," replied Anton happily.

"Shall we eat in or out?" he added. "I serve a *vitello tonnato* to die for."

"Oh, yum, let's stay in then," replied Megan happily, looking forward to resting a bit after her long drive to and from Gmunden.

"Why don't you just stretch out on the couch and I'll go fix dinner for us," Antal instructed, delighted to be host to his old friend from Hungarian Revolution days.

Megan fell into a happy doze, her feet up on the comfortable living room couch. She was gently awakened by the gorgeous ring tone of Massenet's *Méditation*. It was a happy sounding Raiberto Bresaola on the other end. He had been able to secure the roundtrip flight and a reservation at the Seven Stars Hotel. Megan jotted down the flight information.

"You do understand, don't you, Signor Bresaola, that even if the drawings are by Schiele, I will not sign any official document saying so. I can only write you a letter giving you my opinion, even if the opinion is not what you hope to hear."

"That is good enough for me. A letter from you would bear considerable gravitas either way."

After the call was ended, Megan turned to Antal and said: "It's your turn to make flight reservations. Milano, here we come!" The smell of tonnato sauce was beginning to waft toward her and her mood could not have been happier or more expectant.

# 45

Peschka-Schiele had, joyfully, remained behind in Krumau. Ussachevsky had been compelled by business matters to return to St. Petersburg immediately. But, as he had assured Adolf, he would be in touch several times a day. He left a large amount of cash with the bald little Austrian to pay for the cellar excavation process which was to begin the minute the police staff had permanently quit the building.

That had been accomplished in a matter of three days and Adolf had a locksmith come out to change the locks. The real estate agent had recommended a good excavation and building company, and Adolf had them on the job the fourth morning of his stay in Krumau.

He had spent his free days walking around the historic town, breathing in the same air that Schiele once had, and examining architecture that ranged from gothic to ugly modern. His 2014 Baedeker was never out of his hands as he toured and retoured Schiele's favorite town. What other artist had *three* towns with museums dedicated to him? Tulln, his birthplace, Neulengbach, witness to his imprisonment, and Krumau, his mother's hometown. Schiele had painted the "dead city" of Krumau time and again in poignant fragmented views.

The modest hotel Adolf had chosen was close to the former police station, so he was able to be on site early in the morning when two workmen from the excavation company showed up. He gave them the details of what they were supposed to do. No tearing down of anything, simply a careful dislodging of the hundreds of red bricks that had been plastered over in the cellar. The workmen looked at each other in surprise, but they were not about to question a job assignment.

Adolf remained in the basement, supervising the work and admonishing the men to proceed carefully. They were to stop their excavating when they reached what appeared to be the final bank of bricks. They were to go no further. They should try to ascertain when they were there by frequently tapping on the bricks for any possible echo. This method proved to be tenable and by noon two of the arches had been cleared of bricks, except for a final "curtain," left standing, just as Herr Peschka-Schiele had specified. It was surprising how many bricks had been used to wall up the space, Adolf thought to himself.

He realized he absolutely had to keep a cap on his curiosity as to what lay behind the brick screen. He certainly could not remove those final bricks while the workmen were on the scene. After a break for lunch, the men took up their tools again and began removing bricks from the adjoining arch. It was hard going and by six in the evening only two more arches had been cleared. The dislodged bricks were piling up fast in the center of the cellar. The men would cart them off in the morning.

After the workers left for the day, Adolf walked around the basement tentatively touching the exposed final rise of bricks in one of the cleared arches. Here, behind this last brick curtain may be one of the works Schiele intended for his pantheon. Or perhaps it was this wall, he thought, as he moved to the second exposed vertical sheet of bricks. He touched them reverently, then repeated the procedure at the third arch that had been cleared of bricks.

That evening he telephoned his lawyer in Vienna for any news concerning the Milan restitution case. None yet, he was informed, but the delivery papers had been signed for, so not to worry. Signor Bresaola didn't have the ghost of a chance of beating the charges. The portrait of Gerti nude was one of a row of 1910 nudes Schiele had left with Max Oppenheimer in 1912, shortly after his Neulengbach arrest. He had never asked for them back. But that did not mean they *belonged* to Max Oppenheimer or his descendants. They had merely been caretakers. The rightful owner would be a Schiele relative, and he, Adolf Peschka-Schiele as the artist's great grandnephew, was the closest living relative. Not to worry.

But Adolf did worry. He was given to worrying, and often enough he was justified. Just look now, how he was concerned about the excavation going on in the former police-station building. Could either of the workmen be suspicious about his command not to take down the final brick layer? Might he take a peek and see what lay behind? No, Adolf would have to remain diligent. He must not leave the workmen alone for even a minute. But tomorrow should bring the end of their presence; they would have finished the excavating by the end of the day.

The next day Adolf was waiting for the workmen at eight o'clock. They arrived a few minutes afterward and he led them down into the basement with the merest of greetings. Today, tonight would be the great revelation. And at first work seemed to be progressing well under Adolf's watchful eye. But as the workmen pointed out, and as he could clearly see, the cellar itself was becoming impossibly blocked by the ever-growing pile of bricks. Something had to be done. All three men, despite their masks, were coughing from the plaster and dust polluting the air they were breathing.

"Let us haul off the bricks and we can continue excavating the final arch tomorrow," said the older of the workmen.

Reluctantly, Adolf agreed to the reasonable demand. Revelation would have to be put off by one day. He reported back to Boris, who had phoned him several times a day to check on the progress of the work. Ussachevsky too was frustrated by the slowness and now the delay.

"Stay on top of things," he commanded as he hung up. Adolf, to quiet his nerves, decided to take a longer walk than usual around the town. This time he took a new route and followed the inner city wall around to the back of the castle. As the sun began to set, he rounded one more turn of the wall and stopped with a gasp. Stupefied, he could not move.

*There, set into the city wall was an octagonal building.*

Alexandra Azarova was having a crisis of conscience. Ever since the news came out that the Schiele artwork offered her by one Max Valentin—whose identity she had been unable to verify—she had chided herself for not reporting the incident to the police. Her excuse was that she had to leave

Moscow almost immediately afterward to meet colleagues in Kaliningrad. There, when they came upon the body of Sonja Oppenheimer, slaughtered in her own home, they had been subjected to inquisitions concerning the murder.

Not that they were suspects, but the police were hopeful they might have details that would aid their investigation of the event. Most particularly, they wanted to know whether Igor Borodin, Megan Crespi, or she had any idea why a black metal rose with silver tips had been placed next to the corpse. Neither she nor Igor had, but she saw Megan blanch for a moment. Now, she wondered, why had Megan reacted that way? Did she perhaps know something more than she had told the police, or even her?

She thought of phoning Megan, but she was expecting the arrival at her gallery of Jerome Schwartz from Brazil. He was coming to see the double portrait of his father and grandfather which, after restoration, would be shown in Azarova's gallery museum for a short period of time. The slightly faded portrait still had much of its coloration and she was sure Jerome would be thrilled.

And indeed he was, entering the Gallery Rasputin straight from the airport just a few minutes after Alexandra's bout of soul-searching. The two liked each other immediately and Alexandra reveled in the Brazilian's appreciation of Schiele's masterful double portrait of his father and grandfather.

"Ah, but look at the line here, and here," Jerome said enthusiastically, pointing to the angular contour that defined his father's raised arm. The man was gesturing to the other, older man in the canvas, Jerome's grandfather, who seemed to be turning his back on him. And yet, at the head level, both figures were in concord, sharing the same spatial plane and meeting each other's eyes. Schiele seemed to have caught them in intense conversation and the observer of the canvas, even today, felt guilty of eavesdropping.

In the double portrait of Schiele's friend Heinrich Benesch and son Otto, it was the father who seemed to dominate. In this one the son seemed to be the active force. The father was passive with arms folded protectively across his chest as his offspring appeared to pontificate. An interesting psychological interpretation, whether true or not, Alexandra ventured.

"No, quite true. My grandfather was a quiet, passive man lost in the world of thought, whereas my father was very active and garrulous. He dominated conversations and felt obliged to engage with anyone he met. We children used to feel jealous that he was as interested in other people as he was in us."

They gazed appreciatively at the painting for a time, not commenting any further until Alexandra broke the silence. "You are so very kind to allow us to introduce this Schiele to the Moscow public."

"I believe it is important to show the art world that Schiele painted more than just naked people, himself included," Jerome half-joked.

"Yes, it does seem as if most collectors are more interested in acquiring sensationalist works from his adolescent years than from his more mature years, after he married and war broke out.

"And then there are Schiele's riveting landscapes—those pitiful dead trees—and his beautiful, poignant townscapes. I think he turned to painting those subjects for his salvation whenever he was depressed. The jealousies and machinations so typical of Vienna at his time drove him to the consolation of nature, I think," Jerome summed up.

"Oh, I quite agree. Actually I find his later work far more interesting. I think Schiele's portraits of the two Schwartzes and of the two Benesches are the starting point of a greater empathy toward his subjects, rather than beings on which to stamp his own exaggerated agony."

"Yes, you could say that Schiele moved from angst to empathy," mused Jerome.

"Oh, I like that! I think I'd like to use that as the title for our museum exhibition—'From Angst to Empathy.' I have several early Schiele portrait studies which qualify nicely for the angst part and then your double portrait would demonstrate the empathy aspect. What do you think?"

"Fabulous!" responded Jerome, using a word that peppered his enthusiastic manner of conversation. His body language bespoke his openness as he stood with arms out, bent at the elbow, and palms up, sharing his emotions.

"Now I'd like to take some photographs of the painting to bring back with me to São Paulo."

"Oh, I almost forgot! Of course we took photos for you the day your painting arrived here. You're welcome to take your own as well, but let me also give you the ones we made."

The Gallery Rasputin, with its elegant Art Nouveau interior, was host that day to two very happy art lovers. Occasionally on the Schiele front all things were well.

After Jerome Schwartz left the gallery Alexandra, feeling elated and very protective of Schiele, decided to take the step and inform the international police concerning the fact that she had been offered the stolen work by Max Valentin, if that indeed was actually his name. More difficult was whether or not she would also give Boris Ussachevsky's Solovey gallery as a possible outlet for the Schiele. She decided against this, as it would seem like pure professional jealousy.

Anyway, once alerted to the fact that the canvas had actually been in Russia, and might still be, the police would be checking out all major galleries in the country. So it was pretty sure that Ussachevsky would be questioned. She wondered whether that ruthless Schiele fanatic had bought where she refused to buy, and if so where the Schiele could be now. Certainly not at his gallery or his St. Petersburg home?

Her conscience now clear after she made the call, Alexandra turned her thoughts to showcasing the Schwartz double portrait in a small exhibition she would definitely entitle "From Angst to Empathy." A good summary of the artist's tragically short life, she thought.

* * *

Antal Maack had been able to get reservations on the same noon plane to Milan as Megan's, and they had enjoyed a smooth flight, setting smoothly down on the tarmac at Milan's Malpensa Airport. The name Malpensa had always amused Megan, since it could be interpreted as "bad think."

Both she and Antal only had carryon bags and so within a few minutes they were in a taxi headed for Milan's famous Galleria, one glass-covered arm of which opened onto the busy square of the city's great cathedral, the *duomo di Milano*. Giving it an appreciative glance as they paid off the taxi, Megan and Antal entered the Galleria and quickly registered at their hotel, leaving the bags with the concierge. Then they walked past the cafés and boutique stores toward the La Scala end. Under the glass dome the usual line of young and not so young people had lined up on the mosaic floor to grind with their toes the genitals of the bull of Turin depicted underfoot. This was a superstitious act long thought to bring good luck.

More interesting to Megan, poignant even, was the fact, as she pointed out to Antal, that the architect of the Galleria, Giuseppe Mengoni, after twelve years of unremitting labor on the building, accidentally fell to his death from the dome's archway one day before its completion in the 1870s.

"What terrible irony!" exclaimed Antal, looking up at the iron-and-glass dome with new respect. "Sort of makes me think of the architect of the Vienna Opera house. Didn't he commit suicide shortly after the building was finished?"

"That's right. Eduard van der Null was his name, and it was shortly before the edifice was finished. The emperor had made some negative remark about it and the public called it the 'sunken treasure' because the level of the Ringstrasse was raised about forty inches while the Opera house was being constructed. And the other architect involved died of tuberculosis soon after it was built. So it was also called the 'Königgrätz of architecture,' referring to Austria's military defeat at the Battle of König..."

"Here we are!" interrupted Antal, gently pulling the professorial Megan to a halt in front of the Galleria La Scala. No paintings were displayed in the window which was empty except for an animated green ticker tape, apparently a work of art.

"Megan Crespi for Signor Bresaola," Megan announced to the smiling receptionist.

"*Un momento, signora,*" said the receptionist, buzzing the office in the back. Antal looked around the showroom. There were more animated ticker tapes in various colors and on a coffee table was a catalogue to the show, with a red ticker tape on the cover. He looked at Megan and they both shrugged their shoulders in incomprehension. Were they at the wrong gallery?

"*Professoressa Crespi!* Welcome!" A short, clean-shaven man with a

Toscanini halo of white hair eagerly greeted them and Megan introduced Antal. Raiberto Bresaola looked doubtful for a moment then motioned them both into his office.

"Pay no attention to the art outside," he said. "That is for the tourists, and you'd be amazed how many sales we make of those things. We have to pay Galleria-size rent at this site, after all."

"Where shall we start first?" asked Megan, thinking of the complicated Schiele provenance Bresaola had given her over the phone.

"Let us begin at the beginning. Let me show you the Gerti portrait we bought from Simon Oppenheimer."

Bresaola walked to a double door in the back of the office and quietly pulled the doors open. Megan gasped. There on an easel was a beautifully restored Gerti. She stood facing the beholder with her arms wrapped around the upper part of her tawny naked body. Her face was averted, turned to the right, and her eyes were closed. Yes, this was indeed a Schiele.

"Of its genuineness there is of course no doubt, and the restorer has done a superb job, don't you think?" Bresaola asked.

"An excellent job," Megan acknowledged.

"I have brought Signor Maack along because he owns the other nineteen-ten portrait of Gerti nude, although this information is for your ears only."

"*Certo, certo,*" Bresaola assured her, looking at Antal with new respect and interest.

"I am sure you do not mind if Signor Maack, a Schiele *Kenner*, a knower of Schiele, also sees the twenty drawings you have?" inquired Megan in a tone that brooked no dissent.

But Bresaola was only too happy to have two pairs of expert eyes judge the drawings he had on consignment. The source was the same as that of the Gerti portrait, Simon Oppenheimer, but they were not named in the restitution suit, as their existence was as yet unknown to Peschka-Schiele. And Bresaola hoped to keep it that way, he told Megan and Antal.

"Before we look at the drawings may I see the back of the Gerti canvas?" Megan asked.

"But of course."

Megan walked around the easel and leaned forward to examine the canvas. Yes, it was the same weave and thickness of the canvasses the artist used during 1910 and 1911. She was amused to see that in the center of the canvas Schiele had experimented with different signatures, all of them printed rather than written, with the name Egon on top of the name Schiele All of them were boxed in, along with the date 1910 below the large letters of the name. Megan had seen this type of experiment before in Schiele's works but only on paper, not on a canvas. Interesting.

"Now let us look at the drawings," Bresaola said, inviting his guests to sit down at a long mahogany table extending out from his desk. A large flat box was on the table.

Bresaola removed the lid and lifted a sheet of tissue paper off the first drawing, a portrait study. The medium was a black crayon with green and yellow highlights in gouache and watercolor. The artist's signature and date were missing. Megan was intrigued. She instantly recognized the man portrayed. It was Arnold Schönberg. At least three black crayon portrait studies of the composer from 1917 were known, but none with the addition of color.

Oh, yes, even without the customary signature and date, this was certainly a genuine Schiele.

Megan communicated her thoughts to Signor Bresaola, who heaved a sigh of relief. Then he lifted the next drawing out of the box. It too was a study of Schönberg, as were the next ten drawings, all of them highlighted with colors—colors that changed from terse drawing to terse drawing. How exciting, Megan smiled to herself. Wouldn't the Arnold Schönberg Center in Vienna be thrilled to learn of these drawings!

What a pity that, if their existence became known, they would surely become the object of a restitution lawsuit. That Peschka-Schiele man would stop at nothing to acquire works by his great granduncle. She discussed this grim prospect with Bresaola.

"What if Jakob Oppenheimer, who was a musicologist as well as a Judaic scholar, had acquired the Schönberg portrait studies directly from Schiele? They were both alive and well in nineteen-seventeen. They could have known each other through Jakob's brother Max Oppenheimer."

"*Punto*! I love your supposition. If we could prove that, then the drawings would be safe to handle and could be offered publically for sale," Bresaola said enthusiastically.

"I don't want to throw cold water on your argument, Megan, "said Antal reluctantly, "but why didn't Schönberg himself acquire the portrait studies? And was an oil portrait ever painted?"

"That's a good question. Yes, why didn't Schönberg have them? Perhaps because he simply didn't like them, or perhaps, since he was an amateur painter himself, he felt some sense of competition? Remember, Schönberg once wrote a patron asking him to buy his paintings because in fifty or a hundred years they would become very valuable. And he was right.

"As for your second question, no, there is no known oil portrait by Schiele of the composer."

"May we see the other drawings?" asked Antal, who had been nodding silent agreement with Megan's words.

"Oh, yes, of course," said Bresaola, lifting yet another tissue sheet from the next drawing. This time the portrait study, highlighted again with watercolor and gouache, was of a different person. Both Antal and Megan recognized the man immediately.

"That is the composer Anton Webern!" Megan exclaimed joyfully, recalling at least two black crayon studies she knew Schiele had drawn. "He was another sitter the artist had in common with his friend Max Oppenheimer, who actually did create a 'Schielesque' oil portrait of Webern."

They continued to page through the drawings. Three more of them— all unsigned and undated, but obviously from 1917 or 1918—were of Webern. The drawings showed him seated but without the prop of a chair or chair arms, although it was quite obvious that he was sitting and that one elbow was on a chair arm. It was fascinating to Megan that the terseness and lack of distracting detail in Schiele's studies of the man paralleled the shocking brevity—sometimes lasting only two minutes—of Webern's early Expressionist, atonal compositions.

"Now how appropriate it would be," mused Antal out loud, "if the final drawings were of Schönberg's other pupil, Alban Berg."

"Your wish is my command," said Bresaola, whipping off another tissue sheet from the next drawing and revealing a black crayon study, with watercolor and gouache highlights, of a moon-faced young man with heavy-lidded eyes. No doubt, this was Alban Berg. The remaining three drawings were all variations of the man, highlighted again, with gouache and watercolor, all hues that tended toward deep crimson red. None of the portrait studies had signatures or dates, but they didn't need them. They were all clearly by Schiele. Magnificent portrayals by Schiele.

Megan thought about the strange deaths that overtook Schönberg's two pupils in atonality, a word that Schönberg himself never used about his music. Berg died unnecessarily from blood poisoning at the age of fifty, after trying to treat at home a carbuncle caused by an insect sting.

Webern was shot dead ten years later, in 1945, because of an American soldier's mistaken identification of him as a black marketeer being hunted in the idyllic village of Mittersill. Webern, out of thoughtfulness for his sleeping family, had stepped outside onto the balcony of his house to light up a cigar. That was when the soldier, thinking the flame was a signal, shot him. The soldier suffered remorse all his life and died of alcoholism ten years later.

All these ruminations rushed through Megan's brain as she looked at the rich trove of absolutely genuine Schiele drawings. Who would have thought that the artist would have made so *many* portrait studies of the three composers? Usually the count was anywhere from two to five, at the most. Why such care? And wouldn't it be wonderful if they could all be acquired by the Schönberg Center in Vienna. She broached this thought to Antal and Signor Bresaola. They nodded vigorously in agreement.

"I think your work is cut out for you, Signor Bresaola," Megan declared. "You must get together with Simon Oppenheimer and have him go to work looking through family letters, photographs, and documents to see if he can discover any proof that these drawings were in the possession of Jakob Oppenheimer when he died. Perhaps his mother had information about that, perhaps she wrote an account of it somewhere, in a diary possibly. But Simon must do some dedicated, detailed research now if he hopes to sell these priceless drawings to any reputable dealer."

"*Sì, sì, ho capito*," Bresaola said with fervor. "Now would you be willing to write me a letter giving your opinion that these twenty drawings are the real thing, that they are by Schiele?"

"Yes, that I can do. Lend me the use of your computer and I shall do it right away."

While Megan typed away, Anton asked Signor Bresaola how Simon had reacted when told that the Schiele Gerti portrait he had just sold him was now the object of a restitution lawsuit.

"He was shocked, just shocked."

"Well, then, he should be eager to help you prove the legitimate provenance of the painting, especially since these drawings here are dependant on the same heritage."

"I certainly hope so."

Megan finished her letter and Bresaola printed it for her signature. "Remember," she urged, "this is just an opinion. You would do well to obtain Janette Killar's opinion as well. You do know who she is, correct?"

"But of course I know who she is! Look," he said, pointing to the bookshelf behind his desk, "there are both versions of her catalogues raisonnés, as well as her grandfather's initial oeuvre catalogues. Now, may I offer you and Signor Maack an espresso?"

They accepted with pleasure, then took their leave, glancing once again in pained disapproval at the ticker tape "art." Since they were so close to La Scala they decided to visit its fascinating museum devoted to old musical instruments, set designs, autographed scores, costumes, and, above all, portraits of the composers. One of Megan's favorites was the half-figure bronze of a very dapper-looking Puccini. She fondly remembered his breezy words: "*Amo la caccia, adoro l'automobile*—I love hunting, I love cars." The latter love, thought Megan, was odd, since early in his career Puccini and his wife and son had all been involved in a terrible car wreck that almost took his life.

"Your mind seems to be very much on death today," Antal remarked.

"Oh, I don't think so," Megan brushed aside his comment. She realized, however, that, with the resurfacing of the Oppenheimer family, she had involuntarily been thinking again about the terrible fate of Sonja. Out loud she said: "But thinking of the line back from Simon to his grandfather Jakob and what the relationship was of Jakob, if any, to Schiele *has* taken hold of me. I do so hope that Adolf-the-Pest-Schiele doesn't get this bone in his teeth."

When it came time to choose a restaurant for dinner, Megan asked that they go to her grandparents' favorite place, the Giacomo. It was on Via Pergolesi, where they had lived for many years. Although famous for its seafood, Megan would order her favorite gnocchi. Antal acquiesced. After ending with a gelato at a nearby outdoor café, they walked to their hotel back at the Galleria where, just as in olden times, they slept, nestled in each others' arms.

# 47

The Grand Master had dyed his long red hair a dark brown. After admiring his enhanced likeness to his idol, Albrecht Dürer, he left his Vienna flat on the Spiegelgasse where he had parked his Porsche and drove leisurely to Gmunden. No need to bother the baron, now that he had his own meeting house. It was really so much more convenient than the previous situation, in which the Doppel-O meetings took place in one of the Schloss wings. There had always been the chance that the baron might decide to visit during one of the clan's initiation rites. And now the baron and his family were ensconced at their summer house in Italy and the comings and goings at the Doppel-O meeting house would be unobserved.

Now, if he wanted to, he could actually live in the long house. But a more compelling reason was the proximity of the underground replica of Schiele's prison cell, where he could practice the three principles of the Sexual Abstinence Inner Circle of the Doppel-O cult. He would have plenty of time to engage in this activity, with its exhausting culmination, before calling Arnold Moll to come out to Gmunden and bring his laptop with him. It was time to convene a full meeting of the Doppel-O membership, not just the Inner Circle of the S A.

And it was time that they all knew of the heroic self-sacrifice of the

London member who had eaten himself alive in repentance for having engaged in viewing pornography. Also, it was time that they see and rejoice in the beautiful long house with its smoke hole in the roof, ready to waft to the four winds the smoke that would emerge from their ritual ring around the aromatic cedar logs that would be piled and set on fire for the occasion. In short, Wagner was exceptionally eager to show his community what he had accomplished. And on land that was all their own, offering total privacy and solitude.

The one thing still lacking was what he conceived of as The Link. And yet it was within reach, obtainable. Especially now that the baron and his family had vacated the Schloss.

* * *

Peschka-Schiele was in a state of panic. His longer-than-usual walk around the outer city walls of Krumau had taken him to an unwanted and unexpected sight. There, compactly wedged between the brick walls, was a small octagonal building. Yet his workmen were busy excavating the cellar of another small octagonal building, the one in which he believed Schiele's "pantheon" canvases were hidden. What was *this* building? A watch tower? Oh, my god! Were there any more? He began literally running around the city wall, which curved up and down the hills of the town. Yes! There was another one, embedded again in the wall. Adolf made a complete circuit of the outer city walls. There were three octagonal buildings in toto. He was devastated. His single thought was *Ussachevsky must never know.*

After a sleepless night that seemed to last an eternity, Adolf met his workmen promptly at eight in the morning for the final excavation of the cellar of the building that had been until last week the local police station. The building he had guided Ussachevsky into buying.

For the final time, Adolf enjoined the workers not to remove the final screen of bricks in the two last arches. They obeyed his command and soon all seven of the arches were cleared. They loaded up their wheelbarrows and Adolf paid them off, asking that they leave their hand tools and pick them up late that afternoon. The men, pleased by Adolf's generous payment, agreed and left with their loads of brick.

At last Adolf was alone. His phone rang. It was Boris.

"Have the workmen finished?"

"Yes, they just left. I have their tools and will now take down the brick screens. I shall call you as soon as I have results."

"All right. Just keep me informed."

The conversation had left Adolf feeling raw. He *needed* success. Taking up a hammer and two chisels—one small, the other large—he raised his arms high and began carefully chipping away, first the old mortar, then the bricks. He took care to tap the bricks so they would fall on his side of the wall. He did not want a falling brick to gash the face of a possible canvas inside. After about thirty minutes enough of the wall was taken down for Adolf to take a glimpse at what was on the other side. All he saw was heaps of old clothing. What? He brought a chair over and stood on it in order to see better. Again, heaps and heaps of clothing. But he saw something else as well: human skulls.

Desperately he knocked out the remaining bricks and entered the arch. The skulls, with teeth lining their gaping jaws and seemingly smiling, were attached to the clothes and now he could see that there were bones, raw bones extending from the clothing. Arm bones, leg bones, skeletal feet and hands. This was a roomful of skeletons! A dank odor filled the arch. How long had these remains of living persons been here? Graffiti on the far wall gave the answer. Written in several languages were the words: "DIE, JEWS, DIE!"

Adolf sank to the ground. He had no thoughts, he was a shivering blank. He lay motionless for a full ten minutes then sat up suddenly. There was work to do. The other brick screens had to be taken down. The Schieles would be there—they would, they would!

He did not hear himself sob as he hammered at the bricks, more carelessly now, more desperately now. The second arch's screen gave way, the bricks tumbling noisily to the ground. Here would be the Schieles. But no, here were more skeletons, more stinking clothes, more graffiti. Desperately Adolf tore down the remaining five brick screens. Each chamber contained the same gruesome scene. This had been Krumau's short cut to Theresienstadt! Not all the Jews had been shipped out. The ones here had been taken care of locally.

What about the other three octagonal buildings he had discovered last night? There was still hope. Like a madman Adolf grabbed his tools and ran out of the building, leaving the doors unlocked and open. He raced to the first octagonal building he had come upon the evening before. No one was around. He smashed his way inside. The place was empty. Desperately he looked around for a door to a cellar. There was no door, no cellar.

Adolf ran along the deserted city wall to the next octagonal building and repeated his smash-in. Nothing. Out of breath he staggered on to the last octagonal building. The paintings *had* to be here. There *had* to be a cellar. Nothing. He threw himself down on his back in the empty room that had once been a watch tower. It, and the other two octagonals had simply been watch towers, nothing more. He had *not* been wrong about the police station building. Schiele *had* been stationed there. Only he had not hidden his paintings there. Was that Adolf 's fault?

He became aware of his phone ringing. Should he answer it? He knew who it would be. Better not to answer it. He had no explanation. Slowly he walked back to the former police station and returned the tools he had borrowed. Then, in a daze, he walked to his hotel and threw himself on the bed, ignoring the persistent ringing of his phone. What a humiliation! How could he have been so wrong? How could he face Boris Ussachevsky? He began to vomit.

\* \* \*

Boris was standing at his St. Petersburg desk, his cell phone pressed to his ear. He was livid with anger. He may have been a billionaire but he couldn't control everything. Why didn't Peschka-Schiele answer his phone? Did he have bad news? Did he have *any* news? What in hell's name was going on? He would find out and he would find out in person. Calling his standby pilot at the Pulkovo Airport, he instructed him to be ready to take off in half an hour for Turany Airport in Brno, the Czech city he gauged to be nearest Krumau.

When he pulled up at the general aviation hangar, his pilot had his Cessna Citation M2 out on the runway and ready to take off. Boris clambered aboard and they were off for the two-hour and twelve-minute flight. Boris called ahead and a black Opel GT was waiting for him on the tarmac when he arrived. Barely taking time to instruct his pilot to access the hangar and await his return, he jumped into the roadster and sped onto the highway for Krumau.

He made the three-hour drive in two hours and forty minutes. Shortly afterward he pulled up in front of the hotel where Peschka-Schiele was staying. Demanding the room number from the startled desk clerk, he raced to the Austrian's room and pounded on the door. No answer. Boris forced the door.

Too late. Peschka-Schiele had strapped his belt around his throat and was hanging from the ceiling lamp, his neck broken.


# 48

Megan and Antal had enjoyed a leisurely breakfast at their Milan hotel before taking a taxi to Malpensa Airport. They felt the Italian trip had been a triumph. It had been exhilarating to look at so many Schieles at the Galleria La Scala. And Raiberto Bresaola certainly seemed like a decent fellow. They hoped he would have success with the restitution business. From Antal's point of view, and he was a lawyer after all, Bresaola had a good chance at winning the Austrian's lawsuit against him.

Upon their return to Vienna and Antal's flat that afternoon, Megan made phone calls to Dallas to inform Claire and Tina what she was up to and that she had just come back from Milan.

Antal took a look at the day's newspaper which had been delivered that morning to his door. A short article on one of the inside pages caught his attention: "Austrian commits suicide in Krumau."

"Megan," he said urgently, waving the newspaper before her eyes, "come read this when you get off the line." Megan cut the conversation with her sister short, after being assured that her house and Button were both in good shape.

"What's up?"

"Here, read this."

Megan read the article. What? She read it again. The Austrian had been identified as one Adolf Peschka-Schiele. He had hung himself in his hotel room. He had not left a note and there was no known motive for his suicide.

"I can't help but heave a huge sigh of relief," Megan finally said, wondering why on earth this man who had several restituted Schieles and was expecting to win several more, why he would have done away with himself. And why in Krumau of all places? There had to be a Schiele connection. Why else would a fanatical collector of Schiele be there?

Megan decided to call Hannes at the Leopold Museum. He must know the inside details about the suicide.

"Welcome back from Milan," said Hannes, when his secretary told him who was calling.

"Thank you. Tell me what you know about the Peschka-Schiele suicide?"

"Yes, isn't that the most bizarre thing you've ever heard? With all his Schiele lawsuit wins, the man must have been a millionaire several times over. Why would he want to take his own life? And why in Krumau of all places?"

"I was hoping you'd have some answers for *me*," Megan said.

"All I know is what Ludwig told me on the phone when I called him about it. Peschka-Schiele was found with his own belt about his neck. He had hanged himself in his hotel room. No notes, nothing to explain why."

"Do the police know how the suicide was discovered?"

"Yes, and here's the strange thing. His death was discovered by a Russian national who had arrived in Krumau only a few minutes before."

"A *Russian* national? Was it a man or a woman?" Megan asked, thinking of both Boris Ussachevsky and Alexandra Azarova."

"It was a man."

"Ludwig didn't say who?"

"No, but we only talked a few minutes."

"Do you think I could call Ludwig and ask if he knows the name of the Russian?"

"It wouldn't hurt to try."

"All right. Give me his number and I'll get back to you if I have any news. Stand by."

Megan wrote down the number and hung up. She waited a minute, thinking things over. If it was a man, and he was Russian, there could be only one candidate: Ussachevsky. And he would of course have some interest in Krumau because of Schiele's attachmment to the Czech town.

Ludwig answered the phone and immediately corroborated Megan's suspicion. The man's name was Boris Ussachevsky. Megan could not suppress a gasp.

"All we know at this stage is that he gave a statement to the local police and then was allowed to leave. Seems he had just arrived by car and was eager to leave again, now that the object of his visit—Adolf Peschka-Schiele—was dead."

"Did he say *why* he had gone to visit the dead man?"

"Yes, he said it was on a business matter having to do with a building he had recently bought in Krumau. The police checked and sure enough he had purchased a former police station there. So they allowed the man to go. That's all I know. Did they make a mistake in releasing him, do you think?"

"Possibly. Do you think you could check out the dead man's apartment? I know he lives, um, *lived* here in Wien."

"We were going to do that today. His address is on the Brandstrasse in the center of town. Would you like to go with us?"

"If I get to the station, say, in thirty minutes from now would that work in with your plans?"

"Absolutely. We weren't going to go until after three, so come on over."

Megan told the news to a fascinated Antal. Things with his old friend just continued to be lively. He discreetly did not ask to come along, even though he would have been pleased to be in on another Crespi adventure.

Another forty-five minutes found Megan, Ludwig, and a detective named Horst Überfall inside Peschka's-Schiele elegant apartment on the Brandstrasse. The front windows had a view of the back of the Peterskirche. But the den had no windows. And there were no book cases. Only floor-to-ceiling Schiele works on the walls, most of them portrait drawings from the artist's middle years. But two of the works were oils, and to Megan's practiced eye, both from 1914. The signatures and dates inscribed at the lower left confirmed her judgment. The two paintings faced each other across the room. Both were landscapes, one of a low mill building that stretched along green grass in the center of the canvas; the other a lone tree, bereft of leaves, weather-beaten and fragile against a whitish background of faintly articulated low hills. Both were reproduced in Killar, as were all the drawings, to the best of her memory.

"Well, this is *quite* a collection," Ludwig commented finally. Detective Überfall was inspecting the other rooms. He returned to the den and looked through the desk drawers. He held up a sheath of papers.

"Looks like these are all legal documents pertaining to outstanding lawsuits," he said, waving them at Megan and Ludwig.

"What is your procedure here, Konrad?" Megan asked, curious to know what would happen to Peschka-Schiele's papers and properties.

"We'll have to check for any known relatives, and that means interviewing the other occupants of this building, his lawyers, and his business associates. So for now we will have to collect any documents we find that could be useful and then close off the apartment to prevent entry by those who might have a key."

"Then I'll leave you two to your work, Konrad, Detective Überfall," said Megan. She had just discreetly taken photographs of all the den walls' images with her Google Glass, stopping in front of both landscapes to obtain the best view. She wanted to show all these Schiele works to Hannes and Antal, confidentially, of course.

But art historians will be art historians.

## 49

Arnold Moll was still upset that he had come upon Megan Crespi in person when he was involved in that stupid minor accident on the drive back from Gmunden. She might suspect that he was somehow involved in the two failed attempts on her life. No, he could have told her, if I had been the one, you would most certainly be dead. It was that bungling Wolf Schnitt who was after you, not I.

Now Moll had been called back out to Gmunden by the Grand Master. He wondered what was up. Did it have anything to do with the suicide of Peschka-Schiele he had read about in the morning paper? Well, he would know in a few more minutes, he realized, as he turned down the gravel lane that led from the back of Schloss Gemmingen-Eggaberg to the Doppel-O long house.

Kurt Wagner was waiting for him and he was in a most genial mood. Yes, he had read about the Peschka-Schiele affair, but as he was not known to own any obscene works by Schiele, the death did not interest him. It was quite a different matter that had caused him to beckon Moll to Gmunden.

"Moll, my good man, it is time for us to convene the full membership of the Doppel-O. As you saw when you drove up, the long house is finished and I want all our members to see what has been accomplished here on our very private property."

"Ah, at last your efforts will be rewarded, Grand Master. What a fine idea."

"Yes, we will convene all our members, including our man in London who works at Sotheby's and our agent in Milan, reliable Lorenzo Ladro."

"So that's why you wanted me to bring my laptop with me?" Moll asked, knowing that with his firewall it would be next to impossible to hack into it. And even if they did, the code would still be protected by his encryption filter.

"Yes. So make yourself comfortable," Wagner said, gesturing to the chair he had pulled up to the single table in the room.

"And what date would you like our assemblage to take place?"

"Immediately! Let's make it for day after tomorrow, the last day in March."

"March thirty-first it is then," said Moll, sitting down at the long table and setting up his computer. The call to meet would be going out to some forty Doppel-O members, including the S A Inner Circle associates. In the unlikely event of hacking, Moll would be sending out the invites individually rather than as a group, as each member had a different code.

"While you work I'm going to take a walk," Wagner announced.

That was fine with Moll. He always felt a bit intimidated by the presence of the Grand Master. And he had hoped for more praise for the fact that he had brought back from Russia the large Schiele self-portrait. If all the Grand Master saw in him was that he was a computer geek, Moll would be greatly offended. Had he not succeeded where Schnitt had failed?

Glumly, but conscientiously he set to work.

* * *

About an hour after Megan had left the two policemen to do their work sifting through Peschka-Schiele's things, she received an excited phone call from Konrad Ludwig.

"Megan! I think we have found something that will interest you. I'm going to send you a photo of it by e-mail. Let me know what you think when you receive it, okay?"

"Terrific! I'll hang up so you can send it now."

As soon as she saw that Ludwig's e-mail with its photo had come in, Megan opened it up. The photo showed a drawing by Schiele of an octagonal building she had seen once before in the Albertina Museum, the one titled "Mausoleum." This new drawing showed an identical octagon, seen from above, as in the Albertina ground-plan drawing. It was, however, not labeled "Mausoleum" but "Pantheon." Around the sides of the octagon Schiele had written seven words or categories: "Art," "Music," "Literature," "Science," "Medicine," "Philosophy," and "Love."

"This is sensational!" cried Megan, calling Ludwig back. "It means that Schiele had *two* octagonal buildings in mind. That he envisioned one as a mausoleum—goodness knows for what, perhaps the war dead—and the other as a pantheon. A pantheon to the arts and sciences, with a bit of love thrown in as a bonus!"

"I'm pleased that you are pleased," beamed Ludwig over the phone. "And I'll call you if we come across any more finds like that. So far we only have legal documents, a bank account, and credit card enumerations. Nothing special there, except perhaps the *size* of the bank account."

Megan could hardly wait to share this good news as well as her photos of Peschka-Schiele's art trove with Hannes and Antal. She called them both, setting up dinner at the *Wienerwald* on the Annagasse for six o'clock that evening.

In the meantime she had an idea—a brainstorm, really—and she was surprised it had not dawned on her before. Why not go back to Schiele's Wattmangasse building? The new Egon Schiele Museum where the spray painting of photographs of Schiele had occurred was at Wattmanngasse No. 8. Schiele's last studio and home had been at Wattmanngasse No. 6, but as she had discovered when out there to see the Schiele museum, that building was now boarded up. But what if there were a way to access the *basement* of that abandoned building? Perhaps the allegories specified in Schiele's "Pantheon" drawing had been stored in the Wattmanngasse No. 6 cellar.

Never mind that the Pantheon drawing distinctly had the word "Krumau" written on the bottom of the sheet. That may simply have been the site Schiele *wished* to have for his pantheon, not where the paintings for it actually were. After all, his last year of duty was spent in Vienna at the Army Museum, thanks to some strings a highly placed officer friend had pulled. And during the war Schiele would have needed to store them somewhere. Why not in his Wattmanngasse studio, with its garden access to the building's basement?

How come no one in recent times had ever visited the building's basement looking for paintings that might have been left there by Egon after his oh-so-sudden death from the flu epidemic that had claimed his wife Edith just a few days before? Well, of course, in 1918 his mother and sisters had done so when they cleared things out. And probably a few of his patrons had checked out the cellar as well. And had there been any large paintings, even if unfinished, they would surely have been known and mentioned in Killar.

Megan had visited the Wattmanngasse address when she was doing her first research on the artist. But there was nothing to be seen. People there didn't even know who Schiele was, much less which floor he had rented. Megan was pretty sure it must have been the top floor for the light, as with his Hietzinger Hauptstrasse apartment. The thing for her now was to ascertain whether the Wattmanngasse building's basement could be entered. All those old buildings out there had huge cellars. Perhaps she would discover another bonanza, as she had in the Hietzinger Hauptstrasse basement. She hailed a passing taxi. This was far more exciting than sifting through that horrible Peschka-Schiele's papers.

In the taxi she phoned Raiberto Bresaola to tell him the good news that, with Peschka-Schiele's death, the restitution suit he had put into motion against him would most likely be dropped.

"*Meraviglioso!*" he had shouted through the phone, causing her ear to pop. They chatted excitedly for a few minutes more then, as the taxi neared Wattmanngasse, Megan said a merry farewell. She had made one man very, very happy. And now, perhaps, she may well be on the way, some fifty years after the Schiele prison cell discovery, to finding where the artist had stored his Pantheon paintings, maybe even the Mausoleum works. If indeed he had had a chance during the war years to paint such works.

The taxi started to make a left turn onto the Wattmanngasse off the Hanselmayergasse but a large sign blocked entry to the street: CONSTRUCTION ZONE.

"Oh, no! Not already!" Megan couldn't help exclaiming. "I'll walk the rest of the way," she told the driver, paying him off. She had a bad feeling about the way things were turning out and she had a right to worry, as she found out a minute later. *The house at Number 6 was undergoing demolition.*

The whole demolition area was blocked off from pedestrians with construction fencing. It was lined with white plastic that did double duty: to block prying eyes and to protect people from flying debris. Megan walked to a break in the fence where a workman stood talking to the driver of a large bulldozer.

"What's going on? Are you boys going to tear down the whole building?" Megan asked, trying to affect a friendly Viennese accent.

"Yeah. They're going to put in a fancy condominium complex here," answered the construction worker.

"Are you going to dig up the basement as well?"

"Goes without saying."

"Uh huh. And what's your time schedule?"

"We should have this baby leveled by the beginning of next week."

"Does that include digging up the cellar?"

"Nope, not yet. First we have to remove the debris once we get the building walls down. But the excavator is here," said the man, pointing to another heavy equipment machine with a giant iron-toothed bucket at the ready.

Megan thanked the man and walked slowly away, eyeing the containing fence and wondering how she could breech it after the workmen had gone home. Lucky she always wore slacks.

And now she was about to benefit from the way she dressed. Pretty sure that she could climb up and over the fence that very evening, she walked back to the Maxingstrasse and a taxi stand. By six that evening she and Antal were sitting in the *Wienerwald* waiting for Hannes to show up. This he did a few minutes later with a wide grin on his face.

"What do you say about the suicide of Adolf Peschka-Schiele?"

"Well, of course, it's always sad when anybody commits suicide, but in this case it is probably a boon to the art world in general, and to owners of Schiele works in particular," Antal said, priding himself on the fact that his *Gerti*, obtained at the Dorotheum auction so many decades ago, had an impeccable provenance.

"I can tell you that a certain Italian in Milan was thrilled by the 'sad' news," added Megan.

"So is the museum world," Hannes stated in an undertone and with a certain finality.

After they had ordered, Megan turned to them with a mischievous glint in her eyes.

"How would you two like to accompany me on a break in this evening?"

"What sort of break in are you talking about?" asked Antal, who had noticed how excited Megan had seemed when she got back to his apartment late that afternoon.

"Yes, what are you planning now?" added Hannes, knowing that this plucky scholar from Texas, who spoke Italian and German almost without the trace of an accent, was not one to let hurdles, linguistic or physical, get in her way.

"I'm thinking about Wattmanngasse Number Six."

"Schiele's last studio?" Antal asked.

"Why go there, and why break in?" Hannes queried.

"Because they are in the act of demolishing both the building and the cellar to make way for a bunch of condominiums."

"And that should concern us? After all, Schiele's apartment and studio were thoroughly emptied after his death. His mother and his sisters divided up the artworks and the furniture. You know that. You've photographed the sisters with their Schiele works and the black cabinet and its contents that went to Gerti. There's been nothing of his there for decades," Hannes said pessimistically.

"Yes, but did any of these people go into the basement?"

"I think it's very likely that they did, yes," said Hannes. "I don't mean to pour cold water on your nice warm fire, *Liebchen*, but I think your idea is unfeasible."

"I just feel we should take a look and maybe getting a demolition company to help isn't such a crazy idea."

"Okay, if you can persuade them. That should be pretty tough, since they work on a tight schedule."

"Right. So that's why I want to do a reconnaissance this evening after dinner. It wouldn't really be a break in, just a look in."

"I think you're crazy, Megan. And what if we were stopped and recognized? Can't you just see the headlines: 'Crazy American Scholar and Irresponsible Leopold Museum Director Caught Vandalizing Construction Site!'"

They all had to laugh at the prospect.

"But even so, Hannes, I'd truly like to take a look tonight before the teardown gets any worse."

Their dinners arrived and they began to eat. They had all ordered Wienerschnitzel. The conversation turned to other topics related to Schiele, mostly how the slow police investigation of the Doppel-O was coming along. The website master, Arnold Moll, was squeaky clean, Hannes reported.

"Oh, I forgot to tell you, Antal. Hannes and I came face to face with him on our drive back from Gmunden. He'd been in a minor car accident and Inspector Ludwig stopped to check on things. He certainly doesn't *look* as though he might be engaged in criminal activities."

"You should know by now Megan that..."

"...looks are deceiving," Megan completed huffily.

After desert—*Apfelstrudel* for all—had come and gone, Hannes looked kindly at Megan and said: "Look. If you and Antal want to do some nighttime snooping, I can't stop you. But why not wait until the daytime and simply *ask* if you can take a look?"

"Well, that is plan B," replied Megan, "and I promise you that if we come up with anything that suggests demolition be temporarily stopped, we'll go to the foreman immediately."

Antal was only mildly surprised to find he had been included in the nocturnal break in, but he put on a brave face and seconded Megan's plan and promise.

By seven-thirty, as they left the restaurant, Hannes wished them good luck and disappeared down the Annagasse. Antal had his car parked on the next street, the Krugerstrasse, and they walked briskly over to it.

"Yes, not to worry," Antal said as he turned the ignition key, "I do have two very powerful flashlights in the car."

Some ten minutes later they were parked at the top of Wattmanngasse. Hearing their footsteps echo on the empty sidewalk, they walked down to No. 6 and the surrounding wire fence with its white sheeting. They examined the lock where the fence gates were open during the day.

"Doesn't look as though we can get in this way," concluded Antal, gently pushing against the gates.

"That's why I am ready to climb over it and I know just the place to do so. Follow me."

Antal sighed but followed good naturedly.

They went around to the side of the building and stopped at a place where the fence seemed dented inwards.

"Here's the spot I sighted earlier today. I'm pretty sure we can get up and over without scratching ourselves on the wire."

"No, *absolutely* not, ," declared an exasperated Antal. "We're going to walk back to the front gates and try to separate them enough so that you at least can slip in.

As it was, their joint efforts at pushing against the lower part of one gate opened up enough space so that they were each able to squeeze through. With the aid of their flashlights they slowly moved inside the building's shell looking for anything that might signify a basement door. At the back of the building a flight of stairs was picked up by their flashlights. It led downward, below ground level, but the stairs were covered with small irregular pieces of cement that had fallen on them from the demolition work above.

"Let's clear the steps a bit," said Megan, "I think I can get down into the basement." The two friends worked with their hands, hauling the rough pieces of cement out of the stairway. Finally, they had cleared enough debris to make it possible for Megan to inch her way down.

"Yes, this is the cellar!" she shouted up to Antal, who was beaming his flashlight down to illuminate Megan's descent.

"You don't need to come down. I'll just give a look around," she told him. Slowly and methodically Megan began to walk the grid that consti- tuted the basement. It was empty. Nothing was stored there, no suitcases, no boxes, nothing. What a disappointment. Suddenly something moved in the dark. It was a very large rat.

"All right, Antal, let's get out of here," Megan shouted up, starting to ascend the narrow space they had cleared on the stairs.

They walked back to the gates and repeated the process in reverse, with Antal pressing against the lower half of the gate again so Megan could slip through. He followed her.

"Don't fret too much, Megan," Antal tried to comfort his old friend as he drove them back to town and his apartment. "Too many years have passed, that's the problem. And even if Schiele had stored canvases in the

Wattmanngasse basement, they surely would have been removed by his family. Remember Killar does state that some of the unfinished allegorical paintings went to his mother, and others to his sisters."

"Yes, I know, I know," Megan said glumly.

"But you know what? I'm going to go back there in the daylight and talk to the workmen."

"You never give up, do you?"

Late that evening Megan called Claire and Tina to report on things. They both asked the same question: when are you coming home?

"Soon, really, soon, I promise," Megan attempted to mollify them. She hoped she could tie things up in Wien in the next day or two. And surely Button must be wondering where his human was all this time.

The next morning Megan took public transportation back to the Wattmanngasse work site at No. 6. She walked over to the same workman she had spoken to the day before and started up a friendly chat about the weather and deadlines.

"Have all the apartments been completely emptied, or do you sometimes find that things have been left as you knock down walls?"

"Officially they have been cleared of all possessions, but you'd be surprised how many peculiar items literally fall through the cracks."

"Oh, like what?"

"Books, pots, silverware, toys and so on. We don't hold on to the stuff. It's mostly just junk. Except we do keep the toys—in those boxes over there—for any of the workmen who might like to take something home to their families."

"Might I take a look in the boxes?" Megan asked, feeling a strange sort of instinct kick in.

"Yeah, sure, and if you see something you like you can take it home to *your* grandkids."

Startled to be reminded that she looked like and was a senior citizen, Megan paused a moment, then thanked the workman and walked over to the boxes. They were full of stuffed animals, teddy bears being the most popular. Then there were a few dolls, miniature trucks, and trains. Down at the bottom of the second box was a large doll with yellow hair and a little wooden horse.

Wait a minute! *A little wooden horse?*

Megan held it up. It was obviously very old and it had only three legs. *Only three legs?* That is how many legs Schiele's favorite wooden horse had. That is the horse with which he was photographed in 1914 by Trčka. I am holding Schiele's horse in my hand.

Megan felt she might pass out with excitement. She slipped the precious object into her shoulder bag and nodded to the workman in thanks as she walked past him and up the Wattmanngasse. There she paused and withdrew the toy horse from her bag. Did this little three-legged horse have a secret compartment like the one at the Wien Museum? She grasped the little head gently. Yes, it folded back to reveal a small compartment. *And, just like the four-legged horse at the Wien Museum, it contained a key!*

# 50

While Arnold Moll went to work on his computer convening the Doppel-O membership, the Grand Master took a walk. He paced down the gravel lane that led to the back of the Schloss. He had never surrendered his key but found he did not need it. The back door was unlocked. Wagner entered, looking for the footman. He found him in the kitchen and was greeted by him genially. There were no other servants around.

"Where is everyone?" Wagner asked.

"Now that the master and his family are away in Italy we only have a skeleton staff. And tonight we are all going to attend the fireworks festival down in Gmunden."

"I see," said Wagner, delighted by the news he had just heard. "Well, I only wanted to drop off a few items that I had borrowed from the grand ballroom, but thought I should check first to be sure someone was here."

"I'll be here until eight, but after that I'm closing up the Schloss while we all go down to the festival."

"Oh, well, tomorrow will be soon enough."

Wagner wished the man well and went back up the lane to his long house. Moll was in the middle of contacting the membership, so Wagner went to the austere kitchen and made himself some white tea. He used a cast iron red tea pot and drank from a matching iron vessel. He did not bother offering any to Moll.

* * *

Boris Ussachevsky sat in his office reading the St. Petersburg newspapers. There was a short article about Alexandra Azarova's forthcoming exhibition in Moscow. It was going to showcase a "recently discovered" Schiele, the *Double Portrait of Paul and Peter Schwartz* of 1913.

What the article did not address was the ownership of the work, so Ussachevsky presumed that it belonged to Azarova herself, as the show was going to take place not in her gallery but in her museum. What a damnable coup! How could it be that she, and not he, had brought the work to light? He was consumed with envy and hatred. After all, he had so many expensive feelers out, in so many countries. It had to be a question of the woman's sheer dumb luck.

But, he determined, it would be the last lucky thing Azarova would ever encounter. It was time that his major competitor in Russia be put out of business. Permanently. How would he do it? Possibly a devastating fire that would consume her gallery? Yes. He would have to move cautiously but now he had a plan.

# 51

Kurt Wagner suggested to his geek Moll that he plan to return to the long house a couple of hours before the Doppel-O membership convened in two days. Moll was a bit irked that the Grand Master did not invite him to stay over, but on the other hand, there was no place for either of them to sleep on the newly acquired property, just the empty long house. As he drove off, his work done for now, Moll wondered if the Grand Master would be returning to Vienna in the interim as well, or would he be staying at his usual Seehotel Schwan in Gmunden.

It would have been gracious of the Grand Master to offer to put him up at the hotel rather than letting him make the three-and-a-half hour drive back to Wien. And then back out again so soon. No, he shook his head, there was just no two ways about it: the Grand Master did not appreciate him and all he had done for the cause. Even murder.

As it was, the Grand Master did not immediately return to the Seehotel Schwan. Instead, as soon as night fell and the fireworks began in the town below, he took a powerful flashlight and drove to the Schloss. He unlocked the back double doors. No one was around. All the staff were down in Gmunden.

He strode purposefully into the living quarters of the baron and on through to the two-story library. On the far wall, in an elegant gold frame, hung the reproduction of Dürer's self-portrait. Only a true Dürer *Kenner* would realize it was not the real thing. Wagner went straight to the painting and pulled out the large leather volume concealing the lever that afforded entry to the treasure within. He pushed down on the lever and the entire painting panel began to revolve slowly inward, revealing the small inner room Wagner had seen before. There, on the center wall opposite him, was the genuine Dürer returning his reverent gaze.

Wagner, his red, shoulder-length hair freshly dyed dark brown, was now Dürer's twenty-first-century double, and as he worked to liberate the unblinking self-portrait from the wall, he experienced a feeling of blissful approbation for what he was doing—approval from the painter himself.

When he completed his work Wagner revolved the wall panel back until it was flush with the library wall. Then, slowly, he carried the precious painting with him back to the servants' quarters and out the back entry, taking care to lock the double doors again. It seemed to take only seconds to drive back up the gravel lane to the long house.

In another few minutes he had descended into Schiele's prison-cell replica and placed the framed Dürer self-portrait directly underneath the Schiele self-portrait. They both returned his wondering gaze. Oh, such guidance, such merging of meteors could only come from above. This moment was divine. He would have to undergo special punishment for the orgasm that caught him unexpectedly.

# 52

Megan could hardly contain her excitement. In her trembling hands lay Schiele's original three-legged wooden toy horse and it contained a key! Now if only she could ascertain what the key was for. As she walked over to the taxi bank at Maxingstrasse, she took out her iPhone. Whom to tell first? Antal? Hannes? Dietrich? Or call the US: Janette? Claire? Tina?

She decided to call Antal first. He was nonplussed. "How right you were to go back to Wattmanngasse in the daylight and talk to the foreman, Megan. What is your plan now?"

"I'm taking a taxi as we speak and am on my way over to Hietzinger Hauptstrasse right now. There might be more than one trap door down there in the basement. Perhaps this time I'll find something other than empty frames. Wish me luck!" She decided not to call the others until she had thoroughly checked out Schiele's cellar.

When she got to the entrance of No. 101, she realized she did not remember the name of the friendly woman who had let her in to the top floor apartment—Schiele's apartment—and who had let her into the basement on her previous visit there. Maybe if I stare at the name plates it will come back to me, she thought. She leaned forward and cast her eyes down the various names. Ah, there it was, of course. Marie and Oskar Garrard. Megan rang the bell and a woman's voice answered.

"Who is there?" she asked. Megan identified herself and said she needed to give one more look at the cellar, would Frau Garrard mind very much letting her in again?

"Of course not. It would be a pleasure for me. I'll be right down."

"Thank you so very much," gushed Megan. Frau Garrard opened the cellar door with her key and flipped on the light switch. Megan began going carefully around the room looking for a possible second door that she might not have noticed on the first visit. No door. She examined the flooring for a second trap door. Nothing. Well, then it might be in the sub-basement room under the trap door. The two women laboriously lifted up the unlocked door in the floor and Megan descended cautiously into the gloom. The "frames" were still in place, but now her attention was on the walls of the dank cellar. Could there be a door anywhere? Marie Garrard handed down a flashlight and Megan made a second examination of the walls as well as the dirt floor. Nothing. Going back up the narrow flight of stairs, Megan thought to try the key she had found in the three-legged wooden horse in the trap door lock, expecting to turn the bolt. *The key did not fit.*

After trying the key several times in vain, Megan rejoined Frau Garrard and they returned to the ground floor. Thanking her partner in undercover research profusely, Megan walked over to the nearest subway stop and made her way back to Antal's. He wasn't at home so Megan kicked off her shoes, had some green tea, then called Hannes at the Leopold Museum. He was out. How disappointing. She had this wonderful Schiele find—another key—and no one to tell about it. Megan decided to call her other museum director friend, Dietrich Mann of the Wien Museum, where she had made her original discovery of Schiele's four-legged toy horse and its key—the key that *had* opened the trap door at Hietzinger Hauptstrasse.

Dietrich Mann was in. "Greetings, Megan, to what do I owe the pleasure of this call? I didn't think you were still in Wien."

"You owe the pleasure of this call, as you put it, to the exciting fact that I have found another Schiele key!"

"What?"

"Yes, it's true. And from out of Schiele's own *three-legged* wooden horse, the one he's holding with his usual quixotic finger spread in the Trčka photo of him."

"Do you mean to tell me that there are *two* wooden horses?"

"Yes. The one you have there at your museum and the one I just found. And you won't believe where I found it."

"I think I would believe at any locale, as long as it was you who were investigating, Megan."

"Well, it's not that difficult, Dietrich. I simply went back to the Wattmanngasse on a hunch. Did you know they were already at work demolishing Number Six?"

"I had heard that they were going to, but I didn't know they had started now. It's been so long since that building was boarded up. And such a pity the Egon Schiele Museum had to be created next door, rather than in the original building."

"Yes. Well, I made two trips there and talked to the workmen on the job." Megan decided to leave her late night trip out of her account. "The second time I went, a workman directed me to some open boxes on the ground into which the workmen had been throwing the children's toys they found as they leveled the floors. There were all sorts of items in the box, ranging from miniature locomotives to dolls. And at the bottom of the pile in one of the boxes I pulled up an ancient toy—Schiele's *three-legged* wooden horse! It opens the same way yours does and sure enough there was a key in the cavity."

"Well, wouldn't that just be another key to the trap door you found at the Hietzinger Hauptstrasse house?"

"That's what I thought. So I went just now and checked. The key does not fit the lock. Interesting?"

"Extremely interesting," allowed Dietrich.

"So we have to figure out what this new key goes to. Do you have any ideas?"

"None at the moment."

"Okay, but please think about it. I'm going to consult with Hannes. He may come up with some ideas."

"Good thought. Why don't the three of us get together at my museum late this afternoon, if he is free. We could compare your key with the one in our possession and go from there."

"Fine. I'll call and confirm once I get hold of Hannes. And if he can't come, I'll still come over so we can study the keys, if nothing else. Who knows, perhaps it's only the key to Schiele's black vitrine you have there. As I remember though, your key is a bit larger than the one I have."

"Oh? Well that's already interesting."

"Everything about this find is interesting, Dietrich."

Megan was not quite ready to tell Dietrich, or Hannes either for that matter, about the as yet unarticulated idea glimmering on the horizon of her thought process. She couldn't quite pin down the image, but her brain, she could almost *feel*, was working overtime. Let me rethink this, she encouraged herself.

She began to study the photograph she had been sent by Ludwig from Peschka-Schiele's apartment earlier in the day. Schiele's drawing of the octagon titled "Pantheon" was certainly identical to the octagon drawing he had made titled "Mausoleum." While no location had been noted on the Mausoleum drawing, the Pantheon drawing did contain the word "Krumau" at the bottom of the page.

Should she make a trip out to Krumau to see if there could possibly be an actual octagonal building to which Schiele's drawing referred? After all he had been assigned there for almost a year in 1917 during the war. Or, more likely, might this just be a fantasy project for which Schiele was picturing to himself where he would house the ambitious allegories he wished to paint? Megan understood why Krumau could be his town of choice.

On the other hand, she thought, Schiele's final year, 1918, was spent not in Krumau but in Wien, in an undemanding job at the Army Museum, where he had even been allowed to set up his canvas and paint when not busy. Easier to visit it, right here in Vienna, rather than going out on a probably fruitless trip to Krumau, where she had been only recently for an international symposium on Schiele. Who knows, she told herself almost as a joke, the new-found key might open something at the old Army Museum. Or what was it called now, in the twenty-first century? She looked it up on Google. Ah yes, now it was the Heeresgeschichtliches Museum, the Museum of Military History.

She had been there once, decades ago, and her memory of the fortress-like place was that it had on permanent display the open car in which the heir to the Austrian throne, Archduke Franz Ferdinand, and his wife Sophie were assassinated in Sarajevo by the Serbian nationalist Gavrilo Princip. It was his shots "heard round the world" that precipitated World War I. The assassin's pistol and the Archduke's blood-soaked uniform were also on display. Megan used to tell her classes what she had heard about that uniform: that the dying, blood-drenched Archduke had commanded the attending physician *not* to cut the decorative buttons—he did not want his splendiferous jacket to be damaged. How characteristic of an age that placed so much emphasis on the façade.

Megan tried again to reach Hannes at the Leopold. He was still out, so she left a message for him to meet her and Dietrich at the Wien Museum at four in the afternoon, if he possibly could. Hmm. It was now one-thirty in the afternoon. She had time to go out to the Army Museum in the Landstrasse district, not far from the Belvedere Museum, and see if she could talk to the director there. He or she might let her take a look behind the scenes, perhaps the back offices, and most importantly any offices or storage space in the museum basement. She Googled the institution. Aha. The director was one Franz Forelle. She would ask for him.

Realizing she had not eaten any lunch, Megan picked up a frozen yogurt at a Tutti Frutti stand before taking the U-Bahn out to the Army Museum. Entering through the horseshoe arch, she handed over her business card at the ticket desk, asking if they would kindly phone Herr Direktor Franz Forelle's office with the request that she would like to speak to him if possible. The hoity toity answer came in seconds. She would have to make an appointment. Frustrating!

She went ahead and paid the entrance fee to the forbidding garrison, now determined more than ever to explore the rooms as Schiele must have known them. Paying no attention to the exhibits on display, she walked quietly around each room, looking for she was not sure what, but looking—at the ceilings, at the walls, at the strange sequence of cubby holes dug into the museum walls, and at the many interior windows that looked out on a gloomy courtyard. Perhaps there was an octagonal configuration somewhere that she was missing. She tried drawing a floor plan of the old arsenal in her mind but got nowhere. The most she could get was concentric ovals, not octagonals.

Megan repeated her examination of rooms on the next two floors. Nothing jumped out at her. What she needed was to see the basement. And for that she would have to have the director's permission. All right. She would confer with her two museum director friends Dietrich and Hannes and see if one of them could get her in. Which reminded her, if she wanted to get back to the Wien Museum in time for their four o'clock appointment, she should leave now.

Twenty minutes later she was sitting with Dietrich in his office telling him of her non-adventure at the Army Museum. He laughed and said Franz Forelle was famous for being hard to get hold of and that he would make a call to him on her behalf if she really thought it was that important to see what had most likely been Schiele's terrain in 1918.

While they waited for Hannes to arrive—he had left a message that he could come—they discussed various German *Schüttelreime*, shuttle rhymes, that they each knew. Dietrich quoted: "*Ich gehe in den Birkenwald, denn Deine Pille wirken bald.*" "I'm going into the birch forest because your pills are working fast." Megan countered with what was the world's shortest shuttle rhyme in German, she'd been told:

"*Du bist
Buddhist.*"
"You are
Buddhist"

You win, laughed Dietrich. Just at that moment his secretary led Hannes into the office.

"All right, Megan, what do you have for us now?" he asked, rubbing his hands together in anticipation.

The story of her Wattmanngasse discovery was trotted out again and both men evinced genuine interest. Dietrich confirmed that the new key did not match the one in the museum's toy horse; he had taken it out of the vitrine drawer and had it right there in his office. Nor did the Wattmanngasse key fit the Schiele vitrine. The two keys, both metal, were of different sizes. The Wien Museum's key was larger, just as Megan had remembered.

"So what do you think this key goes to, if not anything in the Hietzinger Hauptstrasse basement?" asked Hannes.

"This is truly just a guess. But I wonder if there might be something in the cellar of the Army Museum that this key might fit."

"There is only one way to find out. It's too late to go there now, but I promise you," Dietrich assured them, "that tomorrow morning, first thing, I shall get the three of us—if you want to come along Hannes—an appointment to go down into the Army Museum's basement with the formidable Franz Forelle."

Hannes was brought into the *Schüttelreime* game and merrily added his two cents. Then the three went their separate ways. Megan headed back to Antal's cozy apartment to fix a salad and gnocchi dinner for them both. It had been a long day. And tomorrow could be even longer. When would she ever make her plane reservation to go home? She had to admit to herself that she was having a grand time with this Schiele Hunt, even if, as it seemed, her life had been imperiled for a time.

# 53

In his St. Petersburg office Boris Ussachevsky had now turned to reading the Moscow newspapers and yet another article on Azarova's forthcoming exhibition. It would be held not in the Rasputin gallery but in the adjacent museum. The "gem" of the show was to be a just-unearthed double portrait by Egon Schiele of Peter and Paul Schwartz from 1913. Boris's eyes widened with surprise at the next line in the paper. It said the painting was on loan to the Gallery Rasputin by the owner of the work, a Jerome Schwartz of São Paulo, Brazil, grandson and son of the two men portrayed.

*On loan?* So it was not for sale, as he had thought. He had, of course, planned to buy it from the Gallery Rasputin through an agent. It would have been perfect for his Villa Solovey. What a disappointment. Boris would love to have that work by Schiele, a work that responded so poignantly to the dynamics of a tense father-son relationship.

Boris was feeling a bit unnerved. The Krumau real estate disaster and the unexpected suicide of that fool Peschka-Schiele continued to play through his mind. He would, of course, put the octagonal building back up for sale, but selling it would be on a long hold while the police and the Krumau Historical Society sorted out how the building's basement had come to be used for the incineration of helpless Jews during World War II. No wonder the arches had been bricked up. Would identification of the skeletal remains even be possible?

As for Peschka-Schiele, Boris had been too eager to enter into a project that had not been researched more. The sight of Schiele's hand-writing on the "Pantheon" drawing had thrilled him, as had the idea that there could be an octagonal building in Krumau connected with the artist, perhaps even containing long-forgotten works by him. Boris had been super cautious all his life, and now, for the love of Schiele, he had moved too quickly.

He wanted to get away from it all. Villa Solovey was what he needed. Again he put his private pilot on notice. He would be needing him at noon for the customary flight to Vitkinsk. Boris would stay at his precious villa for a whole week. There he could commune with his spiritual companions Tchaikovsky and Schiele.

Ah, he was feeling better already.

* * *

The gnocchi dinner was a success. And Antal was full of compliments for the tasty tomato sauce Megan had concocted. After dinner they talked over the events of the day, from her amazing find of Schiele's three-legged horse to the mystery key within, to Megan's trying out the key in vain on the Hietzinger Hauptstrasse trap door, to her visit to Dietrich Mann, and finally her unsuccessful visit to the Army Museum.

"I am just sure, Antal, I mean, I have this preternatural feeling that we are going to find something related to Schiele at the Army Museum. Just let me into its basement!"

# 54

Kurt Wagner was almost overwhelmed by his preparations in the long house. Tomorrow evening the entire membership of the Doppel-O would be in attendance. Chairs—some forty of them—had been carefully arranged around the sunken fire pit in the center of the rectangular room. On each chair a black metal rose with silver tips had been laid. Four aisles ran between the chairs toward the pit. At the far end of the building two bridge tables held the red robes which the members would don. Wagner, of course, would be in the Grand Master's black robe, and as there were no initiates this time, the white robe remained in the chest of drawers he had moved over from the Schloss.

Now Wagner was working on the PowerPoint presentation he wanted to show the membership. Detailed architectural drawings included a comprehensive ground plan and a three-dimensional view of the community guest quarters as they would look when completed and fully landscaped. And the membership would be inspired by his granting of the Doppel-O's highest award—belts with a black rose buckle tipped in silver—to the two deserving foreign members who had gone beyond the call of duty, Lorenzo Ladro of Milan and Walter Holloway of London.

The music chosen by the Grand Master to accompany his visuals included, appropriately he thought, those serious numbers with veiled

Masonic symbolism from Mozart's *The Magic Flute*. But the lighting of the fire would be the dramatic climax of the evening. As the smoke rose upward he planned to parade, in his black fur-trimmed robe, down one of the aisles and slowly around the fire pit. Raised for all to see in his hands would be the Dürer *Self-Portrait as Christ*. No one could fail to see the resemblance, now that he had dyed his long red locks of hair dark brown. Allegiance would spring anew in the hearts of his congregation. Yes, the first convocation in the members' long house would be a dramatic success.

But there was still so much to do. In addition to his personal carton of fresh milk, his favorite drink, the kitchen was stocked with bottles of water, heavy brown bread and lard—the only items Schiele had been given in prison. Of course the membership would not be told that this was the reason for the meager fare. Self-denial and fasting were part of the Doppel-O code of conduct. And certainly no one must know of the replica of Schiele's prison cell under the flooring. That was the Grand Master's and his alone. His hallowed secret site for contemplation, repentance, and punishment.

# 55

Boris Ussachevsky had settled into his Villa Solovey for the week, but somehow his spirits were not lifted. Even contemplating his two extraordinary Schiele paintings—the *Self-Portrait Nude Standing* and the townscape of Krumau—had not lifted his spirits. He tried to lose himself in the poignant depiction of the town he had visited so recently in hope of uncovering more Schiele masterworks.

Doing so only brought sorrow. Sorrow and frustration that he had had any dealings with that suicidal man Peschka-Schiele, who claimed to be Schiele's closest relative. No, looking at Krumau right now was not helpful. His eyes turned to the self-portrait and the same melancholy that radiated from the grim image grappling with desires of the flesh, afflicted him.

He too was grappling with desires of the flesh, for the satisfaction of which he paid anonymous young men regularly. But everyone he met nowadays seemed far too young for him. Everything was voiced in slang, and having sex was as ordinary as having a vodka.

As he had done many times before when he felt this way, he donned his beatnik clothes, walked to the Tchaikovsky monument, and sat down on the iron bench in front of it. Sooner or later some sex-for-hire gay would come along.

His thoughts turned to the gratifying decision he had made to burn down Azarova's gallery. His chief competitor would compete no more. This cheered him and his spirits rose. The sun was beginning to set and there were no other people around.

Or so it seemed. All of a sudden, from the left promenade, two fellows noisily approached the statue. They were quite drunk and definitely not gay. They looked up at the statue of Tchaikovsky and began shouting homophobic insults at the effigy. Boris shrank into himself. But the two toughs had spotted him and began to approach him, lurching on the way. Boris felt his skin tingle with apprehension.

"Look, there's one of old Pyotr's faggots right now!" one of the young men cried to the other.

"Let's teach him a thing or two!" his friend shouted back. They broke into a run and reached Boris before he could even get up from the bench. The two men rained blows down upon Boris's head and outstretched hands. Flailing, he fell to the ground where the two toughs then began kicking him in the groin, the stomach, and head. The blows were hard and Boris was bleeding badly at the mouth and from the back of his head.

"Hey, let's get out of here," commanded one of the fellows, noticing a couple coming up the promenade. The two men ran off and a few minutes later a concerned husband and wife were kneeling before the prostate, unconscious figure. They called the police and an ambulance. But help had come too late. Boris Ussachevsky died on the way to the hospital.

# 56

The Grand Master was feeling frustrated. People would be arriving in about three hours and he had worked late into the night completing his PowerPoint presentation. He should have assigned the techie task to Moll. Well, at least he had told him to arrive two hours before the others. In fact here came his car now. He was parking right next to his own, down at the far end of the long house. Moll seemed to be in a petulant mood, almost ignoring Wagner's greeting.

The two men sat at the simple kitchen table discussing things. Two tall piles of black cloth were on the floor. Wagner mentioned that one of the meeting's highlights would be a morale booster.

"How so?" asked Moll with mild interest.

"I am bestowing the award of merit on two of our Inner Circle members tonight."

"And they are?" Moll asked, with a quick intake of air that made his nostrils flare.

"Why, can't you guess?" asked the Grand Master, leaning forward and looking Moll in the eye. "I am honoring our two foreign members, Lorenzo Ladro and Walter Holloway, for having gone beyond the call of duty on behalf of our Doppel-O.

Moll felt the back of his neck tingle as blood rushed to his head. So! *He was being overlooked again!* After all he had done for the Grand Master. He had eliminated the old Russian woman and brought back her Schiele painting for him. And all for no thanks, no acknowledgement. Had he not gone beyond the call of duty for the Grand Master? Neither of the two foreigners had committed murder for the Grand Master. But he had.

"Now I need your help hanging these black cloth drapes around the room," said Wagner, reaching for his carton of milk, completely unaware of what Moll was going through. He took two long gulps, and set the carton down on the table.

Oh, he "needs" my help again, does he? thought Moll bitterly to himself. Obediently, without betraying his roiling emotions, he stood up from the table and followed the Grand Master into the main room. They began with the far end of the hall, working in tandem, Wagner on the ladder, Moll below him, handing up batches of cloth. About half way through the task Wagner, at the top of the ladder, sent Moll back to the kitchen to get the second pile of black curtain cloth.

In the kitchen Moll paused, looking at the carton of milk. Yes. It was time. He would do it. Quickly he opened the small bottle he had with him and poured a good measure of potassium cyanide into the carton, swishing it around vigorously. Then he scooped up the second pile of black cloth and returned to the hall. In another half hour the whole room had been hung with black drapes, affording the privacy so coveted by the Grand Master.

# 51

The meeting with Franz Forelle at the Army Museum had been delayed for one day. He was "indisposed." Both Johannes Ohm and Dietrich Mann said this sort of conduct was par for the course. Rarely did Franz Forelle act in concert with other Vienna museum directors. They would simply have to wait a day.

Exasperated, Megan decided to spend the time at Antal's comfortable flat working on her mystery novel, *Murder for Mahler*. It was delicious work she had put aside last time she was in Vienna, coping with the Klimt situation.

Also she had grievously neglected her e-mail since arriving in Austria and there were a lot to answer, especially from younger colleagues.

That was good. She liked being relevant still today. For one thing, she had been able to encourage and help younger Schiele and Klimt scholars, something that gave her great satisfaction. For another, art matters still required that she engage in quite a bit of travel, an obligation she never minded. For the past two years, for example, she had been engaged with that Egon Schiele Portraits exhibition opening at the Art Austria Museum in Montreal.

The opening was now only a few months away. In fact, just before she left Texas she had gone to a local sound studio to record her part of the museum's audio tour through fourteen stop points. She had been so nervous about speaking spontaneously that during the recording session she had dug her fingers into her legs so vigorously that the sound man had to enter the booth and ask her to stop—the scratching noise was coming through and sounded like a herd of elephants.

That made her think of what caused her to be nervous and what did not. Giving a public lecture, no. Going to a party, yes; socializing was becoming increasingly noisy. Or was she slowly going deaf? Probably the latter. And she was definitely a hermit, just as much of a recluse as Schiele had desired to be. But often life had other plans.

After a few hours of work and lunch, Antal asked Megan if there were not someplace in Wien she would like to visit, considering that she had now finally made her return flight reservations for two days hence. Megan thought, then said yes, she'd like to visit the Arnold Schönberg Museum again. It was not too far from Antal's flat. They walked to the famous Schwarzenbergplatz and entered the building at No. 6. In addition to a wealth of personal effects, books, scores, letters, and documents, there was a fascinating array of portraits of the composer. Some were in the original, others were excellent reproductions.

Among the latter were three large paintings and one black crayon drawing. One of the images was by Richard Gerstl, whose short-lived affair with Schönberg's wife drove him to commit suicide in 1908 at the age of twenty-five. The composer's somewhat chubby figure dominated most of the canvas space and the low couch upon which he was seated, while his glance was keen and direct. Behind him, cut off at the top, was probably a small painting by the composer, as Gerstl had been asked to teach him the rudiments of painting. If so, then the lopping off of part of the little picture within a picture was perhaps, in the age of Freud, a Freudian act on the artist's part.

Next to the Gerstl had been placed a much more dramatic portrait of the composer by Max Oppenheimer. His depiction of 1909 showed the public Schönberg. The composer's glance was apprehensive. A visible correction in the painting of the right arm was a non-too-subtle device intended to make the sitter appear somewhat helpless, with his hands behind his back as though he were being jerked to attention. Oppenheimer was obviously trying to convey the pressures that weighed upon the overburdened but tireless musician.

Facing these two images on the opposite wall were two more portraits of Schönberg, one by Schiele, from 1917, and the other by Oskar Kokoschka, done quite a while after the end of World War I, in 1924. Schönberg posed with his cello for Kokoschka, a pose that resulted in the left hand with its tumbling fingers being held higher—at forehead level— than the right, which was lower and held the bow. Except the painter *left out the cello and bow* in the final portrait. The cello's broadly brushed red echo took up the left hand edge of the canvas. This device endowed the composer with an unusual sense of alertness and concentration. This was something which Kokoschka heightened with a display of agitated brush work filling the animated surround of purple, blue, and black. The colors showered down upon the composer and packed the middle and right side of the picture.

Megan turned to her favorite rendition of the composer—Schiele's black crayon study. She pointed out a contemporary photograph of Schönberg to Antal next to Schiele's signed and dated portrait study and commented on its difference from the gaunt sketch Schiele had made. It was obvious that by 1917 the composer had assumed a rather portly appearance.

Compared to the photograph, Schiele's sketch of the man was a surprise. The gaunt figure in his sketch appeared to bristle with energy. Along with his thoughtful expression, the composer's facial asymmetry had been emphasized by Schiele. This facial asymmetry was something the Nazis later used with unflattering photographs of the man in order to demonstrate that Schönberg's music was degenerate. In Schiele's portrait study a luminous pearly white area streaked like a flash down the top of the head, lighting up a topography of thought. Schiele's recognition of the energy, endurance, and creativity of his model was objective. His response, however, was simultaneously subjective, and he gave Schönberg an emaciated body strikingly similar to his own.

Antal was only too pleased to be the recipient of Megan's impromptu art history lecture, especially since he was not familiar with the Oppenheimer or Kokoschka renditions. What an extraordinary period, what exceptional personalities, and what great creative artists Vienna had produced at that distant, rich period in its history.

That night, reverting to olden times of their own, Megan and Antal spent the evening at home.


# 58

As cars started pulling up to the long house, the Grand Master and his assistant Arnold Moll started up the fire in the middle of the hall. Wagner had added newspaper sheets in between the stacked cedar logs and the fire spread quickly and evenly. The hole in the ceiling funneled the smoke just as it was designed to do. The entire membership was gathered within half an hour as excerpts from Mozart's *Magic Flute* and pieces of his Masonic music sounded solemnly from the overhead speakers. People had donned their red robes and taken seats around the quietly burning fire.

From his console in the kitchen, Wagner began the slide show he had composed and he could hear gasps from the audience. Moll was assigned the duty of doling out the water, brown bread, and lard. Wagner, in full regalia, turned to lift the Dürer self-portrait. To give himself more energy, he took one long sustained swig from the milk carton on the table. Then he took hold of the Dürer with both hands and, holding it in front of him over his head, he progressed slowly to the fire pit, circling it solemnly with measured steps.

The membership gasped out loud at the uncanny similarity between the Grand Master and Dürer. They both had shoulder-length dark brown hair, they both had long noses and high foreheads, and they were both garbed in black fur-lined robes. The effect was everything the Grand Master had hoped for. On all sides he heard people exclaiming: "The new Savior!" and "A Dürer for our times!"

So intent was he on displaying the Dürer self-portrait that he did not realize his complexion was changing from pale white to flaming red. Or if he did, he blamed it on his proximity to the fire flames.

One member did understand the ruddy complexion for what it was: acute cyanide poisoning. He stood to the side of the room, waiting for what he knew would happen next.

It did. The Grand Master suddenly went into a convulsion, tripped, and fell to the ground. The Dürer hit the fire and was consumed within minutes. Members closest to the Grand Master rushed to his aid, but the man was unconscious, his body convulsing involuntarily. Within minutes hypoxia of the neural tissue occurred. The Grand Master was dead.

Bedlam reigned. Some of the members shouted that an ambulance should be called for, others wanted simply to leave the premises, and still others were undecided, looking to Arnold Moll, the second in command, for guidance.

Moll counseled immediate dispersion of the clan. Every member must take responsibility for clearing out of the long house and leaving the town of Gmunden. They should take off in all directions, anything to avoid being associated with the death of the prepossessing giant of a man who had been their Grand Master.

After all of the membership had cleared out, Arnold Moll, left alone, did three things. First, he erased the Doppel-O website from the Internet, destroying all links to any of the membership. Secondly, he set fire to the long house. And thirdly, he finished off Kurt Wagner's carton of milk. The Doppel-O was no more.


# 59

Dietrich Mann and Johannes Ohm arrived in Ohm's car to pick up Megan at Antal's the next morning at a quarter to nine. On the way to the Army Museum they excitedly discussed the sensational news on last night's TV coverage of the disaster at Gmunden. A building in the forest behind the Schloss had caught fire and two charred bodies inside had been identified. They were Kurt Wagner and Arnold Moll, both of Vienna.

"So," said Hannes with satisfaction, "I guess that's the end of the Doppel-O."

"What a relief," Megan sighed.

Pulling up at the Army Museum, they parked at a staff entrance and entered the building through a low slung door Megan had not noticed before. A guard beckoned them to the elevator that took them to the third floor, where the difficult Franz Forelle had his office. An unsmiling secretary motioned them to chairs in the waiting room. Dietrich and Hannes looked at each other knowingly. They had been put through this routine before on Forelle's turf.

After some five minutes of waiting, the inner door to Forelle's office opened and a short man wearing heavy spectacles nodded to them, motioning that they join him in his office. A few cliché remarks were exchanged and then Megan cut to the chase.

"We are most eager to examine that part of the Army Museum where Egon Schiele used to work when he was assigned here during World War I. Of special interest to us is the basement."

"The basement?" Forelle frowned.

"Indeed," Megan said with what she hoped was a winning smile.

"It's of no interest to me. But if you really must have a look then, yes, go ahead."

Megan could hardly restrain herself from running right out of Forelle's office, but she did.

"What is it you hope to find?" fished Forelle.

"We are particularly interested in learning whether or not Schiele might have stored some work down there."

"*Ach, ja*, that is everybody's dream. To find old Schiele paintings somewhere. Good luck," Forelle said sarcastically.

Megan could not stand it any longer. She took the key she had found in Schiele's three-legged wooden horse out of her purse and waved it in front of Forelle.

"We have here Schiele's just-unearthed key to something. We think it could possibly be something in your cellar."

"Well, why didn't you *say* so?" exclaimed Forelle, throwing a cross glance at Dietrich, who had called him for their appointment.

"We shall go down *together*," he added forcefully, standing up abruptly.

Forelle led them out of the office and to the elevator. Behind him as they walked, Hannes murmured to Megan: "This man flip flops like the trout of his surname."

"Do you think that's why his parents named him Franz, for Schubert's *Forelle Quintet*?" Megan whispered mischievously.

"No doubt," Hannes whispered back.

The elevator left them on the ground floor and Forelle led them to a steep staircase that opened onto the basement.

"We go down here," he commanded, nodding to the guard who was looking puzzled at seeing the Herr Direktor leading a group of people around the museum himself.

The cellar was surprisingly well illuminated by modern electric lighting and did not smell of mold. That's encouraging, Megan thought, as she carefully descended the steep cement stairs. A very large basement stretched out in front of them. At the far end was a multi-sectioned rack that held paintings not on exhibit, a common sight in museum basements.

Megan knew this from her feminist days of hunting for women artists' work languishing in museum cellars.

Behind the rack and built flush into the wall was what looked like the front of a multi-drawer horizontal map chest. It had eight metal drawers, each about five inches high, and extended from the floor to about four-and-a-half feet in height. All eight of the drawers had small key holes. *Megan felt the blood race through her body.*

While the men stood examining the storage rack and commenting on the artworks placed there, Megan walked behind it to the wall and pulled out the Schiele key from her purse. Her companions, seeing what she was about to do, fell silent.

Megan tried the key in the top drawer. The lock turned easily. Holding her breath, she pulled the drawer to her. It slid open easily. It held an array of old military maps. She closed the drawer.

She unlocked and opened the second of the eight drawers. This time, in the capacious drawer, some sixty-by-sixty inches wide and deep, was a painted canvas on a stretcher. Cautiously Megan lifted the artwork up and slid it out from the drawer. She held it up to her, grasping it from the back so she could see it. The men, seeing what she saw, gasped.

What Megan silently held up for all of them to see was a completely finished oil portrait by Schiele. It was a self-portrait. The artist, dressed in a dark blue suit with matching tie, showed himself sitting in one of his black chairs. On his lap, facing outward, was a portrait study of his wife Edith in the multi-striped dress she had made from his atelier curtains. The artist, his face serious, with eyes staring unflinchingly at the beholder, held the study with his left hand and pointed to his heart with his right hand. A swatch of lively short brush strokes animated the warm russet surround. The message was unmistakable: *I, Egon Schiele, artist, have created this.*

The four basement visitors stared at the self-portrait in silence. It was unmistakably by the artist and in his late 1917–18 style: no longer agonized but instead emanating maturity and calm. After a few minutes the men joined Megan as she carefully propped the canvas against the wall.

"This is undoubtedly by Schiele and it is surely one of his greatest self-portraits," murmured Dietrich, to which Hannes nodded in vigorous agreement.

"Let's see what the other drawers hold!" commanded a suddenly very engaged Franz Forelle.

Megan inserted the key into the next highest drawer and again easily pulled it out toward her. Another painted canvas on stretchers greeted her eyes. Exercising extreme caution, she drew the artwork out and held it up again for all to see. It was another finished portrait, measuring like the first one, some sixty-by-sixty inches. The person portrayed was instantly recognizable.

It was Arnold Schönberg. He too was in one of the chairs Schiele had built and painted black. Behind the figure was a sketchy indication of the containing room, filled again with short, stubby brushstrokes, this time a mesh of verdant greens. The composer's pose matched the most finished of Schiele's three signed portrait sketches, the one in which the sitter's left arm rested on the chair arm. As in the study, the energized lines of clothing and necktie echoed the intense thought process suggested by the concentrated expression on the composer's face. His right hand rested on his lap and held what looked like a musical score. Written on the top music sheet was the word *Erwartung—Expectation*—the title of Schönberg's Expressionist one-act monodrama. It represented in slow motion the agony experienced by a woman wandering in a forest searching for her lover, only to stumble across his corpse.

But how could Schiele have known of this 1909 work by Schönberg? It was performed for the first time only in 1924. It must have been that the composer told Schiele about the angstful work and its meaning as the artist sketched his studies of him. What a find! As she had with the first portrait,

Megan stood in front of it to take a Google Glass photograph, realizing that it would probably be a long, long time before these works would leave a restorer's studio and be put on public display. But so far the artworks were in excellent shape.

There were five more drawers to go. The men crowded around Megan as she unlocked the next drawer. They helped her pull it out and, yes, there was another completed oil on stretchers. All four recognized the person portrayed. It was the journalist with the acerbic pen, Karl Kraus. This was the man who, in his popular recriminatory magazine, *Die Fackel—The Torch*—had described Vienna as "an isolation cell in which one is allowed to scream!" In fact one of Schiele's 1910 self-portrayals seemed to be in response to this scream image, combining Munch's scream with that of Kraus' analogy. Like the two previous portraits Megan had found, the subject was seated in the ubiquitous black chair, but this time not comfortably so. His hands gripped the chair arms tightly and his small body twisted toward the left as though in impatient response to a question. Very much like the terse manner in which Kraus acted during his public lectures, intense and full of furious energy.

Suddenly Megan saw Schiele's octagon drawing in her mind's eye: in addition to the label "Pantheon" were the words titling each of the seven walls: "Art," "Music," "Literature," and so on.

Yes! This would have to be it! These were the works intended for Schiele's Pantheon. And they were *not* allegories, like Klimt's, after all! They were all going to be portraits. Portraits of individual Austrian achievers in the arts and sciences. Yes, that had to be it! She expressed her thoughts to her three companions. They nodded affirmatively.

What would be next? Megan unlocked and pulled out the next metal drawer with relative ease. She lifted up a fourth canvas. It was the portrait of a bearded man seated with hands stretched out as though playing an accordion. Megan did not recognize him but Dietrich did.

"That's Ernst Mach!" The others looked at him with blank faces. "Of course you know him! The Austrian physicist who studied shock waves and contributed the concept of what we now call Mach numbers for measuring the velocity of sound."

Megan did remember then about Mach and his book *The Analysis of Sensations* that had such an impact on Viennese thought at the turn of the last century. So! That was Schiele's choice for "Science."

"Can we guess who will represent 'Medicine?'" she asked, realizing that they were all in a state of euphoria over these discoveries in the basement of the venerable old Army Museum.

"Freud!" was the unanimous answer. And they were right. The next drawer contained an instantly identifiable image of the physician sitting bolt upright in his chair, both feet on the ground, and his hands joined and folded quietly over a book in his lap. His hair, moustache, and pointed beard were brown and he faced the beholder unblinkingly.

"Interesting that Schiele endows this man who turned the world upside down with his theories, as having somatic integrity," Megan mused, standing back to take, discreetly, her photo.

"And see there," Dietrich pointed out, "one can just make out the title of the book: *Die Traumdeuting—The Interpretation of Dreams.*"

"Perfect!" exclaimed Franz Forelle, growing increasingly excited over the discoveries being made in *his* museum.

"I remember that the book was actually published in eighteen-ninety-nine and not nineteen hundred, as indicated on the frontispiece," said Hannes.

"Yes, he had one foxy publisher to place it at the beginning of the new century," Dietrich said with admiration. "Even though it took ten years before the six hundred copies that were published sold out."

They continued to regard the painting, noting Schiele's newly adopted use of the brush to indicate space. In this painting's case the suggestion of a room was articulated in varying blues.

Megan offered one of her teaching memories: "I used to ask my students to write down the epigram on the original frontispiece when I showed it in class. It was such a wonderful motto."

"And that was?" inquired Forelle.

"*Flectere si nequeo superos, Acheronta movebo.*"

"So true!" cried Johannes. "If I cannot bend the heavens, I shall move Acheron'—the river the dead must cross to get into the underworld."

"Let's take count now," said Megan, marveling before the five Schiele canvases they had placed against the basement wall. "We have 'Art,' 'Music,' 'Literature,' 'Science,' and 'Medicine.' The next one, if they are in the order shown on Schiele's octagon drawing, should be 'Philosophy.' Any guesses?"

"Ludwig Wittgenstein," all three men said at the same time.

"Well, possibly. Although his *Tractatus* was not published during Schiele's lifetime," Megan said thoughtfully. "Of course, they both served in the army during World War I, but Wittgenstein saw action on the front, whereas Schiele did not, so it's not as though they might have met during their army service." The three men appeared unconvinced by her argument.

Then Megan's face lit up. "I think I know! I bet it's going to be Otto Weininger."

"What? That crazy Jewish so-called philosopher who hated both Jews and women?" asked Forelle incredulously.

"I see Megan's point, though," Hannes intervened. "All Vienna heard about him when he committed suicide after the nineteen-three publication of his bizarre book on sex and character, *Geschlecht und Charakter*."

"And he was only twenty-three," Hannes continued. "Certainly, even if Schiele did not read his misogynous, anti-Semitic book, everyone was talking about it, just the way all Vienna talked about Freud's book in nineteen hundred, but few had actually read it."

"And the fact that much of Weininger's book was about the nature of genius. That would have interested Schiele. Plus the 'glamorous' fact that Weininger shot himself in the house where *Beethoven* died. That would certainly have appealed to Schiele," Megan added, becoming more convinced by the minute that she was right.

She unlocked the drawer. Yes, yet another portrait, and yes, it was Otto Weininger. The youthful sitter, formally dressed with high white collar and again posited in a black chair against a lightly indicated wall, was shown staring off into space behind his pince-nez. His high-domed forehead and small moustache made him look older than he was. The suggested room ambience this time was fraught with excessive brushstrokes slamming black after black on the canvas. And sure enough, the volume in the man's clenched hands was titled *Geschlecht und Charakter*.

Franz Forelle whistled. "What a lineup. And the climax, if I may put it that way, ha ha, is going to be 'Love,' I suppose?"

Megan, Hannes, and Dietrich did not dignify his prurient comment with an answer. Without further discussion Megan unlocked and opened the final drawer. Slowly she pulled out the stretched canvas. All gasped at the instantly recognizable image of a beautiful, dark-haired, sensuous woman, dressed in red, sitting in a chair and holding the familiar death mask of Gustav Mahler out and away from her. It was Alma Mahler. And Schiele had painted her during what everyone in Wien at that time knew was her Kokoschka stage. Their scandalous love affair, conducted shortly after Mahler's death, in 1911, had lasted into World War I. In fact, the painter had immortalized their union not only in letters and a bust portrait of her as his own personal Mona Lisa, but in the life-size allegory, *Bride of the Wind* of 1914.

Schiele's depiction of Alma Mahler responded to her beauty with unusual verisimilitude. The choice of a red dress, intimating that it was worn during the widow's supposed mourning period, seemed to be the artist's own personal comment on her behavior.

The images for the seven walls of Schiele's intended octagonal pantheon were now revealed.

How had these paintings been kept secret during his lifetime, to say nothing of after his death? The answer seemed obvious. Instead of painting them at home, either in his new Wattmanngasse studio or the old Hietzinger Hauptstrasse atelier, he had created them here, in the Army Museum, during his light work schedule and down in the basement in the rarely used historic maps room. As part of his job he had the key to the cabinet drawers, and what better place to store his freshly finished paintings, with their smell of varnish, than down in the basement where only he came? What a discovery!

None of the three directors had ever given much thought to Schiele's "Mausoleum" sketch, and of course the matching "Pantheon" drawing was unknown until recently. Hannes was the first to congratulate Megan on her unwavering, almost stubborn, perseverance.

"Just see what you have turned up *this* time!" he said to her with glee.

Dietrich followed suit and praised Megan for acting on her tried and true intuition concerning things to do with Schiele

Franz Forelle looked from the group back to the seven Schiele portraits then back to the group.

"Well, yes, this is a monumental discovery of the highest importance. These paintings must be worth around two and a half million Euros each. And I know just the room upstairs that we can convert for showing the portraits on permanent display."

Hannes and Dietrich both gave a start.

Dietrich spoke first. "You are mistaken, Franz. The Wien Museum is obviously the venue for these Schieles. We already have so much that relates to the artist. And visitors to our museum come by the *thousands* as compared to those hundreds who visit your museum..."

"I'm sorry, Dietrich, "interrupted Hannes. "The Leopold Museum is the *only* possible site for these masterpieces. We already have the largest collection of Schieles in the world and *hundreds* of thousands of visitors pass through our doors every year. It is only right that the works go to our museum. They will round out the image of Schiele for the general public who see him only as a Viennese pornographer."

Hearing grounds for a long, drawn out lawsuit in the making—so typical in the case of Schiele and of Wien—Megan turned away from the arguing men as their voices became louder and more strident.

Reverently, she went up to each Schiele canvas and silently greeted it, in awe of what the artist had wrought, how his mature style and his personality had truly changed from one of solipsistic angst to genuine empathy for his fellow human beings. Now these masterworks which she had been privileged to uncover, fifty years after her first discovery of Schiele's prison cell, would be shared with the world at large.

Now she could fly home to Dallas and to her darling little Button. Montreal would have to wait.

# Readers Guide

1. The Viennese artist Egon Schiele (1890-1918) is considered Austria's greatest exponent of Expressionist art, despite his tragically brief life. In addition to poignant land-and-townscapes, his psychological portraits redefined portraiture at the beginning of the twentieth century. Those who sat for him were represented as gesticulating vessels of angst set in existential voids, rather than within a defining environment. But Schiele turned his most penetrating gaze upon himself. In a 1910 series of life-size naked self-portraits showing himself in the throes of sexual arousal, he went further than had any other artist in history. What did the compositional amputation of his hands signify?

2. The opening paragraphs of *The Schiele Slaughters* find a night watchman's naked body propped up under Schiele's famous *Self-Portrait Nude Sitting* in Vienna's Leopold Museum. The slaughtered guard's hands and feet are missing. A black metal rose, tipped in silver, is on the floor next to Schiele's painting which has been "censored" with black duct tape affixed to its genitals. Are the Jewish restitution demonstrators of the IKG responsible? What does the black rose signify?

3. We meet the book's primary protagonist, Megan Crespi, still agile and engaged at seventy-seven. She is a professor of art history *emerita* and a world expert on Viennese art and music, especially Egon Schiele, about whom she has published several books. Megan is in London on a lecture tour when she receives a call from the Leopold Museum's director, Johannes Ohm, who begs her to come to Vienna to help shed light on the crime. She agrees to fly over the next morning. In the meantime she visits friends at Sotheby's Auction House where a previously "lost" Schiele *Self-Portrait Nude Standing* is undergoing restoration. Who is the anonymous owner of the provocative portrait? And who bid on the Schiele *Krumau Townscape* that Sotheby's recently sold? Was it one of the two billionaire Russian dealers: Boris Ussachevsky of St. Petersburg or Alexandra Azarova of Moscow?

4. An Inner Circle meeting of the Doppel-O, a secret cult devoted to "obliterating obscenity," is taking place at a castle, Schloss Gemmingen-Eggaberg in Gmunden. The Grand Master Kurt Wagner is initiating a new member, Wolf Schnitt, whose proof of compliance is in a black box. What does opening the box reveal?

5. Megan is in Vienna conferring with her friend "Hannes" Ohm in the Leopold Museum's restoration room where the Schiele canvas is being restored. Suddenly a call comes in: Schiele's gravestone has been desecrated! Who could have done this? The IKG or perhaps the Doppel-O sect?

6. We meet Doppel-O member Lorenzo Ladro who has successfully stolen from Sotheby's the Schiele *Self-Portrait Nude Standing*. He delivers it to the Grand Master who informs the baron of the Schloss Gemmingen-Eggaberg, that in exchange for six acres of the castle's adjoining forest land, he will pay him half of whatever he gains from the sale of the offensive artwork in Russia. We learn that the family owns an Albrecht Dürer 1500 *Self-Portrait as Christ*. Is this portentous? Does Lorenzo Ladro's surname indicate anything about him? Will the Doppel-O's Grand Master be able to pay the baron of the castle the sum needed to purchase the six acres he desires for his clan's meeting house? To whom will he try to sell the stolen Schiele?

7. We meet the pushy Éva Vidovszky, owner of a slightly shady Antiquariat in Vienna. Short and slight of build, she could pass as Megan's double. Will this play any role in the future? How soon and under what circumstances do we learn of Vidovszky's irritating nature?

8. Tall, slim, with dark spikes of hair similar to Schiele's, Boris Ussachevsky sits in his St. Petersburg gallery office contemplating the unsigned Schiele *Krumau Townscape* for which he outbid his Moscow rival, Alexandra Azarova. He has just been offered a colossal Schiele "find" by Kurt Wagner under the pseudonym of Max Valentin. Boris contemplates the similarities between his looks and life with Schiele. What are they? Reveling in how well he knows Schiele the man, Boris inscribes the artist's signature and date on the Krumau landscape. Was he right to do this, or is it a criminal act? Is this a common practice in the art world?

9. Talking to Arnold Moll on the phone from Moscow, Kurt Wagner is unpleasantly surprised to learn Megan Crespi is in Vienna. He decides this champion of pornography must be eradicated and orders his second in command, Arnold Moll, to instruct the new initiate Wolf Schnitt to do away with her. Moll is mortified that it was not he who was assigned the task. Will Moll's jealousy play a further role?

10. Megan visits the new Schiele Museum at the Wattmanngasse. Shortly after she arrives someone spray paints the enlarged photographs of Schiele on exhibition in the front room. The museum's founder, Felicitas Geduld, reminds Megan that this could be the work, not of the IKG, but possibly the Doppel-O. She tells Megan that the sect leader, Kurt Wagner, with his shoulder-length red hair, looks exactly like the Dürer 1500 *Self-Portrait as Christ* in the Munich Museum. Will the Dürer play a role in unfolding events? What does Felicitas's surname mean in English?

11. After breakfast in her Römischer Kaiser hotel, Megan visits the Wien Museum. She finds and borrows the key that is hidden in the little wooden horse in Schiele's black cabinet's hidden drawer, about which only she knows. She goes out to Schiele's former Hietzinger Hauptstrasse studio and discovers that the key opens a trap door in the building's basement. Inside the sunken chamber she discovers a number of five-by-five-foot slender wooden beams standing on end in groups of four. She realizes that these boards, all painted black, could be frames. But frames for what? Was Schiele planning a series of allegories like those of Gustav Klimt?

12. Kurt Wagner, alias Max Valentin, visits Alexandra Azarova at her Moscow gallery and shows her the stolen Schiele *Self-Portrait Nude Standing*. She refuses to buy it because he can not provide a provenance for the work. Wagner flies to St. Petersburg and barters with Boris Ussachevsky, who does not care about provenance. After much give and take, Boris wins and pays 100 million dollars for the work. Why does Boris want this particular Schiele? What is a provenance? Why is it so important when selling a work of art?

13. Sonja Oppenheimer of Königsberg in Russia, contacts Megan Crespi. She is disturbed that the Schiele self-portrait she had entrusted via an intermediary, Éva Vidovszky, to Sotheby's has been stolen. Would Megan please come to Königsberg? Whose home town is this Russian city and what is its new Russian name?

14. Dressed in her warm red parka, Megan returns to the Wien Museum to replace the Hietzinger Hauptstrasse key in its secret hiding place. While she is doing this, a tall man with white hair and trim beard loops a trip wire across the top of the museum stairway at foot level. He is Wolf Schnitt, newest initiate of the Doppel-O sect. What happens next? Will Megan survive?

15. Kurt Wagner pays Fritz von Gemmingen-Eggaburg his half of the one hundred million dollar sale of the stolen Schiele and buys the six coveted forest acres from him. Fritz shows Kurt his Dürer self-portrait; Kurt believes his resemblance to it ordains him, as the modern-day Christ, to carry on his work to bring purity to an impure world. What is Kurt, the Grand Master, planning to do with this acreage? Does Fritz have any idea as to the drastic ends the Doppel-O sect will go?

16. A dazed Megan, saved from any broken bones by her padded red parka, regains consciousness. She suffers swollen wrists and elbows, however. In another 48 hours she is so much better that she agrees to fly to Königsberg to see Sonja Oppenheimer's Schiele. From Sonja she learns of the existence of Schiele's great grandnephew Adolf Peschka-Schiele, who pursues all Schiele works with doubtful provenances. Are there restitution lawsuits in the offing? What sort of man is Peschka-Schiele?

17. Megan unwittingly foils Wolf Schnitt's second attempt on her life by suddenly taking a streetcar out to the Upper Belvedere Museum to see a special exhibition. But Schnitt has another chance to kill her when, during a sudden hail storm, he spots her returning to her hotel. What happens next? Who has been slaughtered?

18. Megan, Alexandra Azarova, the Moscow gallery owner, and art restorer Igor Borodin all meet in Königsberg to see Sonja Oppenheimer's remaining Schiele. Why is it such a surprise? Arnold Moll also visits the elderly woman and with what result? What role does a black metal rose play?

19. What is the subject matter of the unusual Schiele drawing Peschka-Schiele finds. Why does it send him to the town of Krumau? Why does Boris Ussachevsky agree to meet him there?

20. What is Wolf Schnitt doing in Dallas? Is his mission successful?

21. The Grand Master has built a special feature into the new meeting hall near the Schloss. What is this feature and why must it remain secret?

22. Back at her friend Antal Maack's Vienna flat Megan receives a call from Milan. She and Anton fly there immediately. What will they find there at the Galleria La Scala? Does it impact Megan's search to find what Schiele's seven images were that would, in his words, "benefit all of Vienna"?

23. Adolf Peschka-Schiele supervises the workmen excavating the blocked up cellar arches in the octagonal building in Krumau that Boris Ussachevsky has bought. Why is it important that the building is octagonal in shape? What are the two startling discoveries that send Peschka-Schiele berserk?

24. The Grand Master dyes his red hair a dark brown prior to the convening of the entire Doppel-O membership. Why is this? What does he take from the Schloss for the meeting? And what sinister act does his subordinate Arnold Moll perform? How does this impact the Doppel-O?

25. Megan, Dietrich Mann, and Johannes Ohm arrive at the Army Museum to meet with the uncooperative director Franz Forelle and go down to the cellar, used now only for storage of paintings not on display upstairs. What connects the Army Museum with Schiele? And what stunning, undreamt-of find does Megan discover in this, the denouement of the book?

CPSIA information can be obtained at www.ICGtesting.com
Printed in the USA
LVOW06s0335150415

434644LV00003B/114/P